the little ones

a novel

Jeanette,

May the Lord bless
you on your life's
journey.
Thank you for all
you do through The Word
Guild to help
Canadian authors!
Lorene

m. d. meyer

THE LITTLE ONES

ISBN-10: 1-897373-64-3
ISBN-13: 978-1-897373-64-4

Published by Word Alive Press
131 Cordite Road, Winnipeg, MB R3W 1S1
www.wordalivepress.ca

Printed in Canada.

"If anyone should cause
one of these little ones
to lose his faith in me,
it would be better for that person,
to have a large millstone
tied round his neck
and be drowned in the deep sea."

-JESUS
(Matthew 18:6)

To all the little girls and boys
In this world
Who have been hurt and abused
And have longed for a
Mommy and Daddy
Who would treat them
As a Mommy and Daddy should.
May you come to know
The friendship of Jesus
The comfort of the Holy Spirit
And most of all be able to sit on the lap of your Heavenly Father
And have His loving arms wrapped around you
He is the one who asked us to call Him...
Abba
Daddy

chapter one

"Dear Lord Jesus,
bless my daddy in jail
and my mommy in the hospital.
And bless my new foster mommy
and my new foster daddy.
And all the people in the whole wide world
except for that stinking whore, Verena."

The little girl sat on the edge of the bed with her eyes squeezed tightly shut, her palms together in front of her face, her voice rising and falling in a sing-song chant. She drew out the last word, "Amen!" in a resounding declaration of completion, opened her eyes and turned expectantly towards her new foster mother.

"Well..." she demanded, "aren't you going to pray too?"

But Sarah was speechless, too stunned by the little girl's words to formulate an immediate response. Finally she took a deep breath. "Yes, Emmeline, I'll pray too. But... I think maybe we need to talk a bit first."

Emmeline tossed her head, sending her long, smooth black hair back in a fluid wave of motion. Her voice was smug as she declared, "They didn't think I knew what was going on, but I heard everything they said about Mommy going to the hospital and Daddy going to jail."

Sarah felt a well of compassion rise up in her. Yes, they would need to talk about that also. Sadly, someone had misinformed the little girl; her mother was not in the hospital but had actually died before they could get her there. Sarah knew she would have to break the news to her somehow but thought that perhaps it would be better to wait until morning—let her get a good night's sleep in her new home before having to face more challenges.

But there was one thing that Sarah felt she could—and should—address tonight. The words that this five-year-old child had used to describe her sister could not be tolerated. Judging by Verena's appearance, there had been more than cruel words heaped on Emmeline's six-year-old sister, but it was all going to end here and now.

Sarah spoke in a kind but firm voice. "Emmeline, honey, your sister Verena was created by God in the same wonderful way that you were. She is very precious to Him—and she is very precious to me as well. So, in this house, you will not be allowed to talk about her in the way that you just did."

"But she's just a—" and to Sarah's horror, Emmeline went on to describe her sister using a string of vile obscenities. Then with a flutter of her big brown eyes and an angelic smile, Emmeline declared, "At least that's what my daddy calls her."

Her daddy... Sarah swallowed back the anger she felt towards him in that moment, and tried to see past his daughter's brazen attitude to the needy child within.

"Well," Emmeline demanded once more, "aren't you going to pray? Don't you believe in God?"

8

Sarah kept her voice soft and low. "I do believe in God, honey, and I would like to pray for you—and for your sister." As she said the words, Sarah moved to put an arm around Emmeline but she was immediately rebuffed.

"I didn't say that you could touch me!"

Sarah let her hand rest on the quilt, halfway between her and the child. She closed her eyes and began, "Dear Lord, I pray for Emmeline and for Verena, that You would help them to feel at home here and…"

Sarah felt the little girl bounce off the bed, and opened her eyes in time to see Emmeline running out of the bedroom. She hurried into the hallway after her but a howl from Verena told her that she hadn't been quick enough. Rounding the corner from the hallway into the combined kitchen and living room area, Sarah quickly scanned the room for the two girls. She saw Emmeline first, standing nonchalantly by the front door.

Sarah hurried towards her, still looking for Verena, and finally spied her cowering in the corner of the room, huddled up, crying, against the large desk adjacent to the door.

Sarah rushed forward to comfort the little girl but stopped short at the look of terror in Verena's eyes. She swung around, ready to ward off Emmeline, but Emmeline had maintained her position, a faint smile on her lips, her eyes issuing a bold challenge. Turning back to Verena, Sarah was shocked to realize that it was *her* that the little girl was terrified of—not Emmeline!

Sarah hesitated, unsure of how best to handle the situation. She was certain that Emmeline had hurt Verena in some way but she was equally certain that Emmeline would flatly deny it. And Verena, terrorized by her sister as she was, would never tell on her.

Then Sarah remembered something that her sister-in-law, Jamie, had told her about how she'd coped with her daughter Rosalee's difficult teen years. "You choose your battles," Jamie had said.

Maybe, Sarah thought, this was not the best time for a confrontation. The two children had been in their new foster home for less than an hour—it was late and they were all tired. And although Emmeline had been cooperative in taking a bath and putting on her new pajamas—and even saying her prayers!— Verena had refused to be drawn further into the house, even the few feet from the living room into the kitchen. She had remained with her head bowed, standing close to the door, while Emmeline had walked boldly past her, eagerly taking in everything there was to see.

Sarah had tried to coax Verena to at least sit down on the end of the sectional which was closest to the door. Finally, she had decided to "divide and conquer," by getting Emmeline ready for bed first and then later coming back for Verena.

Sarah decided that this was still a good plan. She turned her attention to Emmeline. "It's late, and you've had a long day. You head off to bed now. When Colin gets back, I'll send him in to say goodnight to you."

"No, he can't—I won't let him!" she answered defiantly, her eyes narrowing as she spoke.

"Okay." Sarah tried to make her voice sound cheerful. "Goodnight then—we'll see you in the morning."

Emmeline stood for a moment longer, her face settling into a frozen glare before she spun sharply on her heel and marched out of the room.

Sarah sighed as she heard the bedroom door slam shut. *What in the world had she got herself into?*

Verena was still cowering in the corner, her knees drawn up tightly to her chest, her terror-filled eyes watching Sarah's every move.

Sarah understood a little better now why Verena had arrived in the state that she had; her hair matted and her clothes dirty and torn. Likely, none of the other caregivers had been able to get close to Verena either.

Sarah had no idea how she was going to coax the little girl into the bathroom but it would have to be done. The smell emanating from her was strong enough to make Sarah feel slightly nauseous.

At least the children had been given supper already. The social worker, who had been waiting impatiently for Colin and Sarah when they had stepped off the plane, had told them that she'd finally taken the girls to the hotel restaurant when she realized that no one was coming to pick them up.

Sarah had been so embarrassed—their first day as foster parents and they'd blown it already! They hadn't been expecting the girls to arrive until the following morning so had decided to take the later flight into Rabbit Lake. The girls and the social worker had arrived at the airport at 4:00 pm; Colin and Sarah hadn't arrived until 7:00 pm!

And although they had been a little prepared, having been told that Verena, although thirteen months older, was smaller in size than her sister, they hadn't expected such extreme differences in their health and hygiene. It was obvious that Verena had been severely neglected and abused. She was too thin, her eyes had a dull, haunted look—and although she wore long sleeves and pants, Sarah had caught glimpses of some fresh and old bruises and scars on her ankles, wrists and shoulders.

Sarah knelt, hoping she would appear less intimidating, and smiled gently at the cowering child. "Verena, sweetheart, I won't hurt you. Please don't be afraid of me. Your sister's had a bath and is in bed. Would you like to take a nice bath too? I have some bath toys and bubbles..."

But as Sarah spoke, the little girl's fear seemed to escalate. She was trembling now and making low whimpering noises. The sound drove deep into Sarah's heart and tears filled her eyes. She couldn't ever remember feeling so powerless. Was there nothing she could do to help this little girl?

The door opened, startling them both.

"Colin!" Sarah exclaimed, "I'm so glad you're home. Verena is..." Sarah's voice trailed off as she got a clear look at her husband.

Colin's warm, brown, eyes, usually twinkling with good humor, were dull and smudged with grief and fatigue. His smooth, handsome face that lifted so easily into his trademark lopsided grin, was looking drawn and haggard, as if he'd aged ten years in the one hour that he'd been gone.

They had known about the passing of Colin's dear friend and mentor Tom Peters, since Friday afternoon, and it was Monday now, but Sarah and Colin had been in Winnipeg all that time. Colin had been unable to grieve with the family up until now...

"How is everyone?" Sarah asked.

Colin sank down onto the sectional and shook his head. "Not good," he replied wearily. "Missy is the most upset. It seems as if Joshua has disappeared."

"What!"

Colin nodded. "She said she left several messages on our answering machine. She doesn't feel that the police have tried hard enough to find him."

The police. As Chief of Police in this small Ojibway community, Colin had the full weight of responsibility for everything that was done—or not done—by his officers, even while he was preoccupied with family concerns 300 miles away.

Suddenly, Colin's focus shifted to Verena. "What's happening, Sarah? I thought you were going to bath the girls and put them to bed."

Sarah glanced at Verena, who was looking more curious than scared now. "Emmeline had a bath and is in bed," Sarah told him. "But Verena seems to get really afraid whenever I try to get close to her."

Colin sighed wearily. "She's got to go to bed sometime, honey. And she definitely needs a bath first. Just pick her up and bathe her, Sarah," he advised. "I'm sure that she'll be fine."

Sarah hesitated a moment, then slowly leaned towards the little girl, keeping her voice soft and low. "It's okay, sweetie," she said, "I'm just going to give you a little bath and then you can snuggle down under some nice warm blankets with your new teddy bear..."

Verena continued to cower trembling in the corner as Sarah spoke. But the instant that Sarah touched her, Verena struck out like a wild cat, raking the jagged edges of her fingernails across Sarah's face.

Colin jumped to his feet and grabbed Verena, who instead of striking out at him as she had Sarah, went completely limp and almost slipped out of his grasp. He quickly repositioned her, cradling her in his arms as he gently laid her on the sectional.

The violence of the attack had shaken Sarah to the core and she was trembling and weeping as Colin knelt down, wrapped his arms around her, and whispered words of comfort.

After a moment, he pulled back a little to examine her face. "We should get something on those scratches," he said in a voice that shook a little. Gently, he raised her to her feet. But as they stood together, they were transfixed by the sight of the little girl lying on the sectional. It was as if she were in a trance or some sort of catatonic state. Her eyes were open but they were fixed and staring at the ceiling.

"Colin..." Sarah whispered hoarsely.

He shook his head. "I don't know what's going on," he said anxiously. "But honey, you're bleeding..." He kept one arm around her as he led her towards the bathroom, but Sarah hesitated at the doorway, turning to check on Verena. "She'll be okay, hon," Colin said softly. "She even seems calmer now."

It was true. In her trance-like state, the look of wide-eyed fear was gone. Verena no longer cowered or trembled. She could almost be asleep if it were not for the fact that her eyes were open.

In the bathroom, Colin gently cleaned the scratches and applied antibiotic ointment to them. Fresh tears flowed down Sarah's cheeks and around his fingers as he worked.

"I don't know what I did wrong," she said. "She's so afraid of me. And—and I don't think I did so well with Emmeline either. I think she might have hit Verena. But—but I just didn't know what to do... Oh, Colin, I don't think I know how to be a mom... Maybe I'm not cut out for this..."

Colin drew her into his arms once again. He stroked her hair and spoke tenderly to her. "You're going to be a great mom, Sarah. We're going to get through this. It's going to be okay."

Colin led her back out into the living room where they stood for a moment watching as Verena lay still as a statue. "Maybe…" Colin began. "Maybe we shouldn't worry about a bath tonight. Maybe she could just sleep in her clothes. I'll just slip her into bed beside her sister——"

"No!" Sarah exclaimed. "Emmeline might hurt her. She can—she can sleep in the baby's room."

The baby's room…

"Are you sure?" Colin asked.

Sarah lifted her chin and nodded bravely, but Colin still hesitated.

The baby's room… It had been years since he'd even set foot in there. It had been closed up for so long that Colin could barely remember what it looked like, but Sarah could probably have described every inch of it.

She had begun decorating the "baby's room" the moment that the walls had gone up on the new addition they'd built onto his grandfather's old cabin. With joyous abandon she had painted, wallpapered, built shelves and made baby quilts. Together they had filled the room with a crib, dresser, change table and a multitude of toys. But as the months passed slowly by and still the hoped-for child failed to arrive, Sarah's focus had gradually shifted to decorating the other rooms, and sewing quilts for their own bed and the guest room. There were numerous trips down south to doctors and specialists, but to no avail. And when the months turned into years, Sarah's focus had shifted again to outside of their home—to helping others in the community.

It had been especially hard on Sarah when her mom, Gracie Waboose, had passed away. Added to the grief of her mother's death was the sorrow Sarah felt knowing how much her mother had been looking forward to grandchildren.

It was a week after her mother's funeral when Colin had arrived home to find the door to the baby's room shut. Sarah hadn't gone in there at all since that day and Colin had respected her feelings and stayed away from the room as well.

When they'd made the decision to take in foster kids, Colin hadn't been too surprised when Sarah had prepared just the guest room...

As Colin gently scooped Verena up in his arms, her face still fixed in that inscrutable mask, he mulled over the fact that Sarah must really be convinced that Emmeline could hurt her sister, to be willing to sacrifice the baby's room for Verena's safety.

Not expecting Sarah to follow him, Colin walked into the narrow hallway with its doors leading off to his right, and shifted the little girl's weight slightly in his arms as he turned the doorknob of the first bedroom—the "baby's room."

It had been closed up for too long—a thick layer of dust covered all the surface areas. Colin sighed; he would have to at least change the sheets on the crib. The rest could wait until morning. He glanced around the room, wondering where Sarah might have put the spare crib sheets—she certainly wouldn't have put them in with their regular linens.

As Colin turned towards the door, he was surprised to see her standing there, watching him. "I need to change the sheets," he said.

Sarah smiled wanly and walked towards the closet. "I'll help you." But her voice had a sad, hollow sound to it as she opened the closet door and lifted some sheets and a blanket down from the top shelf.

To Colin, it all felt so unreal—the limp child in his arms, and being with his wife in this room after so many years. He watched as Sarah quickly and efficiently made the bed and then walked out of the room without speaking another word.

The crib was a full size one that converted into a toddler's bed and there was lots of space for Verena's small body. Colin laid the little girl down on the bed and pulled the covers up over her. It was the end of July but this far north in Canada, the nights could still get cool.

Sarah had put the side rail of the crib down to make the bed. Colin left it down and moved a little stool over so that Verena could get out of bed easily if she wanted to. He stood awkwardly for a moment, looking down at her. Could she even hear him in that trance-like state of hers?

"Verena," he began haltingly, "you can use the bathroom if you need to. It's just back a bit toward the big room where we were before. I'll keep your door open and the hallway and bathroom lights on. If you need a drink or anything…" But even as he spoke, Colin realized that it was unlikely that she would leave the room. He only hoped that she wouldn't stay frozen in the same position all night.

A sound at the door made him turn. Sarah had come back with a bucket of water and a rag in her hand. She dipped the cloth into the soapy water, squeezed it out and advanced toward the crib.

Colin heard a cry of fear and turned back to see Verena clutching the blanket like a shield in front of her. The eyes that had been blank and expressionless a moment ago were once more wide open with terror.

"I—I just want to get rid of some of this dust," Sarah said, running the damp cloth across the top of the crib's headboard.

Colin gently put his hand over hers and pulled it away from the crib. "Let's wait and do that tomorrow, honey," he said softly. "For now, I'll just open the window to let some fresh air in."

Colin pushed aside the brightly patterned curtains and opened the window, thankful for the screen that would allow a cool breeze in from off the lake, without letting in all the mosquitoes as well! With summer at its peak, the mosquitoes and black flies were also at an all-time high.

The days were at their longest as well. Although it was almost nine o'clock, the sun was just setting on the horizon, bathing the sky, the lake and the trees in a warm orange glow. Colin drew in a deep breath, savoring the beauty and tranquility around him, thankful that when they'd put the addition onto his grandfather's cabin, they'd set all three bedrooms in a row so that each could have a window facing the lake.

Sarah's low cry of despair startled him back into the reality of the moment. He turned to see her still standing where she had been, cloth in hand, her eyes fixed on Verena, who continued to regard her with a look of stark terror.

"Why?" Sarah's whispered cry drove deep into Colin's heart.

He closed the distance between them and gently guided Sarah towards the door, swallowing a lump in his throat before he could speak. "Tomorrow—maybe things will be better tomorrow."

He glanced back as they left the room, and was surprised to find Verena looking at them intently, her eyes filled more with curiosity than fear. Colin tentatively smiled at her but immediately her eyes moved to the ceiling again. Colin sighed, his heart aching as he and Sarah walked down the hall into the bathroom, where she put away the bucket and cloth. He stood in the doorway, watching her, wondering what either of them could possibly do to help the little girl.

Suddenly a thought came to him. "Sweetheart, didn't you have a teddy bear for Verena?"

"Oh, I forgot!" Sarah exclaimed. "It's in the room where Emmeline is sleeping—up on the dresser I think."

Colin quickly walked back down the hall, past the baby's room, and quietly opened the door to the guest room. Emmeline was asleep on the big bed but it might just as well have been a small one. She was scrunched up against the wall with the blankets drawn close around her.

The floor squeaked beneath Colin's foot and Emmeline was instantly awake. She sat up straight, pulling the blankets up close to her chin. But there was no fear in her voice as she demanded, "What are you doing here?"

Colin bit back the retort: *This is my house; I live here!*

"I was just getting Verena's teddy bear," he spoke kindly as he made his way over to the dresser where the stuffed toy sat propped up against a table lamp.

"Why?" Emmeline demanded.

Colin was at a loss for words. *Why what?*

As he picked up Verena's teddy bear, he noticed that the one they'd given Emmeline was lying on the floor. Colin set it up on the bed. "I'm really glad that you've come to live with us," he said, "and I hope that you'll like it here."

Emmeline's eyes narrowed. "When are you going to leave?"

Colin still tried to keep his voice light and cheerful. "Now, I guess."

"Shut the door when you go!"

Colin's heart went out to her as he saw past her hostile words to the little girl who remained pressed against the wall, the blankets still clutched tightly against her chest.

"Goodnight, sweetheart," he said.

As Colin walked into the baby's room, he was immediately struck by the similarity between the two girls. Although Colin had yet to hear a word from her, hostile or otherwise, Verena too was huddled up in the corner of her bed, her covers tightly held in front of her chest.

It was as if she had been watching for him, waiting for his next move. Colin could only pray that sometime during the night the little girl would relax enough to go to sleep. Maybe the teddy bear would help.

Slowly, he approached the crib, desperately hoping that he would not make her more frightened than she already was. "I brought you a teddy bear, Verena," he said. "I'll just put it here beside you."

As Colin leaned over to set the bear down on the bed, Verena's arms dropped by her sides and her gaze became fixed on the ceiling.

Colin immediately moved away from the crib, his heart in his throat. He would never grow accustomed to seeing the death-like trance that she fell into whenever he touched her—or even came close to her!

His voice shook a little as he backed further towards the door. "Goodnight, Verena. I—I hope you have a good sleep."

With a heavy heart, Colin made his way slowly into the kitchen.

Sarah was sitting at the table, where she had set out a pot of tea and a cup for each of them.

Colin gazed at her beloved face, tracing his eyes over the high cheekbones and full lips that revealed her Ojibway heritage, and the curly brown hair and lighter complexion from her father's side. Even with the scratches on her face, she was beautiful. Her beauty wasn't only skin-deep either—she was warm, compassionate and caring, with even her career choice of nursing reflecting her concern for other people.

Sarah reached up and took his hand, drawing him into the chair beside her.

Colin looked into her chestnut-colored eyes, saw the sadness there and asked, "You okay?"

Her attempt at a smile was made more difficult by the scratches on her cheeks. "I didn't think that they would be so... *damaged*."

Colin withdrew his hand. "It's not their fault, Sarah."

She was instantly apologetic. "I didn't mean it to sound that way. I know it's not their fault. It's—it's just a bit of a shock, that's all."

Damaged... Colin's spirit recoiled at the word. To him it implied rejection and unworthiness. But that wasn't what Sarah had meant—or had she?

chapter two

"I'd like Emmeline and Verena to stay with us," Colin said.

"I would too," Sarah spoke quickly. "But..."

Damaged... Unworthy... Rejected... Voices from the past invaded Colin's head, taunts and jeers that had no place in his life now. Irritated with himself, he shook the voices out of his head. "But what?"

He could sense her hesitation. "I don't know if we are what they need, Colin. I can't even get close to Verena, and Emmeline seems to hate me already. Maybe they need psychiatric help or something."

"What they need," Colin said in a voice that trembled with emotion, "is a Mommy and Daddy that will love them and take care of them. I—I'd like to give them that, Sarah."

She leaned towards him and spoke earnestly, "I would too. I guess I'm just feeling a little overwhelmed right now, that's all."

Colin smiled wryly. "Me, too."

"May we should pray," Sarah suggested, smiling warmly back at him.

Colin nodded, and together they joined their hands and hearts, asking God for the wisdom and the love they would need to parent the two little girls.

Then Colin's thoughts turned towards the Peters family and he prayed for them also. When Colin had been up there, everyone had appeared to be exhausted, at the end of their resources both physically and emotionally.

Jeff, the eldest son, had left his wife behind in a Chicago hospital, dying of cancer. He and his sister Coralee had rented a van for their two families to make the twenty-four hour long journey north from Chicago, around Lake Superior and further north to Ear Falls, where they had left their van in long-term parking and taken the half-hour flight to Rabbit Lake. They had all arrived tired and disheveled to grieve with the family members already there: Martha, Tom's widow; Bobby, the youngest son; and Missy, Tom's granddaughter.

Colin prayed for each of them by name. When he mentioned Missy, he heard Sarah gasp and when he ended his prayer, her question was immediate. "Oh Colin, I forgot! You said that Joshua had disappeared—and Missy thinks the police haven't been looking hard enough for him? You left Keegan in charge, didn't you?"

Colin nodded. He had felt confident leaving the Assistant Police Chief, Keegan Littledeer, in charge of the unit while he was in Winnipeg. "But he had to leave also," Colin told Sarah. "Randi had some bleeding on Saturday evening and they thought at first she might be having another miscarriage."

"Oh, no!"

"She's okay," Colin quickly reassured her, knowing that Sarah's own hopes for a child made her more sensitive to others

23

who were trying to have one. "They did fly her out Saturday night, and they kept her under observation at the hospital for a couple of days, but she was released earlier today."

Sarah looked relieved. "Oh, that's good," she said

"Randi and Keegan got home just before us," Colin continued. "They came in on the early flight."

It still felt a little strange to Colin that there were now two scheduled evening flights into Rabbit Lake. For years, there had just been one, arriving at 4:00 pm and departing at 4:30 pm. But the demand had increased to the point where Rabbit Lake Airlines had added the extra flight that arrived in at 7:00 pm and departed half an hour later.

"That's right," Sarah commented. "He was the one who called to tell you that the girls had come in on the early flight."

"Keegan left Constable Adams in charge while he was gone," Colin resumed.

"Constable Adams!"

Colin sighed. "He *is* highly qualified."

"...To work down south!" Sarah declared. "From all that I've heard, he's pretty clueless about people in general and he knows nothing about life here in the north."

Colin had to agree. The man seemed to specialize in trampling on people's feet. And although he had married a First Nations woman, he had met her while she was at school in Winnipeg, and so had never spent more than a couple of days at a time in the north prior to arriving at his post in Rabbit Lake just a week ago. Fortunately, Colin hadn't had any direct dealings with the man since, so far, they'd been on opposite shifts since his arrival.

"Apparently he didn't take Missy's concerns seriously," Colin said. "And Jeff hasn't been much help. He thinks Joshua is out drinking with his buddies, either grieving for Tom or celebrating the inheritance that he received from him."

Sarah shook her head in confusion. "Drinking?—Joshua! And what inheritance are you talking about—Tom left him some money? That wouldn't make Joshua go out drinking. Doesn't Jeff know his future son-in-law at all?"

Colin sighed. "Apparently not. They haven't actually had that much contact with each other through the years. Jeff's been down in Chicago and quite busy with his work and then preoccupied with Jenny's illness. And…" Colin hesitated. "And maybe there are still some unresolved issues… that are maybe clouding his judgment right now."

He could see by the look in her eyes that Sarah didn't understand.

Colin wasn't sure he understood either. His voice remained hesitant as he attempted to explain. "It had something to do with Jeff being white and his adoptive parents being African-American. *They* accepted him and loved him but I guess Jeff was teased at school and in some ways, he just felt like he never lived up to his father's expectations."

"But Jeff's a pediatric surgeon. Tom must surely have been proud of him!"

"Yes, I know that he was. And I'm not sure where the disconnect came from. You know Tom was always so big and loud and… decisive."

Sarah laughed. "That's one way of putting it!"

Colin smiled too but his heart ached with the knowledge that he would never again hear Tom's "big, loud and decisive" voice. Oh, how he would miss him!

"Jeff was always sensitive," Colin continued. "He was a thinker; Tom was a doer. Jeff was a bookworm; Tom was an athlete."

"An NBA champion and then a coach for many years," Sarah added.

Colin nodded. "And Jeff grew up in his shadow. And there was always a lot of media attention, people speculating about the white boy adopted by the black basketball player, asking if he would ever be able to follow in his father's footsteps and learn how to play basketball like him…"

"You know," Sarah mused, "in all the times that Jeff has been up here to visit, I don't think I've ever seen him play. I know Bobby loves to join in whenever there's a game on."

Colin thought that maybe it was because Bobby was born with Down's syndrome. "Yeah, but it might be easier in some ways for Bobby," Colin said. "Everybody always praises him whenever he has any small successes. He's not under the same kind of pressure as Jeff would be."

"You mentioned an inheritance," Sarah prompted.

Colin nodded. "Yes, Tom named Joshua as his primary beneficiary."

"Primary?" Sarah questioned. "Instead of Martha?"

"Yes," Colin replied. "Martha and Bobby have a settlement. It's quite a large amount. They won't have to worry about money ever—they'll be able to live quite well off the interest."

"And Joshua…"

"Joshua got everything else—the lodge, all the property and all the rest of Tom's money, which is a lot."

"But the lodge…" Sarah exclaimed. "That's Martha and Bobby's home."

"Joshua would never force them to leave," Colin said, feeling as if he were stating the obvious. "And Tom and Martha were planning to move out of the lodge anyways when Joshua and Missy started up the youth program there. They wanted to still stay close to support Joshua and Missy—probably in one of the cabins or the house by the lake—but this whole thing of Joshua taking over the lodge is not new." Colin felt a pang of grief. "It's just… early."

Sarah reached over and gently squeezed his hand. "But Colin… I still don't get why Jeff would assume that Joshua is drinking. It's been years, hasn't it?"

"Yeah, seven years to be exact. He quit drinking right after his father died. And to my knowledge, he hasn't touched a drop since."

"So why…?"

Colin sighed. "I guess things were pretty tense there Saturday night. Tom's death was such a big shock—to all of us. We knew that he had some heart problems but he was always so big and strong—I guess we all just thought he would live forever." Colin shook his head, trying to shake away his grief but it stuck like a burr. "Anyway," he continued wearily, "everyone was also really tired from traveling. And you know how Coralee is—always trying to organize everything and everyone. Of course, she felt the will needed to be read that night. It was just the wrong timing, I guess. There was quite a bit of… heated discussion. A lot of the family didn't agree with Tom's wishes. Missy said that her dad even talked about hiring a lawyer and contesting the will. So when Joshua left the lodge that evening and didn't return, I guess everyone thought maybe things had just got too hot for him."

"The Joshua I know wouldn't run away from his problems like that," Sarah declared.

Colin smiled gratefully at her. Joshua was like a little brother to him and it warmed Colin's heart to have Sarah defending him. "Missy didn't think he ran away either. She wanted to call the police right away but her father insisted that he take a look around first. That's when he found the empty beer bottles scattered around outside the lodge."

Sarah frowned. "And he jumped to the conclusion that Joshua was off on some drinking binge?"

Colin sighed again. He couldn't ever remember being so bone-weary tired. "Yeah, that's about the size of it."

Sarah stood to her feet. "I should call Missy."

Colin remained where he was as Sarah dialed the lodge's number. Missy must have picked up at the first ring for Sarah started speaking almost right away. "I'm so sorry about your grandpa, Missy."

Sarah's face filled with concern as she listened. Then she spoke again, "Yes, honey. Yes, he's here. Yes, of course."

Sarah handed Colin the phone. "Hey, Missy," he said gently.

"Colin..." The young woman's voice broke into a sob. "Colin... what if he's hurt? What if he's dying?"

Before he'd left the lodge, Colin had assured Missy that he would organize a full search party for Joshua in the morning, and Missy had seemed okay with that. But now as he heard the desperation in her voice, Colin realized that she needed him to do something now—tonight.

"It's the third night, Colin! Tomorrow's Grandpa's funeral. Joshua would never do this. You know he wouldn't."

And suddenly the extreme urgency of the situation hit Colin. Missy was right. Joshua would never of his own volition abandon Missy—or Martha and Bobby—at a time like this. He'd been missing for two full days. Anything could have happened in that amount of time!

"Missy," he said quickly, "I'm going to call in the Emergency Response Team. I don't think they'll send in their helicopters until after sunrise either but at least they'll be ready to get going at first light. And I'll start calling our local people too."

Missy's cry of thanks broke into a sob again and Colin assured her that he would call her back after he had begun the preparations for the search.

He started with the contact list of local people, thankful that they had developed this a few years back. It made it a lot easier for him to just call the top three people on the list. Each of those three were responsible for calling three others, who would then call three more each.

Colin also called Keegan, to begin a chain that would notify all the police officers in the detachment.

Once the two contact chains were activated, he placed a call to the regional Emergency Response Team. They agreed to help out, and asked for more information about Joshua.

Colin was able to give a fairly good description of him: 23-years-old; five foot ten; about 150 pounds; long black hair, usually worn in a pony tail or braid down his back; dark brown eyes… But he had no idea what Joshua had been wearing on Saturday. He

didn't even know the exact time that he'd gone missing—
something that he would normally have found out right away at
the beginning of any investigation.

He called Missy, telling her that plans for the search party had
been put in place. Then he asked her the questions that he should
have already asked.

Missy described what Joshua had been wearing. In honor of
Tom—and knowing that all the family would be arriving—Joshua
had worn a black short-sleeved cotton dress shirt and a pair of
black dress pants. He had a pair of black casual leather slip-on
shoes. No jacket—it had been a warm summer evening and he
hadn't been planning to go out…

Colin questioned Missy on this last point. How did she know
that Joshua was not planning to go out? Obviously, he *had* gone
out.

"He was just answering the door," Missy explained. "And then
he stepped outside to talk to them and that was the last I saw of
him."

This was news! "There was someone at the door?" Colin asked
excitedly. "Who was it?"

"I don't know," Missy said hesitantly. "I thought I heard
Joshua say his brother Russell's name…"

"No, it couldn't have been him," Colin said. "He was arrested
in Winnipeg Thursday night."

"Arrested?"

"Yes." Colin hesitated, wondering if he should burden Missy
with all the details.

But she continued in an anxious voice, "Maybe he was
released by Saturday."

"No, there's no way that he would have been. His wife…" Colin lowered his voice and moved further away from the hallway so that if Emmeline or Verena were awake, there would be no possibility of them overhearing him. "His wife took their children to a child protection agency and signed a statement accusing her husband of child abuse. Then she left the two girls in the waiting room, went alone into the bathroom and slashed her wrists. They didn't find her right away, so by the time they got her to the hospital it was—it was too late."

"Russell's wife…?" Missy asked in a dazed voice.

"Yeah, I don't think most of us even knew that he was married. I had heard that he got released from jail after only serving a few months, though." Colin sighed deeply. Russell should still have been serving his prison term even now—instead he'd been out scot-free for the past seven years. "I heard he was living out in Edmonton…"

"Russell's wife…" Missy said again in a slow, sad voice. "She would have been my sister-in-law—after Joshua and I were married. Now, I'll never have a chance to even meet her."

"I'm sorry, Missy," Colin said, regretting that he had told her when she already had so much else to deal with. "Sarah and I went to the funeral on Saturday in Winnipeg. We thought maybe the girls would be there."

"Girls?"

"Russell's kids," Colin explained. "He has two children; they're staying with us now."

"That's good," Missy said, still sounding a bit overwhelmed by it all. "So it couldn't have been Russell…"

"No, I did see him Saturday but I think he was just out on a pass for his wife's funeral. I'm sure that this time they're gonna

31

lock him up and throw away the key." Colin, thinking about the two little girls, found himself fervently hoping that this time there would finally be justice.

"I just don't understand who it could have been," Missy said, her thoughts on Joshua again. "And I don't understand why there would be all those beer bottles out behind one of the cabins. My dad said there were a lot of them. Someone must have been there."

Colin shook his head. "I don't know," he said. "But Missy, I need to ask you another question: Can you tell me what time it was that Joshua left?"

Missy hesitated. "I don't remember exactly…"

"Just an approximate time then…"

"Well, everyone arrived a bit after seven," Missy began. "Aunt Cora got everything organized right away and figured out where everyone would sleep. There was lots of food that people had dropped off for us so she got us all to sit down and eat together. Then after we were done with that, even though everybody was tired, she insisted that we had to read Grandpa's will. We gathered at the end of the lodge by the fireplace and she gave it to my dad to read. And after he read it, everybody started to argue. And Grandma started crying because everyone was fighting. And Bobby got all upset. Oh, Colin, it was just so awful!"

"I can well imagine," he spoke grimly. "So do you think it might have been around nine o'clock or so when Joshua left?"

"Maybe…" Missy said thoughtfully. "I know my dad asked for a flashlight when he went outside to look. But that was a while later."

"Okay, that's near enough anyway," Colin said. "Listen, I've got to go. I need to call the Emergency Response Team back. You try and get some rest, okay?" Leaving Missy with some more reassurances, Colin then contacted the Emergency Response Team to pass on the information he'd gained. They confirmed that they would arrive the next morning and Colin informed them that there would be a group of local searchers ready to help out also.

He hung up the phone and sank wearily down onto the sectional. Sarah came and sat beside him. "You should try to get some sleep," she said. "Tomorrow is going to be a long day."

Colin nodded. "We should be ready to start by six o'clock at the latest. And some of us will have to pull away from the search for the funeral at eleven o'clock."

"You think you'll still be searching by then?" Sarah asked.

Colin sighed wearily. "I don't know. There's hundreds of miles of bush around us. He could be anywhere."

Sarah took his hand. "We should get some sleep. It's been a long day—a long couple of days."

A long couple of days... What had they been like for Joshua? An image of the young man rose in Colin's mind. And suddenly he knew that he couldn't sleep until he knew that Joshua was safe.

"I'm going to go look for him," he said.

Sarah's eyes opened wide in surprise. "Now?"

"Yes. Will you be okay while I'm gone?"

"Of course!"

"The girls..." he reminded her.

Sarah looked towards the hallway and hesitated. "Maybe they're asleep by now."

Colin smiled reassuringly. "C'mon, let's go check on them together," he said.

They almost made it in and out of Emmeline's room without waking her. She was huddled against the wall as before, her teddy bear once more on the floor.

"Can't you just leave me alone?" her petulant voice demanded as they were just about to close the door.

"We won't bother you again tonight, honey," Sarah spoke gently. "We just wanted to make sure that you were okay."

"Well, I'd be a lot better if you wouldn't come in here waking me up every five minutes!"

"We'll see you in the morning," Colin said as he shut the door.

They walked silently into Verena's room. A sliver of light from the doorway fell across her sleeping form. It was the first time that Colin had seen the little girl relaxed and peaceful. And she was holding the teddy bear that they had given her.

Colin glanced over at Sarah and his heart soared as he witnessed the look of pure joy on her face. He put his arm around her and they quietly left the room together.

chapter three

Colin pulled the high-powered searchlight out of the storage box in the back of his truck and wondered what else he might need. Sarah had offered him coffee and sandwiches. He probably should have accepted the coffee at least. He hadn't slept much the past few days, worrying about the girls—and worrying about Tom's family.

He realized now that it would have been better if he'd stayed in touch with them the whole weekend—then he would have known about Joshua's disappearance. But after the initial phone calls to the lodge, Colin had felt so helpless that he had decided to wait until he could comfort Martha and Bobby in person. He'd never been really good at expressing his feelings over the phone.

Colin sighed. He hadn't been able to offer much comfort in the end, anyway—both Martha and Bobby had been inconsolable. But Missy and Joshua... Perhaps there was something that he could do for them.

Even if he didn't find Joshua tonight, just the fact that someone was out looking would be a consolation to Missy.

But where to begin?

The lodge, of course! Again, Colin realized that he wasn't fully functioning as a police officer right now. His judgment was clouded with emotion and even the things that should be second nature to him, he seemed to be forgetting. Of course, he should begin at the spot where Joshua was last seen. And there were perhaps some more questions that he should ask Missy... if he could just push past this fatigue and the huge weight of grief that threatened to crush him.

He started to climb into his truck, but then thought that maybe he should instead walk up to the lodge, and search along the shoreline on his way. Joshua might be there.

But then again—he might be anywhere!

With sudden decision, Colin shut the truck door and strode down towards the lake. He would search the shoreline and then search around the lodge property.

The wind was blowing from the east down the hill toward the lake and as Colin picked his way along the shoreline, he occasionally caught a whiff of smoke. Not normally an unusual thing since many people had woodstoves, but it was the end of July and most people would have fans going to keep them cool, not fires to keep them warm.

It could be a group of kids. They tended to hang out a little ways from the main community but not too far as most of them were on foot. They usually went this way north of the community towards Goldrock Lodge or east of the community up behind the airport.

If it were kids, they had likely lit a fire to keep themselves warm while drinking or sniffing solvents or getting high on some new drug being imported from the south. Many of them were malnourished and wouldn't have a lot of body fat to keep them warm. And they would be sitting or standing around for hours instead of moving about as Colin was.

As he continued along, shining the powerful searchlight in one direction and then another, Colin couldn't get the kids off his mind. For so many years, they had tried so hard as a police force and as a community to protect their kids from substance abuse. Rabbit Lake had long been declared a "dry reserve," a place where alcohol was banned. And they had instituted stiffer fines and longer jail terms for those caught selling illegal drugs.

Of course, it was recognized that drinking and drugging was only a symptom of a much deeper problem but everyone seemed to have different ideas about the solution. All kinds of programs had been developed and various activities were planned for the Arena and the Community Center but these programs never seemed to touch the neediest of the youth.

Colin's thoughts returned to Joshua. Having battled with drugs and alcohol himself, Joshua had a real heart for these kids. He'd worked for many years up at the lodge with Tom Peters. They had been running a youth camp every summer but it had been mostly for kids from the south. This summer was to be their last. After that, the winterized cabins would be used for a year-round program for troubled youth. The ratio of campers to staff would be quite high: two to one. They would be given help with schooling but a lot of their growth and development would come from real life experiences as they were taught a variety of skills. Instead of just learning how to drive a boat, they would learn how to maintain an outboard engine as well. The same would be true in the fall and winter with ATV's, chain-saws and snowmobiles. The youth would learn carpentry as they worked on maintaining the cabins, cooking skills as they prepared food, and health and hygiene as they kept themselves and their living environment clean.

But what would make the camp stand apart from many other good programs would be the emphasis on the spiritual as well as the physical, mental and social. By introducing the young people to their Creator and to His Son Jesus, the staff would be in a position to offer real hope and healing to these kids who had been hurt so deeply in so many ways.

There wasn't really a decent trail along the lake between Colin's house and the lodge property but it was easier going than if Colin had tried to travel directly through the bush. Almost as impenetrable as a jungle, machetes sometimes were the best way to break a new trail through the dense pine forest, thick with poplar and birch saplings struggling to fight their way up towards the sun. The terrain was rough too. Besides the risk of tripping over protruding roots or fallen trees, there were frequent rock outcroppings and the land itself was uneven, so that Colin found himself continually walking either uphill or down.

It also didn't help that it had rained recently. Colin ended up slipping off a rock and getting soaked past the knees at one point—and trudging through sticky mud at another. The mosquitoes were bad too, drawn by the glow from the search light. Another big disadvantage of searching for someone at night!

Colin was relieved when the house on Sandy Point finally came into view. The lights were on so obviously some members of the Peters family were staying there. He passed Charles Kakegamic's houseboat, docked in Macaroni Bay, but there were no lights on there. Colin knew that Charles had been away from Rabbit Lake on a book tour but was expected to arrive in time for the funeral, if not before. Likely there would be a lot of people arriving back on the early morning flight. Colin's sister, Jamie, and her family were due back then, too. They'd been out in Regina getting Colin's nephew, Andrew, signed up for the RCMP training there.

Colin passed the cabins in a row around the southern curve of the bay and Goldrock Lodge came into view. A powerful floodlight at each end of the building illuminated the two-story-high building with its tall glass windows, skylights and rooftop deck. Built flush against a huge rock outcropping, Goldrock Lodge was always an impressive sight, whether by day or night.

The door was unlocked and Colin stepped in without knocking. All the lights were off but a voice spoke out of the darkness. "Hello? Who's there?"

"Hi Missy, it's me, Colin."

Blind since birth, Missy had no need of lights so often forgot to turn them on. Colin flicked the switch on a small light near the entrance, rather than turning on the huge overhead crystal chandeliers extending down from the cathedral ceilings, just in case everyone else was already in bed.

He turned to his left and walked over to where Missy was huddled in what had been her grandfather's favorite chair, in front of the stone fireplace that dominated the south end of the lodge.

As Colin approached, he switched on another small table lamp.

Unlike her sister Jasmine, Missy bore almost no resemblance to either her adoptive father or her birth mother. Where Jasmine had a pale complexion, wavy blond hair and blue eyes, Missy had dark skin and black, tightly curled hair that she often wore in African braids. Missy had not let her blindness stop her from looking her best—she always made sure that her clothes were matched and that her makeup was flawless. Tonight, though, she hadn't taken her usual care with her appearance. Her hair was pulled back into a pony tail and she wore faded blue jeans and a T-shirt that Colin recognized as Joshua's.

As he closed the distance between them, Colin spoke with compassion. "How're you doing, Missy?"

She opened her mouth to reply but dissolved into tears instead.

Colin leaned over and put his arms around her. She wept on his shoulder for a moment before gaining control of her emotions and her voice once more.

"Thanks for coming over," she said.

Colin eased down into the sofa close to her chair. "I was out looking for Joshua..."

"Oh Colin!" Missy exclaimed. "You're looking for him? You're really looking for him?"

Colin had to swallow past the lump in his throat. "Yeah, I'm looking for him."

She began to weep again. "Thank you," she murmured. "Thank you so much."

Colin grimaced. He didn't deserve such effusive gratitude. When someone was lost, it was the responsibility of the police to find them. There was for sure something wrong with this picture.

Colin looked around. Even now—where was everyone? If they weren't out searching, they should at least be keeping vigil with Missy, not leaving her alone, when her fiancé might be lying dead in the bush somewhere!

"Where is everybody?" he asked with some irritation in his voice.

Missy waved her hand towards the door. "They all left shortly after you did. Dad and my sister are staying at the house on Sandy Point. Dad wanted me to stay there too—he said we should be together as a family at a time like this. But—but Joshua is the one I want to be with."

"And your Uncle David and Aunt Coralee...?" Colin asked.

"They're staying in one of the cabins. They said they wanted to get my cousin, Alisha, to bed. They're all so tired—from the grieving, and from their long drive." And before he could ask, she added, "And Grandma and Bobby went upstairs too. Everyone seems so tired..." Her voice trailed off. She herself sounded exhausted.

Colin stood to his feet. "Missy, I'm going to start by looking around outside the lodge. When Joshua went to answer the door, it was the main door, right?"

He was surprised when Missy answered, "No, it was the side door off the hallway by the kitchen."

Now that was interesting... Most people came to the front door. "Okay, I'm going to start there," Colin said.

Missy jumped up. "Take me with you!" she pleaded.

Colin bit his lower lip. "Umm... Missy..."

"I know I'm blind!" she shouted. "I know I can't really help you. But please... please... take me with you. I just can't stand to sit here any longer, just waiting and doing nothing. Please..."

Colin thought about how he would feel if it was Sarah who had disappeared three nights ago. And for Missy to be blind and unable to search for Joshua herself... "Okay," he said with a deep sigh. "You can come with me."

"Thank you!" Missy exclaimed, her words broken by sobs.

She was already moving towards the door when he noticed she didn't have her white cane. He spoke hesitantly, "Missy, it's pretty rough terrain out there in some spots…"

She turned around, impatience on her face and in her demeanor. She strode confidently around the tables and chairs that were in the large dining area and retrieved her white cane from a shelf by the door and stuffed it into a backpack, which she slung over her shoulder.

"And you should let someone know that you are leaving," Colin suggested.

"They're all asleep," Missy retorted.

"I'll leave them a note," Colin offered.

"I'll do it," Missy snapped, moving back past the front door into the other sitting area where there was a computer, stereo and television set. Colin walked over to join her as she sat down at the computer, typed a quick message and printed it out.

Missy stood to her feet. "Anything else?"

There was more anguish than anger in Missy's tone and Colin understood that. He looked at her dry, chapped lips and said, "Just one more thing."

Missy reluctantly followed him into the kitchen as Colin poured a glass of water for each of them. Over Missy's protests, he asked, "When did you last eat or drink anything?"

"When did *Joshua* last eat or drink anything?" she countered. She grabbed up two water bottles, stuffed them into her backpack, and walked away, refusing the glass of water he offered her.

He allowed her to stride past him and out the side door before catching her arm to slow her down. "Missy, I know you're feeling anxious for Joshua but a proper search takes time. I'm not going to be running; I'm going to be walking. I'm going to be trying to find any clues I can as to where he might have gone."

Missy nodded and said in a subdued voice, "I understand."

Colin looked carefully around the side of the building but if there had been anything to see, the recent rain had obliterated it.

"Where did your dad say he found those bottles?" Colin asked.

"Just over behind the first cabin," Missy said.

But although Colin looked there and around the other cabins as well, there was no sign of them.

"Did your father pick them up?" Colin asked.

"Not that I know of."

"Well, someone did," Colin replied grimly. Maybe the same *someone* responsible for Joshua's disappearance.

"He didn't drink very much," Missy spoke softly.

"What?" Colin spun around to face her. "What did you say?"

"We talked about it earlier," Missy continued in a sad, quiet voice. "You asked how much I had to eat and drink in the last few days…"

"Oh, I thought you meant—never mind."

"When everybody got here, Aunt Cora made us all sit down to eat," Missy explained. "But Joshua didn't—he couldn't. He got up from the table and went over to sit by the fireplace. I started to go with him but Dad and Aunt Cora made me come back. They kept bugging me till I ate something. But they just left Joshua alone…"

And that, Colin thought, just about summed up how the visiting Peters family had treated Joshua.

"He didn't have much to eat or drink before then, either," Missy said. "We were so much in shock after Grandpa died. I remember Joshua saying that every time he tried to even drink anything, his throat would just close up. I know he couldn't eat."

"So, it's not just been two days," Colin said grimly, "but almost four days."

"We've got to find him!" Missy exclaimed, walking rapidly towards the Mine Road.

"Missy!"

She stopped and walked slowly back towards him.

"I want to search the old mine buildings too," he said. "And running around like chickens with our heads chopped off is going to get us exactly nowhere." As Missy stifled a sob, Colin continued in a gentler voice, "Joshua's been missing for over two days now. A few minutes one way or the other probably won't make that much difference to him."

And at this point, it didn't...

chapter four

When they'd first bound him with his arms behind his back and his legs bent up behind him, the duct tape wound over and over between his wrists and his ankles so that he couldn't move at all, every second had felt like a minute and every minute had felt like an hour. The steady drone of insects and their frequent piercing bites, combined with the intense pain in his limbs from being constrained in one position, had made time into a crueler enemy than death itself.

But Joshua had long since given up praying for death. He had long since given up praying for anything. As the minutes had passed into hours and the hours into days, his thoughts, once coherent and linear, were now just a confused jumble. Nothing made sense anymore. Dehydration had begun to take its toll, and disorientation and confusion had replaced any rational thoughts that might have lingered.

Russell noticed the difference this time. When he had put his fingers on his brother's wrist and demanded as usual, "Still alive, eh?" there had been no answering response—no flinch or even a faint twitch of a facial muscle—nothing. Maybe his brother *was* dead! He hadn't really been serious in his "pulse check"—he'd started it when Garby and the others had complained that Joshua could die without water. And Russell had enjoyed suddenly coming up to his brother, grabbing him by the wrist and startling him into movement—movement that caused him intense pain as his frozen muscles were forced into action.

But up until now, Russell had not really considered that his treatment of Joshua could result in his death. It wasn't actually possible to feel his pulse beneath the layers of tape but there'd always been some kind of response when Russell grabbed his wrist.

Through the flickering firelight, Russell watched, and felt relieved to see Joshua's chest slowly rise and fall.

He rocked back on his heels and looked down at the inert form. Maybe it was time for his brother to be found. First degree murder had never been a part of the plan. He'd just wanted to teach the little wimp a lesson.

Russell had been mostly staying away from Rabbit Lake, making a name for himself first in Edmonton and then in Winnipeg. People on the street knew him, feared him and respected him. The new drugs that were available were in high demand by the young, rich snobs in the city and Russell had enough money to make himself a favored guest among the elite. He had friends. He had power. He was *somebody!*

He'd expected Joshua to still be rotting away in Rabbit Lake, still at his beck and call, cowering, cringing...

Instead, he'd been told that Joshua was up at the Big House, living like a king, planning to marry the Big Man's granddaughter, no less! And now to top it all off, it seemed that the old man had died and Joshua had inherited the whole kit and caboodle!

Russell had decided that maybe he should go up there with his brother, Garby, and a couple of his friends to help Joshua celebrate. They'd even brought some hard liquor that he'd smuggled in on the plane.

But then the little twerp had acted embarrassed to be seen with them! He'd shut the door and gone outside to try to get rid of them!

Russell had been angry alright. He'd wanted to teach his kid brother a lesson about respecting his elders. But that didn't mean that he wanted to kill him... Maybe it was time for an anonymous tip to be passed on to the police.

They sure hadn't been having much success in finding him so far—not that anyone seemed to be trying all that hard. There hadn't been any large scale search and rescue effort; the Emergency Response Team hadn't been called in. And Russell had taken great delight in keeping Joshua up to date on the non-progress of the police.

Joshua hadn't believed him at first and though his mouth was taped shut, he had managed a muffled protest when Russell had gleefully told him that not even his precious fiancée had gone out looking for him. But as time passed, Russell could see that the message was finally getting through to his baby brother. No one cared at all that he'd gone missing! Russell enjoyed watching the defeat and depression grow, knowing that he was finally breaking Joshua down.

"Oh, how the mighty are fallen!" He'd said that more than once over the last few days! And if he thought his brother hadn't heard him, he'd kick him a few times till he was sure that Joshua was awake enough to hear. "Oh, how the mighty are fallen!"

He'd taped Joshua's eyes shut after just a few hours. Where there should have been hate there had been only sorrow, and perhaps even pity. Russell hadn't been able to stand those eyes watching him and accusing him by their very non-accusation.

Garby and his friends had drifted off earlier in the day, after all the booze was gone. Russell had been glad to see them go. They were starting to whine and complain too much and Russell had got tired of their talk about freeing Joshua. He would let him go when he was good and ready!

Russell flipped the steak over. It smelled good. In the beginning he had taken great pleasure in knowing that Joshua could smell the food and was no doubt craving what Russell described in detail as he ate. Now Joshua was too far gone to even notice. Russell thought that maybe he could have prolonged things if he'd loosened the tape around Joshua's mouth and given him some water now and then.

Yeah, it was probably time that the little twerp was set free. Russell knew there would be no danger of Joshua squealing on him to the cops. He'd shown him who was boss and Russell was pretty sure that Joshua wouldn't ever forget it again! And Garby and his friends wouldn't say anything that would implicate them. They didn't have a bunch of lawyers feeding at the trough the way that Russell did. And his aunt would stick up for him, no matter what.

A half-formed plan churned around in Russell's mind. What if he was the one to "find" Joshua? Could he make it convincing enough? Already, he knew, there was some sympathy for him in the community. His aunt had made sure that the police knew he was a grieving widower. Russell grinned as he thought about *that* scene. His Aunt Yvonne could be pretty convincing when she wanted to be. When that cop had come around asking if anyone had seen Joshua, he'd wanted to talk to Russell, too. That's when his aunt had told him that Russell was off in the bush, grieving—and it would be wrong for the cops to go out there and disturb him. If he knew his Aunt Yvonne, Russell figured she had probably also thrown in a grand performance as the grieving mother-in-law—even though she'd never even met Russell's wife.

Well, Russell could continue the good work his aunt had begun. He might even decide to stick around Rabbit Lake. He'd heard his daughter was going to be sent up here to a foster home—he'd get her back soon enough—his lawyers were working on that already. Yeah, maybe a new life up here with just his daughter and *without* that sniveling piece of trash and that pile of garbage that was always clinging to her. It was time to make a new start.

A grieving widower... And Russell figured he could also easily paint himself as the victim in the case of his daughter's "abduction" by the children's "protective" services. His lawyers were all prepared to back him up. They'd done a good job of getting him out of jail already. And they were pretty certain that his wife's testimony could be invalidated—the ranting of a crazy woman, now dead—who would believe her?

And his wealth was sure to impress everyone—everyone liked it when a reserve kid "made it" in the big city—and came back loaded.

Now to add to his "homecoming," he'd be the one to find poor lost Joshua. If he could lead the police to this spot... maybe say that he noticed some smoke off in the bush...

Russell looked around. He'd have to get rid of any evidence that might point to him or any of the others. He gathered up all the bottles and garbage strewn around the area, and with a pine branch swept away all the recent footprints, noting with satisfaction that the recent rain had already done a pretty good job of washing away any evidence of their presence. The grass that had been trampled had sprung up again, and the rocks and fallen logs, where there might have been evidence of spilled food or drinks, had been washed clean.

Russell kicked Joshua but didn't get any response—not even a groan or a flinch.

He kicked him again. "Wake up, little brother! You're going to be released soon."

There was still no response but Russell once again noted that Joshua was at least still breathing.

He took one final look around. He'd clean up his own footprints as he went. His plan was taking shape. He'd go to the police station and tell them that he had smelled smoke over behind the airport and thought it was his civic duty to report it. Russell chuckled to himself as he thought about his possible reception at the police station. The irony of the situation hit him; it was the first time he'd ever gone to *that* place voluntarily!

chapter five

Colin and Missy finished searching around the old mine buildings of the former Goldrock mine, now all Goldrock Lodge property. But all the buildings had been secured long ago and there was no sign that the locks had been tampered with.

Colin felt unsure of his next move, torn between the urgent need to continue searching and his usual practice as a police officer to go down to the station and read through any documentation there might be of any search efforts already undertaken. The Emergency Response Team would be expecting a full report in the morning when they arrived.

Colin tried, without success, to persuade Missy to return to the lodge or to stay with Sarah, but the young woman was determined to continue with the search.

As they walked along the Mine Road back to his house, Colin shone the light to and fro through the trees, and Missy called out Joshua's name.

They stopped in to see Sarah, and although Missy was willing to accept a hug and words of comfort from her, she was not prepared to abandon the search for Joshua.

"I can't just sit around and do nothing, anymore," Missy explained. "I've been doing that for two days now. And maybe I can help somehow…"

Colin sighed deeply. Sarah and Missy both looked exhausted. What they all needed right now was some sleep. They could join the organized search in the morning…

But Colin knew that before the Emergency Response Team arrived, he needed to at least see the reports of what had been done so far to search for Joshua.

"I just need to go down to the station for a bit," he said.

"And I'm going with you," Missy declared.

Colin, not knowing what else to do, finally relented and drove down to the police station with her.

Inside, he was shocked to find Russell Quill!

He was sitting nonchalantly in Colin's desk chair, pulled out of his office and placed in front of Constable Adams' desk. Russell reeked of citified wealth. His hair was slicked back and he wore a thick gold chain around his neck and a single gold earring in his left ear. He had on a black leather jacket over top of a purple shirt that looked like it was made of silk, and his jeans, just touching the top of his brown suede loafers, actually had a front crease in them!

"What's *he* doing here?" Colin demanded.

Constable Adams raised his eyes inquiringly. "And *you* are?"

"I'm the Chief of Police."

Russell smirked. "Congratulations."

Constable Adams kept his stiff demeanor, flicking his eyes over Missy for an instant before focusing them on Colin once more. "And she is?"

Colin felt at a distinct disadvantage. He was out of uniform, his clothes were torn and muddy from his search, and he was tired, so very tired, both emotionally and physically.

He turned to Russell. "What are you doing here?"

Constable Adams spoke in a stiff official voice, "Mr. Quill has come to report that he observed smoke in the general vicinity of the Rabbit Lake Airport terminal building."

A sneer covered Russell's face as he stood and walked towards Colin and Missy.

"What's *she* doing here?" He stabbed a finger into Missy's chest.

Missy gasped and took a step backwards. Colin grabbed Russell's arm, berating himself for not anticipating something of the kind. He stepped in front of Missy, effectively shielding her from further assault.

Russell feigned innocence. "Hey, I was just wondering why you'd brought your lady friend along to work with you. I thought you already had a woman—or did you trade her in for a younger model? You should have checked your warranty—didn't you notice, she's blind as a bat?" Russell added in a stage whisper, "And black as one, too."

Colin unconsciously tightened his hold on Russell's arm.

The gleam in Russell's eyes brightened. "Now, now. Police brutality!"

"Maybe I should wait outside in the truck," Missy said hesitantly.

Constable Adams came around from behind his desk, glancing from Colin to Russell and back to Colin again. His eyes narrowed suspiciously as he asked, "You two know each other?"

Colin gave him an exasperated look. "Of course I know him! I've lived here all my life. I know every single person in this community."

Russell leered at him. "Yes, but you have to admit that you do know me better than most." He turned toward the young police officer and then let his eyes casually travel back to Colin. "He accused me of sexual assault. Maybe I was guilty," Russell spoke languidly.

The young police officer looked from one to the other. "I think that maybe we should call in somebody else on this— someone impartial."

"But what about Joshua?" Missy protested.

Russell raised his eyebrows in her direction. "Ah, so that's who you are! Joshua's woman. Worried about him, are you?"

Colin could stand it no longer. He grabbed Russell by the shirt collar and spoke through gritted teeth, "If you know something about where he is..."

"All right, none of that!" Adams said, surer than ever of his authority now.

Colin pulled his hands away from Russell, strode to the phone and jabbed out a seven-digit number.

His voice softened a little when he realized that he was speaking to Keegan's wife. He'd woken her—and that likely meant that Keegan was asleep as well. "I'm sorry to wake you, Randi, but we need Keegan down here at the police station—yes, right away—thanks."

Colin hung up the phone and led Missy to the other end of the room, as far away from Russell as possible.

They all sat in silence for the ten minutes that it took for Keegan to arrive. Constable Adams busied himself with something on his desk while Russell sat eyeing Missy and Colin, a self-satisfied smirk on his face.

When Assistant Police Chief Keegan Littledeer entered, Constable Adams rose to his feet in obvious respect for the man to whom he had been reporting for the past week. Keegan, in contrast to Colin, was dressed in a clean, wrinkle-free uniform, his closely cropped curly hair not requiring any combing.

Keegan looked around the room, taking in Russell's insolent attitude, Colin's frustrated demeanor and Missy's expectant air. He glanced at the young police officer but spoke first to Colin. "You needed me?"

Colin smiled wryly. "Conflict of interest," he spoke succinctly. "It seems that our friend here feels that I may have a personal vendetta against Mr. Quill and that it would be wise to call in another officer on the case."

Keegan turned on the young man, his eyes blazing. "Constable Adams…"

The young man snapped to attention, fearful for the first time that he might have made a mistake.

"In this community, there is *no one*…" Keegan Littledeer advanced toward the junior constable and repeated the words, raising his voice for emphasis, "There is *no one* more well respected than this man sitting right here. If you have *any* questions about his leadership capabilities, you might want to find yourself another detachment to work for.

"As for this man…" Keegan turned towards Russell. "He is a criminal—and a liar."

Keegan picked the report up off the desk and read quickly through it. Then he turned to Colin. "Did you want to check this smoke thing out?"

Colin stood to his feet and sighed deeply. "Yeah, I think maybe we should." He shook his head. "I wouldn't normally but I did smell the smoke myself earlier and..." He glanced over towards Russell. "I just have a strange feeling about all this."

"Right," Keegan said, "let's go then."

Colin hesitated. The last information that he'd had on Russell was that he had been remanded into custody. "I'd like to make one quick phone call first," he said.

"Colin," Missy pleaded, "can't we just go?"

"She's right, you know," Russell spoke flippantly. "Her lover boy could be dying even as we speak."

Colin made a quick decision. He told Keegan and Constable Adams about what he knew of Russell's arrest in Winnipeg, then ordered Adams to call the Winnipeg police and find out Russell's official status. He grabbed a radio phone and told the constable to call him as soon as he had the information.

Keegan picked up a radio phone as well and told Constable Adams to stand by to arrange for any additional help that he and Colin might require.

Colin decided that Missy should travel to the airport with him in his truck. Keegan could follow with Russell in the cruiser.

It was only a matter of minutes to the airport. They got out of their vehicles and Missy took Colin's arm as they all headed out behind the large terminal building.

"I saw the smoke back of the runway somewhere," Russell said, taking the lead.

Colin had every nerve alert—to be out here in the dark of night following Russell seemed the height of folly. *He was not to be trusted!* Colin wished that he'd left Missy back at the police station. She wouldn't have been happy about it but at least she would have been safe!

"Just over here…"

Colin heard Russell's voice ahead of them. "Walk behind me," he said to Missy.

Keegan held the searchlight, illuminating the way ahead of them as they continued along the runway. Suddenly, Russell veered off into the bush and as they followed, Colin reached back and grasped Missy's hand.

When the dying campfire, and a dark shape on the ground beside it, came into view, Colin dropped Missy's hand and hurried forward but she quickly grabbed his arm and kept up with him.

Her voice was frantic. "Colin, what do you see? Please tell me!"

He knelt down and Missy knelt with him.

"It's Joshua," Colin said in a voice he didn't recognize as his own.

With a little gasp, Missy began to feel around in front of her. "Where?" she cried.

Colin placed her hands on Joshua's face.

"There's tape…" Her voice shook. "And he's so cold… Joshua… Oh, Joshua…"

"I'm getting my knife out." Colin tried to keep his voice calm but he couldn't stop the storm of emotions from sweeping over him—anger toward those who had hurt Joshua—and fear that they might have arrived too late.

But he felt as Missy did. *They had to get this tape off!*

Keegan held the search light over them as Colin sawed through the tape that was wound around Joshua's ankles and wrists but even after his arms and legs were freed, Joshua remained locked in the same position. Missy picked frantically at the tape around Joshua's mouth but still there was no response from him at all. And Colin knew that it was time to call for additional help…

"Keegan, get hold of Doctor Peters. Give him directions to where we are. Tell him it's an emergency! And call the station. I need more officers down here. I want a full scale crime scene investigation."

Missy was weeping now, calling Joshua's name over and over. Colin reached for his pulse—he'd been delaying the moment—when suddenly Russell grabbed Joshua's other limp wrist and cheerfully asked, "Still alive, eh?"

The reaction from Joshua was dramatic and totally unexpected. His limbs flailed out in all directions, striking both Missy and Colin. Then as his overtaxed muscles contracted into painful spasms, an anguished moan came muffled from behind the tape still binding his mouth.

Recovering quickly from the shock, Colin got to work on the tape around Joshua's mouth while Missy began to gently massage his arms, trying to ease the painful cramps out of his muscles.

They talked to him all the while, Missy's words coming in short, quick gasps. "It's okay. Josh, we're here. It's going to be okay. You're going to be okay, Josh. You're going to be okay…"

Colin worked at keeping his voice slow and calm. "Hang in there, buddy. Help is on its way."

He was grateful that Keegan kept on holding the light above them even as he made the necessary phone calls. The tape had been wound over Joshua's mouth and around behind his head and Colin chose a bit of a looser spot just below his ear to begin cutting. It was slow, difficult work to get the knife under the tape without causing any further injury. Finally Colin cut all the way through, and freed an end that he could pull with. Slowly he began to ease the tape off.

But Joshua reached up and tried to tear it away faster, ripping skin off his lips and causing himself further pain by using the contracted muscles in his arm. And he seemed to be half-drowning in the terrible gulping sobs that shook his entire body.

Missy, her hands feeling Joshua's frantic fumbling, tore the remaining tape from off his mouth and stroking his face, bent over him, speaking words of comfort, trying desperately to calm the nearly hysterical young man.

Colin thought that she was having some small effect. Joshua was still trembling violently but he no longer was gasping for breath and the painful, rasping sobs were subsiding.

Colin turned as he heard the sound of a vehicle and someone calling out.

Jeff Peters…

Keegan went to meet him, directing him through the bush towards them.

"You didn't take long!" Colin exclaimed, a grateful tone in his voice.

But as Keegan's light returned, Colin could see that Jeff was not in a particularly good mood. His thick blond hair, usually combed neatly, was standing on end in places and his grayish blue eyes were clouded with anger. In a gruff voice, he demanded to know what his daughter was doing out here.

"Dad, we found Joshua!" Missy exclaimed.

"Would have thought that was a job for the police," Jeff spoke tersely.

He nudged Colin aside as he bent over Joshua and put a stethoscope on his chest. "Why is this tape still on his eyes?" he demanded.

Colin found himself fumbling for words. "I was—we were just going to…" As he spoke, he reached for his pocketknife again. Jeff put out his hand for it and Colin gave it to him.

As Jeff began to work on the tape, he spoke to Missy. "You should be home with your grandmother."

Missy didn't answer.

"Did you hear me?"

"Yes," Missy responded in a barely audible voice. If Colin hadn't been holding his breath waiting for the faint reply, he wouldn't have heard it at all.

As Jeff pulled roughly at a large section that was wrapped around Joshua's head, pieces of his hair were torn away also. Joshua cried out and Jeff tersely commanded Colin to hold Joshua's head still.

"Be careful!" Missy exclaimed, tears running down her cheeks as she reached out to smooth down Joshua's hair.

"Don't bump me," Jeff berated her. "Do you want me to put this knife through his eye? What's he got all this long hair for anyways? What a mess!"

"Go!" Missy spoke in a deep-throated voice, still clogged with tears. "Just go and leave us alone."

Colin watched as the look of impatience on Jeff's face turned suddenly into remorse, and he knew that Missy's words had hit home. In all the years that Colin had known Jeff, he had never seen the man be purposely cruel to anyone. But he *had* seen him lose control of his emotions and unintentionally hurt others, as he was doing now.

Jeff quietly handed the knife back to Colin and gently pulled the rest of the tape away from Joshua's eyes.

Joshua flinched and tried to turn away from the light, and Keegan quickly shifted the powerful searchlight so that it wasn't shining directly into his eyes.

Jeff leaned forward and pulled one of Joshua's eyes open.

Joshua moaned and tried to pull away, and Missy angrily demanded, "What are you doing now?"

"I need to see into his eyes," Jeff said gently.

Joshua stopped struggling and looked at Jeff. And in that moment, Colin realized the emotional toll that the kidnapping had taken on the young man. All the confidence that Joshua had gained in the past seven years seemed to have been stripped away from him. The look of hopeless despair drove deep into Colin's heart.

Jeff couldn't help but be affected too—but his first concern was for his daughter. "Missy," he said softly. "I want you out of this. Leave it for the police to handle. C'mon, let's go."

"No!" Missy flared. "*You* go! I'm staying with Joshua."

Jeff rose slowly to his feet and spoke in a dispirited voice, "Colin, make sure he gets some water… Frequent, small sips… You don't want to overload the depleted cardiovascular and pulmonary systems. And I'll call an order in for some cream for those insect bites."

Missy latched onto the one word. "*Water!* I have water in my backpack. I left it in the truck."

"I'll get it," Jeff said.

"No!" Missy shouted, starting to rise to her feet.

Colin stopped her with a hand on her shoulder. "Let your dad go," he said softly. "You stay here with Joshua."

Missy sank down again. She smoothed back Joshua's hair and ran her fingers over his face, her only way of "seeing" him. Tears sprang suddenly to his eyes and Missy sobbed out his name, "Joshua, oh, Joshua…"

"It's because of the light," Colin said, almost convincing himself that it was true. "If he's had that tape on for two full days, the light will bother his eyes. Keegan, move it away a bit more."

Joshua smiled faintly at Colin and his eyes conveyed gratitude for a brief instant before darkening with despair once more.

"Well, this has been fun—but I really should be going now."

Russell…

Colin had forgotten that he was even with them! He turned towards the voice and Keegan tilted the light a little so that he could see Russell sitting on a log, surveying the scene with a smirk on his face.

Colin looked up at Keegan. "Any news from Winnipeg?" he asked.

Keegan spat on the ground. "They say he's free to go."

Colin turned back to Russell who returned his glance with a wide grin and a smart salute. "See you later—'pee-pants'!"

That almost forgotten taunt from so long ago!

When Colin had first arrived at the Quill house as a foster child, he'd been so frightened, in an unfamiliar place, his parents recently killed in a plane crash…

He wasn't frightened now. Colin glared at Russell but it didn't seem to faze him one bit. Colin could hear him laughing as he sauntered away.

Colin felt shaken and, at the same time, angry with himself for allowing Russell's comment to bother him.

62

M. D. MEYER

Keegan kicked up some dust with his boot and spat on the ground again. "What a jerk!"

Colin glanced up at him, grateful for the support from his colleague. Keegan had been on the wrong side of the law as a youth and had come a long ways since. He was a good police officer now, well respected in the community.

Jeff returned with Missy's backpack. He gently spoke Missy's name, handed her one of the bottles, and gave the other to Colin.

"Thanks," Colin said. "Missy, we'll hold Josh's head up a little, okay?"

The instant a drop of water touched his lips, Joshua's hands fumbled frantically for the bottle.

"Take it slow," Colin cautioned.

Joshua nodded but still some involuntary reaction took over, and he gasped and sputtered as he tried to take in huge gulps of water all at once.

Colin pulled the bottle away for a minute to let Joshua catch his breath.

Joshua reached out for the bottle that was in Missy's hand and she, feeling the tug on it, quickly unscrewed the cap, ran her fingers along Joshua's cheeks to his mouth, and held the bottle to his lips. Colin, seeing what she was doing, helped her to hold it to Joshua's mouth. "He needs to take it slow," Colin reminded her.

Jeff had been standing by, silently watching them. "I'm going now," he said in a weary voice. "Unless you need help..."

"No!" Missy snapped. "We don't need your help at all."

Jeff sighed resignedly and turned to go.

"Jeff!" Colin stood to his feet. "Thanks."

Jeff turned back, smiled faintly and gave him a small salute before disappearing into the trees back towards the airport parking lot.

In his wake, two police officers emerged, arriving in response to Keegan's summons. Jonathan Quequish and Richard Meekis were both competent, experienced officers. They'd brought additional high powered search lights, which combined with Keegan's, illuminated the entire area.

Colin glanced around, for the first time taking in the fact that the ground had been swept clean. His eyes rested for a moment on the log where Russell had been sitting.

"We'll need to find some solid proof," he said, trying to suppress his rising anger. "Something that will stick when it comes to trial. Keegan, I'm putting you in full charge of the investigation. Just keep me informed of any new developments. Oh, and be sure to call the Emergency Response Team right away. Let them know we found Joshua."

Keegan nodded his assent and Colin spoke to one of the other officers. "Jonathan, can you give me a hand here?"

"Where we taking him?" Jonathan asked, as he linked hands with Colin behind Joshua's back and under his legs, forming a kind of chair.

"Just to my truck," Colin answered.

But as they carried Joshua through the bush and along the airport runway, Colin thought about their final destination. He was quite certain that Joshua would not want to go to the Health Center and besides, if Jeff had thought that he needed hospitalization, he would have said so. Sarah was a nurse; she would know how best to care for him...

When they got to the truck, Missy moved ahead of them and opened the driver's side door, then slid over on the wide bench seat to be ready to help them pull Joshua in.

Colin saw that what she had decided made sense. He released Joshua to stand for a moment supported against Jonathan. Then he reached in to tilt the steering wheel column up out of the way and then backed off himself so that Jonathan could, assisted by Missy, get Joshua into the driver's seat.

Colin thanked Jonathan, who went back to the investigation, and then helped Missy move Joshua into the middle seat between them, where he would be cushioned and supported as they traveled.

He then made a quick call to Sarah, shifted the truck into gear, and headed out onto the Airport Road.

chapter six

Missy felt the weight of Joshua's head on her shoulder and a chorus of gratitude sprang up within her.

He's alive! He's going to be okay! He's alive! He's alive!

They hit a bump in the road and Joshua made a low moaning sound. Missy tightened her hold on him and spoke comforting words in his ear. "It's okay, my darling. It's okay. Everything's going to be okay now."

"Hang in there, buddy," Colin added, patting Joshua on the knee. "We're on the Mine Road now. Almost at our turn-off…"

It wasn't really that far from the airport to Colin and Sarah's house; at least Missy had never thought so. But now, as she noticed each little bump and turn in the road, and worried about Joshua's discomfort, their journey seemed to just go on and on forever.

When Colin finally eased on the brakes, made a sharp turn and headed downhill, Missy knew that they had turned off onto the long driveway that led down to his house by the lake.

Sarah must have been watching for them because no sooner had they stopped than Sarah was opening the door on Missy's side of the truck.

"How is he?"

The compassion in her voice shattered Missy's composure. "They—they tied him up, Sarah! And he didn't have anything to drink. There was tape on his eyes and on his mouth..."

Sarah put her arm around Missy and leaned towards Joshua at the same time. "He has a lot of bug bites, too." Her voice was etched with concern as she spoke Joshua's name.

He didn't answer but Missy felt his head move slightly and wondered if Joshua had opened his eyes and was looking at Sarah.

If so, his look did nothing to reassure her, for the anxiety in her voice had increased as she said, "Let's get him inside."

Missy heard Colin's door open. "Are we taking him out the same way he came in?" she asked.

"Missy..." Sarah said gently. "It would be better if you let us do this."

It was frustrating—and worse because Missy knew she was just as strong and capable as Sarah. But she obediently slid out of the truck and let Sarah take her place at Joshua's side.

She pulled her white cane out of her pack and tapped it in front of her. At least Colin had parked right in front of the door...

Joshua's anguished groan caused Missy to spin around towards the truck again.

"Just a couple of steps," Sarah said. "You can do it, Josh."

"You're making him walk!" Missy exclaimed.

But it *was* only a couple of steps—and once again, Missy found herself in the way. She walked quickly inside the open door and past the sectional—that was likely where they would let Joshua sit down again.

As she heard them ease him down onto the cushions, Missy moved quickly to his side. She pulled the half-empty water bottle out of her backpack, unscrewed the cap, touched his face, and held the bottle to his mouth.

Sarah's voice sounded close above Missy and she felt another hand on the water bottle. "Good idea, Missy. Just a sip, Josh…"

But once again, Joshua's desperate thirst made him try to grab for the bottle and swallow the water all at once. He coughed and sputtered, then groaned as the muscles in his arms seized up.

Missy gentled massaged his arms, easing the tension out of them as Sarah continued to hold the water bottle and speak to him. "Just a little sip. That's it… Okay, now just a bit more… Okay, Josh, it's empty now. Colin, is this all he's had since you found him?"

"There were two bottles…"

"He finished one out there," Missy spoke up. She turned towards Colin. "This one here is the one that you had set down. I picked it up and brought it with me."

"Good," Sarah said. "Now, I think a hot bath would help a lot with the stiff muscles. Josh…?"

Again there was no verbal response and Missy felt frustrated at what they could see and she could not. And it frightened her, as nothing else could, that Joshua was making no effort to communicate with her.

"It's not that far, Josh," Sarah was saying.

"It's a long ways!" Missy protested.

"It would be better if he moves around a bit," Sarah insisted.

And before Missy could say or do anything else, they were lifting Joshua to his feet again.

Missy walked quickly around them and grabbed hold of the desk chair that she knew was up against the desk on the adjacent wall. She rolled it towards them. "Here, use this at least."

To Missy's great relief, she felt Sarah take the chair from her, and heard them speaking as they eased Joshua down into it.

Missy followed them through the kitchen and into the hallway but Sarah stopped her at the bathroom door. "Missy," she said, with some irritation in her voice, "let us handle this. I'm a nurse. If Josh was in the hospital, you'd be out in the waiting room. Maybe… maybe you could make a pot of coffee."

Missy swallowed back a retort and strode into the kitchen.

They'd left the bathroom door open, and even with the water running in the background, Missy could hear every step of the process. She winced every time she heard Joshua groan in pain, even though it sounded like Sarah and Colin were trying to be gentle…

"Lift up his arm a bit, Colin, and I'll get this sleeve off…"

"Just raise your foot a bit, Josh, so I can take off your shoe…"

Missy turned resolutely towards the task she had been assigned, finding the coffee pot where Sarah usually kept it. Missy knew where the coffee was, too.

She had just sat down in the big wooden rocking chair that was between the kitchen and living room, when Joshua's cry of pain, followed by a splash, made her jump to her feet again. And when a child's terrified scream came from the same general direction, Missy hurried towards the sound.

She felt the child brush past her and Missy turned back towards the kitchen. By the time she'd walked to the center of the room, the terrified screams had subsided into gasping sobs and Missy could hear that the little girl had gone into the furthest corner of the living room, over behind the desk.

Missy walked over to the rocking chair and sat down. She didn't want to frighten the child more by moving too close to her.

She waited a moment before asking gently, "Could you tell me what's frightening you? I can't see at all. Is there something that I should be afraid of?"

"Bath—water," the little girl said in a trembling voice. "They're hurting him!"

"No," Missy said gently. "No, they're not, honey. It's because he was tied up for a long time and it hurts him to be moved at all."

The sobs had subsided into deep trembling breaths and Missy listened, waiting for the child's response to her words.

It was a moment before the little girl spoke again and when she did, it was not what Missy had expected. "You—you can't see anything at all?"

Missy smiled in her direction. "No, I can't."

The voice sounded closer this time. "Why?"

Missy hesitated, finally deciding on an abbreviated form of her story. "When I was born, I had an operation done that resulted in me losing my sight."

The little voice was quite near now. "But you have eyes…"

"Yes," Missy carefully explained, "they're prosthetic eyes."

"Pros—pros…" the little girl struggled to pronounce the unfamiliar word.

Missy smiled. "Prosthetic," she said again. "They're artificial eyes made out of acrylic plastic. I can't see through them but the ocularists try to make them look like real eyes."

A series of low groans and the sound of sloshing water came from the direction of the bathroom. Tears sprang to Missy's eyes. *Joshua… Oh, Joshua…*

Missy felt a small hand tentatively stroke her wet cheek. "How come you can cry when you've got no eyes?"

Missy stifled back a sob and answered the child's question, glad that this topic could provide a distraction for the frightened little girl. "My eyes are gone but the tear ducts are still there—and they work just fine."

There came a louder slosh of water and a deeper cry of pain and the child beside Missy began screaming again, "No! No! No!"

Quickly Missy reached out and pulled her up into a tight embrace. "Oh, honey, it's okay, it's okay," she cooed softly. "They're not hurting him. They're just helping him out of the tub. They're his friends. I'm his friend. I wouldn't let anyone hurt Joshua…"

Missy's voice trailed off.

She *had* let someone hurt him. Missy searched her heart. Was there anything more she could have done?

If her father hadn't been so convinced that Joshua was out drinking, his judgment clouded because he was so worried about Missy' mother…

And if everyone else hadn't been so preoccupied with the will…

They were all so sure that Joshua was at fault somehow. But it had been Grandpa's decision, not Joshua's. The whole way that things had been done was so typical of her Grandpa. He'd been of the "old school"—fiercely independent, having had to fight his way up in life. He hadn't believed in boards or corporations or partnerships. He'd been the sole owner and when he died, he wanted Joshua to be the sole owner!

And if Charles hadn't been gone on his book tour… Charles would have stuck up for Joshua. He was Grandpa's best friend—he knew the will was something that Grandpa Tom would have done.

And if Grandma hadn't been so crushed down with grief and so overwhelmed by all Aunt Cora's questions...

What did it matter what songs were sung at Grandpa's funeral? If Grandpa was alive, he would have been the first one out there looking for Josh.

If she could have reached Colin sooner... but he hadn't been available, and even Jamie and Bill had been out in Saskatchewan. And former Chief of Police Sammy Rae, another good friend of Grandpa's, was also out of town. Even Keegan had been gone... And instead, every time Missy had called the station, there had been that same complacent voice, patronizing her, minimizing her concerns about Joshua.

Voices in the hallway brought Missy back to the present.

Then there was complete silence.

Missy strained her ears, wondering what was happening, feeling increasingly more uncomfortable. Then someone moved and Sarah's voice sounded quite near, speaking in a breathless whisper, "She's asleep."

Missy realized that Sarah must be talking about the child on her lap.

"She looks..." Sarah continued to whisper, her voice filled with awe. "She looks so at peace there."

Colin spoke then. "Missy, do you think that you could carry her back to her room without waking her?"

Missy smiled. "I'll try."

"I heard her scream," Sarah continued in a quiet voice as Missy rose with the little girl in her arms. "Then I heard you talking to her. But I never dreamed that you'd be able to get her to go to sleep."

As Missy walked down the hall, she felt a little guilty about all the praise. She hadn't been really thinking about the little girl at all. She'd been rocking her but all her thoughts had been on Joshua.

Colin directed her. "One more step to your left—you're at the crib now—we put a little stool on the floor in front of it."

Missy felt the stool with her foot and leaning forward, felt the edge of the railing. She eased the little girl down onto the bed and felt for covers. There was a teddy bear there, too and Missy tucked it in as well. She smoothed back the little girl's hair and kissed her forehead.

A thought struck her suddenly. This would be her niece—after she and Joshua were married. And she didn't even know her name.

"What's her name?" Missy whispered, turning back to the others.

"Verena," Sarah answered in a voice that sounded as if she were holding back a great deal of emotion.

Missy began to walk toward the door. "Where's Joshua?" she asked.

"We put him in our bed," Colin spoke up.

Missy walked out and turned to her right, running her hand lightly along the wall until she came to the last bedroom door. It was open and Missy walked in. She'd been in here before and unless they'd changed things...

"We moved the chair over beside the bed," Colin told her.

Because there were glass patio doors that faced the lake, Colin and Sarah had an easy chair that was usually set over by them.

Missy felt for the chair that was now close beside the bed and sat down in it. Sarah's voice came close beside her. "Colin, will you bring a glass of water in for him? Missy, we need to keep giving him sips of water. I'm going to head over to the Health Centre and get the medication that your dad ordered."

After Sarah and Colin left, Missy leaned forward, softly speaking Joshua's name. When there was no response, she touched his face with her fingers and was shocked when she found that his cheeks were wet.

"Joshua…" she called out softly once more, her heart in her throat. "Josh, is the light bothering your eyes?"

She felt him shake his head slightly but instead of relief, Missy felt increased anxiety. Joshua wasn't someone who cried easily. Even this past Friday and Saturday, he'd kept a tight control on his emotions, trying to be strong for everyone else.

Missy reached out for his hand and found that it was trembling. She wondered if it was because he was cold or if it was an aftershock of his experience. The muscles in his arm were tense and she wondered how much pain Joshua was experiencing.

Colin arrived with a glass of water and Missy asked him if there was some Tylenol or something that they could give to Joshua.

"I'll call Sarah," he said, and a few seconds later, Missy heard him speaking to her on his cell phone. After he finished, Colin told Missy, "Your dad ordered a muscle relaxant for Joshua—Sarah thinks that will help a lot."

Colin had put a straw into the glass of water. Missy leaned towards the bed. "Josh, here's some more water for you…" She reached out to touch his face so she could hold the straw to his mouth. This time there was no mistaking the fresh, warm tears on his cheeks.

Unmindful of the tears streaming from her own eyes, Missy forced a smile to her lips as she held the straw for him. She felt the cold water in the straw and heard him swallow. Joshua drank down the whole glass and somehow it made her feel a bit better.

She set the glass down and took his hand again.

"Missy…" Colin spoke hesitantly.

She turned towards the sound of his voice. "Yes?"

"I—I think that Joshua and I need to talk—alone."

Missy felt as if he'd struck her. Or that Joshua had…

Talk? Would Joshua really talk to Colin when he wouldn't talk to her, his fiancée? Colin sounded pretty sure of himself. And once again, Missy wondered what he was seeing that she was missing. Joshua hadn't spoken one single word since they'd found him—and now he and Colin were going to have a cozy little chat—without her.

"Joshua…" she whispered hoarsely, "Joshua, is that what you want?"

"He's nodding his head, Missy," Colin said gently.

She swallowed back the tears that threatened to spill over again, released Joshua's hand and stood unsteadily to her feet. She made her way towards the door, walking too far one way and bumping into a wall before finding it and passing through into the hallway.

chapter seven

Colin was suddenly thrust back to a time when a much younger Joshua had lain in this very same house after having been beaten to a pulp by his older brothers. It had been Grandpa Pipe's cabin then, and the kind old man had offered sanctuary to Joshua as he had many years before to Colin.

But Joshua had been too afraid of his brothers to move out from under their tyranny. And he'd been too afraid to seek any kind of medical attention, knowing that if he went to the Health Center, they'd have to report his injuries to the police—and if that happened, his brothers would hurt him even worse.

Colin and Grandpa Pipe had done their best, bandaging up the cuts and taking care of the boy for as long as he'd stay with them. But Joshua always returned to his brothers... until the day that Tom Peters had put a stop to it all.

At almost seven feet tall, with the bulk to match his height, Tom had been a powerful ally for Joshua. Together they had stood up to the brothers and, after that, none of them had ever hurt Joshua again.

Until perhaps now...

"Josh…" Colin said gently. "Was it Russell? Was he the one who did this to you?"

Joshua shut his eyes, closing out the world as he had done so many years before.

Colin leaned towards him. "If you could talk about it, I know that it would help you."

His eyes remained closed but slowly Joshua shook his head.

"Let me help you," Colin pleaded. "A burden is always lighter carried by two people instead of just one."

"It might be too soon, honey." Sarah's soft voice came close behind him and Colin felt her hand on his shoulder.

Sarah… his dear precious wife who had walked with him through so very much.

"He needs rest. I think we all do," she said gently.

Colin sighed and stood to his feet. Sarah was probably right.

"I talked to Doctor Peters and he thought that it might be a good idea to give Joshua an IV also," Sarah said. "And something to help him sleep. He likely hasn't slept much since Friday night."

Colin watched as Sarah started an IV in Joshua's arm, gave him an injection, and rubbed some ointment on his bug bites. She gave him a few more sips of water and then straightened out his blankets and pillow, gently sweeping his long, still damp, hair out from under him and off to the side. They hadn't attempted to brush it out at all; there were still bits of tape clinging to it and it was hopelessly tangled—something that would have to be dealt with when Joshua was stronger. For now, Sarah was right—he needed rest. "May the Lord give you peace, my little brother," she said as she bent over and tenderly kissed him on the forehead.

Colin was deeply touched by her words. She'd never called Joshua her brother before. Technically, Colin had only been

Joshua's foster brother but this young man, who had lost his mother as a child and his only sister and father as a teenager, desperately needed a family to help shelter him from life's storms.

Colin put his arm around Sarah as they walked out of the room, leaving the door open so that they could hear if Joshua woke and needed anything.

Missy was sitting in the rocking chair looking tired but composed. Colin greeted her and she asked anxiously, "Did he talk to you?"

"No," Colin replied wearily.

Missy stood to her feet. "I have to go to him…" She spoke the words as if in a daze and she staggered a little as she walked towards them.

Colin reached out a hand to steady her.

"Missy," Sarah said, "maybe it would be better if you rested."

"No!" Missy exclaimed frantically. "I *have* to go to him."

Colin nodded over Missy's head at Sarah, then said, "Okay, Missy, here, take my arm, though. You look like you're about ready to drop." He helped Missy towards the bedroom and into the chair that he'd just vacated, and she immediately ran her hands over the covers until she located Joshua's hand, and clung to it. The medication seemed to be taking effect—Joshua was already asleep.

Colin found Missy a pillow and blanket. He touched her shoulder in parting. "If there's anything that you need…"

She smiled wanly up at him. "Thanks, Colin."

Out in the living room, he found Sarah was already lying down, curled up on the smaller end of the sectional that faced the hallway.

"No, no," he said as she started to get up, "you should rest. Lay back down. I'll get you a blanket."

"What about you?" she asked as Colin placed a cushion under her head and draped an afghan over top of her.

"I'll just lie down here too, I think," Colin said, stretching out on the longer piece of the sectional that ran along the front wall of the house.

Sarah's eyes closed right away and a moment later her deep, even breathing indicated that she was asleep. But with so much on his mind, sleep didn't come as easily for Colin. How could he convince Joshua to give evidence this time? He had to find some way to persuade Joshua to stand up against his abuser, or else Joshua would remain in bondage, forever the victim. It was unthinkable!

Colin stood quickly to his feet, too agitated now to attempt sleep.

He walked quietly over to the sink, poured himself a glass of water and drank it slowly, standing at the kitchen counter. He thought back over his own life and the changes that had occurred through the years. As a youth, he had been enslaved to alcohol and had lived in fear of his older foster brothers. Then they'd gone to jail and he'd been free for a while—but then they'd come back, and the nightmare had begun all over again.

But as Colin carefully searched his heart, he knew that he was no longer afraid of them—no longer in bondage. What had made the difference in his life? What was it that he could share—*must share*—with Joshua to enable him to experience the same freedom?

They were both Christians, and had begun their journey of hope in Jesus' forgiveness and unconditional love. Colin knew that people had been instrumental in his healing as well. It had been important—no, essential—that someone had taken the time to really listen to his story with total acceptance and love, and had given him the opportunity to grieve. Tom had been the first and then Sammy. But as the layers of pain had been peeled away, it was to Sarah that Colin had turned for comfort. And to the Lord—some things could perhaps never be completely understood by another human being. And there were things that he would never wish for Sarah to understand—for to understand, she would have had to have experienced some of what he had, and he would wish that on no one.

Colin's thoughts returned to Joshua. Maybe he was reading too much into that bleak look of despair. Surely Joshua would rally again. He couldn't have lost all those years of growth in one bad experience. The Christian life was a progression and God only allowed trials in the life of a believer to strengthen them—not to crush them.

Colin found his Bible on top of the microwave and opened it. He flipped through until he found the eighth chapter of the book of Romans and the twenty-eighth verse:

"We know that in all things God works for good with those who love Him, those whom He has called according to His purpose."

All things...

Colin thought about the many events in his life that he could wish had never happened—but they had shaped him into who he was now.

And Joshua's life—could God use even the events of the last few days to work together for Joshua's good?

Colin knew that He could—and would.

Colin glanced down again and his eye fell on the last two verses of the chapter:

"For I am certain that nothing can separate us from His love: neither death nor life, neither angels nor other heavenly rulers or powers, neither the present nor the future, neither the world above nor the world below—there is nothing in all creation that will ever be able to separate us from the love of God which is ours through Christ Jesus our Lord."

Colin's eyes had grown heavy as he read the last few words. He returned the Bible to the top of the microwave, turned off the light beside the rocking chair, remembered to lock the front door, and finally switched off the small lamp on the table by the sectional.

As Colin closed his eyes and finally succumbed to sleep, he smiled. Nothing in all creation could separate him from the love of God. Nothing…

Colin woke to the sound of someone knocking on the front door. He groaned, pulled himself to an upright position and staggered over to open it.

It was his niece, Rosalee. "We got back as soon as we could," she said. "Dad and Mom are over at the lodge. I've brought you some donuts we picked up before we left this morning."

As he squinted in the bright morning sunlight streaming in through the open door, Colin felt as if he were trying to fight his way out of quicksand. He mumbled what he hoped was a satisfactory reply and sank wearily down on the arm of the sectional close to the door.

Rosalee stepped in and shut the door as she continued in a more hesitant voice. "I was told by Doctor Peters to give you a message. He says that Missy absolutely has to attend the funeral and that he, uh, expects the rest of you to be there too—especially Joshua, since he inherited—"

Colin put his hand up. "That's okay," he said, unable to keep the irritation from his voice, "I think we get the idea."

Why couldn't the man have come over and told them himself if it was so important to him?

"Guess we shouldn't shoot the messenger," Sarah quipped wearily. Colin glanced over at her. She was sitting up, but looked as tired as Colin felt. Her naturally curly hair was sticking up every which way and her clothes were rumpled from having been slept in. The scratches on her face stood out in bold relief.

Rosalee couldn't help but notice them. She stepped forward and asked, "Aunt Sarah, what happened?"

chapter eight

Rosalee was surprised when no one answered her question. Finally, Uncle Colin said in a hesitant voice, "One of our new foster daughters—she was frightened—and her nails need to be trimmed."

Rosalee took a moment to digest the information before asking, "Is there anything I can do?"

Aunt Sarah smiled wearily. "A cup of coffee maybe?"

Rosalee laughed and moved towards the kitchen. "I think that could be arranged." She set the donuts down on the table and was about to walk further into the kitchen when she stopped, horrified at what she saw before her.

"Uh, Uncle Colin, Aunt Sarah…" she called in a voice that shook a bit. "There's a little girl in your kitchen and she's…"

Rosalee had never actually seen anyone eat food from a garbage can before.

Her aunt and uncle had both sprung to their feet as if they'd been struck by lightning, and were at her side in an instant.

"Verena…" Aunt Sarah spoke in a weak voice.

Uncle Colin just groaned and knelt down beside the child.

Rosalee was surprised to see the little girl cower away from them both. The look of terror in her eyes was unmistakable. Rosalee looked behind her aunt and uncle, thinking there had to be something else that the child was afraid of—but it was *them*!

Aunt Sarah turned away, fumbling for a chair to sit down on. She looked as if she might be sick.

"Verena…" Uncle Colin had finally found his voice. "Verena… You don't have to eat… I'll get you something else." He stumbled to his feet, spied the box of donuts, grabbed them and knelt down by the child again.

He was going to offer her one but Rosalee spoke up. "Do you think maybe I should take her to wash her hands first?"

Uncle Colin looked up at her as if he'd forgotten she was there, and Aunt Sarah said in a trembling voice, "She won't let you."

Rosalee remembered a foster child that her parents had a couple of years back. The little girl had been sexually abused by her father, and her mother had reacted by giving her scalding hot baths and scrubbing her skin almost raw. She had been so afraid of baths when she'd arrived at her new foster home that it had taken days before they could even get her hands and face washed.

Rosalee turned towards her aunt and uncle. "I'd like to try," she said gently.

Receiving a slight nod from her uncle, Rosalee took the little girl's hand and led her to the bathroom. She kept up a steady patter as they headed down the hallway. "Your name is Verena, I think I heard them say. Verena is a very pretty name. You remind me of a foster sister that I used to have. Her name was Nadia."

They were at the bathroom now. Rosalee lifted her up so that she stood on the closed toilet seat; the little girl felt light as a feather. Rosalee turned on the faucet and noticed Verena's eyes grow wide with fear. She kept chatting, keeping her tone light and cheerful. "Here's a pretty blue washcloth. I'm just going to get it wet and then put some of this nice smelling soap on it. Now I'm just going to wash your hands. That wasn't so bad, was it? Can you hang onto the sink and look into the mirror? Would you like to wash your face too? Take the washcloth... Yes, you can do it yourself. Good! Okay, just another little spot above your eye... Wow, you did a really great job!"

She waited a moment while the little girl gazed pensively into the mirror.

Rosalee looked and saw her face reflected back side by side with Verena's. The lighter patches on her dark skin, showing malnutrition, and the dull hopelessness in the little girl's big, sad brown eyes contrasted sharply with Rosalee's smooth, healthy skin and the sparkle of light and life that was evident in her eyes. Rosalee's hair was black like Verena's, but it hung soft and shiny while Verena's was dirty and dull and tangled.

Rosalee gently pulled some strands of hair away from Verena's face. The little girl looked confused but didn't protest as Rosalee lifted some more hair and gently made a loose braid, being careful not to pull any of the tangled strands apart. "Do you like your hair in a braid?" she asked.

There was no answer but Rosalee felt sure that she saw the slightest flicker of a smile. She reached up and took two butterfly clips out of her own hair and gently clipped them into Verena's hair, one on each side in the front where she would be able to see them in the mirror.

"There!" Rosalee smiled widely into the mirror and this time the returning smile from Verena was unmistakable. For a brief instant, it lit up her face and transformed the homely pinched features into those of a beautiful little girl.

Verena's smile faded as quickly as it had appeared but Rosalee kept hers as she asked, "So what about some clean clothes now?"

Verena looked down at her dirty, smelly clothes and kept her head bowed even as Rosalee lifted her gently down off the toilet seat. "Hey, we'll find something, okay?"

"She's garbage. Don't give her new clothes. She'll just wreck them!"

Rosalee turned toward the door. Another young girl stood with her hands on her hips and an angry scowl on her face. She wore what was obviously a brand new T-shirt and jeans. A tag was still attached to the T-shirt and was hanging out from the back of the neck. Rosalee reached out for it, speaking as she did so. "You have a tag…"

The little girl jumped back, shouting angrily, "Don't touch me! I didn't say that you could touch me!"

"You gonna run around all day with a tag hanging off your clothes?" Rosalee asked, nonplused.

But the little girl was already struggling to twist her shirt around enough to pull the tag off.

Rosalee turned to Verena, who had shrunk back into a corner of the bathroom. "Okay pretty girl, let's go find some new clothes for you, too."

The child in the doorway shouted, "Her name's not *pretty girl*; it's *garbage*!"

"No," Rosalee spoke firmly, her chin held high. "I have changed her name. Now it's *pretty girl*." And without any further argument, she took Verena's hand and walked with her out of the bathroom, down the hall, and into the kitchen.

Aunt Sarah was sitting in the rocking chair with a cup of coffee and Uncle Colin was making pancakes. Both of them stopped and stared as Rosalee and Verena walked in.

"Your hair looks very pretty," Aunt Sarah spoke hesitantly.

"Yeah," Uncle Colin added, "I like those little things..."

Rosalee laughed. "Butterfly clips," she informed him.

"Oh," he said, sounding just as mystified as before. Then he turned quickly to flip over a burning pancake.

"Do you have some clothes...?" Rosalee began but before she could finish, her aunt had jumped up and was hurrying towards them.

"Oh, yes, I do," she said eagerly. "I have several outfits that you could choose from—some T-shirts and pants—and some cute little tops and skirts and there's a sweater if she gets cold and..."

Rosalee laughed as she followed her down the hallway. "Just one outfit will do for now," she said.

They went to the second bedroom, the one that Colin and Sarah used as their guest room. Clothes and toys that were obviously new had been ripped out of their packages and strewn around the room. The little girl that Rosalee had seen before stood defiantly in the doorway.

"She can't come in. She'll stink up the room!"

Rosalee glanced at her aunt but she was staring at the clothes and toys, a slightly dazed expression in her eyes.

"Are there two different sizes here?" Rosalee asked.

"Yes," Aunt Sarah answered weakly, "I was told that Emmeline was about a size 6 and that Verena was about a size 4."

Rosalee nodded and started searching through the mess for a size 4 outfit. She found a cute blue velour shirt that said "princess," a pair of blue jeans, socks, shoes and underwear.

Ignoring the still defiant little girl, Rosalee took the clothes and walked out of the room. Verena was peeking around the doorway of the first bedroom, a look of apprehension on her face.

Rosalee smiled and went to join her.

"These are some new clothes that Aunt Sarah and Uncle Colin bought for you," she said, holding them out for Verena to take.

But instead of reaching out for them, the little girl took a step backwards, her eyes wide and her mouth open as if in shock.

Rosalee smiled and took a step forward into the room. Verena, in turn, took another step backward and then another. There was a little stool over by the bed; Rosalee pulled it into the center of the room and set the clothes down on top of it. "I'll be right back," she spoke gently.

Rosalee went into the bathroom and, looking under the sink, found what she wanted... a plastic wash basin. She filled it with warm water, added a bit of fragrant bath oil, dropped in a clean face cloth, and chose a fluffy pink hand towel.

Verena was still staring wide-eyed at the new clothes when Rosalee returned, but then she spied the water and started backing away. Rosalee kept a bright smile while she squeezed out the washcloth and explained to Verena that it was just like when she'd washed her face. She could use this water to wash the rest of her body and use the towel to dry herself.

Verena continued to stare at her nervously and Rosalee wondered if the little girl understood what she was saying. "And after you've washed," Rosalee continued to smile as she spoke, "you can put on these new clothes. They're for you. Aunt Sarah and Uncle Colin bought them just for you."

Rosalee paused. Verena still hadn't moved an inch. But Rosalee felt it was important to at least give her a chance to take care of her own personal hygiene. "I'll be back in a few minutes," she said. "I want to see what you look like in those nice new clothes."

Stepping into the kitchen, Rosalee came upon what, at first glance, looked like a pleasant family meal. Aunt Sarah and Uncle Colin sat one on either side of Emmeline and they were eating pancakes and sausages. But as Rosalee approached, she could see that her aunt hadn't touched any of her food and that her uncle had just taken a bite or two. Emmeline was the only one who seemed to be truly enjoying the meal.

They all stopped and looked up at her as she came into the room.

"Verena?" Aunt Sarah asked.

"She's just getting changed," Rosalee answered, hoping that was indeed what was happening.

"Thanks for all your help," Uncle Colin said. He stood up. "Would you like some pancakes? I made lots."

"No thanks," Rosalee answered. "I'm going to go back and check on Verena in a minute. Maybe I'll just have something to drink." She sat down with them and sipped on some orange juice, wondering how long she should give Verena.

But it was Aunt Sarah who stood up first. "Maybe I should just go check…"

Rosalee shook her head. "It's okay. I'll go."

She found, to her delight, that Verena was fully dressed in her new clothes. The murky water, wet washcloth, and damp towel bore testimony to the fact that Verena had at least bathed herself to some extent. There was still a noticeable odor but Rosalee thought that it might just be the wet sheets and dirty clothes. She gathered these up, determined to wash them as soon as possible.

Verena followed her out into the kitchen, where Rosalee asked her aunt if she could put a load of clothes into the laundry. Too late, she realized that it would have been better to have gone back later for the wet sheets and clothes—and to have spoken about the laundry more discreetly.

With a gleeful look on her face, Emmeline stood up on her chair and, pointing down at Verena, began a sing-song chant. "Pee-pants! Pee-pants! Verena is a pee-pants!"

chapter nine

Colin's head whirled—it was as if the past and the present were colliding in some sort of strange time warp. His heart felt as if it was being squeezed in a vise. He should have felt anger, but as the awful chanting continued, what he felt most was… shame.

"That is enough!" a woman's voice rang out with authority.

Sarah…

"There will be no name-calling in this house. It ends here and now."

There was surprise in Emmeline's eyes when she looked at Sarah—and for the briefest of instants, there was a flash of respect as well. Then the insolent expression returned and Emmeline jumped off the chair, marched over to the sectional and sat down hard, her arms folded in front of her. She stared straight ahead, her lips pursed, her eyes narrowed.

Colin glanced at Verena. She was looking up at Sarah with frank admiration in her eyes.

Colin felt the same.

Sarah showed Rosalee where the laundry soap was and Colin bent down to give Verena a friendly grin. "Hey, I bet you didn't know I was the best pancake maker in the whole wide world?"

But if he felt some kinship to Verena, she as yet felt none towards him. Her shoulders drooped and she bowed her head.

Colin felt a great well of sadness followed immediately by a sense of determination. He would do whatever it took to win the friendship of this little girl! And he would do whatever it took to ensure that she would never be hurt again!

Sarah put a couple of pancakes on the plate that had been set for Verena but when she put a hand on her shoulder to guide her, Verena winced and pulled quickly away. It hurt Colin to see the pain in his wife's eyes. He was happy in one way when Rosalee took Verena's hand and led her to the table, but he wished that it could have been Sarah that had been able to do this one small thing.

Colin wanted to sit down with Verena but knew that she would probably eat better if he wasn't involved in any way. Rosalee and Sarah seemed to have the same idea; they got a cup of coffee each and wandered over to look out the window, chatting about the weather.

Colin began to tidy up the things that he had used for cooking, occasionally stealing a glance at Verena as he worked.

She sat stoically for two or three minutes then quick as a flash, her hand darted out and she pushed a whole pancake into her mouth! Then she held tightly clenched fists over her mouth so that no one could see her chew, all the while looking furtively around to see if anyone was watching.

It hurt Colin in a way he couldn't have described—a deep stab of pain that turned quickly to anger as he thought of what this little girl must have endured to cause her to eat this way, more like a wild animal than a child. Colin averted his glance, afraid that

Verena might try to swallow the food all at once if she caught him watching her.

"Colin…"

Sarah's warm touch and soft voice came unexpectedly and Colin almost broke down crying. His voice trembled as he sought to gain control over his emotions. "Russell has a lot to answer for," he said.

"Yes."

There wasn't anything else to say and Colin was grateful that Sarah didn't feel the need to speak further. Her hug meant more to him than any words possibly could.

Colin glanced at Verena and looked quickly away again. She was drinking the glass of milk they had set out for her—and he didn't want her to hurry with that and possibly choke. When Colin looked again, the glass was empty and she had the cutest little milk mustache. He just had to smile!

Afterwards he couldn't have said for sure that she'd smiled back—it was too fleeting—like a small ripple on the water or the rustle of leaves in the springtime. It was there and then it was gone.

But it gave him hope.

"Will you be bringing the girls with you? If not, I could watch them for you."

Colin hadn't noticed that Rosalee had come over to join them until she spoke the words in a quiet voice.

For a moment, Colin drew a blank and then he remembered. The sorrow hit him afresh as he thought about how much he would truly miss Tom Peters. They had been friends—and more than friends—for almost seventeen years. Tom had been like a father to him, giving him spiritual guidance, helping him in his battle with alcoholism, supporting him in his decision to become a police officer...

"I'm not sure," Sarah's voice interrupted his thoughts. "What do you think, Colin?"

She was asking him if he thought that the girls should come to Tom's funeral. Colin sank down into one of the kitchen chairs, his eyes traveling from Verena's nervous pose to Emmeline's defiant one.

And what if Russell was at the funeral?

Rosalee had offered to watch the girls. But what if Russell came to the house while everyone else was at the funeral?

"Colin...?" Sarah sat down beside him.

He glanced over at Verena, then turned away to whisper to Sarah, "Russell is here."

"But he couldn't be!" she exclaimed.

Both of the girls were watching them closely now. Colin made his decision. "Thank you, Rosalee. That would be great if you could stay here with Emmeline and Verena. Sarah and I will go to the funeral."

"My mommy's funeral?" Verena asked, her lower lip trembling.

"Oh no, honey!" Sarah's voice was filled with compassion and she made a move to put her arms around Verena but stopped just inches away.

"She's so stupid!" Emmeline said, her eyes filled with scorn.

"No, she's not," Colin immediately countered.

But Sarah's voice was tender as she took a few steps towards Emmeline. "This isn't your mother's funeral. But, sweetheart, I need to tell you that they didn't get your mommy to the hospital in time..."

"No, she's not dead!" Emmeline jumped up. "She's not! You're lying!" The little girl stood with her feet spread apart, her hands balled into fists at her side, and her face tight with anger. "I hate you! And I hate her! She was stupid—stupid like Verena!"

"Oh, Emmeline…" Sarah's heart broke for the little girl.

"You're stupid, too. You don't know anything. I'm going back home. She'll be there. And my daddy, too." As Emmeline shouted the words, she was moving towards the door.

Sarah stared helplessly at her, wondering if they would have to somehow physically stop her from running away. As Emmeline's hand reached the doorknob, Sarah made a move forward but Colin's calm, practical voice stopped her—and Emmeline too. "The next flight out of Rabbit Lake doesn't leave until four-thirty."

"I'll walk home!" Emmeline flung back.

"You can't, sweetheart," Colin said. "At this time of the year, the only way out is by boat and even then it's not so easy; there are portages and you have to leave a vehicle at Mike's landing and drive part of the way on an old logging road…"

The little girl eyed him defiantly. "I don't care!"

"And in the winter," Colin continued in a calm voice, "you can go over an ice road using a snowmobile and later when the ice is thick enough, a truck. It's best if you have four-wheel drive but I did go out once in a little Chevette."

She was taking in the information as fast as it came and Sarah could see a spark of interest in the little girl's eyes. Then like a knight's face armor, the steel visor closed shut once again. With head held high, Emmeline walked to the sectional and sat down, her arms folded and her eyes set in an angry glare.

Colin sighed deeply. "Maybe we should stay home."

Sarah focused her attention back on him. "No, honey, you need to be there."

Rosalee looked at her watch. "It's almost nine-thirty. The funeral is at eleven. Maybe I should see how Missy is doing. Her father..."

"Joshua!" Sarah jumped out of her chair and hurried down the hallway.

Colin followed, noting first that Rosalee was watching over the girls. He heard Sarah mutter something about being a terrible nurse. "Not so terrible," he said, catching up with her. "Just a little preoccupied at the moment with other very urgent matters."

Sarah put her hand up for silence as they entered the room. Both Missy and Joshua appeared to be asleep. Missy had her head resting on Joshua's chest and he had both arms wrapped around her.

Sarah went quietly around to the other side of the bed, lifted Joshua's wrist, held it for a moment as she felt for his pulse, and checked his IV. After a moment she signaled to Colin that they should leave.

"What about Missy? Shouldn't we wake her?" Colin asked when they were out of the room.

Sarah shook her head. "She's exhausted, poor girl. She probably hasn't slept in days. I certainly won't be the one to wake her."

But as they entered the kitchen, Colin realized that there was someone who had every intention of doing just that!

Jeff Peters was loudly demanding to know where his daughter was. Rosalee looked relieved when she saw Colin and Sarah. Jeff directed his question to them, "Where is Missy? And for that matter, where is Joshua?"

Sarah stepped forward and said in a calm professional voice, "Neither one of them is well enough to attend the funeral. They are both physically and emotionally exhausted."

Jeff narrowed his eyes. "I think I can be a judge of that. I am a doctor—"

"Not right now, you're not," Sarah said gently. "You're a father and you're a grieving son."

But Jeff was past the point of being able to receive her sympathy. He marched through the kitchen and down the hallway, glancing into each room as he went.

Colin and Sarah hurried after him.

"Missy!" Jeff thundered as he entered the last bedroom.

She was startled awake and Joshua's arms fell away as she sat up straight. Joshua opened his eyes but he looked disoriented and confused.

"You can sleep after the funeral!" Jeff spoke loudly.

Missy, who still seemed half asleep, stood up and took a few steps toward Jeff's voice.

"Funeral..." Joshua muttered groggily. Before anyone could stop him, he was pushing himself up from the bed and trying to stand up. In the process, he got his feet tangled in the bed sheets and ended up crashing to the floor. The IV tubing twisted under him as he fell and the needle was ripped out of his arm, causing it to bleed.

Sarah and Colin rushed forward, narrowly avoiding Missy who had turned back to help Joshua and was searching for him, frantically calling out his name.

"Missy, let's go!" Jeff ordered. "They can take care of him. You're only making matters worse."

"No!" Missy cried out. She'd found his arm and felt the warm blood flowing where the IV had been. "Joshua! Joshua!" she sobbed, near panic.

Joshua misunderstood her cries and tried to rise to his feet, prepared to fight off some unknown assailant. He called her name in a voice slurred from the medication but unmistakably full of terror on her behalf.

Colin said in a clear, calm voice, "She's okay. Just relax, Josh." Colin put an arm around his shoulder but it was thrown off as if *he* might be the assailant!

Sarah grabbed hold of Missy's arm. "Tell Joshua that you're okay!" Sarah commanded. "Tell him now."

The message got through finally. "I'm okay, Joshua," Missy said but her voice still trembled as she asked, "Are—are you okay?"

"Tell him again," Sarah urged.

"I'm okay, Josh," Missy said, this time with more reassurance in her voice. Joshua stopped struggling. His vision seemed to clear and he focused in on her face and then slowly on the rest of the room.

"His—his arm—it's bleeding," Missy cried.

"It's okay," Sarah quickly reassured her. "The IV came out, that's all."

Jeff bent down and put his hands on his daughter's shoulders. This time his voice was gentle. "Sarah and Colin can take care of him. We need to go."

Missy pulled away from him. "Joshua…"

Joshua's voice was weak but steady. "Go," he said.

Missy hesitated only a moment, her hand reaching for his. He circled his fingers around hers as she solemnly told him, "I will go to the funeral, Joshua. I will go for both of us."

She bent forward to kiss him then rose to her feet to follow Jeff out the door.

As soon as she was gone, Joshua seemed to collapse in on himself like a deflated balloon. Colin caught him as he sagged forward and together he and Sarah helped him back into bed.

Sarah restarted the IV on Joshua's other arm, then cleaned and put a bandage on the one that was still bleeding slightly.

When she was done, Colin said, "We're going to the funeral, too. Rosalee will be here and the phone is right by your bed. Just press number one on the speed dial—it's my cell number…"

Colin wondered if Joshua was taking in anything that he was saying. The young man's eyes were closed and his face impassive.

"He mostly just needs to rest now," Sarah said gently as she touched Colin's arm. "We should get ready."

Colin, with one final look at Joshua, followed his wife's example as she quietly gathered up some clean clothes and left to get ready for the funeral. Colin offered to let Sarah use the shower first, and continued on into the kitchen.

Rosalee was there, patting out some bannock dough on the table and the two girls were sitting one on each end, watching her with rapt attention.

Colin stood looking on for a moment, imagining Sarah in Rosalee's place standing there with their two foster children, showing them how to cook. The social worker had said that the girls would quite likely become permanent wards of the court, and would therefore be eligible for adoption. Perhaps soon Sarah would have the family that she'd always wanted…

"I made a fresh pot of coffee," Rosalee said, smiling at him.

"Thanks," Colin replied. He poured himself a cup. The girls' eyes were on him now—Emmeline's filled with malice and Verena's with fear.

It hurt in a way that Colin could never have expected and as he moved past them towards the living room, the question resounded like an echo through his heart: *Why? Why? Why?* Rosalee had slipped so easily into a friendly relationship with them—why couldn't he and Sarah? Were they simply trying too hard?

"You can come back for this bannock later," Rosalee said. "Maybe I can throw together a casserole, too."

"Thanks," Colin replied, sinking down onto the sectional facing the kitchen. "If one of us can't make it back, we'll send someone else."

The girls kept their eyes fixed on him as Colin took a sip of coffee and then set the cup down on the small table beside him, but when Rosalee spoke to them, they turned their attention to her again.

Colin put his head back and closed his eyes, the ache in his heart settling into an intense bone-deep weariness.

chapter ten

Rosalee was frying a second pan full of bannock when Sarah came out into the kitchen. She had fixed her hair and put on a bit of makeup so that the scratches were not as noticeable. Her forest green blouse matched well with her dark brown hair and she was wearing a long flowing black skirt and a pair of dark brown sandals.

Rosalee smiled. "You look very nice."

"Thanks!" Aunt Sarah gave her a smile in return. "You girls sure are busy."

"Would you like to try a piece?" Rosalee asked.

"No, no, it's okay," Aunt Sarah spoke quickly as she continued on into the living room. "I should really wake Colin up."

She bent down to kiss her husband and he opened his eyes and looked sleepily up at her.

"We should be going soon," she said.

He groaned but stood to his feet and stumbled off to the bathroom.

Rosalee rolling out another piece of bannock dough, glanced up to find her aunt gazing wistfully at them.

Aunt Sarah, catching her eye, spoke quickly, "Maybe I'll just go check on Joshua again one more time before I go."

She hurried down the hallway and Rosalee, turning back to the job at hand, asked Verena if she would like to try cutting out some bannock. The little girl shook her head vigorously, so Rosalee turned to ask Emmeline the same question. With a smug look on her face, the younger girl took the jar lid and expertly cut out round circles from the dough. If Verena had done it, Rosalee knew that she would have praised her highly, but something about Emmeline's cocky attitude made Rosalee hold back and she ended up just politely thanking her for her help.

When her uncle emerged from the bathroom a few minutes later, he looked a little less groggy than he had before. He'd put on a pair of dress pants, a short sleeved shirt and a tie. He went down to check on Joshua also and a few minutes later, Rosalee noticed him supporting Joshua as he walked down the hall to the bathroom.

It was getting pretty close to eleven o'clock by the time that both her aunt and uncle were ready to go. Still they seemed hesitant to leave.

"Could you check on Joshua occasionally?" Aunt Sarah asked. "He's had some pain medication and he should sleep…"

"Are you sure you can manage everything?" Uncle Colin asked with concern in his voice.

"We'll be fine," Rosalee assured him.

"We really appreciate this…" Colin began.

"It's no problem, really," Rosalee said with a smile. "I enjoy baby-sitting. And it's much more important for you to be there than it is for me."

They both thanked her again, said goodbye to the girls, and finally left for the funeral.

As the door closed behind them, the house seemed suddenly to be much too quiet. Rosalee looked from one silent child to the other and made a quick decision. What they needed was music! Wiping off her hands, she went over to the CD player, chose a worship CD and turned the volume on low. The songs were familiar to her and Rosalee felt her spirit rejoicing along with the singers as they lifted their voices up in praise to the Lord.

She smiled at the two girls. "I think that we should try making a macaroni and cheese casserole when we're done with this," she said.

"I don't like cheese," Emmeline spoke sullenly.

"Well," Rosalee answered cheerily, "You don't have to eat any of it; we're going to make it for the funeral feast."

Verena's eyes filled with tears as she asked in a tiny voice, "Did my mommy have a funeral?"

Rosalee stopped what she was doing. "I—I don't know. I'm sure she did." Rosalee thought that the girls, young as they were, should still have been at their mother's funeral. "We'll ask Uncle Colin and Aunt Sarah when they get home, okay?"

"She's so stupid!" Emmeline spat out the words.

Rosalee felt her jaw tighten as she looked across the table at her. "No," she said in a stern voice, "your sister is not stupid." Her voice softened. "You and Verena should have been told more about what happened to your mom. And—and if you want to talk about it some more, we can do that."

But neither of the girls said another word. Verena sat with her head bowed while Emmeline folded her arms, pursed her lips and stared straight ahead.

Rosalee continued to work on the bannock, dropping more pieces of round circles of dough into the hot fat. When asked, Emmeline flatly refused to help cut any more dough and chose instead to alternately glare at Verena and then Rosalee.

She could feel the venom in those looks but Rosalee continued to force her thoughts on more pleasant things. There was now a full tray of bannock to show for their efforts and she covered it with a clean towel to keep it warm. Hopefully, her aunt or uncle would remember to come and pick it up, or at least to send someone.

Pouring a glass of milk for each of the girls, Rosalee took a box off the counter and placed it on the table. "I think that we should eat some of these donuts before they go stale," she declared with a smile, setting one down on a napkin for each of them.

But neither Verena nor Emmeline touched theirs. Emmeline continued to sit with her arms folded, glaring at the food as if it were rat poison; Verena remained with her head bowed.

Rosalee decided not to worry about whether they ate them or not. They'd had a good breakfast and she would make them a nice lunch in a little while.

Then she suddenly remembered another responsibility she'd been left with. "You two wait here," she said. "I just need to go check on Joshua."

He seemed to be asleep and after watching his even breathing for a moment, Rosalee tiptoed back out of the room.

She was walking quietly down the hallway when the sound of a loud crash made her break into a run. Rosalee berated herself. *She shouldn't have left them alone—even for a moment!*

As she skidded into the kitchen, she spied Verena huddled up against the counter by her overturned chair, crying. Rosalee knelt down beside her, about to ask what was wrong, when suddenly she felt something brutally hard smash down on top of her head.

Momentarily stunned, Rosalee stared in bewilderment at the glass mixing bowl now shattered in pieces on the floor beside her. Then a half-empty bag of flour hit her square on the back of the head, and as the flour cascaded around them like snow, Rosalee instinctively bent over Verena to protect her. A hard blow on her right shoulder preceded the sound of the rolling pin dropping to the floor and then milk was tossed over them, followed by the sound of the glasses shattering around them.

"Put that down!" a strong male voice rang out.

Rosalee looked up.

Michael...

Rosalee couldn't remember the last time that she'd seen her childhood friend—a couple of years at least. He'd grown a beard and filled out some too. His shoulders were broader. Rosalee felt as if she needed a pair of broad shoulders just then.

But Michael's attention, at least for the moment, was on Emmeline. "Now, you come sit over here and don't you even think about getting up until I say you can!"

Rosalee watched as the girl released her hold on the frying pan and moved away from the stove...

The hot grease! She had been going to throw the hot grease!

Rosalee felt all her remaining strength drain away.

"Hey," Michael said gently, "you two okay?"

Rosalee looked up into his compassionate eyes. The aftershock of the assault hit her and she burst into tears.

Michael helped Rosalee to her feet and put his arms around both her and Verena, who clung fiercely to the older girl.

Rosalee tried to explain to Michael what had happened but the words didn't make sense, even to her. The attack had been something she had been totally unprepared for her. "She—I—shouldn't have—but—but had to check on Joshua—I can't believe she would—the grease was still hot—"

"Shh, shh," Michael consoled, drawing her into a closer embrace. "It's okay now. It's okay now..."

He led her to the rocking chair and Rosalee, with Verena still in her arms, sank gratefully down into it. Her knees still felt a little wobbly and her head was starting to throb.

She glanced over at the sectional where a sullen but subdued Emmeline sat in her usual pose, arms folded, staring straight ahead.

Michael pulled a kitchen chair up beside Rosalee, positioning himself so that he could still see Emmeline. He raised an inquiring eyebrow.

"So whatzup?" he asked. "And who's the little vixen on the couch over there—and what's she got against you?"

Rosalee put a hand up to brush some of the flour off her face and hair, thinking about how awful she must look. She glanced over at Emmeline again and struggled to frame a reply to Michael's question. Rosalee could think of no reason why Emmeline should attack her. But she had no idea why the little girl should have been hurting her sister either...

Fortunately Michael didn't seem to need a response of any kind. He nodded towards the counter where the tray of bannock remained untouched. "I was supposed to get something from you to bring back to the funeral feast but you wouldn't believe the mountains of food they've already got there."

Rosalee smiled. "Yes I would," she said. For any event, but especially when people knew there would be a lot of visitors, the community was always very generous in the amounts of food that were prepared.

"You're feeling better." Michael sounded pleased.

"Yes," she said, realizing that it was true. Something inside of Rosalee that had grown cold in the face of Emmeline's hatred was being warmed now by the kindness and concern she heard in Michael's voice.

His face relaxed into a wide grin. Then one eyebrow shot up. "You're still looking a little pale though." He leaned back as if assessing her before concluding, "Definitely white."

Rosalee had to laugh. He was referring, of course, to the flour that clung to her face and hair but it had always been a mark of their friendship that they could freely talk, and even joke, about their skin color. Both of them had been adopted and neither had any knowledge of who their parents were but it was clear that Rosalee had some Native American ancestry and Michael had some African American ancestry. When they'd been younger, Rosalee remembered putting their arms side-by-side, comparing skin tones. She had always been a little lighter than the First Nations children in their community and Michael had always been just a little darker.

"I'll see if I can find my Native roots," she quipped, standing to her feet. "I think, in this case, a washcloth will help." Verena sprang up into Rosalee's arms, burying her face in her shoulder.

Rosalee paused in the entrance to the hallway and glanced nervously over at Emmeline, but Michael must have noticed.

"I'll keep an eye on her," he said reassuringly.

Rosalee found some clean clothes for Verena and then slipped quietly into her aunt and uncle's bedroom to borrow a clean shirt for herself. In the bathroom, she set Verena down to stand on the closed toilet seat as she had before. With the door closed between them and the outside world, Verena seemed comfortable enough to be separated from Rosalee but knowing Verena's fear of water, Rosalee thought it best to not try cleaning her face and hair just yet.

Turning instead to assess the damage done to her own appearance, Rosalee was appalled at the image she saw reflected back from the mirror. *Michael had seen her like this!*

"I've got to get cleaned up!" But even as she spoke the words, she was moving past Verena to put the bathtub plug in and turn on the faucets. She added some bubble bath and made sure that the temperature of the water was okay before straightening up again. "This might be a good time for you to think about having a bath, Verena," she said in a gentle voice.

The little girl didn't respond. Rosalee would have been surprised if she had! Turning her attention back to the mirror, Rosalee mused, "I'll have to wash my hair but maybe I should brush some of this flour out first."

Her head hurt from where the heavy glass bowl had struck and when she lifted her arms to brush her hair, her back ached where the rolling pin had hit her. Still she managed to get a lot of the flour out. She washed her face, still talking as she worked and occasionally glancing at Verena, who stood transfixed, watching her.

The tub was almost full when Rosalee turned off the water. "Why don't you hop in?" she suggested. "I'm going to wash my hair first and then I'll wash yours."

Verena just stared at her.

"Hey, I'm not going to argue with you," Rosalee spoke matter-of-factly. "If you want to walk around with flour in your hair for the rest of your life…" She smiled. "But I'm going to wash mine 'cause there's this guy out there whom I happen to like a lot."

She wasn't sure what she'd expected—it was hard to know what to expect when it came to Emmeline and Verena. But when Rosalee finished rinsing her hair in the sink, and looked around for a towel to wrap it in, she was more than a little surprised to find that Verena had followed her instructions.

The little girl was sitting in the tub of water, bubbles up to her chin and looking just a little surprised herself!

"Would you like me to wash your hair?" Rosalee asked.

Verena's eyes grew wide with fright.

"Maybe later," Rosalee quickly amended. She found Sarah's blow-dryer and began drying and brushing out her hair, thinking that maybe Verena did best when no one was paying attention to her. Well, that's what she would do, at least for now…

chapter eleven

Michael heard the bath water and rightly assumed that the girls would be a while. He looked again at the tightlipped, hostile child in the living room and wondered what Rosalee—or more specifically Colin and Sarah—had gotten themselves into. *Who were these kids?*

He took the kitchen chair that he was sitting on, carried it into the living room, flipped it around backwards, and sat down facing the little girl.

"So what you got against my friend Rosalee?" he inquired casually.

The dark eyes flashed, the lips grew tighter, and the little girl began to swing her legs out, kicking at the chair with the toes of her shoes.

Michael moved his chair out of range of her feet and tried again. "She probably would have got third degree burns if you'd let that hot grease fly."

"So!"

Well, at least he'd got some sort of dialogue going!

"So..." Michael leaned forward and enunciated each word slowly and carefully. "You were hurting someone whom I am very sure has never ever hurt you."

"She's a—" And the little girl let loose with a string of obscenities.

Michael felt his jaw stiffen. He'd done some volunteer work helping street kids and he'd heard this kind of language before— but he couldn't ever recall hearing it from someone this young. And to have the words directed towards Rosalee filled him with an anger that he could barely suppress. It took him a moment before he could even speak but when he did, his voice was calm and controlled. "No, she is not," he said.

A stony silence enveloped the little girl once more.

Back to square one!

"This all started as a fight between you and your younger sister..." Michael prompted, trying to resume some dialogue on the subject.

Lifting her head, the girl spoke with disdain, "She's not my younger sister."

Michael couldn't keep the surprise out of his voice. "She's not?"

"No," the girl proudly declared, "I'm thirteen months younger than her."

"How is that possible?" Michael wondered aloud.

"She's just garbage," the little girl said in a dismissive tone.

Michael took a deep breath, trying to gather his thoughts.

"No one," he began in a slow, steady voice, "no one is garbage. God, the Creator, made each and every person in His own image and likeness. We were created to be friends with God. He loved each and every one of us enough to send His Son Jesus to die for us so that our sin could be taken away and we could be friends with Him. He loves you and He loves your sister, too."

"No one loves her. She is garbage!"

Michael couldn't ever remember encountering anyone so filled with hate. Silently he prayed for wisdom, then stood up and searched around the room, finding what he was looking for on top of the microwave.

Opening the Bible to the book of Mark, he told the little girl that he was going to read about a time when Jesus was on the earth. He began at the tenth chapter and the thirteenth verse:

"Some people brought children to Jesus for Him to place His hands on them, but the disciples scolded the people. When Jesus noticed this, He was angry and said to His disciples, 'Let the little children come to Me, and do not stop them, because the Kingdom of God belongs to such as these. I assure you that whoever does not receive the Kingdom of God like a child will never enter it.' Then He took the children in His arms, placed His hands on each of them, and blessed them." Michael closed the book and set it down—just those four verses were enough.

"If Jesus were here right now, He would take your sister in His arms." Michael paused. "If He were here right now sitting in this chair, Jesus would take you in His arms."

"No, He wouldn't," the little girl said defiantly. "I wouldn't let Him."

Michael sighed. "Yeah, that's what it comes down to, you know. God made us. He loves us. He wants to be friends with us—but we don't want to be friends with God."

"I don't have friends. Friends are stupid."

And in that instant, it was as if Michael's eyes were opened and he saw beyond the tough exterior to the frightened little girl inside, crying out for friendship—crying out for love.

But he had no idea what it would take to reach across the barrier of anger and hatred that she had built up over such a short lifetime. Some sort of miracle, he was sure of that.

For now, though, what they most needed was a truce.

And from working with tough street kids, Michael knew how important it was to command respect without putting the child on the defensive. He stood to his feet.

"We need to clean up the mess that you made," he declared. "C'mon."

She did her best to stare him down, but in the end, his authority and good humor won out and she followed him into the kitchen and reluctantly started picking up what she had thrown. He swept while she held the dustpan for him, then he filled a bucket full of water and showed her how to squeeze out the mop and wash the floor.

They ended up cleaning the whole kitchen together, clearing off the table and counter and washing and drying the dishes. Michael was pleased with what they were accomplishing. He was beginning to wonder, though, what could be keeping Rosalee so long...

She was ready.

She had fixed her hair and even applied a bit of makeup, knowing her aunt wouldn't mind her borrowing it. She'd also washed and styled Verena's hair, weaving the strands into two French braids that joined together in the back, adding some pretty mauve butterfly clips that matched the little girl's new purple and white outfit.

They were ready.

But Rosalee didn't want to go out there again. She looked down at Verena and read the same message in her eyes.

The hatred and rage coming from Emmeline had been like a physical force...

But Michael would be there...

Rosalee squared her shoulders and patted Verena on the back. "You'll like Michael," she said cheerily. "C'mon."

Rosalee opened the door and they walked hand in hand toward the kitchen. She could hear Michael whistling but was still surprised by the sight of him wiping off the table and even more surprised to see Emmeline, standing on a chair, putting away the dishes as she dried them.

Michael looked up and saw them but seemed at a loss for words.

Rosalee smiled. "Hey," she spoke in greeting.

Michael still seemed a bit tongue-tied. "You—you've changed."

Rosalee had to laugh. "I've changed? Well, I was covered with flour and milk and stuff."

"No, no, since I seen you last," Michael fumbled over the words.

Rosalee lifted her eyebrows. "A few minutes ago?"

"No, I mean—since I saw you last—you've got older—and uh, prettier." Michael relaxed a little, his characteristic grin falling easily into place. "What I mean to say is you look fine. You look real fine."

Rosalee flashed him a wide smile. "Thanks!" She glanced down at Verena, who still held tightly to her hand and kept her head bowed. Then she looked over at Emmeline, carefully putting a coffee cup away in the cupboard. "And thank you, Michael, for helping out here."

"Hey, no problem!"

Rosalee looked around. "It's so nice and clean in here," she said, keeping an eye on Emmeline, not wanting to say anything that might set her off again. "You two did a really good job."

Michael moved towards where Emmeline still stood on the chair. He smiled at her and picked up another dishtowel and a wet glass before turning back to Rosalee and thanking her for the compliment.

Rosalee was surprised by how nervous she felt. She was usually a very competent baby-sitter but somehow things had gotten out of hand...

"Come sit down," Michael said gently, pulling a chair out for her. "Can I get you a drink or something?"

Rosalee smiled. "Sure."

Michael pulled out a chair for Verena as well but the little girl continued to cling to Rosalee. Michael shrugged and pushed the chair back in again. He smiled at Verena and said, "Nice hair!"

"Could you pass me two glasses please?" he asked Emmeline, then amended the request to include two more. Emmeline handed him four glasses, then stepped off the chair and dried and put away the last two items, a fork and a spoon.

Michael set the glasses on the table and bent to look in the refrigerator for something to serve. "We got us some Pepsi, some

7-Up, some O.J. and for those of us who might need a calcium boost, some 2% milk." He looked up inquiringly at Rosalee.

"Maybe some Pepsi," she suggested.

"And for you, darlin'?" he asked Verena.

The little girl didn't reply but only grew more nervous as Michael waited for her answer.

"She can drink the dirty dishwater," Emmeline spat out vindictively.

Michael spun around on his heel. "And what would you like—some witch's brew?" He was immediately repentant. "Oh man, I'm sorry." He spoke directly to Emmeline, "I shouldn't have said that. I'm really sorry."

But the young girl had taken her usual stance, arms folded, eyes narrowed, and lips held tightly together. Rosalee felt her heart go out to Michael. He must have worked very hard to get the kind of rapport going that had been necessary for them to clean up the kitchen together. Now it had all vanished as if it had never been.

"It's okay, Michael," Rosalee said gently. "If it's all right with you, maybe we'll all just have a glass of Pepsi. Emmeline, honey, why don't you sit down? You must be tired after all that work you did."

Emmeline sat down hard on a chair at the other end of the table, a sulky expression on her face. Michael took the bottle of Pepsi from the refrigerator and served everyone. Rosalee smiled at him as he filled her glass but the two girls didn't look up at all. Michael sat down and took a sip of his drink.

There was a moment of awkward silence, then Michael whipped a deck of cards out of his pocket and asked enthusiastically, "Anyone up for a game?"

"Sure," Rosalee said, grateful for his suggestion.

Michael began to shuffle the deck and even the two young girls started to take an interest as he did a few fancy maneuvers with the cards.

Rosalee wondered how she would have ever managed if Michael hadn't shown up. Hopefully, none of his family were missing him and hopefully Sarah and Colin wouldn't be too upset when no food showed up from their house.

chapter twelve

But food was the last thing on Sarah or Colin's mind at that moment. Throughout the funeral they had been keeping an eye on Russell, who had made his presence very obvious at both the service and the burial. Now, at the funeral feast being held at the community center, Russell moved through the crowd like a politician, shaking hands with everyone he met. He was dressed like a politician too—or maybe a drug lord. His suit looked like it had been bought at some specialty men's shop, his hair was slicked back, his silk tie a bright magenta and his shoes shone as if they were brand new.

It wouldn't have bothered Colin so much if it weren't for the fact that he had just received Russell's two daughters into his home, one of them malnourished, ill-kempt and dressed in rags!

As Russell continued to work the crowd, he came within earshot of Colin and Sarah. "Yes, I'm a father now too," Colin heard Russell brag. "Would you like to see a picture of her? She'll be starting school this fall."

"Oh, then I guess I'll be getting to know you." A young man joined in, reaching out to shake Russell's hand. "I'm the principal of the school here. How old is your daughter?"

Russell pumped his hand. "She's only five years old but she can already read and write," he boasted. "She's smart just like her old man."

The principal smiled and looked around. There were quite a few kids amongst the crowd that looked as if they could be about that same age.

"She's staying with her uncle at this time," Russell pointed with his lips towards Colin. He dropped his eyes and spoke with obvious emotion in his voice. "You see, my wife just died recently."

"Oh, I'm so sorry," the young man said quickly.

Russell pursed his lips and nodded, leaving a suitable amount of silence before replying somberly, "She'd been sick for a while. It was a blessing when she was finally taken." Russell glanced slyly at Colin, almost daring him to challenge his account of events.

Colin clenched his jaw so hard that it hurt—*the man was lying through his teeth!* But what angered Colin the most was that in addition to neglecting and abusing his eldest daughter, Russell was now publicly denying her very existence!

Colin could stand it no longer! He had to say something, make the truth known! He was about to speak when suddenly he felt Sarah urgently tugging at his arm. "Martha's heading over this way," she whispered.

Colin followed her gaze and as he focused on the older woman approaching them, his heart went out to her. She seemed so lost without Tom at her side. Her salt and pepper hair was beautifully set and her dress was new—Coralee would have seen to that—but all the joy and life seemed to have drained out of her. Her red-rimmed eyes were fixed on Colin but it appeared to be taking every ounce of her remaining energy to make her way through the crowd, like a fish swimming upstream against the current. People kept stopping her, hugging her, speaking to her...

Colin quickly pushed his way past the people between them.

"Martha..." Colin took both her hands in his.

"I need you to do something for me," she said in a quick urgent voice.

"Anything!" Colin exclaimed.

Martha smiled at his eagerness and seemed to relax a little. "It's Missy," she said, directing his attention to where her granddaughter sat alone, close to the front door.

It felt strange to see her so isolated... Missy and Josh were usually surrounded by people wherever they went, enthusiastically discussing the new youth program at the lodge. Colin wondered what would become of Josh and Missy's dreams now.

"She should be with him," Martha said softly. "Time is so short. You never know when..." Her voice trailed off.

How like Martha, Colin thought, to be concerned about someone else even in the midst of her own great loss. He squeezed her hands and nodded his assent, too overcome with emotion to speak.

"Uh, Colin... what about Jeff?" Sarah interjected hesitantly.

Colin glanced at Martha, wondering how much she was aware of the recent conflict between Missy and her father.

But the older woman seemed to understand. She smiled fondly in Jeff's direction. He was deep in conversation with his brother-in-law, Dr. David Rodriguez. "He's very protective of Missy," Martha said softly. "And," she added, "he can be a little overbearing at times—just like his daddy." She reached up and wiped a tear from her eye.

"Mom!" Coralee negotiated the crowd to reach her mother's side. "Mom, you don't have to be walking around. People can come to you. And you haven't had a bite to eat yet and—"

"I'll be fine, dear," Martha said, stemming the tide of words coming from her daughter's lips. "I just wanted to talk to Colin for a minute. We're done now."

Colin smiled reassuringly at Martha. "I'll take care of what you asked," he said.

As Coralee led Martha away, he and Sarah went over to speak with Missy.

Sarah put a comforting arm around the younger woman while Colin sat down on the other side of her. "Your Grandma thinks that you should be with Joshua," he said. "We'll take you there now if you like."

Missy jumped to her feet, and a sound halfway between a cry and a laugh burst from her lips. Then she shook her head wonderingly and smiled. "Grandma," she whispered, "thank you."

Sarah was glad to have an excuse to leave. She had done a pretty good job of covering up the scratches with makeup but they were still visible up close. A few people had commented, but most had been too polite or too preoccupied to say anything. All the same, she would be glad to get home.

She was exceptionally tired, too. Even though the last few days had been quite taxing, Sarah thought she might be coming down with something as well. Her stomach had felt queasy all day.

And she was worried about the girls. Maybe she shouldn't have left Rosalee all alone with them. And Joshua should have had someone with nursing experience...

"You okay?" Colin took one hand from the steering wheel to close his fingers gently around Sarah's.

"Guess I'm just worried about Rosalee and the girls." She turned toward Missy, who was sitting beside her in the cab of the truck. "And Joshua," she added.

"We'll be home soon," Colin reassured her. "And they're probably doing just fine. I've had my cell phone on; they would have called if there were any problems."

And it seemed as if Colin was right. Even before they opened the front door, Sarah could hear laughter coming from inside the house. But the sound was so discordant with Sarah's present mood that she found herself slightly annoyed by it, and even more so when she saw Michael sitting at the table, joking and playing cards with Rosalee...

"Your parents were wondering where you were," Sarah spoke to him more harshly than she'd intended.

Michael, looking up, seemed surprised by her tone of voice. "I, uh, felt like I was needed here."

"He *was* needed here!" Rosalee exclaimed.

Colin stepped forward. "And we do appreciate the help you were able to give." He set down the dish of food he was holding and reached his hand out toward Michael. "I haven't actually had a chance to talk with you much yet. It's nice to see you again."

Michael stood to his feet to shake Colin's hand. "I just wish it could have been under better circumstances," he said. "Grandpa was one in a million. There isn't anyone who could ever take his place."

Colin agreed. "I will miss him."

Michael moved toward Missy, speaking her name in greeting before giving her a hug. "I didn't have a chance to talk to you either," he said. "How're you doing?"

"Okay, I guess," she said hesitantly. "But I'm worried about Joshua."

"Rosalee said he'd been hurt..." But Missy was already moving towards the hallway. "I'll go with you," Michael offered. "Tell me what happened."

Sarah picked up the casserole dish that Colin had set down. "Maybe I'll just put this food in the refrigerator; I don't imagine anyone is hungry right now."

Passing Rosalee, sitting with Verena snuggled up on her lap, Sarah thought to ask, "You did make them lunch, I suppose?"

Sarah was surprised when Rosalee hesitated. Everyone always talked about what a good baby-sitter she was...

"I did offer them some donuts but they didn't eat them." Rosalee looked around. "I think maybe they got thrown out."

Sarah set the dish of food back down on the table. "I didn't leave specific instructions," she said, measuring her words carefully, "but I did assume that you would prepare a meal for them."

Rosalee stood to her feet and tried to set Verena down but the little girl clung tightly to her neck and kept her legs wrapped around Rosalee's waist. "We were... busy," Rosalee said through tight lips, looking wounded by Sarah's disapproving tone.

Sarah glanced around, noting the full tray of bannock. "Yes, I appreciate you making some food for the funeral but Michael was supposed to bring it over. I can understand that you might want to visit with him instead but—"

With a cry of frustration, Rosalee began to stride towards the door then stopped to try once more to disengage the little girl. But Verena was clinging onto her, as if her very life depended on it.

"I'll take her," Colin offered.

As soon as he touched Verena, the little girl became limp. He took her in his arms and set her down gently, propped up in the corner of the sectional.

Rosalee walked slowly away from the door, back towards Verena, a look of horror in her eyes.

Sarah remembered what a shock it had been for her when she'd first seen the little girl go limp like that. "Rosalee..." she said gently.

"What's *wrong* with her?" The younger woman spun around to ask the question, then moaned and put her hand on the back of her head. "I gotta go," she said in a dazed voice.

"She's okay..." Sarah spoke slowly, as the realization began to dawn on her that something was wrong *with Rosalee*. If she hadn't been so preoccupied, she would have noticed it before. Rosalee was wearing one of Sarah's T-shirts and she still had her hand on the back of her head, and she looked as if she was in pain....

Colin must have noticed something as well. His voice was filled with concern as he asked, "Rosalee, what's wrong? What happened here?"

"I'll tell you what happened."

As Michael's clear, strong voice rang out across the room, Rosalee suddenly burst into tears. Sarah put her arms around her and gently guided Rosalee over to the rocking chair.

She kept her hand resting on Rosalee's shoulder as the young woman's sobs subsided.

Colin and Michael both pulled up kitchen chairs to sit close by Rosalee, who made a visible effort at controlling her emotions. "I—I'm okay now," she said.

"Sure you are," Michael spoke soothingly. "You're going to be just fine."

Colin, his face still tight with anxiety, said, "You were going to tell us what happened…"

Michael took a deep breath and began. "I'm not sure what all happened before I got here but Rosalee was on the floor bent over this little girl…" He nodded his head toward Verena. "Protecting her from this other one…" Michael motioned towards the table where Emmeline sat.

"I'm so sorry, Rosalee," Sarah said, giving her shoulder a squeeze. "We shouldn't have left you alone—" She broke off suddenly when Rosalee winced and pulled away from her.

"Emmeline," Colin spoke sternly, "what did you do to Rosalee?"

Emmeline looked slyly out of the corner of her eye. "I was bad," she said drawing the last word out into a malicious grin.

Colin's jaw tightened. "What did you do?" he asked again.

Emmeline seemed pleased with herself. "I could show you," she offered, slipping down off her chair and heading for the kitchen cupboard.

"No!" Michael commanded. "You sit right down again!"

Colin shot a surprised look at Michael, then waited for the little girl to speak again once she was back in her seat.

But Emmeline had said all she was going to say. She folded her arms and lifted her chin triumphantly.

"She pushed Verena off her chair," Rosalee said in a quiet flat voice. "I was kneeling down to help her up when Emmeline threw a glass mixing bowl at my head—and a rolling pin—it hit my shoulder—and she threw some glasses—and—and other stuff."

Colin leaned towards her. "Rosalee, I'm so sorry."

"It wasn't your fault, Uncle Colin."

"We shouldn't have left you alone!"

Rosalee gave a small smile. "I volunteered, remember? And I'd do it again."

"No!" Sarah exclaimed. "From now on, either Colin or I will stay here with them."

"Aunt Sarah," Rosalee said in a gentle voice, "I think that you guys are going to need some support now and again. I do want to help."

"Me too," Michael added.

Rosalee smiled at him before continuing, "And I'm sure that Mom and Dad, once they know what you guys are going through..."

Sarah's eyes grew misty. "Thanks," she said.

Colin's voice was hoarse with emotion. "Yeah, thanks."

Michael stood to his feet. "Can I give you a ride home?" he asked Rosalee.

She nodded and stood also.

Michael looked down at Colin. "You call me—*anytime*," he said. "I don't have anything on my agenda for the next little while. I had been thinking that I might hang around after the funeral and see if Joshua needed me for his project up there at the lodge." He hesitated before adding, "I think there might be some delay now with that."

Michael and Rosalee were at the door when suddenly Verena leapt up and ran towards them. Sobbing uncontrollably, she clung to Rosalee's leg.

Rosalee gasped in surprise and looked helplessly at Colin and Sarah.

Sarah felt tears prick her eyes. "She—she seems to have become attached to you."

Rosalee laughed shakily. "Yes, quite literally attached."

Colin stepped forward and plucked the little girl up in his arms. She immediately went limp again and Sarah heard him groan in dismay.

Tears filled Rosalee's eyes as she looked at the little girl. "Is there something I can do?" she asked. "Maybe I should stay for a while..."

Sarah shook her head. "It's okay."

Michael put a hand on Rosalee's back, gently guiding her through the door, and closing it behind them.

Sarah turned back to see Colin still standing, staring down at the child in his arms, the deep pain he was feeling evident in his eyes.

"Maybe she's better left..." Sarah began.

"No," Colin said with sudden decision. He walked with Verena over to the rocking chair and sat down, cradling her limp body in his arms.

Sarah blinked back her tears and gently kissed her husband on the forehead.

"Maybe I'll warm up some of this extra food we brought home," she said, and picked up the casserole dish and placed it in the microwave.

"Are you hungry?" she asked Emmeline, who was still sitting where Michael had ordered her to stay. But the little girl didn't acknowledge her words in any way, her gaze remaining fixed on an empty spot on the wall beside the refrigerator.

Sarah turned sadly away, thinking that although the two girls were as different as night and day, Emmeline could be just as numbed to her environment as Verena.

chapter thirteen

Sarah went over to the entertainment center and put on one of her favorite CD's by *The Kry,* entitled "YOU." As she passed Colin, he smiled sadly up at her and Sarah bent and kissed him again. Colin had shifted Verena into a sitting position so that her head rested on his chest but her gaze was as blank as before.

Sarah started towards the hallway to check on Joshua but stopped when she came to Emmeline. "You can come with me," she said in a voice that held no room for argument.

Emmeline slid off the chair and walked stiffly behind her. But as they were about to pass the bathroom, Emmeline suddenly darted inside, slamming and locking the door behind her.

Sarah was startled and then dismayed. *What now?*

A moment later, she heard the toilet flush and right after that, the door reopened. Sarah felt a wave of relief—the child had just needed to use the bathroom. But didn't Emmeline feel free to even ask for this—how long had she been waiting without saying anything?

"Emmeline, honey," Sarah said in a gentle voice, "you can use the bathroom whenever you want." She paused. "I would like you to wash your hands, though."

Emmeline looked defiantly up at her. "I already did," she declared.

"Maybe we'll just do it together again, okay?" Sarah moved past her to turn on the water faucet.

Emmeline put her hands behind her back.

Sarah waited a moment, unsure of what to do next.

Suddenly Emmeline thrust her hands under the faucet, rubbed some soap over them and rinsed again. Then she darted out of the bathroom once more. Sarah had no choice but to follow her. She quickly turned off the tap and went out into the hallway.

Emmeline was almost at the doorway to the master bedroom. Sarah called out to her, "Emmeline, wait please," and miraculously, the little girl obeyed.

Through the open door, Sarah could see Missy sitting on the chair beside the bed, holding Joshua's hand. The younger woman looked completely exhausted.

Sarah walked quietly in. "Is he still sleeping?" she asked.

Missy hesitated before answering, "I think so."

Sarah put a hand on her shoulder. "Why don't you go lie down, honey; we'll stay with Joshua for a while."

Missy looked confused. "We?"

"Emmeline is here with me," Sarah explained.

"Oh," Missy said in a tired, lifeless voice, "how is everyone?"

"We're fine," Sarah answered. "Emmeline, you wouldn't mind if Missy used your bed to rest on, would you?"

The little girl shrugged her shoulders and looked disinterested.

"Maybe I will take you up on that offer." But Missy remained where she was, sitting on the chair, holding Joshua's hand.

"Missy..." Sarah prompted.

A ragged sob from the younger woman compelled Sarah forward. She put her arms around her and held her as she wept.

When Missy finally spoke, it was as a plaintive cry. "He should be awake by now, shouldn't he? I—I just want to hear his voice, that's all. I just want to hear his voice."

"Missy…"

Both women turned towards the hoarse rasping sound and Sarah immediately moved to get Joshua a glass of water. Missy bent over to embrace him, crying again and saying his name over and over. Sarah watched as Joshua, with great effort, lifted first one arm and then the other to encircle his fiancée. His eyes traveled up to meet Sarah's.

She realized he was trying to communicate something to her, that he didn't want Missy to know about. He inclined his head toward Missy, rested his gaze on her a moment and then looked up at Sarah again. This time there was a clear appeal for help in his eyes, and a kind of wild desperation.

Sarah set the glass of water down and put her hand on Missy's back. "I think that he just needs some rest, dear. I'm going to give him another dose of pain medication. Maybe you could talk with him later tonight…" But when Joshua gave an almost imperceptible shake of his head, and implored her with those quietly desperate eyes again, Sarah amended her words. "…Or maybe tomorrow."

There was a flash of unmistakable gratitude in Joshua's eyes.

"You've both been through a lot," Sarah continued gently. "I think you'll be surprised at how much better you'll feel after you've had some sleep."

Joshua eased his arms back down again. Missy kissed him on the cheek then stood slowly to her feet and quietly left the room.

Emmeline was sitting on the floor, leaning up against the wall.

"You can sit over here on the chair," Sarah offered.

Emmeline didn't reply but just stared straight ahead, her body rigid.

Sarah sighed wearily, suddenly wishing that she could have been the one to go and take a nap. She turned back to Joshua and noted that his eyes were closed again. Even so, she told him at every step what she was going to do as she timed his pulse and respirations, checked his IV, gave him a dose of pain medication and put some more ointment on his bug bites.

When she had finished, she sat down on the chair that Missy had vacated. "I'll be right here if you need anything, Josh," she said. "But you can just rest too. You don't have to talk. The pain medication should take effect soon."

She only wished that there was a medicine for the heart that she could give him—and Emmeline. Sarah sat watching the girl for a few moments, then stood to her feet. Somewhere in the closet, on the top shelf...

Sarah found what she was looking for... a favorite story book that had been read to her as a child. Her adoptive parents' marriage had failed gradually over the years—they had finally separated when Sarah was in her late teens—but this book was from the good years when they had been happy together. Sarah smiled as she flipped through the pages. The pictures were so comical and the book itself was what Sarah's mom had called "just plain silly."

Sarah sat down as close as she dared next to Emmeline, leaned back against the wall, opened the book and began to read:

"There once was a boy named Jimmygojumpin'. He got this rather peculiar name because every day when he would come home with his hands and face and ears all dirty from playing outside, his mother would meet him at the door, put her hands on her hips and declare, 'Jimmygojumpin' that tub and get yourself cleaned up.'

"Then later, after he'd had his supper, bed-time story and prayers, she'd give him a kiss good-night and say, 'Jimmygojumpin' that bed and go to sleep now.'

"And in the morning, when it was time to go to school, guess what his mom said...? Yep, she'd hand him his lunch bucket, pat him on the head and say, 'Jimmygojumpin' that bus and study your lessons good.'"

Sarah laughed softly. "I remember after we read this book, always wanting my mom to say 'Sarahgojumpin' bed' and 'Sarahgojumpin' the bath.'"

Sarah hazarded a glance down at Emmeline, expecting her to say something like, "That's stupid!" Instead the little girl maintained her pose. But Sarah, in that quick glance, thought she had detected a slight relaxing of her muscles, a small release of tension.

With a smile on her face, Sarah resumed reading.

"One day, Jimmygojumpin'..."

Colin wondered if he was doing the right thing. How long could a little child remain in this state—disassociated from everything around her? Did she even know that he was there? Was it possible for her to learn what good touching was—that a hug could be healthy and healing?

For the first seven years of his life, Colin had known what it was to be loved by both his mother and his father. Then they had been killed in a plane crash and Colin had been thrust into an abusive foster home, where he had been sexually abused by the father, Amos Quill, and by the three oldest sons, Russell, Garby and Bryan.

Joshua, the youngest son, had only been a baby when Colin had escaped from the Quill household, and Rebecca not even born yet. Still Colin, throughout the years, had tried his best to help Joshua and Rebecca, to protect them from their own family, but he felt like he had failed them both. Especially Rebecca… the memory of her still stabbed like a knife in his heart. She had only been eleven years old when she'd been driven by despair to take her own life…

Colin looked down at the child in his arms, Russell's child, and wondered what chance she had in life. He doubted that she had ever really known the security of being loved and cherished by her parents… he feared that Amos' cruel legacy had been kept alive in Russell's home. Colin wished with all his heart that he could turn back the clock and swoop in and rescue her before anyone had had a chance to hurt her in any way.

But here she was in his arms… damaged… broken…

He felt so helpless!

"God!" he cried out in silent prayer. "There's got to be a way! There's got to be a way to reach her."

He lifted his eyes to the heavens and tears began to roll down his cheeks. "Oh God! There's so many hurting people. And it's just going on and on. It's the third generation now. And I thought that Joshua was healed but now I'm afraid… And I thought that I was healed but I'm feeling as if I've been shot full of holes…"

The CD that Sarah had put on was still playing softly in the background but suddenly the words of the song began to penetrate Colin's heart and mind. It was as if God Himself was gently whispering the words to Colin and they flowed over his soul like a healing balm:

> He won't let you go
> the moment that you say
> come and live in me
> take me all the way
> what He said is true
> He will never leave you
> forever by your side…it's true
>
> He won't let you go
> though the seasons change
> He's never been so close
> He's just a prayer away
> when you hear the Father's call
> when He's calling to you
> run into His arms
> don't hesitate to do it
>
> He won't let you go
> when He's forever by your side
> He wants you to know
> Jesus has paid the price
> He wants you to go
> forever in paradise
> getting close to Him

is really all you have to do
and even when you die
He will still be by your side

He won't let you go
His love will never change
let Him hold you close
closer everyday
He would have died for you
had you been the only one
don't you ever doubt...it's true

He won't let you go
forever by your side
He wants you to know
Jesus has paid the price
He wants you to go
forever in paradise
give your heart to Him
is really all you have to do
and even when you die
He will still be by your side
getting close to Him
is really all you have to do
even when you die
He will still be by your side

He will never let you go
this, I know
He will never let you go

through the ages
time after time
He will never let you go.[*]

As he listened, Colin felt that he was indeed running into his Father's arms and letting Him hold him close. Even though his earthly father was gone, Colin knew that his Heavenly Father would hold him in His arms forever. He would never let him go.

And as he rested in his Father's love, slowly the deep well of sorrow that had been in Colin's heart gave way to a fountain of joy. Tears were still running down his cheeks but now they were tears of healing and of hope.

Suddenly Colin felt two tiny arms encircling his chest. He looked down into Verena's eyes and saw, to his amazement, that they were filled with compassion—and something else that he couldn't put his finger on. A bond, perhaps? A link of understanding between them of shared suffering?

Colin grew still, hardly daring to breathe, sensing that any small movement on his part might break this gossamer thread of trust that hung between them.

Somehow his deep sorrow had penetrated the barrier that Verena had built up between herself and an unbearable reality.

And in that moment, Colin was suddenly transported back to the little house where he had grown up, and for the first time in twenty-five years, Colin remembered what it felt like to sit on his daddy's knee. His father had been a great story-teller and Colin had sat enthralled at the tales he had been told of life on the trapline in the winter, or out on the fishing boats in the summer.

---

[*] Words and Music by Jean-Luc Lajoie, www.thekry.com

As Colin looked down at the little girl in his arms, he began to search his mind for one of the stories that his father or grandfather had told him, or better yet, a tale of his own. If he could remember his life before his parents had died, some story he could tell Verena...

Suddenly Colin remembered! The robin with the broken wing...

He smiled down at Verena and asked in a gentle voice, "Did you know that I once had a pet robin?"

Her eyes opened wide as she slowly moved her head side to side.

"Well, he wasn't exactly a pet..." Colin felt laughter bubbling up from deep inside. *He was telling his foster daughter a story just like his dad had told him stories so many years ago!*

"This little robin," Colin continued enthusiastically, "we called him 'Tweeter.' He was just a baby when I found him." Colin looked down in time to see a tentative smile forming on Verena's lips and joy bubbled up in him once more. "Tweeter was so tiny that I could hold him cupped in my hands—and I was just young myself then, maybe only four or five. Jamie, my sister, was older—she must have been about ten or eleven at the time."

A shadow fell across Verena's face at the mention of a sister and Colin hurried on. "Jamie was really cool; she didn't mind helping me find worms. And she taught me how to take care of Tweeter. I thought he would be happy in a box in my bedroom but Jamie knew that it would be better if he stayed outside." Colin paused. "Did I tell you that he had a broken wing?"

Verena made a slight motion with her head indicating that he had not.

"Oops, sorry. Well anyway, that's why he needed someone to take care of him, because he had a broken wing."

Verena said in a tiny voice, "I had a broken arm. I got throwed down the stairs."

Overcome with emotion, Colin could barely speak. "I'm sorry, Verena. I'm sorry that happened to you."

"It doesn't hurt anymore."

But Colin could see the remembered pain in her eyes, and his heart broke for her. He wished there was something—anything—that he could do for her.

As if reading what was in his heart, Verena asked in a tentative voice, "Can I keep my teddy bear for always?"

"Oh, yes!" Colin exclaimed. "It's yours, Verena. Would you like to get it now?"

Slowly she nodded her head, but there was fear in her eyes as she looked towards the hallway.

"We'll get it together, okay?" Colin suggested. He stood to his feet as he spoke, and Verena rested her head on his shoulder and put her arms around his neck as they walked to the bedroom to get her teddy bear. On the way back, she held onto it with both hands, hugging it close.

Colin suddenly remembered the teddy bear that he'd had as a child, and how much it had meant to him. But it had gotten lost somehow, either during his parents' funeral or when they'd emptied out the house. People had been so busy arguing about what should be done with him, nobody had seemed to care about what he'd really needed.

Colin sat down in the rocking chair again, and Verena rested her head against his chest and hugged her teddy bear.

"Did Tweeter have a mommy and daddy?"

She said the words so quietly that Colin almost missed them. He paused for a moment to think... Verena had already identified herself with the bird with a broken wing, by telling Colin about her broken arm. What was it that the little girl most needed to hear?

Colin chose his words carefully. "Yes, Tweeter had a mommy and daddy but they weren't able to take care of him."

Verena looked intently at him. "The lady with the big purse said that our mommy and daddy weren't able to take care of us anymore."

Colin translated "lady" to mean the social worker and the "big purse" her briefcase. "The lady was right, honey," he said in a gentle voice.

Colin kept his feelings to himself about Russell. He was getting off too lightly—he certainly could care for his own kids if he wanted to!

"Did Tweeter get a new mommy and a new daddy?"

"Not exactly," Colin said, once more choosing his words with care. "But I guess maybe Jamie and I were like a mommy and daddy to him. We took care of him."

The little girl was silent for a moment. Then she said, "My mommy's dead."

Colin hugged her close. "Yes," he said in a voice filled with compassion.

"My daddy hurt me..."

Colin groaned, feeling her pain as if it was his own. "Oh, Verena..."

"Lots of times," she added.

"I'm sorry, Verena. I'm sorry that happened to you."

She looked up at him and in a slow, serious voice, declared, "I think I need a new mommy and a new daddy."

A huge wave of emotion crashed over Colin. With every fiber of his being, he wanted to cry out that Sarah and he would be Verena's new mommy and daddy! But so far they had only been granted temporary custody of the children. The social workers had been confident that the children would become eligible for adoption, but that surely had changed now that Russell had avoided prison. And by the way he was talking at the funeral, he seemed determined to at least regain custody of Emmeline...

"Verena..." Colin began in a voice hoarse with emotion. "Sarah and I are your foster mom and dad. In a way, we are your new mommy and daddy but we don't know for how long. You might not be able to stay with us..."

Her sharp cry of pain drove deep into Colin's heart. And when she began to weep, tears fell from his eyes also.

She looked up at him with pleading eyes and cried, "I need a new daddy! I need a new daddy!"

He didn't know how to answer her, as he didn't want to give her false reassurances, but his silence was having a devastating effect on the little girl. Her eyes widened in terror and she began to tremble and moan, "No, no, no..."

And in that moment, Colin realized that she wasn't just asking for a new father but for some assurance that she would not be returned to her old father.

Colin knew all too well what it was like to live in fear of Russell and suddenly he resolved to do whatever it took to ensure that this little girl was never hurt ever again—by Russell or by anyone else! He would fight for her. He would gain custody. He would take care of her. He would be her daddy. And no one would ever, ever hurt her again!

"Verena!" he cried in a voice choked with tears. "Verena, no one's going to hurt you ever again. Do you hear me? No one's ever, ever going to hurt you again. I promise you. I promise you."

She had fallen back onto his chest again, still trembling but weeping silently now. Colin held her close and began to gently rock her, speaking all the while, "You're safe now, Verena, you're safe now. No one's going to hurt you. You're safe..."

How long before her trembling and weeping ceased, and how long before Colin's own tears stopped falling, he couldn't afterwards have said. The minutes merged and folded into one another and it wasn't until some time later that he realized that he was holding a sleeping child. She had fallen asleep in his arms— trusting him completely.

There was such a look of peace and repose on her face that it broke Colin's heart again. "Oh God," he prayed, "help me to keep my promise. Help me to protect her..."

A sound at the front door startled him and woke Verena. He felt her fear like a tangible thing.

But it was only Jamie.

Colin slowly let out the breath that he'd been holding.

She flipped back her long, silky black hair, kicked off her sandals and asked with raised eyebrows, "Who were you expecting?"

Colin shook his head and grinned sheepishly. "Not you, I guess."

As she came closer, Jamie's eyes filled with concern and Colin knew that she could tell that he'd been crying. He could see her big sister instincts kicking in as she pulled up a chair and asked in a gentle voice, "You okay?"

"Yeah." He smiled reassuringly. "I'm fine." He looked down at Verena, including her in his smile. She was facing Jamie and had only to look up to see the warmth in her eyes.

"This is Jamie, my sister. Remember, I told you that she was the one who helped me with Tweeter."

The little girl looked shyly up at her as Jamie laughed and said, "I remember Tweeter! All those disgusting worms I had to help you find—and then he wouldn't let you get close enough at the beginning—and I had to feed them to him!"

Colin laughed too. "You didn't seem to mind at the time—or at least you never showed it."

Jamie rolled her eyes. "Well, I did have an image to keep up. I was your big sister, unafraid of anything, remember?"

Colin smiled. He did remember. If only they hadn't been separated after their parents had died, his sister could have continued to be his ally. But he'd been all alone and then bad things had started to happen...

And now it seemed as if it had started all over again for Joshua...

"Jamie," he said in a more serious voice, "you heard what happened to Joshua?"

She nodded and stood to her feet. "Yes, that's why I came over. I thought maybe I could help Sarah."

Colin smiled up at her, grateful to his big sister for her continued friendship and support.

chapter fourteen

Jamie's first impression of Emmeline surprised her. From Michael and Rosalee's description of events, Jamie had expected the child to be bigger and meaner looking. What she saw was a sweet little girl sitting and listening to her foster mother reading her a children's storybook.

Jamie stood for a moment in the doorway taking in the scene. Then she must have made some slight sound or movement for the little girl turned her way. Her relaxed demeanor froze into a look of suspicion, which in turn twisted into a glare filled with intense hatred. Jamie drew in a sharp breath and Sarah turned towards the sound.

"Jamie…" Sarah rose quickly to her feet. "Jamie, I'm sorry about what happened to Rosalee."

Tearing her eyes away from the child, Jamie tried to give Sarah a reassuring smile. "It's okay," she said kindly. "It wasn't your fault. And Bill and I would like to help in any way that we can. He was going to come over with me but then Jeff called and…" Jamie paused. "Jeff's going through a really rough time right now."

Sarah shook her head and spoke angrily, "He's the one that spread the rumor that Joshua was off on a drinking binge and he seems determined to break up the relationship between Missy and Joshua!"

Jamie glanced over at Joshua but he appeared to be asleep. "Jeff is very protective of his daughter..." she began.

But Sarah just shook her head again, effectively ending the discussion.

"I can watch over Joshua for a while if you'd like," Jamie volunteered.

Sarah looked grateful as she nodded in agreement. She turned to speak to Emmeline but the girl had slipped out unnoticed.

"I'd better go!" she exclaimed, rushing out the door.

Jamie followed her into the hallway, fearing some new catastrophe. But they both stopped as they saw Emmeline standing quietly in the kitchen entrance. As they quietly moved closer, they could see what Emmeline was staring so intently at: her sister in Colin's arms in the old wooden rocking chair.

Jamie watched Sarah's anxious look melt into a warm smile of love as she went to join her family.

Jamie walked back into the bedroom and quietly observed Joshua. Something about the stiff position of his body made Jamie realize that he was awake after all. She approached the bed and softly spoke his name.

He opened eyes that were bleak with despair and Jamie wondered if it was Tom's death that had affected him so deeply— or if he was suffering from some kind of post-traumatic depression.

She leaned toward him. "Is there anything that I can get you, Josh?"

"Bathroom," he said in a hoarse whisper.

Jamie nodded and helped him up into a sitting position.

"Colin..." he rasped.

Jamie had been about to assist him to his feet. She stopped but said, "I think that we can manage. You should be able to walk on your own soon."

"Colin..." Joshua spoke more insistently.

Jamie patted him on the shoulder. "I'll get him for you."

Everyone was just sitting down to the table but Colin jumped up right away when Jamie told him that Joshua was asking for him.

Together, the two of them supported Joshua to the bathroom and back. He walked stiffly, each step an effort.

After Joshua was back in bed, Colin turned to go.

"Stay—please..."

Colin bent over his friend. "Both of us?" he asked.

Joshua shook his head.

Jamie had been watching and immediately stood to her feet. Joshua's eyes spoke of his gratitude. She smiled at him, touched Colin's shoulder lightly in farewell and left the room.

Colin slowly sat down, wondering why Joshua would want to see him alone. The look of despair in the younger man's eyes frightened Colin. How close was Joshua to doing something desperate?

It was clear that Joshua wanted to ask something from him. It was as if he was gathering up his strength—or courage.

"A drink..." he finally rasped.

Colin jumped to his feet as if he'd been stung. "No!"

He immediately realized his mistake as Joshua flinched, reacting as though Colin had physically slapped him with that one word. And he heard it in the bitter tone that Joshua used when he said, "Water."

Colin's throat constricted and his own mouth grew as dry as dust. "I'm sorry," he whispered.

Joshua tried to smile but the hurt look remained in his eyes.

Colin quickly picked up the glass of water and held it to Joshua's lips. He took several swallows before motioning for Colin to take it away.

Colin set the glass down on the bedside table and waited for Joshua to say what was on his mind. But it seemed as if the words were still sticking in his throat and Colin grew afraid again.

"Josh, what is it?"

"Missy…" Joshua spoke in a trembling voice.

"Yes…?" Colin prompted.

Joshua flung the words out in a burst of emotion. "She has to go home!"

"Right now?" Colin asked in a bewildered voice. "She's resting right now. I could take her later…"

Joshua's chest heaved with emotion. "To Chicago… She has to go home to Chicago."

Colin felt his mouth go dry again. "Why?"

Joshua shook his head, despair clouding his eyes once more.

"Joshua—why?" Colin demanded.

"I—I can't…"

"You're breaking off the engagement?" Colin felt anger burn through his heart like a torch. Joshua was giving up! Just like that, he was giving up!

Joshua's voice was raw with emotion and each word was forced out as if with a great effort. "I can't protect her. She's not safe. I can't…"

Colin felt like shaking him!

"Joshua! What about your dreams? You and Missy were going to build a youth camp for kids that had gone through what you had gone through…" Colin's voice trailed off. He could see the answer in Joshua's eyes.

"No camp." The words were spoken in a sigh. Joshua shook his head. "I couldn't guarantee the kids' safety."

Russell! Colin thought angrily.

Was there no end to his destructive force?

So many dreams had been wrecked, so many lives destroyed…

And now would Russell win yet again?

Colin bowed his head. The anger faded away as if it had never been. Despair, his companion of so many years ago, settled back in as if to stay.

Then like a gentle breeze blowing back the curtains of his soul, from across the room came a voice, clear and sweet, pure and innocent.

"Daddy…"

Colin spun around to face the door, his heart in his throat.

She stood, clutching the teddy bear, her eyes wide open, looking expectantly towards him.

"Verena…" He spoke her name in a whisper, hardly daring to breathe, afraid that the moment might vanish like a dream.

It was as if they were both afraid to make the next move.

Then Colin opened his arms wide and Verena ran into them.

They clung tightly to each other. Then Colin felt her grip relax. She pulled away a little and looked up at him. Her eyes were shining and a slow smile spread across her face. Colin thought it was the most beautiful smile that he'd ever seen in his life!

Feeling as if his heart might burst with all the pride and joy that was welling up inside of him, Colin turned towards Joshua.

"There's someone that I'd like you to meet," he said.

Joshua managed a smile as he reached out his hand to greet the little girl. "Hi, there," he said.

From the safety of Colin's lap, Verena let him take her hand and shyly lifted her eyes up towards him.

"That's a really nice teddy bear you have there," Joshua said. "Does he have a name?"

Verena snuggled in even closer to Colin. A faint smile remained on her face as she shook her head slowly side to side.

Joshua looked up at Colin. "I knew you were thinking about foster kids…"

Colin nodded in affirmation. "Yes, and the Lord has blessed us with two little girls. This is Verena, and her sister's name is Emmeline."

"Verena, that's a pretty name." He smiled at her. "And my name is Joshua."

Colin hesitated, wondering if he should let Joshua know that Verena was his niece. But then, he'd have to bring up Russell's name, and that would upset both Verena and Joshua.

Colin made a quick decision. "Would it be okay if Verena called you 'Uncle Joshua'?"

The younger man's face broke into a wide grin and for an instant, the old Joshua was back. "Well, since she's calling you Daddy…"

Colin smiled, feeling at a loss for words.

He knew it was premature, and went against what they'd been advised by the agency: to have the children call them by their names instead of using "mommy" and "daddy." But after her desperate plea for a "new daddy," Colin found himself incapable of rebuking Verena when she addressed him that way. If she needed to call him "Daddy," then so be it. And he prayed earnestly that someday he would no longer just be her foster father, but her adoptive father as well.

"You're hoping to keep her for a while?" Joshua asked quietly.

Colin felt a strong protective instinct rising up in him once more. "Yes," he declared.

Joshua smiled his approval. "I always thought you'd make a great dad," he said. Then, as Colin watched, Joshua's eyes drooped and his face sank into repose as the medication took effect again.

Verena looked at Joshua and then up at Colin, a question in her eyes.

"He's just asleep," Colin reassured her.

A noise in the doorway made them both turn. It was Sarah. She kept her voice low as she said, "Bill's arrived—and Jeff's with him."

Colin sighed. He could have done without Jeff tonight.

He managed a smile for Verena though. "We need to go talk to some people," he said, sliding her off his lap to stand on the floor. But she sprang back up into his arms, her eyes wide open and fearful. Colin patted her shoulder reassuringly and rose, shifting Verena onto his hip.

Sarah's voice was wistful as she said, "You two are getting quite attached."

"She'll warm up to you," Colin said, putting an arm around his wife. He kissed her and then grinned. "You're irresistible, you know."

His words brought a smile to her lips and together they walked with an arm around each other down the hallway to meet their guests.

As they entered the kitchen, Colin took a quick glance around. Jamie was making a pot of tea, Bill was leaning against the kitchen counter and Jeff was pacing around the room like a caged animal. Emmeline sitting in the corner of the sectional, surveyed everyone through narrowed eyes.

As soon as Jeff caught sight of Colin, he came striding over. "Where's Missy?" he demanded.

"She's resting," Sarah spoke up.

"She needs to get ready. I want her on the flight out tomorrow morning."

"What!" Colin shouted and felt the little girl in his arms begin to tremble. He looked down and saw the terror in her eyes. "It's okay," he said gently. Ignoring Jeff, he continued to speak comforting words to Verena as he walked over to the rocking chair with her and sat down.

On the periphery, he heard Sarah and Jeff arguing. Jamie seemed to have joined in as well. Colin continued to focus his attention on the child in his arms. "He's just worried about his daughter," Colin tried to explain to Verena, as the voices rose in pitch and intensity.

Verena's trembling ceased. "Why?" she asked in a tiny voice.

Colin shook his head. "I guess it's just what daddies do. But he shouldn't be worried about her. She's an adult. She can make her own choices."

When Verena looked more intrigued than upset, Colin judged it safe enough to call out to Jeff. But he had to speak Jeff's name twice before he was heard above the argument. Everyone stopped and turned towards Colin.

"You're frightening the children," Colin said, making the word plural so as to include Emmeline. "And you're going to wake Missy and Joshua."

Jeff stood for a moment like a moose caught in the headlights. Then Bill stepped forward and took him by the arm. "Come and sit down," he said.

Bill had obviously taken over the task that Jamie had begun. There was a pot of tea on the table and cups laid out. He'd even set out a plate of the bannock that his daughter had made earlier in the day.

Jamie and Sarah took their cue and followed Bill and Jeff over to the table.

Colin waved away Bill's invitation to join them.

Jeff took a swallow of the tea that Jamie placed in his hand, then set the cup down. He sighed and pushed his fingers through his hair. When he spoke, his voice no longer held antagonism, just fatigue.

"Colin, you're a policeman. You tell me. Is she safe here? Have you caught the perpetrators? Can you guarantee that the same thing that happened to Joshua won't happen to her? Especially since I've heard that Joshua knows who his assailants are and isn't willing to assist the police in identifying them." Jeff paused and when he spoke again, his voice was filled with passion. "I am her father. I want to protect her, keep her safe. Can you at least try to imagine what that must feel like?"

chapter fifteen

The room fell silent. Sarah abruptly stood, pushing her chair back with a screech. She walked over to the cupboard, keeping her back to everyone as she reached for more cups.

Colin swallowed hard… even with the comforting weight of the child nestled trustingly in his arms, Jeff's words were like a jagged knife being twisted into his gut. He took a deep breath. "Yes, I can imagine," he said.

Jeff blundered on, unmindful of the pain he had caused. "I cannot condone a relationship that wreaks such havoc on her emotional well being. Missy already has so much to deal with because of her handicap; she needs a strong husband that will take care of *her,* not the other way around."

Colin watched as Sarah poured two glasses of juice and began to walk towards him. Their eyes met and he could see his grief reflected there. The children they had hoped to have together… to nurture… to love…

Jamie was speaking to Jeff but her words barely registered on Colin. Something about Missy not being a child any more… He had to let go…

Sarah offered one of the glasses of juice to Verena and Colin was pleasantly surprised when the little girl accepted, though she didn't raise her eyes to meet Sarah's.

Colin thanked her and gently touched her arm. They exchanged wan smiles before Sarah moved over to Emmeline, who quietly accepted her glass of juice also. Colin was more than a little surprised that she didn't move away when Sarah sat down beside her.

"Colin?" Jeff said impatiently. "Are you even listening to me? I was saying that in the last few days, a great deal of responsibility has been placed on my shoulders. This is in addition to the heavy load I am already carrying with regards to my wife's illness. I also need to consider what's best for Martha and Bobby. And I do have other responsibilities at work as well. I have patients under my care and as head of the neonatal surgical unit—"

"I get the picture," Colin interrupted tersely.

Jeff gave a deep sigh. "The lodge was given to Joshua but I feel responsible, as my father's son, to be certain that he is capable of managing and maintaining this legacy. I need to weigh everything, consider everyone and make the right decisions for all concerned." He stopped, and looked around at the others. "So I've decided to close down the lodge for now."

"What?" Colin interjected angrily. "You can't do that!"

Jeff continued on as if Colin had not spoken. "Missy will have the list of people that need to be contacted. She can write or call them to let them know that this—treatment center, or whatever it's supposed to be—is on hold for now.

"Furthermore, I *will* be taking my mom and brother with me tomorrow when I leave."

"No, Jeff!" Jamie gasped. "Do they even know what you're planning for them?"

He didn't seem to hear her either. "I *have* to get back to Jenny. I need to leave on the flight tomorrow morning—and Missy needs to go with me."

They were back where they had started.

Bill and Jamie both stood at the same time.

"We should go," Jamie linked her arm with Jeff's, and Colin was once again reminded of a large bull moose staring into the headlights of an oncoming car. Jamie tried to steer Jeff away but he stood his ground.

"Missy has to come with me *now*. She has to pack," he insisted.

Colin rose to his feet and gently deposited Verena on the chair. He walked over to Jeff, hooked elbows with him, and together he and Jamie walked him towards the front door and away from the children. Colin's tone was quiet but authoritative as he said, "Missy is an adult. Yes, she is your daughter but she is also promised in marriage to Joshua. If she chooses to stay with him, then she has the right to do so. And yes, Martha is your mother and Bobby is your brother but that doesn't mean I will tolerate you bullying them into leaving their home." Colin let Jeff's arm drop. "You're not the only one who loves them, and wants the best for them."

Jeff's jaw tightened and he seemed about to resume the argument but Bill stepped in front of them, put his hands on Jeff's shoulders and said, "Come on, Jeff, let's go. We'll talk about this again in the morning when everyone is rested."

"But then we'll miss the morning flight," Jeff protested.

"I can fly you out whenever you're ready," Bill said.

It took a moment for the words to penetrate but finally Jeff nodded wearily and allowed himself to be led out the door.

Bill popped his head back in after everyone else was gone. "I can bring over a foam mattress if you need one. It's just a single..."

Colin nodded. "That'll be fine. Thanks, Bill."

As the door closed, Colin turned towards Sarah, still sitting on the sectional beside Emmeline. He sat down beside them and beckoned to Verena. She slid off the rocker, carrying her teddy bear, and walked cautiously over to them. He held out his arms and she climbed up into his lap. Leaning back, Colin slowly put his arm around Sarah, acutely aware that this was the first time all four of them had sat so close together. He didn't want to move—didn't want to risk shattering this precious moment.

He let his gaze rest for a moment on Sarah's beautiful face, lit now with the joy of maternal love. Her focus was on Verena, who was completely taken up with her teddy bear as she smoothed her fingers over the soft fur, satin ribbon and button eyes.

A slight movement made Colin shift his gaze to Emmeline and he was startled by the deep pain and longing in the child's eyes as she watched Sarah focus on her sister.

"Emmeline," he said softly, longing to draw her into the family circle, and Sarah lifted her arm to place it around Emmeline. But the little girl bounced angrily away from her, folded her arms, and eyed the three of them with hostility.

Colin sighed. The joyous moment was gone. He felt instead a keen disappointment and a growing sadness. "I guess they should go to bed soon..."

He looked over at Sarah expecting a weary reply. He was surprised instead to see a mischievous grin lighting up her face. He was further surprised when she sat up straight, put her hands on her hips and declared with an exaggerated southern twang, "Emmygojumpin' that bed of yours!"

And then, for the second time that day, Colin felt as if he was witnessing a miracle. He held his breath as a slow smile spread across the little girl's features, then she jumped to her feet and darted from the room, as carefree as any child should be.

Sarah turned and grinned at Colin, then suddenly shot to her feet. "Oh no! Missy's asleep on Emmeline's bed!"

Together, they rushed towards the guest bedroom... but no one else was in the room besides Emmeline. And the little girl's defenses were firmly back in place. "What are you guys staring at?" she demanded.

"We thought that Missy might still be in here," Sarah explained. She smiled at Emmeline. "We'll leave you now. There are pajamas if you'd like to wear them—with pretty blue flowers on them."

Her words were met with stony silence.

"We'll see you in the morning then," Colin said gently.

They backed away from the door and Sarah closed it before turning to Colin. The pain in her voice was palpable. "We were so close... I thought..."

Colin put his arm around her. "And we'll be there again. Don't worry. She responded to you once, she'll respond to you again."

Sarah rested her head on his shoulder for a moment and then smiled at Verena. "I guess we should get this little one to bed, too."

But instead of an answering smile, a look of wariness filled Verena's eyes. Sarah flinched as if she'd been struck and Colin felt her pain as if it was his own.

Before he could speak to comfort her, though, Sarah pasted a bright smile on her face and said, "I'll get the sheets from the dryer for you. Maybe you and Verena can make her bed together. Missy is probably with Joshua. I should go check on them..."

As Sarah stepped into the master bedroom, her eye was caught by the scenic beauty of the lake and trees framed by the glass patio doors. The sky was lit up a brilliant orange and a warm glow spread across the still water. Sarah felt her spirits lift a little.

It was also good to see that Joshua appeared to be asleep. Missy was sitting beside him, holding his hand.

Sarah pulled a second chair quietly up beside Missy's and tenderly asked her how she was doing.

Missy gave her a weak smile but seemed unable to frame a reply to Sarah's question. When she did finally speak, her voice held a plaintive note. "When I hold his hand, I feel there is still some kind of connection between us. Maybe if I could see..." She shook her head sadly. "I don't even know when he's awake." She hesitated. "He—he spoke to Colin, didn't he?"

"I don't know," Sarah answered honestly.

"He spoke my name once and even hugged me. But his arms were so stiff..."

"Missy, he was tied up for over two days," Sarah gently reminded her.

"I know," Missy spoke the words in a half-cry, moving her hand up to massage Joshua's upper arm.

Sarah laid her hand over Missy's. "You're going to wake him, honey," she cautioned. "The pain medication will be easing the muscle cramps."

Missy sat back in the chair, releasing her hold on Joshua. "I just feel so helpless," she cried. "I couldn't help him then and I can't help him now!"

"The best way that you can help him now," Sarah said gently, "is by getting some rest yourself. Then you'll be better able to cope with tomorrow's problems." She hesitated, choosing her words carefully. "Joshua will be okay here. Colin and I will check on him."

"If you think I'm leaving..." Missy's voice rose.

"Okay, okay," Sarah spoke in a soothing whisper.

"I want to stay right here beside him." Missy's voice was choked with tears. "Don't you understand? I feel like I'm losing him. Like—maybe I've already lost him."

Sarah put her arm around the weeping young woman. "You'll never lose Joshua," she said. "You two were made for each other. You guys hit it off right away as soon as you met—and you've built a solid relationship based first on friendship and then on romantic love. You two have shared common goals and dreams together. You both love the Lord and want to serve Him. And you always seem to be having so much fun when you're together. You bring joy to those around you."

Sarah's words seemed to be having some small effect on Missy. "I do love him," she whispered.

"And he loves you," Sarah affirmed.

But Missy was shaking her head doubtfully. "I don't know anymore," she said in a tiny, broken voice. "Ever since we met, he's always been honest with me. He'd never laugh at me or try to trick me. And we could always talk about my blindness. He'd always say that we all have handicaps of one sort or another. He helped me to find and develop my strengths. And now—and now, he doesn't even want to—to talk to me."

"Of course, he wants to talk to you!" Sarah exclaimed. "The pain medication is making him sleep and that's a good thing. The more he rests, the quicker he will get better. What we all need to do now is give ourselves one good night's sleep."

She stood to her feet and it was then that she saw the fresh tears in Joshua's pain-filled eyes. He was awake!

Sarah didn't trust herself to speak so began to tidy up the bedside table, lifting and setting things down and opening and shutting the drawer.

Finally, she sat down beside Missy and put her arm around her again. "Honey, just think, this time last night, you didn't even know that Joshua was still alive and would be found. Be thankful for the moment and give yourself—and Joshua—time to heal."

Missy was nodding. And in Joshua's eyes, mingled with the pain, Sarah could read gratitude.

She felt a little guilty for not letting Missy know that Joshua was awake, but he seemed to want—or need—it that way.

"In the morning," she said. "You two can talk in the morning." Joshua nodded in thanks but the despair in his eyes deepened.

Sarah turned towards Missy, who was retrieving the pillow that had been tucked down beside the chair and the blanket that had been slung over the back of it.

"Let me know if there's anything you need, honey," she said.

Missy nodded and reached up to squeeze Sarah's hand. "Thank you," she whispered.

Sarah patted her shoulder and went to find Colin.

Both Emmeline and Verena's doors were shut, and Colin was in the kitchen making two cups of hot chocolate.

"How is Verena?" he asked.

Sarah was momentarily confused.

"I left her with her pajamas a little while ago," he explained. "I thought that maybe you would check the girls on your way back."

Sarah shook her head. "I'll go check now, though."

Colin followed behind her. Sarah stopped at Emmeline's door, hesitated a moment, then quietly peeked in. The little girl seemed to be asleep and Sarah quickly shut the door again.

They went on to the next room and tiptoed in. Verena also seemed to have fallen straight asleep after putting her pajamas on and getting into bed. She was clutching her teddy bear and had the blankets pulled up around her chin but there was a look of serenity on her tiny brow. Sarah and Colin exchanged smiles and quietly walked out again.

Back in the kitchen they sat at the table and luxuriated for a moment in the peaceful silence. Colin took a sip of hot chocolate then asked about Missy.

"She's pretty upset," Sarah began slowly. "She thinks that Joshua doesn't want to talk to her but that he has talked to you."

"He *has* talked to me," Colin admitted.

"He was awake when I left," Sarah continued.

"Did Missy know?"

Sarah shook her head.

Colin sighed deeply. "He wants her to leave. He wants to give up on the camp, on their marriage, on everything."

Yes, from the abject despair that she'd seen on Joshua's face, she could well believe that he'd given up on everything. And she remembered a time seven years ago, when she'd seen that same defeated look in Colin's eyes as he fought an apparently losing battle with alcohol. He'd also been ready to give up on everything, including her. Sarah had almost let him do it. If it hadn't been for Tom... Sarah shuddered to think what might have happened if she'd run away and left Colin to battle alone against the forces of darkness.

"Missy *needs* to stay," Sarah declared.

Colin shook his head. "We can't force her."

"No, but we can encourage her..." Sarah's voice softened, "...the way that Tom encouraged me to stand by you."

Colin laughed. "*Encouraged*? From what I heard, a more appropriate word might be bullied!"

Sarah laughed too. "He was pretty mad at me," she admitted. "But I deserved it." Her smile faded. "I let you down when you needed me the most."

Colin reached over and took her hand. "Neither one of us handled things as well as we could have. We were young..." he lifted an eyebrow and grinned, "and foolish."

"And now we're not young anymore—just foolish!" Sarah laughed.

Colin began to sing off key, "Oh, I'm just a fool for you..."

They stood up and ballroom danced as Colin continued to sing tunelessly, "Just a fool for you..."

The front door opened, revealing Jamie and Bill carrying a foam mattress between them. Colin glanced over at them, but continued to twirl Sarah around the room one more time before planting a kiss on her lips.

When he turned to greet his guests, they were wearing mischievous grins. "You did tell me that you just needed a single mattress, didn't you buddy?" Bill asked.

"Bill!" Jamie scolded him but ruined the effect by laughing.

"Yes," Colin sighed theatrically and hung his head. "I have to sleep on the couch tonight. We had this terrible fight. Sarah told me that when I sing, I sound like a braying donkey."

"I never said that!" Sarah laughed. "I might have *thought* it but..."

Bill shook his head, his good-natured grin still evident. "Guess we'll leave you two guys to duke it out." They leaned the mattress up against the couch then headed for the door. As an afterthought, Bill reached into his pocket for a coin and tossed it to Colin. "Here, you can flip for it!"

"C'mon!" Jamie laughed, pushing him outside. "See you kids in the morning!"

The door closed behind them.

"Kids!" Colin exclaimed, pretending to be insulted. "Did you hear what she called us—'kids'!"

Sarah was about to reply when a quiet voice interrupted.

"Joshua wanted to talk to you, Colin," Missy said. "I think he's worried that you guys might not have a place to sleep tonight."

"It's okay," Sarah began, "Jamie and Bill brought us..."

"I'll go talk to him," Colin offered. "Sarah, maybe Missy would like a cup of hot chocolate or something."

Colin found Joshua sitting on the side of the bed, swaying slightly as if he was going to fall over at any moment! Colin rushed across the room and placed his hands on Joshua's shoulders to steady him. "Whoa there, buddy—what are you trying to do?"

"I already took your bed one night." Joshua's voice was as feeble as his efforts to climb off the bed. "I can sleep on the couch... or somewhere."

"Here, lay down again." Colin pressed lightly on his shoulders and Joshua collapsed back onto the bed. He looked drained, as if the effort of sitting up had cost him every last ounce of energy. Colin helped lift his feet up and repositioned the pillow and blankets.

"Josh, relax. We have an extra mattress. Jamie and Bill brought one over. We don't mind if you have our bed another night. We're more concerned that you get well."

As Colin turned to go, Joshua grabbed at his arm. "I've got to tell her tonight!" he rasped.

"No, you don't," Colin said in a calming voice. "It can wait for the morning. You need to give yourself time to heal, emotionally and physically, before you make those kinds of decisions."

But Joshua was looking past Colin, towards the doorway.

Colin, following his gaze, exclaimed, "Missy!"

She smiled wanly. "I didn't want any hot chocolate. I want to be with my fiancé..."

"Missy, I..." Joshua faltered.

With her head held high, Missy moved past Colin and sat down. She adjusted the pillow and pulled the blanket up around her. Her voice held a quiet determination as she declared, "I am *not* leaving you, Joshua Quill."

chapter sixteen

Joshua felt her presence like an aching wound. He listened to each breath and wished that he had the courage to speak to her. He finally drifted off to sleep only to awaken a short while later to the sound of her crying. Every fiber of his being longed to comfort her, but he had to think of her long-term welfare. Tom had been a giant of a man. No one had even dared to put graffiti on the buildings, let alone harm any of the occupants. But with Tom gone, Joshua couldn't guarantee anyone's safety—not Missy's, not the campers, not Martha or Bobby's...

It was as if everything had gone back to the way it was before he became a Christian—before he went to work at the lodge—before he met Missy...

He'd never trained for anything else. He'd never wanted to do anything else.

He'd worked at the camp alongside Tom for the past seven years, knowing his destiny was wrapped up in that place and in those people. He had felt fulfilled, happy...

Now there was nothing. Nothing at all.

It had been many years since Joshua had entertained thoughts of suicide but they pressed around him now... beckoning... promising a quick, easy solution... a way out.

It would solve everything. Missy's father could do what he wanted with the lodge—he'd probably sell it and take everyone down to Chicago with him... Martha and Bobby... And Missy... Yes, he'd surely take her back down there, too. And find her a more suitable husband—someone from a good family—someone who could keep her safe. Missy was so beautiful and talented—with Joshua out of the way, she'd soon find herself another man.

Colin would miss him for a while. But he had Sarah, and now the beginning of a new family... Those two little girls would need a lot of love and care... It would be better if Colin could focus on them and not have Joshua around to worry about.

Everyone would be better off without him.

The demons of suicide danced and swirled around in his head, enticing, luring, beckoning him...

Missy woke feeling stiff and sore from sleeping in the chair. She felt her watch and "read" the time—7:14 a.m.

She listened for the sound of Joshua's deep, steady breathing and was glad that he was asleep. It seemed to Missy as if they had both been awake most of the night. Though she had remained apart from him physically, not even touching his hand, she remained attuned to each small movement and breath he took. Strangely enough, it was when he was perfectly still that Missy knew he was awake, trying hard to keep her from knowing it.

Though Missy longed for this barrier of silence between them to be broken, she dreaded it also; well aware of what Joshua would say to her when he did speak. He was going to insist that she return to Chicago with her father!

Missy did want to see her mom again. Her dad had told her that her mom's condition had deteriorated, and that there was no way she could travel up to Rabbit Lake for Missy's wedding. But Missy was still hoping that she would rally again and somehow be well enough by then to make the trip. Her mother's journey with cancer had been such an up and down roller coaster ride, filled with long stretches of good days followed by an equal number of bad. But maybe her dad was right... He was a doctor. He would know. Maybe her mom *was* a lot worse.

Missy felt a sudden urgency to call her, hear her voice.

She stood, listened again to Joshua's breathing, and assured that he was still asleep, walked quietly out, and down the hall into the living room.

She called Sarah and Colin's names in a low whisper and, getting no response, felt her way to the desk and picked up the cordless phone. She was familiar with the keypad and knew the phone number of her mother's hospital room. Walking halfway back down the hall, she slid down onto the floor and dialed the number.

Missy was relieved when it was her mom that answered; that meant she was awake and feeling well enough to speak on the phone.

They talked a little about the funeral, her mom expressing how much she'd wanted to be there, and Missy telling her about some of the people from out of town who had attended. "Doc Ryley was there and Charles... He sat by Bobby the whole time...

Bobby is really broken up about Grandpa." She paused before adding, "Dad wants to bring Grandma and Bobby back down with him."

There was a long pause. "Mom..." Missy spoke urgently.

Her mother's voice came back shaky and filled with sadness. "Missy, please tell Dad that—that he shouldn't wait. He—he needs to come down—now."

Missy gasped. What was her mom saying? Did she think that she might not live long enough to see him if he didn't get down there right away?

Her mother was continuing on. "Maybe Grandma and Bobby could come down later with Uncle David and Aunt Corrie..."

"Yes," Missy quickly agreed, "I'm sure they could."

"I—I need him."

"I'll tell him, Mom," Missy promised. "I'll tell Dad what you said."

"Are you coming down too, honey?" her mom asked.

Missy's instant reaction was a defensive one and she had to consciously remind herself that her mother wasn't trying to separate her from Joshua as her father was; she just wanted to see her again. "I don't know, Mom," she said. "Maybe Joshua and I could come down later, when he's well enough to travel."

"How is Joshua, dear?"

If her mother had asked that question in a strong clear voice, Missy would have broken down and told her everything. But her mother sounded weak and frail, and Missy could not bring herself to place another burden on her shoulders. "He's doing fine," she said. "They've given him a muscle relaxant and he seems to be sleeping better... sometimes... He—he's able to talk a bit, too... sometimes."

Missy stopped, knowing that her voice was betraying her.

Her mother's voice was gentle and filled with tenderness. "Missy, give Joshua time to heal. And Missy... *be there for him.*"

Suddenly, she sounded hurried and fretful. "I've got to go. They're waiting to give me a needle. And my nurse has that scolding look of hers. They think I'm overdoing it just by being on the phone."

"I'll let you go then, Mom," Missy said quickly. "I love you, Mom."

"Take care of Joshua, honey," were her mother's parting words.

Missy heard the click and then the dial tone. She fumbled for the off button, trying to digest all that her mother had said.

Silently, she began to pray for the strength that she would need for the upcoming day. Her mother's words echoed in her head. *Be there for him.* It was what Missy herself knew she needed to do. She stood to her feet with new resolve; the confusion of the night had passed and her vision was clear.

She walked quietly back into the living room, not knowing if Colin and Sarah were awake yet. She set the phone gently down on the corner of the desk and was about to leave again when Sarah's sleepy voice reached her ears. Her "good morning" sounded as if it was spoken in the midst of a huge yawn.

Missy smiled in her direction and offered to make coffee.

"That would be nice," Sarah said with another yawn. "Maybe I'll just lie down again for a little while."

Missy smiled again as she moved toward the kitchen.

"Help yourself to whatever you'd like to eat," Sarah said. "I' not feeling quite up to snuff yet or else I'd cook you somethin

"It's okay," Missy replied, "I can manage."

She put the coffee on then searched for what she might cook for breakfast, thinking not of herself but of Joshua, acutely aware that this would be his first meal since the kidnapping. Familiar with Sarah's kitchen, Missy easily found bread, eggs and bacon to cook. The settings on the stove were easy for her; she always gave the dials exactly one-half of a revolution, cooking everything on medium heat and baking everything at 350 degrees, a rule that seemed to work for just about everything.

After preparing a heaping plate of food, Missy poured a glass of orange juice and grabbed a knife and fork. "Coffee's ready!" she called out to Sarah before heading back to the bedroom.

As she set the plate, silverware and glass down on the bedside table, Missy wondered if Joshua was awake yet.

"Joshua..." she called softly.

"Missy..." he rasped.

She could hear the desperation in his voice and for an instant felt her courage falter. Then with a false cheeriness, she proclaimed, "I brought you some food. I know you must be hungry. You haven't eaten since—since—in a long time." She swallowed hard and began again. "We'll start with the orange juice, unless you'd like some eggs first, or toast or—"

"Noth—nothing..." he protested feebly.

But Missy already had the glass in her hand. She put the straw into the juice and leaning over reached out to feel for where Joshua's face was. His cheeks were wet and once more, she almost gave way to her own feelings. She didn't trust herself to speak but held the straw to his lips.

She was grateful when he took a swallow and then another. When she heard the gurgle of the last few drops of juice being sucked up into the straw, she felt like jumping up and dancing around!

"Now, how about some bacon, eggs and toast?" she announced with a flourish.

"Missy, I need to talk..."

"Not before breakfast!" Missy declared firmly. She rested her wrists on the edge of the tray, felt for the knife and fork and the rim of the plate. She had placed the strips of bacon on the toast and covered it with the fried egg. She positioned the knife and fork and expertly cut a square inch of toast, bacon and egg. She speared it with the fork and with her left hand felt for Joshua's face again. She touched his cheek and let her hand slide down to where his mouth was. Then she moved her other hand with the fork in it towards his mouth.

She felt his smile at the moment that she felt his hand gently grasp hers. He guided the fork full of food into his mouth. She still had one hand on his cheek and could tell when he chewed and then swallowed.

He sounded like the old Joshua that she knew when he said, "Maybe I could just feed myself. That fork coming towards me was pretty scary."

Missy protested. "I knew exactly what I was doing. I had it all lined up..."

Joshua took her hand from his cheek and kissed her fingers. "I know. I know," he said tenderly. Releasing his hold on both of her hands he continued with a smile in his voice, "But I'm twenty-three years old and I can feed myself."

Missy felt joy bubbling up inside her but kept this emotion in check as well, allowing herself just a small smile as she set abr cutting another piece of toast, bacon and egg. With the forkful of food, she extended her arm towards him.

But Joshua gently pushed her hand back. "You need to eat too."

"No, I ate yesterday," she protested, then laughed in spite of herself as she realized what she'd said. "Okay, but the next bite is yours," she declared, popping the food into her mouth. It did taste good and Missy realized that she had been very hungry.

They continued taking turns until the plate was empty.

Missy set down the knife and fork, and reached for Joshua's hand, dreading this moment but feeling a need for some connection with this man she loved. If only she could see his face and watch his expressions change...

"I'm going up to the lodge now," she began with more confidence in her voice than she felt. "I want to shower and change and I need to make sure my dad gets on the morning flight out. I promised my mom."

"Go with him!" Joshua implored her, the desperation in his voice a tangible thing.

Missy took a trembling breath but when she spoke, her voice was clear and strong. "Not now." She took a breath. "Not yet." She breathed again. "And not without you."

"Missy!" He spoke her name in a groan of despair.

She fell into his arms, overwhelmed by the pain she heard in his voice. "I'm never going to leave you! I'm never going to leave you..." she said over and over as she wept on his shoulder.

Gradually she became aware of his repeated response. "You have to! You have to..."

She raised herself up, swiped at the tears on her cheeks, and stood to her feet. "I'll be back in an hour or so."

Then, ignoring his protests, she walked resolutely out of the room.

Sarah and Colin were in the kitchen. "I'm going up to the lodge," she told them.

There was a moment's hesitation, and then Colin said, "I'll drive you."

"It's okay. I can walk."

"I'd rather drive you."

She could hear the concern in his voice but felt irritated nonetheless. Would he be this overprotective if she was sighted?

Sarah's voice sounded quite near. "We just don't want anything to happen to you right now."

"Nothing's going to happen to me!"

There was a pause before Colin spoke in a resigned voice. "You do have your whistle, don't you?"

"Yes, it's clipped right here on my backpack," Missy said irritably. She felt for her watch. "Nobody will even be awake yet. You think I'll be attacked at this hour of the morning? This isn't downtown Chicago!" She pulled her white cane out of her pack. "See, I even have my cane so I won't get lost!"

With her hand on the doorknob, she sighed and turned back, a softer tone in her voice. "I do appreciate everything you've done for Joshua—and for me," she said. "I won't be long—maybe an hour at the most."

Colin and Sarah stood watching at the window for a moment as Missy tapped her way past their truck and on up the hill towards the main road.

Then Sarah took his hand. "C'mon Daddy," she said with a smile. "We have two little girls waiting for us. It's a new day—a new beginning!"

They walked hand-in-hand down the hall, hesitating only as they reached the first bedroom door. Colin thought how easy it would be to go to Verena's room first. Verena—the easy child to love.

But Emmeline needed them too. Colin knocked lightly on the door and then opened it slowly. She was waiting for them. He could see the flash of relief in her eyes before she slammed shut the window of her soul once more.

Colin hesitated, unsure what to do next but Sarah stepped boldly into the room and cheerfully said, "Emmygojumpin' that bathroom and get yourself washed up for breakfast!"

Colin had seen it before but was still amazed at the little girl's response. Emmeline giggled—actually *giggled!*—then bounced up from a sitting position to a standing one and jumped off her bed onto the floor and ran out the door.

Sarah's laugh was one of pure joy. "I'd better be waiting for her in the kitchen. If you want to go get Verena..."

Colin kissed his wife affectionately on the cheek before heading into the other bedroom.

Verena was still asleep and Colin paused, wondering if he should wake her. She looked so peaceful.

He walked across to the window that was still open. A light breeze blew in. Colin looked out over the lake and felt grateful to the Creator of all things. The water glistened in the morning sunshine, a sparrow chirped its morning song, and Colin could hear the haunting cry of a loon somewhere far out on the lake.

Suddenly, the calm was shattered by the shrill sound of a man-made whistle.

Missy!

chapter seventeen

Colin's loud cry of dismay woke Verena, who gave a frightened whimper, clutched her teddy bear and retreated to the corner of her bed.

Colin stifled his rising panic enough to speak a soft, "It's okay, honey," to her as he scooped her up in his arms and dashed from the room.

He almost collided with Sarah coming the opposite way. He grabbed his radiophone from off the desk and quickly called, "All units report!"

"Keegan here. I heard it."

Colin breathed a prayer of thanks that there was a police cruiser on patrol in the vicinity. "It's Missy Peters," Colin said. "She's on the Mine Road, probably about half way to the lodge."

"Okay," Keegan replied, "I'm on the Mine Road. Just approaching your place—do you want me to pick you up?"

Colin heard a loud clatter from the master bedroom and hurried in that direction as he replied to Keegan, "No, just report back to me right away!"

Joshua was leaning against the patio door, fumbling with the handle, trying to open it. The IV pole had fallen to the floor but fortunately there was enough slack in the tubing so that it had not been pulled out of Joshua's arm. Sarah was trying unsuccessfully to calm him down and lead him back to bed.

Colin entered the fray. "Joshua, relax! Keegan's on his way to her!"

His words didn't seem to have any more effect than Sarah's, but when Keegan's voice came across on the radiophone, Joshua stopped struggling long enough to listen.

"I've spotted her. She looks okay," Keegan said.

Joshua almost collapsed in relief, and willingly allowed Sarah to guide him back to the bed. He didn't lie down though but sat, anxiously listening for further reports from Keegan.

Colin glanced down at Verena and her faint smile reassured him. He saw Emmeline standing hesitantly in the doorway, and asked her, "You okay?"

The little girl met his eyes and then turned away.

Keegan's voice came over the radiophone again. "There's someone with her. It's Russell!"

Joshua sprang to his feet and cried out, "No! Missy! *Missy!* Oh, please dear God, no! Not Missy!"

As Joshua stumbled wide-eyed towards the patio doors again, Colin passed Verena to Sarah, dropped his radiophone on the bed and intercepted the younger man. He stood squarely in front of him and placed his hands on Joshua's shoulders. He had to shout his name to get his attention and even then Joshua, between sobs, kept insisting that he had to go help Missy.

"Colin!" Keegan's voice rose above the din.

Colin pushed Joshua back towards the bed. "If you want to help, let me do my job!" As Joshua sank weakly back down on the edge of the bed, Colin grabbed up the radiophone and spoke brusquely into it. "Colin here."

"Doctor Peters just drove up," Keegan said. "I'd appreciate if you'd send reinforcements. We might have a confrontation on our hands."

"Will do," Colin said.

Another voice sounded. "Officers Adams and Quequish here. We're at the station. Do you want us to head out to Mine Road?"

"Affirmative on that." Colin replied, then added, "Officer Adams, our object is to *diffuse* the situation."

There was a noticeable pause and when the young officer replied, there was a subtle note of hostility in the standard response. "Copy that. We're heading out to Mine Road now."

Colin glanced around the room to see how everyone was faring and, to his surprise, found both Emmeline and Verena sitting alert but calm in the big easy chair with Sarah.

Colin smiled briefly at them before turning his attention to Joshua, who was once more struggling to his feet, a look of determination in his eyes.

Colin put his hands on Joshua's shoulders again and said firmly, "Missy's going to be okay, Josh. Her father is with her, and so are three of my officers."

"I need to go, too," Joshua insisted stubbornly.

"No, you don't!" Colin almost shouted the words. Then in a softer voice he added, "Josh, you're in no condition to go anywhere. Missy's going to be okay. Keegan will call us back soon with a report. We're all just going to sit tight here and wait. He's a good officer. I'm sure he has the situation well under control."

But that young man had his hands full. Everyone was shouting at once.

"So now it's against the law for me to accidentally bump into someone?" Russell loudly demanded just inches away from Keegan's face.

"It wasn't an accident!" Missy declared.

"If you hurt my daughter...!" Jeff Peters yelled.

"I wasn't hurt, Daddy," Missy said in a quieter voice.

"No, Daddy," Russell mocked in a falsetto, imitating Missy's voice, "your little girl wasn't hurt." His voice returned to its normal pitch as he leered at Missy and added, "I was just having a little fun with her... wanted to see if she'd like to play house with a real man instead of that wimpy little brother of mine."

Jeff roared and tried to charge him. "If you so much as touched her...!"

Keegan restrained Jeff as Russell wagged a finger in Jeff's direction reprovingly, "Temper, temper..."

"Doctor Peters," Keegan interjected quickly, "I'd like you to take your daughter back up to the lodge. I'll send Constable Adams along with you to get a statement from her."

He watched as Adams took a firm grip on Jeff's arm and steered him and Missy up towards the lodge, waiting until they were out of sight before turning back to Russell. "Mr. Quill, you can give your side of the story to Constable Quequish here."

Keegan moved away from them a little to report to Colin on the radiophone. "Missy's gone up to the lodge with her father and

Constable Adams. He'll take a statement from her. I have another officer getting a statement from Mr. Quill."

"Do you have enough to detain him?" Colin wanted to know.

"I don't think so," Keegan said regretfully.

There was a short pause. "I appreciate your quick response. Keep me posted on any other developments. And... anything to report on the other investigation?"

Keegan knew what other investigation he meant—the investigation into Joshua's abductors. "Unfortunately, no. We've gone over the area quite thoroughly... but someone had been very careful to ensure that there wouldn't be anything there for us to find."

He could hear the disappointment in Colin's voice. "Okay, keep me posted."

After ending his call, Keegan walked back over to Russell and Constable Quequish. The interview was already over, and Russell seemed anxious to be on his way.

He eyed Keegan from head to toe and back up again, wearing his usual smirk. "You must like me," he said in a mocking voice. "We're always bumping into each other."

Keegan carefully controlled his anger and kept his voice calm and authoritative as he ordered, "Stay away from Missy Peters."

Russell, with a final smirk in Keegan's direction, turned and walked away.

Keegan once again reined in his anger and motioned for Constable Quequish to follow him into the patrol car.

The older man was also carefully controlling his feelings and offered no comment on Russell's words or actions. "Where we headed?" was all he asked.

"Up to the lodge," Keegan replied. "If there's something in Missy's statement that we can use to press charges..." He left the sentence unfinished, the meaning clear.

All the way back to the lodge, Missy's father had lectured her about walking alone. Why hadn't she called someone? And didn't she see that this proved once and for all that she needed to return to Chicago with him?

Missy had kept silent, knowing that his angry bluster masked a deep concern for her. But now, as she tried to give her statement to the police, Missy wished that her father could somehow refrain from constantly interrupting!

And she wished with all her heart that she had let Colin drive her up to the lodge this one time. Grandma and Bobby didn't need all this commotion on top of everything they were already dealing with. Keegan and Officer Quequish had arrived almost immediately after she and her father had, bringing the total of police officers to three.

"So you weren't actually hurt?" Constable Adams asked her for at least the third or fourth time.

Keegan Littledeer, hearing the question for the first time, interrupted him. "Constable Adams, we need a complete statement from the victim. We don't need opinions or judgments. Now I know that you are aware that an 'assault' does not necessarily imply bodily harm. If there is a physical injury, it is 'aggravated assault' which carries a maximum penalty of fourteen years."

Missy, feeling slightly overwhelmed, said in a quiet voice, "He frightened me and he pushed me."

"We'll need to make an audio recording of your statement," Keegan said. "So later today, if you could come down to the station, I'd appreciate it."

"She's not going to be here 'later today'!" her father declared.

Keegan sounded tired. "I'll need to see you before you go, then." He paused. "If you need a ride anywhere..."

"I'll be sure to ask someone," Missy quickly promised.

"How's Joshua?" Keegan asked her.

The question threw Missy into a whirlwind of emotions. Keegan had asked with such compassion in his voice that she almost broke down, and poured it all out to him—that Joshua was in the depths of despair—that he was ready to throw away everything—including her!

"Is he able to talk yet?" Keegan asked in a gentle voice. "We need to get a statement from him as soon as he's able."

"Yes," Missy said with a deep sigh, "he's able to talk."

"Good. Maybe I'll head over there now then."

"Oh!" Missy exclaimed as a sudden realization hit her. "Did you call them on your radiophone? Do they know that I'm okay? They might have heard the whistle. I don't want Joshua—"

"Yes, they know you're okay," Keegan quickly reassured her. "I'm heading down there now. We'll come back and get you if you're needed."

"She's needed right here!" Missy's father declared.

Keegan patted Missy's arm. "Talk to you later," he said in parting.

Missy heard the door close and then her father's voice again—"So, are you all packed and ready to go?"

Missy was about to loudly protest when her sister, Jasmine, answered, "I just have one load left in the dryer." Missy sighed in relief—the question had not been directed towards her.

Anxious to return to Joshua, Missy hurried upstairs to her bedroom to get some clean clothes to wear. She showered and dressed, choosing a set of clothes that had been pre-matched. She always had someone help her shop for clothes, and when she did laundry someone would also help her put on hangers the tops and bottoms that would go well together.

But Missy sometimes still worried that she might have done her buttons up wrong or made some other blunder that she was unaware of, so when her sister came into the room, Missy asked her how she looked.

"You look gorgeous—as always!" Jasmine declared.

"What color am I wearing today?" Missy asked.

It was a kind of game they had played since they were children. Missy had never seen any colors in her life and so Jasmine had become imaginative in describing them to her.

"The blouse that you're wearing is the color of the sky on a cold, clear day in January. Your pants are white like freshly fallen snow."

Missy laughed. "Brrrr! Now I feel cold."

"Well, that's a good way to start the day," Jasmine said, "because I've heard that's it's supposed to get pretty hot later on."

"Oh, it never gets really bad here so close to the lake."

"Yeah," Jasmine said with a sigh, "I'm not really looking forward to going back to Chicago in the middle of a heat wave."

"I don't know when I'll see you again," Missy said.

"I'm going to be back for your wedding in just a few days!"

Missy shook her head. "I hope so," she whispered.

"I will be!" Jasmine declared.

But Missy's thoughts were running on a different line. *If there even is a wedding...*

"I told Dad that I would have to be back here Saturday at the latest. That only gives us a week until the wedding, and we've still got so much left to organize. You still haven't told me if you want those tiny, white Christmas lights on both the spiral staircases and the balcony—or just the spiral staircases—"

"Jasmine," Missy interrupted her, "could we—could we just talk about it later, please?"

Jasmine gave her a quick hug. "Sure. Oh, there's Dad calling for me. I'd better go."

Missy swallowed back the tears that had been about to fall and sank down onto her bed. With her sister gone, the room felt empty, as if all the energy had been sucked out of it.

People often said of Jasmine that she had been born smiling. Though that was perhaps an exaggeration, there was never any dispute that the vivacious curly-haired blond had been blessed with an unusually sweet temperament. Missy, on the other hand, was more like their father—headstrong and with a fiery temper to match.

As they were growing up, Jasmine had always seemed to have an endless number of friends. And while Missy had friends, too, sometimes it had been hard for her to tell whether they really did enjoy her company, or whether they were just being nice because they felt sorry for her. But from the moment that she'd met Joshua on the beach when she was fourteen, Missy had known that he was a true friend.

Since Joshua lived in Rabbit Lake all year round, while Missy only visited during summer and on holidays, their friendship had mainly consisted of long hours spent on the phone and the Internet, until Missy had moved up to Rabbit Lake the previous summer. That's when their close friendship had blossomed into love...

"Missy..." Jasmine's returning voice interrupted her thoughts. "Dad wants to know if you've got everything packed and are ready to go."

"No, I haven't, and no, I'm not," Missy snapped—but was immediately repentant. "Oh, I'm sorry." She reached out and clasped her sister's hand. "But Jas, you know I'm not going with you..."

"Yes, I know," Jasmine said gently. "But I don't think Dad does."

Missy clung to her hand a moment longer. "Will you talk to him for me—please?"

"I'll try," Jasmine promised.

As Missy headed out onto the landing, she could hear Martha talking in low tones to Bobby, who responded back in a tearful voice. Missy wondered if her dad was rushing everyone unnecessarily—Bill had said that he would fly them down whenever they were ready to go.

She made it down the stairs and through the kitchen without meeting anyone and entered Joshua's bedroom, feeling his presence there as a tangible thing. She ran her fingers over the top of his dresser and picked up his hairbrush and put it in her bag. She touched the double bed that would have been *their* bed in just a few short days... Missy stopped there for a moment as a wave of sorrow swept over her. Then she resolutely walked into the bathroom and gathered up Joshua's shampoo, shower gel, toothpaste, toothbrush and deodorant.

"What are you doing?"

Her father's harsh voice startled her and Missy almost dropped her backpack. "Just getting a few things for Joshua," she said defensively.

"You should be packing your own things, not his."

Missy walked past him and began opening drawers and placing things into her backpack. She felt the Goldrock insignia patch on a sweatshirt and scooped that one up, knowing it was one of Joshua's favorites. And a pair of jeans…

"Jasmine says that you're not coming with us," her dad's voice thundered loudly in the small room.

"No, I'm not," Missy said.

The silence around them was deafening. Missy wished that she could see her father's face. "I talked to Mom this morning," she said in a gentle voice.

Missy heard her father groan and when he spoke again, his voice was quite near to her and held a note of appeal. "Don't you see that we need to be together at a time like this? She needs all of us."

Missy reached out to take his hand. "She needs you, Daddy," Missy said gently. "And Joshua needs me."

Her father abruptly released her hand and spoke brusquely. "I've got to see if the others are ready."

"Daddy, please can we talk…?"

"I think we have talked and you've made yourself very clear."

"It's just that maybe Grandma and Bobby could use a little more time. The funeral was just yesterday. Maybe they could wait and travel down with Aunt Corrie and Uncle David."

"So you'd have time to convince them to stay in this God-forsaken place as well?"

Missy's voice was quiet but strong. "God hasn't forsaken this place and He hasn't forsaken us either."

Missy waited for his rebuttal but there was none, and a moment later she realized that he was gone.

And suddenly Missy didn't care who left and who stayed—she just wanted to be with Joshua.

She slung her backpack over her shoulder and strode through the kitchen and back up the stairs, praying she would not meet her father again. Upstairs, she found Jasmine, their grandmother, and Bobby together in his room. Bobby was asking to bring his computer and hockey card set and Missy's grandmother was patiently explaining to him that they wouldn't have room on the plane.

"Jas, can I get you to drive me over to Colin and Sarah's, please?" Missy asked.

Jasmine quickly agreed and Missy moved forward to say goodbye and give a hug to her grandmother and Bobby.

"Oh, Missy," her grandmother exclaimed as she embraced her, "I haven't been much of a help to you or to Joshua..."

"Grandma, it's okay," Missy said affectionately. "I just wish I could have been more of a support to you."

She hugged a weeping Bobby and assured him that everything was going to be okay.

"Don't let Daddy push you into going if you don't want to," Missy said to her grandmother in parting. They embraced again and Missy could feel that her grandmother's cheeks were wet with tears.

Jasmine touched her arm, indicating that she was ready to go, and Missy followed her down the stairs and out the door to the car, thankful to have not encountered her dad on the way.

Outside Colin and Sarah's, Jasmine declined Missy's invitation to come in. "I should get back," she said. "Dad will be wondering what happened to me."

Instead of using the front door, Missy first tried the patio doors into the master bedroom and was pleasantly surprised to find them unlocked.

"Missy!" Joshua cried out the moment she stepped into the room. "Missy, I was so worried about you!"

She set down her backpack and came forward to embrace him. He put his arms stiffly around her and Missy smiled sadly, thinking that this time last week, he would have welcomed her with a kiss, even if he hadn't been worried about her as he said he had been.

As they drew apart, Joshua said with obvious relief in his voice, "You've got your backpack stuffed full! So you're all ready to go with your dad?"

Missy smiled wanly. "I packed some stuff for you in here. And I'm *not* going with my dad."

"Missy!" Joshua's voice trembled. "You *have* to go! Missy, you *have* to!"

Missy felt tears sliding down her cheeks but kept her voice steady as she asked, "For how many days—or weeks—or months? Are you breaking off our engagement?"

There was a long pause followed by a hoarsely whispered, "Yes."

It felt like he had driven a knife through her heart. And maybe something had died in that moment... something that would never live again...

Nooo! Missy fought back against the pain. "God help me!" she prayed silently. "God help us!"

"I'm not leaving you, Joshua," she said, gritting her teeth to keep her voice from shaking. "At least not until you're well enough to make a decision—about us."

"So you think I've gone crazy too?"

"No!" she protested.

"That's what Keegan thinks," Joshua said bitterly. "He thinks I'm crazy because I won't tell the police who did this."

"I don't think you're crazy, Joshua," Missy whispered, sitting down in the chair beside his bed. "I think—I think, maybe you're afraid."

He didn't answer her.

The silence hung between them like an iron curtain.

Talk to me Joshua! Please talk to me! I can't see you. I don't know what you're thinking! "Joshua…" she implored.

She felt his hand reach for hers and at the same moment heard a stifled sob. *Joshua was crying!*

"Oh, Josh," Missy groaned, as she leaned forward and wrapped her arms around him, each painful sob tearing through her heart like a bear's claw.

They clung tightly to each other, Missy feeling as if they were survivors of a shipwreck out on the ocean being buffeted by the waves. But together… still together…

She heard his sobs subsiding and felt him pull away a little. Her face was still just inches from his. Missy felt his fingers gently brush away the tears and knew that he was looking at her. What did he see, she wondered?

"If anything happened to you…" he said huskily, "I wouldn't be able to go on, you know."

"Yes, you would," Missy replied gently. "As I would go on if something happened to you."

She could hear the smile in his voice. "Oh, you would, would you?"

Missy swallowed back the tears that were threatening again. "When you were—when I thought you might be..."

Joshua tenderly kissed her on the forehead. It gave Missy the courage she needed. "When I thought that you might have died, I felt as if I wanted to die, too. Then it was as if the Lord came and just held me in His arms like a little baby, and I felt His comfort and I knew—I *knew* that I could go on."

"I don't know if I have that kind of faith," Joshua said.

"You have to!" Missy cried. "Don't you see? Joshua, I need to be free. You can't protect me from all harm. You can't be everywhere at once. You're not God. I might get hurt. I might get cancer like my mom..."

"No!" he gasped.

"Joshua..." She smiled and reached out to stroke his hair. He had thick, silky smooth hair that she loved to run her fingers through. "Let's just enjoy each moment that has been given to us."

Her fingers hit a tangle in his hair and Missy remembered the brush she had brought for him. "I've got some of your things for you, Joshua," she said. "Clothes and your shower gel and shampoo... and your brush. I could brush your hair now or wait until after you wash it..."

He took her fingers from his hair and lightly kissed them. "Thanks," he said.

"Missy, you're here!" Sarah's voice sounded from the doorway. "When did you get back?"

Joshua gently squeezed Missy's hand and let it go.

"I've only been here a few minutes," Missy said.

"She brought me some clean clothes," Joshua added. "May I use your shower?"

"Of course!"

Sarah and Missy walked on either side of him down the hallway, with Missy carrying the backpack. They left him in the bathroom and continued on to the kitchen where Colin was busy making pancakes for the second morning in a row.

"Can't seem to convince Sarah to make breakfast anymore," Colin complained good-naturedly.

"It doesn't hurt you to help out once in a while, Mr. Macho Man," Sarah teased back.

Missy listened to their light-hearted bantering and though the two girls were silent, she knew they were present also, as Sarah and Colin included them in their conversation.

But Missy's ears were tuned for the sound of the bathroom door being opened and as soon as she heard it, she hurried back down the hallway.

"Oh, I'll help you," she heard Sarah say from behind her.

It was easier with the two of them since Joshua was still unsteady on his feet and they had the IV pole to contend with. But after Sarah got Joshua settled into a chair outside on the deck, she left the two of them alone again.

Missy could feel the warmth of the sun and the gentle breeze off the lake and felt a moment of contentment. She dug Joshua's hairbrush out of her backpack and was about to start brushing his hair when he put his hand over hers. "There's some glue from the tape still," he said. "I couldn't get it out. I don't know if you'll get the brush through it."

Missy set the brush down and ran her fingers through his hair, stopping often as her fingers caught on tangled strands that seemed permanently glued together. "Maybe we'll have to cut some of the tangles out," she said.

Joshua's voice, when he spoke, was filled with a sudden sadness. "Or just cut it all off."

"Is that what you want?" Missy asked.

His voice was a bare whisper. "Yes."

Missy was aware of the Native tradition of a person cutting off their hair to show grief over the death of a loved one, and she wondered how much Tom's recent death was affecting Joshua's decision.

"I'll ask Sarah for some scissors," she said.

Sarah, who was used to cutting Colin's hair, was able to find Missy a pair quite easily and soon Missy was setting about the task.

She started by doing a blunt cut all around, working silently, sensing Joshua's sadness as huge chunks of his hair fell to the deck around them.

Missy was about half-way through a closer cut of the rest of Joshua's hair, carefully holding each strand a finger's width away before cutting it, when she suddenly heard a loud gasp followed quickly by Jamie's horror-struck exclamation.

"Missy! What are you doing?"

Joshua reached up for her hand and held it over his mouth so she could feel his smile and they could share the private joke between them.

Missy giggled. "Cutting Joshua's hair."

Joshua chuckled softly. "She does a great job."

"But... but..." Jamie sputtered.

Missy and Joshua were both laughing now as Jamie continued to sputter, "But..."

Missy could barely suppress her laughter. "It's easy—once you know how. I just measure a finger-width of hair—and snip!"

"She cuts Bobby's hair all the time," Joshua cheerfully added. "And she used to do mine before I decided to let it grow long."

"Well, I'm glad to see that you're feeling better this morning, Joshua," Jamie said in more normal tones. "Maybe we could get that IV out of your way now."

"That'd be great," Missy said, and Joshua heartily agreed.

"I'll come back in a bit... uh... when you're done," Jamie said.

Missy stifled a grin. "Okay."

She finished cutting his hair and went to get a broom and dustpan to sweep it up while Joshua lay down again, his energy depleted.

Missy had just stepped back inside and was dumping the cut hair into a trash can when she heard a vehicle pull up outside, loud music blaring from its sound system. The engine was turned off, the music stopped and she heard boots crunching on the stones in the driveway. Then she heard the front door open and a voice call out, "So how is my little girl behaving for you, Colin?"

Missy flew to the patio doors, shutting and locking them. Then she hurried to lock the bedroom door also.

With trembling limbs, she made her way back over to Joshua, pushing the easy chair up closer to the bed as if it might afford even more protection. She sat down and he took both of her hands in his.

"Don't be afraid," he said tenderly, but Missy could hear the fear in his voice as he spoke.

"I know that it was him that hurt you, Josh," Missy spoke in an urgent whisper, glad now that she couldn't see his reaction to her words. "That night that we found you, we were at the police station and he hinted that you might be dying... And that whole thing about spotting a campfire... And there's no one else you'd be so afraid of. It's—it's because of what he did when you were young, isn't it?"

Joshua didn't say anything but drew her into a close embrace.

chapter eighteen

Colin couldn't believe Russell's words. *So how is my little girl behaving for you?* To imply that Colin was merely baby-sitting and that he, the caring father, had come to check on them! And why was he bothering with this pretense anyway? There were no schoolteachers or social workers around to impress. There was just Jamie, Sarah, the girls and himself.

And once again, Russell was implying that he had only one child. It angered Colin to have Verena so disregarded. "*Both* of your children are doing fine and you are not welcome in this house," he said.

With a sardonic gleam in his eye, Russell moved from his casual stance of leaning against the doorjamb, took two steps into the room and stood squarely before Colin. "And who's going to stop me?"

Colin realized too late that he'd made the mistake of issuing a challenge to a man who loved fighting and who thrived on violence. He quickly changed his voice and manner to that of a negotiator. "It's a beautiful day outside. We can talk down by the lake. Or go for coffee."

Russell laughed in his face and focused his attention on the group assembled around the table. "So how's my little girl doing?"

Emmeline smiled slyly. "I've been bad—*real* bad."

Russell roared with laughter. "That's my girl!"

"You have *two* children," Jamie spoke through gritted teeth.

Colin wished she had remained silent for now Russell's attention shifted to Verena, who cringed away from the look of hatred in her father's eyes.

"We bin' i gun!" Russell spat the words at her.

Emmeline stood up and began chanting, "Garbage, garbage, Verena is garbage."

Colin silenced Emmeline, "Gego!" and Sarah reached over and drew Verena onto her lap.

Russell pursed his lips in Verena's direction and cursed her, "Kaamacentaakositc!"

Colin said in a gentle voice, his eyes on Verena also, "Gaawiin! Minwentaakosi!"

Sarah stared at Jamie, who did a whispered translation, "No, she is not hated. She is liked."

"Kaamacinaakositc!" Russell snarled.

"Minonaagosi!" Colin responded.

"Not ugly but pretty." Jamie spoke the words as a blessing over the child.

Russell looked around for allies and found none. Emmeline's eyes were on Colin. "Aan enaabadiziyin?" Russell asked her.

"And what are *you* good for?" Jamie whispered.

Colin pursed his lips in Emmeline's direction. "Minwaabadizi!" he said gently.

"Useful," Jamie translated.

"Kihci-inentaakosi!"

"Important!"

"Shawentaakosi!"

"Blessed!"

Emmeline was walking towards Colin, drawn to him like a magnet. There was not yet love in her eyes, but there was a need for love. Colin read the message there and knew that he would do anything and everything to deserve the trust she was giving him.

"You can't have her!" Russell thundered as he lunged towards the little girl and, before Colin could stop him, picked Emmeline up by one arm like a rag doll.

The little girl screamed as her arm was wrenched and Colin reached out to pull her from Russell's grasp. With an angry snarl, Russell flung Emmeline across the room towards the door. "Get into my truck!" he ordered as she struggled to her feet.

Sarah ran towards her with Verena still in her arms. In the background, Colin could hear Jamie calling the police station.

"Russell! Stop! You are under arrest for assault of your daughter, Emmeline." But he had to run after Russell even as he spoke the words because Russell, cursing loudly, was running after Sarah and the girls.

"I'll kill her! I'll kill them all!" Russell yelled.

Sarah had made it to the truck and was frantically getting herself and the children inside. Russell grabbed hold of the driver's door.

"Get away from them!" Colin yelled.

Russell turned and swore at him, still hanging tenaciously onto the door, preventing Sarah from shutting it. Colin threw himself in a full face-on tackle on top of Russell, knocking him to the ground. Sarah slammed the door shut and the truck sped off.

Russell went momentarily still as he hit the ground, and Colin quickly placed his hands either side of Russell and started to lever himself up. Suddenly, Russell's arms shot up and he grabbed Colin around the neck and squeezed hard. Colin tried to pull away and managed to get up on his knees, but couldn't dislodge Russell's grip. Using a technique that he'd learned in "non-violent crisis intervention," Colin thrust his arms inside of Russell's and struck with sudden force against them, breaking himself free from Russell's grip. Unfortunately, in the course of this action, Colin's fist struck Russell's jaw and his head hit the ground again.

Colin scrambled quickly to his feet. Russell was not one to give up easily though. Still muttering oaths and threats, he rolled over onto his hands and knees, and started to push himself up.

Colin was shocked to see blood dripping from the back of Russell's head. He looked past him and saw a flat rock embedded in the ground. It was covered with blood also.

"Jamie!" he called.

She appeared in the doorway just as Russell made it to his feet.

"Jamie, call an ambulance!" He turned back to see Russell staggering towards him, his fists clenched and a murderous look in his eyes.

"Russell!" Colin yelled. "You're bleeding! You need to sit still."

"What?" Russell demanded angrily. He reached up and touched the back of his head, looked in surprise at the blood on his hand then crumpled to his knees with a moan.

Jamie rushed towards them, the cordless phone still in her hand.

"Don't try anything!" Colin warned Russell as Jamie quickly examined the back of his head.

"Is there a first aid kit in the house?" Jamie asked.

"In the bathroom," Colin told her, still keeping a wary eye on Russell.

As Jamie disappeared inside, a police cruiser swung down the hill. The brakes were slammed on and two uniformed officers jumped out—Adams and Quequish.

"Assault on a police officer now?" Constable Quequish asked as he pulled Russell's hands behind his back and slapped handcuffs on him.

"No," Russell moaned. He focused on Adams and spoke in a weak mumble, just clear enough to be understood. "He assaulted me. I didn't do nothing."

Adams quickly knelt beside Russell. "This man needs medical attention! Quequish, get these cuffs off him!" He glared up at Colin. "Didn't think to give him first aid?" he snapped.

"Of course!" Colin protested. "Jamie went to get a first aid kit. Here she comes now."

Adams completely ignored him. "Call an ambulance!" he barked at Quequish, who was unlocking the cuffs.

"I already did that," Jamie informed him as she knelt down and opened the first aid kit.

Adams snatched a compress out of the kit and pressed it to the back of Russell's head. "Come here and hold this in place!" he ordered Quequish.

Jamie shook her head in disgust and moved out of the way so that the older man could take her place beside Russell.

Constable Adams and Jamie both stood to their feet at the same time. Adams returned Jamie's angry glare as he flipped open his notebook. Then he focused his attention on Russell again. "We'll need a statement—if you're feeling well enough to talk."

Russell moaned again. "He banged my head against..." He turned his head a little and looked down and they could all see the bloodied rock on the ground. "On—on that," Russell continued in a weak voice. "I think he was trying to kill me."

Adams glared up at Colin. "Your personal vendetta again?"

"No, of course not! This man is under arrest for assault of a minor. He also uttered death threats, and assaulted a police officer who was attempting—"

"That police officer would be *you?*" Adams glanced around meaningfully.

Colin sighed in exasperation. "Yes."

"And the subject's weapon—you have that in possession?"

"There was no weapon. The subject—"

"The *subject* is the one requiring medical attention," Adams said pointedly as he stood to his feet. "Now, where I come from, this would be a clear case of police brutality. It's what gives the force a bad name. I know you people up here think you can all be Rambos, using excessive force with no repercussions from the law—shielding each other from prosecution with your 'Blue Code of Silence' but where I come from—"

"Maybe you should go back to where you come from."

Adams smiled maliciously. "Not just yet, my friend. Not just yet." He turned back to Russell. "You are aware, sir, that you can press charges against this officer?"

"This is ridiculous!" Colin growled. "What was I supposed to do—stand back and do nothing while he further assaulted the children—and my wife?"

"Ah, your wife—is that what this is really all about?"

"No!" Colin shouted. "I was protecting the children."

"*My* children!" Russell interjected.

Adams scribbled away in his notebook. "So…" his tone was disbelieving, "you were protecting this man's children—from whom?"

"From *him*!" Colin shouted

Adams looked affronted. "I can hear perfectly well without you raising your voice. Now I will assume that you had some right to be protecting these children from their father?"

"Yes, I'm their foster parent." Colin struggled to keep his voice low. "And I refuse to be interrogated by you!"

"You people seem to think you can pick and choose who is investigated and when," Adams spoke derisively. "But be assured that I will be writing up this report—with or without your full cooperation—*sir*."

Colin was saved from responding by the arrival of two Emergency Medical Technicians. Colin recognized Saundra McKay and Orson Fobister, both long-time residents of Rabbit Lake.

Russell groaned and suddenly his head slumped forward, causing Constable Quequish's hand to slip. The compress dropped and fresh blood poured out of the wound and ran down Russell's face.

The two EMT's quickly snapped on gloves and knelt either side of Russell. Saundra took his pulse while Orson began to cleanse the head wound and apply a temporary dressing. Saundra shone a light into first one of his eyes and then the other. Then she looked up at Colin. "What happened here?"

"Mr. Quill was assaulted," Adams stated.

"He was trying to hurt Sarah and the children," Colin countered. "He had hold of the truck door, preventing them from escaping. I tackled him. He must have hit his head on that rock—"

"And that would explain the contusion on his jaw as well?" Adams asked pointedly.

"No, that's when I hit him."

"When he was already down?" Adams queried. "Not very sportsmanlike of you."

"He was threatening to kill my wife and our two foster children!" Colin shouted.

"So you thought you'd kill *him* first, is that it?"

"No, of course not," Colin said, carefully bringing his voice back under control. "I was just trying to stop him."

"Well, you certainly did that," Adams replied sarcastically.

Saundra and Orson were helping Russell to stand but he appeared to be unsteady on his feet as he half-shut his eyes and moaned.

"What are you doing?" Adams demanded. "Don't you have a stretcher you can put him on?"

They ignored him as they continued assisting Russell into the back of the ambulance, and helped him lie down. Orson turned to address Constable Adams. "We're taking him over to the Health Centre. You can question him there later."

Adams poked his head into the back of the ambulance. "Mr. Quill, I'll be over in a few minutes to get your full statement, and will be happy to assist you should you wish to press any charges."

He stepped back and turned to face Constable Quequish. "I want a proper crime scene investigation. No slacking off. No favoritism..."

Colin watched as Orson secured Russell onto the stretcher while Saundra climbed into the driver's seat. As Russell continued to moan, Colin wondered if perhaps he might be seriously hurt after all. But just as Orson turned his back on Russell to close the ambulance doors, Russell caught Colin's eye and winked broadly.

Colin didn't know if he felt relieved or just plain angry.

As the ambulance pulled away, Adams accosted Colin. "We need an exact location of where the victim was standing when you assaulted him."

The victim. Colin gritted his teeth but maintained a calm voice as he said, "Russell Quill was standing right about where you are standing. He was holding onto the door of my truck."

"And you didn't like him touching your vehicle, is that it?"

Colin turned away in disgust. *Let the man think whatever he wanted to think!*

He looked over at his house, wondering where Jamie had got to. Then he remembered Joshua and Missy…

The patio doors were locked and the curtains drawn, and there was no reply when Colin knocked. He dashed along the side of the house to the main door, ignoring Adams who was ordering him to come back. Colin hurried on through the living room and down the hallway, stopping as Jamie emerged from the master bedroom.

"Everyone's fine," she told him. "Missy was opening the door for me while you were knocking on the patio doors."

Colin followed her into the bedroom, seeing for himself that Missy and Joshua were okay before noting that the glass patio doors were now open.

"Hill!" Constable Adams stepped into the bedroom through the patio doors. "You still haven't finished explaining what happened after you found Mr. Quill touching your truck."

Colin shook his head. The man was as persistent as a deer tick and could burrow under his skin just as effectively. "I used empty-hand control to physically prevent him from assaulting my wife and our two foster children," Colin patiently explained.

"Mr. Quill was injured in the altercation. Perhaps you might clarify exactly what you mean by empty-hand control."

Colin stared at him. *Did the man really not know police force regulations and procedures?* Or was he just feigning ignorance to further irritate him? Colin eyed him with disfavor and said in a carefully modulated voice, "As I'm sure you are aware, this is a stage on the use of force continuum that is a standard for police officers. I did not have a weapon. I pushed the subject away from the truck using a full body tackle. I used reasonable force considering the circumstances and my prior knowledge of the subject."

"Ah, yes, your prior knowledge of the subject..."

Colin gritted his teeth. "I knew the subject well enough to ascertain that he would carry out his threats to further harm the children."

"Ah, yes, the children. *His* children. You didn't think to politely ask Mr. Quill to move away from your truck?"

Colin rolled his eyes. "No, that thought did not occur to me."

"So you knocked him to the ground, didn't notice or didn't care that you had injured him, but instead proceeded to hit him— once or more than once?"

"I only hit him once," Colin said.

"Did Mr. Quill at any time lose consciousness?"

Colin thought back to that brief instant when Russell lay quiet—just before he fastened his hands around Colin's throat. "There might have been a very short time…" he answered honestly.

"That would be when you took the opportunity to hit him?"

"I'm heading back to the station," Constable Quequish said. He had entered the room just behind Constable Adams and had stood there quietly up until that point. His comment greatly surprised Colin. A quiet soft-spoken man, who had joined the police force to help out the kids in the community, Jonathan Quequish typically went along with whatever he was asked or ordered to do.

"You can't leave just like that!" Adams said. "We're in the middle of a crime scene investigation."

Quequish shook his head. "No, we're not."

And that was as far as he would go in criticizing a superior. But as Colin watched him go, he knew that Jonathan Quequish would follow these words with action, walking back to the station, a distance of a couple of miles at least.

"Perhaps you should leave, too," Jamie said to Constable Adams.

Colin put a hand on her arm. "It's okay, Jamie. What I really need you to do is find Sarah and the girls. I'm concerned about Emmeline."

"I think they probably drove over to my house. I'll check there first," Jamie said.

As she left, Adams surveyed the room, taking in the other occupants. "Are these the *children* you were protecting?" he asked, pointing towards Missy and Joshua.

Colin could hardly believe how thick-headed the man was. "No, of course not!" he exclaimed.

"Oh, you must be the young man who was kidnapped." Adams eyed Joshua suspiciously. "So when are you going to squeal on that friend of yours who did it?"

"He's not my friend!"

Adams snorted in disbelief. "So why are you protecting him then?"

"He's not," Missy spoke up. "He's protecting himself."

Colin sighed. "Now would be a good time, Josh," he advised.

Constable Adams looked contemptuously around, eyeing each of them in turn. "So you all know who he is and you're all afraid to turn him in." He pursed his lips and nodded at Colin. "Some justice system you all have up here."

Colin was saved from trying to answer that as a car skidded to a noisy halt just outside the open patio doors. A moment later, Jeff Peters came striding in, calling out his daughter's name. Colin groaned. Jeff would just be the icing on the cake!

"Dad!" Missy exclaimed. "I thought that you were already on your way! I promised Mom…"

"I'm still leaving today—hopefully within the hour. Grandma and Bobby are planning to travel down later with Aunt Cora and Uncle David. But I want you with me on this flight, Missy."

"Dad, I told you—I'm not going."

Jeff sighed heavily and ran his fingers through his hair. "Missy, I don't know what all is going on here. But I want you out of it."

She began to protest but he forestalled her. "If you won't leave him, then we'll take him with us." Jeff looked toward Colin. "From what I hear, it might not be a bad idea to get this young man out of harm's way anyhow."

Colin heartily agreed.

Joshua looked confused. "You want me to go with you to Chicago?" he asked.

Missy's voice was hesitant. "Maybe it would be good, Josh. Just for a few days. I'd like to visit with my mom. Dad said that she might not be able to make it up for our wedding—"

"There's not going to be a—" Joshua began.

"Just for a few days, Josh," Missy said. She turned towards her dad. "Just for a few days—and then we're coming back here— *both of us*."

"Missy, you'd be safer if you—" Jeff began.

"I'll go with you," Joshua suddenly interjected, his voice sounding surprising strong and confident.

Jeff nodded appreciatively in his direction. "Bill will be ready to leave in about half an hour."

"Wait a minute," Adams interrupted. "I need to call my superiors first to see if you can go."

"I *am* your superior!" Colin almost shouted. "And he's not a suspect. He was the *victim*! Unless you think he tied and gagged himself!"

Suddenly weary, Colin waved an arm in Joshua's direction. "Go—and if you have a chance, don't come back. Sometimes I think there *is* something wrong with this place."

Jeff gave Joshua a brief examination before withdrawing the IV, pocketing the bottle of pain medication, and helping him to his feet. Colin quickly moved to assist him and together they walked Joshua out to the car, with Missy following close behind.

"I'll need to pack a few things," Joshua said.

"I'll help you," Colin offered.

Constable Adams cleared his throat. "You're not going anywhere except with me to the police station."

Colin spun around. "You want to hand-cuff me while you're at it?"

"If you think it will be necessary," came the haughty reply.

"I'll pack Joshua's clothes," Jeff said as he checked that Missy and Joshua were settled into the back seat; then climbed in behind the wheel and put the key in the ignition. "Missy will need to pack too," he added. "Bill will wait for us as long as we need him to."

Colin followed him around to the driver's door and reached in through the open window to shake Jeff's hand. "Thanks," he said.

Jeff grinned wryly and gestured towards Adams. "Is there anything I can do to help out here?"

Colin grimaced. "How about a character reference for a new job?"

"Hey," Jeff said gently, still gripping his hand, "things have gotten bad before and you've always hung in there. I know from personal experience that you don't give up easily." Jeff released his hand and shifted into gear. "Keep your head above water there, buddy!"

Colin knew that Jeff was referring to the time that Colin had rescued him from drowning many years before. Even though they had often clashed in the intervening years, the resulting bond between them from that incident always remained.

Colin reached through the window to shake Joshua's hand as well. "Take care," he said, feeling a well of emotion that he couldn't express. He'd looked out for Joshua ever since he was a little kid, and it felt strange to be letting him go just when Joshua seemed to need him the most. But he had Missy now, Colin reminded himself; maybe it was the right time to step back in order for Joshua and Missy's relationship to grow stronger.

Colin shook Missy's hand too. "You take care of each other now.

"Give Jenny our love," he said to Jeff. "Tell her we're praying for her every day."

Jeff nodded solemnly as Colin stepped away from the car and with a final wave, they were on their way.

His cell phone rang.

"Emmeline is fine," Sarah said. "We were all a bit shook up but we're doing okay now. Jamie's here…"

Colin looked over at Constable Adams, who was waiting impatiently for him by the squad car. He sighed. "Sarah, sweetheart, I have to go. I'll call you back as soon as I can."

He strode over to the squad car, ignored Adams' smirk and the back car door that was being held open for him, and took his place instead in the front passenger seat. It gave Colin some small pleasure to know just how much this irked the younger officer. But his confidence ebbed away as a message came through from the station: "They ordered a Med-i-vac for Russell Quill. Apparently there seems to be some internal bleeding or something. It's causing pressure on his brain…"

Constable Adams climbed into the driver's seat and turned towards him with a smug grin. "Still think you'll get out of this with your badge intact?"

chapter nineteen

As Colin silently took in the news about Russell's medical condition, he did indeed wonder if this could be the end of his police career. If Russell died...

Thankfully, Derek Adams didn't speak again until they pulled up in front of the station. "We're here," he announced triumphantly.

We are indeed. Colin stepped out of the vehicle and strode on ahead of Adams. The place was as familiar to him as his own house—perhaps even more so since his home had been renovated in the last seven years and the old police station hadn't changed since Colin was a boy.

He was surprised to find the office empty—unusual for this time of the day. He checked the roster to see who was scheduled and then looked at the sign-out sheet. Both Cromarty and Quequish had taken cruisers and were out on patrol.

"If you're ready..." Adams spoke impatiently, eyeing him from his seat behind the computer. "Let's have it from the beginning this time—not all jumbled up the way you told it to me at the scene of the crime."

"Colin, what's going on?" Keegan's friendly voice was like a balm to Colin's spirit.

But Adams intercepted the question. "I am taking a statement from Mr. Hill. He has injured someone, perhaps fatally."

"Russell…" Keegan spoke it more as a statement than a question.

Colin nodded. "He was Med-i-vac-ed out a few minutes ago."

"I see that you're off-duty," Adams addressed Keegan, who was dressed in street clothes. "There's no need for you to be here—I've got it all under control."

Keegan motioned towards Colin. "One of the two of us is on call at all times," he spoke flatly. "This isn't Toronto."

"You left *me* in charge," Adams said peevishly.

Keegan eyed him with disfavor. "Yes, just once when *Chief of Police* Hill and I were both occupied with urgent family matters outside of the community."

Colin heard a plane take off and hoped and prayed that Missy and Joshua were aboard…

"Well," Adams spoke brusquely, his fingers on the computer keyboard. "I have a report to file. If you will please sit down, *Mr. Hill*…"

Colin sat down and tried to think—he *had* injured Russell badly, although he hadn't intended to. How could he possibly begin to make this man understand?

"Let's start with the witnesses. Were there any?" Constable Adams demanded.

"My wife, my sister and the two foster children," Colin answered quietly.

"Any *independent* witnesses that could give an objective view?"

"There—there were no other witnesses," Colin spoke slowly, his confidence melting away. Maybe it was because he was sitting on this side of the desk, bringing back memories of when he'd been in trouble with the law as a young teen...

"Well, let's get on with it!" Adams' tone was contemptuous. "Or are you busy devising a—" He stopped mid-sentence. Keegan had reached over behind him and pressed the power button on the computer.

Adams jumped to his feet as if scalded, moved to the other desk and began dialing a number.

"Colin," Keegan said wearily, "it's okay. I'll take care of things here. You go see Sarah and the girls. Jamie says they're pretty shook up by the whole incident."

"You're letting him go?" Constable Adams demanded. Then the person on the other end of the line must have answered for he changed his tone dramatically. "Yes, this is Constable Derek Adams speaking..."

"Go," Keegan spoke softly. "I'll catch up with you later."

Colin headed out the door just as Adams said, "Yes, we have a situation here..."

Colin ran all the way to Jamie's house, feeling that time was at a premium, but gave himself a minute to catch his breath before walking in. He entered without knocking and no one noticed him at first.

Jamie was in the kitchen cooking something on the stove. Sarah was... Sarah was sitting with both of the girls on her lap, reading them a story! Colin's heart skipped a beat as he watched them. Sarah with her curly brown hair bent over the two children with their darker, straighter hair—much like his own.

"Daddy!" a little voice exclaimed.

212

Colin looked at Verena—but it was *Emmeline* who had spoken!

Colin grabbed a kitchen chair and pulled it up to sit in front of them, his knees touching Sarah's. "Emmeline," he said tenderly, "how are you? Are you hurt?" He looked closely at her but could see no cuts or bruises from when Russell had thrown her across the room.

She smiled at him. "No, I'm okay. Mommy was just reading to us about beavers…"

Sarah took hold of his hand. "And you're not hurt either? Jamie told us a little about what happened…"

Jamie came over to join them. "We heard that Russell was Med-i-vac-ed out."

"You beat him up real good!" Emmeline's eyes sparkled.

"I only tried to stop him from hurting you," Colin said firmly. "If there was any other way… If I could have reasoned with him…"

"I was real scared," Verena said in a small voice.

Colin released Sarah's hand, and leaning forward, gently placed first one hand and then the other on Sarah's arms, effectively embracing the girls as he did so.

He expected that, at any moment Emmeline might revert back to her old ways and pull away from them both. But she remained relaxed and comfortable, her head resting on Sarah's shoulder.

Colin looked into his wife's eyes and saw reflected there the joy that he himself felt. "It's like a miracle," he whispered.

Sarah nodded tremulously, her eyes misty with tears.

Colin knew there would still be difficult days ahead. The effects of five years of abuse couldn't begin to be eradicated with just a few days of love. It would take years and, Colin knew, in some ways the effects would last a lifetime, with complete healing only happening on the other side of eternity.

And there were other things they would be facing in the coming days. Even if Russell's condition improved, it seemed as if Constable Adams was determined to pursue the "police brutality" charges that might result in lengthy court battles and an interruption in his duties as the community's Chief of Police.

But what Colin feared most was that these two precious girls might be taken away from them. If Adams was successful in getting charges laid against him, it could well be the end of his and Sarah's brief stint as foster parents.

Jamie was moving back towards the kitchen.

"Wait, please." Colin looked up at his sister. "Will you pray with us?"

"Of course." Jamie smiled and pulled up a chair beside them.

Colin made a quick decision. These two little girls had lived through so much already and hiding the truth from them might only cause them more pain later. He leaned back a bit, holding onto Sarah's hands now, still forming a kind of circle around the girls. "Emmeline, Verena, I might have to go to jail for what I did to your father," he said.

"No!" Sarah gasped.

Colin looked away from the pain in her eyes down to the fearful faces of the little ones. "We have a great God, though," he told them. "He's already done some miracles for us. He brought us together. And He helped us so that none of us got hurt." Colin looked from one girl to the other. "And He loves us very much," he told them.

Emmeline turned towards her sister and spoke matter-of-factly. "If Jesus was here, He'd take you into His arms."

Colin stared in amazement. *Where did that come from?* He smiled at Emmeline and agreed, "Yes, that's right, honey."

Sarah cuddled her closer but Verena stared wide-eyed at her sister.

"And He'd take me into His arms too," Emmeline told her. "When the little children came to Jesus, He placed His hands on each of them, and blessed them."

"Yes, that's right, Emmeline," Colin said in a gentle voice. "But how did you come to know this?"

"Michael told me!" Emmeline spoke brightly. "He read it out of a book."

A cheerful voice chimed in—"What's that you accusing me of, baby girl?"

Colin looked up to see Michael and Rosalee.

"You told me about Jesus!" Emmeline declared, craning her head to see him.

"Yes I did!" Michael exclaimed. "And you-all remembered. That's cool!"

"Rosalee," Jamie interrupted, "I heard the plane taking off. Did everyone get on okay?"

Rosalee nodded. "Dad, Doctor Peters, Jasmine, Missy and Joshua."

Colin gave a sigh of relief. At least they were safely out of harm's way.

"We were just about to pray," he said. "Would you two like to join us?"

"Daddy might go to jail because he beat up our other daddy," Emmeline declared.

Colin exchanged glances with Michael and Rosalee.

"Yeah, we'll pray with you, man," Michael said, as he and Rosalee came around to sit on the couch adjacent to them.

All of the adults prayed in turn, beginning with Colin and ending with Michael. He ended his prayer as his Grandpa Tom always had, "Thy kingdom come, Thy will be done, we love You, Jesus."

Everyone opened their eyes but then Emmeline announced that she still hadn't prayed.

"Okay," Sarah's voice was hesitant, "you can pray too if you want."

The little girl squeezed her eyes shut and began in a sing-song chant.

> "Dear Jesus,
> Please bless Mommy and Daddy
> And my sister Verena too..."

Then her voice changed and there was more feeling and expression in her tone as she continued:

> "And make Daddy not go to jail
> Because he was just trying to help us.
> And nobody's ever tried to help us before.
> Except for our first Mommy and she died.
> And if Daddy's in jail, he can't be a policeman
> And put all the bad guys in jail.
> And You do want all the bad guys in jail, don't You?
> Well, I guess that's all—so—amen."

Emmeline opened her eyes and looked straight into Colin's.

"Don't cry, Daddy," she said. "I prayed and Jesus is going to make it all better."

"I know, Princess," he said, smiling through his tears. "But did you know that sometimes people cry when they're happy too?"

"They do?" she asked, her eyes open wide in amazement.

Colin nodded.

"Are you happy because I prayed?" Emmeline asked.

"Yes," Colin bent over and hugged her, "I'm happy because you prayed."

Colin released her but Emmeline clung to him. "Can I sit with you?" she asked in a small voice.

Colin looked into Sarah's eyes; they were glowing with happiness. "Sure you can, Princess," he said.

As he scooped her up into his arms, Colin glanced at Verena and saw such a look of devastation and despair on her face that it almost broke his heart. "Verena," he said gently, "come sit with me too. There's lots of room. There'll always be room for both of you."

Sarah stood up, lifting Verena with her. "Here," she said, "I'll help Jamie with lunch. You guys can have this chair. And we were reading this book about beavers..."

Colin settled into the big easy chair with both little girls on his lap, one arm around each of them. "So let's see, where did you stop reading?"

"Baby beavers are called 'kits,'" Emmeline informed him.

Colin looked down, found the spot and began to read, "Baby beavers are called 'kits.' There are usually four to a litter..."

It seemed no time at all before Jamie announced that lunch—grilled cheese sandwiches and tomato soup—was ready. She had added two extra chairs around the table, so all seven of them could eat together. Colin prayed before they ate, thanking the Lord for the food and asking Him for His divine protection on all of them.

"Where's Kaitlyn?" Rosalee asked as she passed the plate of sandwiches to her mother.

"Over with Bobby," Jamie replied. "Charles brought him a new computer program but he didn't have time to show Bobby all the different levels yet. He had to leave this morning; he's in the middle of a book tour..."

The conversation flowed around the table but Colin's mind was never far from his problems and when the phone rang, he jumped up as if he'd been shot.

"I'll get it!" The phone was only a couple of steps away but Colin felt out of breath as he answered with a hurried, "Yes?"

It was Sammy. He'd been Rabbit Lake's Chief of Police for almost twenty years, before retiring so that Colin could step into his shoes. Sammy didn't waste time with small talk. "I just got a call from Kenora. There's some pretty heavy-duty charges being laid against you."

Colin leaned against the counter, feeling all his strength ebb away. When Sarah came up behind him and put her hand lightly on his back, Colin pulled her close, drawing new strength from her love and loyalty.

"Colin...?" Sammy's voice sounded in his ear again.

He took a deep breath before answering. His voice sounded hollow and seemed to echo in the now silent room. "What should I do?" he asked.

There was a brief pause before Sammy answered. "A voluntary leave of absence might be a good idea for the time being. Keegan is young but he's a fine police officer."

Colin took a moment to absorb the words from his old friend and mentor. When he finally spoke, he had to work to keep his voice from trembling. "I don't care about myself," he began. "Sometimes I think I don't even care about the job any more. But—but we're foster parents now. We've got these two little girls and I don't want to lose them. Sammy…" Colin's self-control shattered. "I'd do anything—*anything*—for them!"

He tried to focus on Sammy's reply as he swiped away tears.

"They've been saying that you're not cooperating with the investigation—that you refuse to even give a statement," Sammy said in a heavy voice.

"But…"

"What I would suggest," the older man continued, "is that we make it very clear that you are more than willing to cooperate. That you are, in fact, willing to go out of your way to aid the investigation."

"How?" Colin breathed.

"We go together to the district police headquarters in Kenora. Let them know that you mean business. And…" Sammy paused. "At least there you'll have someone objective taking your statement."

Colin knew that was as close as Sammy would go towards criticizing Constable Adams. He tried to think clearly. What Sammy was offering him was his support and the weight of his reputation. *We go together…*

"When?" Colin asked.

"As soon as possible. I've got a flight lined up for us. The pilot's been wanting an excuse to go to Kenora—he wants to pick up some parts for his truck or something. Anyway, I'll pick you up in half an hour. You'll be ready?"

"Yes, thanks," Colin said, feeling more gratitude than he could possibly express.

Sammy asked about Joshua, and Colin told him that he and Missy had already left for Chicago.

"And Sarah...?"

"She's here," Colin said. "You don't think there's any danger...?"

Sammy hesitated. "Maybe it would be best if Sarah and the girls stayed with Jamie and Bill while we're gone."

"Maybe I should just stay here."

"You asked me for advice," Sammy reminded him.

"Yeah." Colin sighed in resignation.

"I'll pick you up at one."

Sammy rang off and Colin turned towards Sarah. "I'm going to Kenora with Sammy, to give my statement. He thinks you and the girls should stay with Jamie and Bill—if that's okay with you, Jamie?"

As Jamie nodded her agreement, Sarah anxiously asked, "How long will you be gone?"

Depressed by the conversation with Sammy, Colin shrugged his shoulders and there was a tinge of bitterness in his voice as he replied. "Maybe a few hours—maybe a few years."

"Nooo!" Emmeline screamed, launching herself towards him. "No! No!"

Colin knelt down to embrace her but Emmeline beat with her fists against his chest, sobbing. "You can't go! You *can't* go!"

chapter twenty

Too late, Colin realized that he shouldn't have spoken so bluntly around the little girls. "I'm sorry, Emmy," he said, trying to put his arms around her.

But she continued to beat her little fists against his chest, protesting against all the losses she'd already suffered in her short life.

"No matter what happens..." Colin lifted his voice above her cries. "I'll always love you. I'll always love you..."

He drew her a little closer—and then a little more—and finally she stopped fighting and fell sobbing into his arms.

"I'll always love you," he said again. "No matter what happens."

He picked her up and sat down at the table with her. "And Mommy is still going to be here," he said, as he gently stroked tear-wet strands of hair away from her desolate face.

But even as Sarah bent over to hug Emmeline, Colin wondered if that was true. Would either of them be granted a license to foster if Colin was convicted of an indictable offense?

As that possibility tore at his heart, he tried to console himself with the fact that even if he and Sarah weren't permitted to continue fostering the girls, the children would still remain in Rabbit Lake. The social worker had made it clear that the agency's intention was to see the children placed in their home Reserve.

"You'll have Aunt Jamie too," Colin continued in a soothing tone. "And Michael and Rosalee…"

Michael stood up and reached across the table, a wide grin on his face. "Yeah!" he declared, reaching out to give her the fancy handshake that Colin remembered he used to do as a kid— hooking his right thumb around Emmeline's, then grabbing her fingers, sliding his hand down past her wrist. Then he took his other hand to help her turn her palm upwards to meet his, slapped his palm against hers and then shaped her hand into a fist to knock it together with his.

"A special handshake for true friends," Michael declared to a now smiling Emmeline.

Colin slid her off his lap back onto the chair she'd previously had beside him. "These sandwiches sure are good," he said, reaching for the platter. "I think I'll have another one."

The cold grilled cheese sandwich stuck in his throat but it was worth the effort of swallowing it because the mood was now lighter around the table and others were following his example, resuming their meal.

Colin made a conscious effort to not talk about his trip to Kenora again, as they all lingered around the table after they were done eating, the adults sipping tea and talking about mundane things like the weather.

But all too soon, Sammy was at the door. Colin greeted the former Chief of Police with a handshake. Sammy was dressed in casual clothes. He'd worn his hair longer than regulation length even when he'd been a police officer and he still had his trademark mustache that drooped almost to his chin. He walked with a slight limp, the legacy of a childhood accident.

He stepped in and closed the door but didn't sit down as Colin turned back to say goodbye to Sarah and the children.

The girls were standing one on either side of Sarah. Colin knelt down to hug Emmeline. "You're going to be real brave now," he encouraged her.

But already, Emmeline's lip had begun to quiver. Colin, glancing at Verena, was amazed that she seemed to be more in control of her emotions than her sister was. But then he remembered that Verena had had a lot of practice shutting down her emotions.

"Both of you…" Colin extended an arm out to encircle each of them. "Remember that I love you. Nothing will ever change that."

Colin wished that there were something that he could give them—a picture or a memento of some kind, something that would remind them of his promise. He took out his wallet and looked inside, but there was only a picture of Sarah, and one of Jamie and Bill's family.

Colin made a quick decision. He took his police identity badge out of his breast pocket and handed it to Emmeline. "You keep this for me till I get back," he said.

"Colin!" Sarah and Sammy both exclaimed at once.

But Colin winked at Emmeline and she smiled back. Their reaction had just tripled the value of what he had entrusted to her.

Colin reached into his wallet and took out his Indian Status Card. With a smile, he handed it to Verena. "You won't lose this, will you?" Solemnly, she shook her head. Colin pointed to the photo on the card. "I don't really look that awful, do I?"

Verena shook her head again. "No," she looked up at him with adoring eyes. "You're beautiful."

Colin threw back his head and laughed. Then he gave her a big hug, lifting her off the floor as he did so.

"Handsome," Emmeline corrected her older sister, "the word is handsome."

Colin set Verena down and gave Emmeline a hug as well. Then he turned to his wife. They embraced for a long time. Finally, Colin pulled away.

He wished that he could tell her not to worry—that he'd be right back. But he just didn't know...

Michael shook his hand solemnly and Jamie and Rosalee each gave him a hug.

"Quite the send-off!" Sammy remarked with a low chuckle after they were outside.

As Colin climbed into Sammy's truck, he swallowed a lump in his throat before he could reply. "Yes... I've got an awesome family."

They drove in comfortable silence the rest of the way to the airport.

As they boarded the plane, Colin wondered how Joshua had made out on his flight. He wasn't really well enough to travel yet—but he was being escorted by a doctor. Colin hoped that Jeff would remember to be kind to him.

Jeff was enjoying the flight—it felt good to be freed from the burden of decision-making for a short time. He'd always liked flying, especially in little bush planes: they were just as safe as the big Airbus A380s but the noisy little Otters, Beavers and Cessnas *seemed* more dangerous, which, for Jeff, only added to the excitement. And he liked that the cockpit wasn't closed off as in larger planes. He could see Bill working the controls and Jasmine, in the front seat beside Bill, was asking questions as he flew. Jeff smiled, foreseeing yet another career goal change ahead... he sometimes thought that Jasmine changed her career goals as often as she changed her clothes!

Joshua had fallen asleep almost immediately after take off—he'd been exhausted just by the walk from the car to the airplane. He was sandwiched between Jeff and Missy on a bench seat and Jeff had been careful throughout the trip to avoid any large movements that might awaken Joshua.

Missy was sitting quietly, with her head back and her eyelids closed. Jeff didn't want to speak to her in case she was asleep; the past few days had been stressful for all of them.

There had been some turbulence throughout the trip but as the plane hit a down-draft, there was a sudden drop in elevation and Jeff was reminded of roller coaster rides he'd enjoyed as a child. But it had a much different effect on Joshua, who started thrashing his arms and legs about and crying out in torment, "No! *No!* Stop!"

"Josh, cut it out now! Calm down!" Jeff shouted, trying to grab his arms to prevent him from hurting Missy.

But as soon as he touched him, Joshua seemed to curl up into himself, and his cries trailed off into whimpers. "Please, please stop..." His head bent forward and his shoulders hunched as if to ward off a blow.

Missy wrapped her arms around him. "Joshua, it's okay. Shh, shh, it's okay. It's okay, my love."

Jeff stared at them. Joshua's cries had subsided but Missy continued to tenderly cradle him in her arms and speak soothing words to him. *He was still asleep*, Jeff realized grimly! What kind of marriage partner would this fellow make with these deep-rooted unresolved psychological problems? To be fair, this episode might be a post-traumatic response to Joshua's recent kidnapping experience. But Jeff was still sure that Joshua was partly responsible for that, too. The empty beer bottles that he'd found proved that *someone* had been drinking... and drunks often did turn on one another...

"Missy," he said, "I'd like Joshua to check into the hospital for a day or two."

She didn't answer and Jeff spoke her name more sharply than he'd intended. *"Missy!"*

He could hear the careful control in her voice as she answered, "We really haven't had a chance to make plans much yet. When Joshua wakes up, you can discuss it with him."

What's to discuss? Jeff thought angrily. *I'm a doctor. She should respect my medical opinions, if nothing else!*

They didn't speak to each other again until the plane began a slow descent towards the airport. "You should probably wake him up," Jeff told her.

"Josh..." Missy spoke close to his ear. Joshua startled suddenly and for a moment Jeff was afraid of a repeat episode of his previous behavior.

But Joshua only opened his eyes slowly and asked in a sleepy voice, "Where are we?"

"International Falls!" Bill announced.

226

A customs official met them as they landed, and inspected everyone's photo identification. After questioning them about their citizenship, and the reason behind their visit, he granted them permission to enter the USA.

They didn't have to wait long for their connecting flight to Chicago's O'Hare International Airport, and upon landing in Chicago took a taxi directly to the hospital where Jeff worked— and where his wife was a patient.

"Joshua," Jeff said, forcing a casual tone as they exited the taxi, "I'd like to admit you for a day or two, if that's okay with you?"

Joshua smiled wanly as Jeff and Missy each took an arm and helped him inside. "I don't think I have the strength to argue with you, even if I wanted to."

Once inside, Jeff scribbled doctor's orders and his signature on some forms and was prepared to leave Joshua in the hands of the admitting clerk. But of course, Missy refused to leave him!

"Daddy," she insisted with such a tender smile that it melted his heart. "It's you that Mom wants to see. Jasmine and I will come up in a few minutes."

Jeff waited impatiently for an elevator for a full minute before abandoning that mode of transport in favor of the stairs. She was only on the third floor...

He ran up both flights, pausing only briefly to catch his breath before entering the ward. He didn't want to alarm anyone by running down the halls. But his entire being was pressing forwards towards *her*.

A nurse spotted him and hurried forward. "Doctor Peters, you're back! Jeremy in Room 211—"

"Later!" Jeff barked. Then, realizing how harsh he'd sounded, he apologized and quickly explained that he just wanted to see his wife first.

"Of course," the nurse answered. It was her turn to be apologetic.

Jenny had a private room. At least he'd been able to do that much for her. It had been a constant source of frustration to Jeff that, even with all his medical training and experience, he had been helpless to combat this enemy that was slowly but surely taking his wife away from him.

Even though it was only four o'clock in the afternoon, Jenny's curtains were drawn and she appeared to be asleep. Jeff walked quietly in and stood looking down at her, not wanting to disturb her rest.

She looked so beautiful! Even without her luxurious thick auburn curls, she was still the woman of his dreams. He remembered the day that her hair had begun to fall out. He'd found her crying in the bathroom and it had taken all his persuasive powers to convince her that he would always love her, no matter what.

She was wearing one of her colorful turbans—purple irises on a bright yellow background—and the matching nightgown. Coralee had designed and sewn three different sets for Jenny, each in a different pattern and color.

Her chart was in a metal clipboard at the end of the bed. Jeff flipped it open and scanned through the recent entries. The words "palliative care" jumped out at him and Jeff recognized the term as something he himself used when there was no longer any reason to hope that the patient might recover. *Palliative care*—just make them as comfortable as possible, and help prepare the family for a future without them.

Jeff honestly could not imagine a future without his beloved wife by his side. It would be utterly unbearable.

The battle had been going on for three years now, but the oncologist claimed that the cancer had gone undetected for at least five years before that…

Long ago, Jeff had stopped asking the question "why?" and replaced it with "how?"—How were they going to get through the next round of chemo, the next operation… the next day? How many hundreds of times he had wished he could change places with her—take her pain and make it his own instead. For Jeff, that was perhaps the worst part of the whole ordeal—this awful, overwhelming feeling of *helplessness!* He was a doctor but there was nothing—*nothing*—that he could do to help the person he cared most about in all the world!

His presence was the only really tangible thing he could do for her. He'd been reluctant to leave her, even to go to his father's funeral, but Jenny had insisted that she would be fine for a few days—his mother and brother needed him more than she did. But he was back now—back to stay.

"You're here!" Her voice seemed even weaker than usual but the joy at his return was clearly evident.

Jeff dropped the clipboard and rushed to embrace her. She felt so frail. He was careful not to hurt her as he gently put his arms around her.

"I missed you," she sighed, as he pulled up a chair beside her bed.

"I missed you too," he attempted to say but his voice failed him half-way through and the words sounded more like sobs.

Her eyes filled with compassion, Jenny reached a hand up to take his.

"How is your mom doing?" she asked.

Jeff shook his head. "It was such a shock, Dad's death coming so suddenly. It's like she can't seem to take it in. She almost seems as if she's walking in her sleep. I tried to get her to pack some stuff and come down here with me. I think she'll come down with Cora and David..."

"And Bobby?" Jenny asked as Jeff's voice trailed off.

Jeff shook his head again. "Poor guy. He's a bit like Mom— it's as if he doesn't know what hit him. They're both so lost without Dad..."

"And you?" Jenny asked softly. "How are you?"

The question pierced his heart like an arrow. In all of the days since his father's death, it seemed as if no one had thought to ask him that question. They'd asked about his family and talked about the funeral, the food, the weather... but never about what he was feeling. Maybe he projected too much of a tough-guy image.

He wasn't a tough guy now. The tender compassion in Jenny's eyes shattered his defenses and he could do nothing to hold back the sob that tore from his throat. And as she gently stroked his cheek, catching a tear that was trickling down, the dam suddenly burst and Jeff crumpled forward and began to sob uncontrollably.

But when his two daughters came into the room a few moments later, and rushed over to comfort him, Jeff quickly brought his emotions back under control.

"It's okay, Daddy," Missy said gently. "It's okay to cry."

Jeff sat up straight, shrugging off their comforting hands as he surreptitiously tried to remove the evidence of his tears.

"Mom, is there bad news?" Jasmine asked tremulously.

"No, hon," Jenny replied in her sweet, gentle voice, "we were just thinking of Grandpa. But come closer so that I can hug you. Oh, it's so good to have you all here with me!"

"Joshua came with us, too!" Missy exclaimed. "Dad talked him into it."

"But where…?"

"Fourth floor," Jeff said, clearing his throat to remove the last vestiges of grief from his voice. "I've ordered some tests and consultations for him."

He pushed back his chair and stood as his name was paged for the second time. "You girls can visit with your mom for a while. I really need to check on a few patients." He added in a theatrical whisper as he turned to go, "I think they've discovered I'm here."

"Jeff, wait… Is it time yet?"

Jeff groaned, the pain etched in Jenny's voice piercing deep into his soul. He stumbled past his daughters, fumbling for her chart and trying, with eyes blurred with tears, to decipher when her next dose of pain medication was due. "I—yes, I'm sure," he stammered. "I can ask—it should be okay. I'll find out."

Frustrated, he dropped the chart, and the metal clipboard clattered against the steel bed frame as he headed towards the door. "I'll get you some. I'll get you some now. I'll—"

But Missy had caught at his arm. "Let me go, Dad, please."

For a moment he stood there, feeling confused and overwhelmed. Then he looked toward Jenny, saw the need in her eyes, and was drawn to her like a moth to light. "My darling," he whispered hoarsely, dropping into the chair beside her once more.

On the periphery, he heard Jasmine say that she would go with Missy.

"And tell them…" Jeff struggled to keep his voice steady. "Tell them I'm not available for any consultations yet!"

Missy and Jasmine stopped by the nurse's station and reported that their mother needed some more pain medication. They also passed on their father's message that he would be unavailable for a while.

Jasmine wanted to go to the cafeteria to grab a bite to eat but Missy was anxious to check in on Joshua first, so they arranged to meet later.

Missy hurried up to the fourth floor and, stepping into Joshua's room, called out his name. "I think he might be asleep," a stranger's voice answered.

"Oh, hi, I'm Missy," she said, smiling in his direction.

"Name's Matt," he responded. "Your friend was out like a light as soon as his head hit the pillow. Say, was he on one of those survivor programs or something? He sure looks as if he has a lot of bug bites. I always thought that would be the worst part about being on one of those things. I mean, they're not allowed any bug spray or anything, are they?"

"I don't know," Missy answered, trying not to be irritated by the constant patter. "Joshua wasn't on a survivor program. He was kidnapped and held captive for almost three days."

Missy regretted her words the moment that they were spoken.

"No kidding!" Matt spoke excitedly. "Did they catch the guys yet?"

"No, uh, I have to go," Missy backed away. "I'm meeting my sister for lunch." She lowered her voice. "Josh, you're not awake yet, are you?"

"Hey, you're *blind!*" Matt exclaimed. "I just realized that! You sure do well—for a blind person I mean. Say, what's it like being blind? How do you know where——?"

But Missy escaped out the door, breathing a sigh of relief as she headed towards the cafeteria. One thing was for certain, she reflected wryly as she punched the elevator button, Joshua's excessively talkative roommate would provide him with the motivation to get better real soon!

Colin and Sammy's flight to the small city of Kenora had taken less than an hour. Without Sammy's pilot friend, they would have had to wait for one of the regularly scheduled evening flights out of Rabbit Lake, and then travel by car an additional 200 kilometers south down Highway 105 and then east on the Trans-Canada highway.

Colin was anxious to get the whole thing over with, so as soon as they landed in Kenora, they rented a car from the airport and drove straight over to the district police headquarters.

They were both well known at the station but Colin was still surprised at the commotion created by their entrance. Everyone stopped what they were doing to come forward to greet them, but there was something odd in their voices and their sideways glances.

Then Peter Owens, who'd recently transferred down from Rabbit Lake, approached Colin and asked in a low urgent voice, "What's going on? There's an APB out on you. They're saying that you could be armed and dangerous!"

Suddenly, the room fell silent as every eye turned to watch the rapid approach of their most senior officer. Even before he reached Colin, Sergeant Paul Melton's voice thundered across the room. "Come to turn your badge in, have you?"

chapter twenty-one

Before Colin could speak, Sammy stepped in front of him. "Just hold on now! There's been a bit of a misunderstanding—and we're here to sort it out."

Sergeant Melton greeted Sammy by name and shook his hand solemnly. "Wish we could be meeting under better circumstances." He turned and scanned Colin from head to toe. "Guess you wouldn't be stupid enough to come in here with a concealed weapon?"

"No, sir," Colin said respectfully.

"Better come into my office," the sergeant growled as he spun on his heels, and strode back down the corridor.

Colin and Sammy followed him into a well-lit office overlooking the Lake of the Woods. The sergeant sank heavily down into his office chair in front of the window, the late afternoon sun giving his gray hair a silver sparkle.

Colin, whose heart had been racing since he'd heard about the APB, felt his spirit grow calmer as he looked out over the water.

Sammy spoke first, motioning out towards the lake. "How's the fishing down here this year, Paul?"

Sergeant Melton leaned back in his chair and smiled. "Landed a big one last weekend," he boasted. "A five pound pickerel. Twenty-two inches long." He spread his hands apart at least three feet.

Sammy chuckled softly. "Pretty big fish," he said.

The senior officer waved a hand in Colin's direction but addressed the question to Sammy. "So what's going on?"

"It's a long story," Sammy began.

"I've got the time," Sergeant Melton answered with a sideways glance at Colin, who remained silent, content to let Sammy do the talking, at least for now.

"He's one of my best officers," Sammy stated, as if he were still in charge of the unit. "He has a heart—you know?" Sammy tapped two fingers on his chest as he spoke. "Not all police officers have this special combination to understand the law and understand people, too."

Sergeant Melton sighed. "I am aware that you have always held Officer Hill in high regard."

"As have you."

"*Have*—past tense. I'm assuming that you've seen the charges?"

"I *know* Colin," Sammy replied with conviction. "As to the accusations against him..." Sammy waved his hand dismissively.

Sergeant Melton's chair squeaked as the senior officer leaned forward to hand a sheet of paper to Sammy. Colin looked over at his mentor and friend, and felt his heart lurch as Sammy's face clouded over.

Silently, he passed the paper over to Colin to read as well.

The list of charges was formidable—and ridiculous!

"Criminal negligence causing bodily harm?" Colin protested. "Aggravated assault? Excessive use of force?—I had to stop him!"

"Well, you certainly did that now, didn't you?"

Colin remembered that Adams had used almost the same words and sarcastic tone when Colin had tried to defend his actions to him earlier that day. But Sergeant Melton was nothing like Adams! Colin had always felt the deepest respect for Paul Melton as a police officer and as a person.

"I didn't know that he fell on a rock," Colin said.

"*Fell?* It says here that you *pushed* him!"

"I pushed him away from my truck. My wife and our two foster children were inside. Russell was threatening to *kill* them!"

"So you decided to kill him first!"

Again Colin had to force himself to not dwell on the fact that Adams had used the same words when interrogating him. "I didn't decide to kill him, sir," Colin replied in a respectful tone. "I was only trying to prevent him from injuring my family."

"*Your* family?" Sergeant Melton snorted. "It says here that Mr. Quill was on a parental visit with *his* children—a visit that *you* objected to—strongly enough, I presume to risk both your career *and* your personal freedom."

"No!" Colin gasped, fear climbing up his throat. *His career... His personal freedom...*

"Paul..." Sammy appealed.

The senior officer held up his hand towards Sammy and kept his eyes boring into Colin's. "And after committing an unprovoked bodily assault against the children's father in their presence..."

"No..." Colin protested weakly.

237

"*And then* refusing to be interviewed by the officer who attended the scene of the crime, you, with the help of Constable Littledeer, escaped custody and now—"

"Paul!" Sammy appealed more urgently.

Sergeant Melton turned his glare upon him. "You expect me to just dismiss all of these charges just because you two are buddies?" His voice softened a little. "Just because *we're* friends..."

"No," Sammy spoke firmly. "I expect you to dismiss these charges because they are *false* charges that have been laid against one of your very best police officers."

Sergeant Melton waved his hand wearily. "Yes, yes, you've said that before. But even the *very best police officers* can let their emotions get out of control and do things they very much regret later..." His focus had returned to Colin as he spoke.

"I don't regret what I did," Colin said.

Sergeant Melton gaped at him. "You don't regret that you might have killed an unarmed man simply because you wanted to prevent him from seeing his children?"

Colin sighed deeply. "I regret that Russell might die. I don't regret preventing him from injuring Sarah or Verena or Emmeline."

"And you *knew* this was his intention?"

"Yes, sir, I knew that was his intention."

Sammy leaned forward again. "Paul, don't you think it would be better if Colin could tell you the whole story from start to finish?"

Melton held Sammy's eyes for a moment before giving a resigned sigh. Then he turned to glare at Colin once more. "But, you'd better make this good—real good!"

Colin nodded as his thoughts raced. Where should he begin? When he and Sarah had first been given custody of the children? Did the sergeant know that Russell had recently been accused of child abuse? That he had been convicted and sent to prison for the same crime ten years ago?

"Russell came to your house this morning..." Sammy prompted gently.

Was it just this morning? It seemed like longer ago than that!

Silently, Colin prayed for wisdom, for peace, and for the right words. As he looked across at the stony face of Sergeant Melton, Colin reminded himself that his superior officer was a caring and just man.

"I knew Russell was back in the community," he stated, sitting up straighter as he felt the fear start to slip away. "I saw him for the first time the night that he led us to Joshua..."

"*He* led you to Joshua?" Sammy broke in.

Colin suppressed a smile. Something that Sammy hadn't known—in a community where everyone knew everything about everyone else almost before they knew it themselves!

"Aren't we getting a little off track?" Sergeant Melton prompted.

"No, sir," Colin said respectfully, "I think that it's important that you know a bit of background."

The senior officer looked meaningfully at his watch and Colin took the hint and hurried on. "Russell Quill is a suspect in Joshua's kidnapping."

"The victim is not on trial here."

"Neither am I," Colin said firmly, looking his superior directly in the eye. "But it is important to note that Russell Quill has a criminal record and that ten years ago he was convicted and imprisoned on charges of sexual and physical abuse of minors. He was not convicted on the related kidnapping charge, as there was not enough evidence due to the fact that the victim, Bobby Peters, was unable to offer a clear testimony because of his disability."

"I remember that," Sergeant Melton said thoughtfully. "Was it not partially your testimony that convicted him?"

"Yes, sir, it was."

"So I'm guessing this is part of the *personal vendetta* that Officer Adams alludes to?"

"No, sir," Colin stated clearly, "there is no personal vendetta. I am a police officer. Russell Quill is a repeat offender."

Captain Melton waved his hand wearily. "Continue!"

"Last Thursday, Russell Quill was also charged with the abuse and neglect of his own two children. That is why they were placed in foster care."

"And you had something to do with that, too?"

"No, only that his children were placed in our care—my wife, Sarah, and myself."

"Quite a coincidence! You arrest their father and you get to keep the kids."

"I didn't arrest their father!" Colin protested. "I didn't even know he was their father until after we'd agreed to take the children."

"And you didn't see it as a conflict of interest when you did find out?"

Colin shook his head in confusion. *Conflict of interest?* "No, of course not. It was..." Colin tried to remember exactly what he had felt when he'd learned that Russell was Emmeline and Verena's father. "I thought of it as a privilege," he said. "You see, I was a foster child myself in the Quill family. I would almost consider myself an uncle to the two girls."

The sergeant snorted in disbelief, shaking his head. "These small northern communities! There's far too much intermingling!"

"I would have to disagree with you there, sir," Colin said. "It is a great benefit to a community if people feel a kinship with one another and can pull together in time of need."

Sergeant Melton waved his hand dismissively. "Continue!"

"This morning, Russell Quill verbally abused both of his children in my presence and physically abused his youngest daughter, Emmeline. He held her up by one arm and then threw her across the room. My wife fled with both children and the assailant ran after her. I warned him to stop and told him he was under arrest. When he refused to stop, I pursued the assailant—"

"This *assailant* would be the victim now in critical care?" Sergeant Melton interrupted in a sarcastic tone.

"He is not the victim. He is the perpetrator."

The sergeant sighed deeply as he shifted through the papers on his desk again. Finding the one he wanted, he said, "Constable Adams also states in his report that you struck the *victim* while he was unconscious."

Colin kept careful control of his emotions. "I struck Russell Quill because he had his hands around my neck and seemed quite determined to kill me. He was certainly not unconscious."

"Did he, at any time during this entire incident, lose consciousness?" Sergeant Melton pressed.

Colin tried to answer as honestly as he could. "There was a brief instant when he was quiet but his eyes were still open. He might have been stunned by the fall…"

"But that was not the moment that you chose to strike him?"

"No."

"But you did strike him when he was lying on the ground and the result was that his head was smashed against a rock for the second time?"

"I didn't know the rock was there."

Sergeant Melton eyed him coldly. "Not very observant, are you?"

Colin could think of no response.

The sergeant looked down at his notes again. "There's also the charge of resisting arrest, refusing to cooperate in an investigation and escaping custody..."

"I was never formally arrested," Colin said. "I did cooperate with the investigation, just not to the satisfaction of Constable Adams. And I did not escape custody—I went to check on my family. I was worried about them."

"And after you found out they were okay, you decided to skip town."

"That was my idea," Sammy volunteered. "I knew he would receive a fair hearing here."

Sergeant Melton shuffled the papers on his desk and cleared his throat. "What we've discussed today—I want it on paper. A full report! Am I making myself clear?"

Colin snapped to attention. "Yes, sir!"

The sergeant looked satisfied. "Now, what about this young man..." He reached over and opened another folder. "Joshua Quill?" His eyebrows shot up. "Any relation to Russell Quill?"

"His half-brother," Colin replied.

"Ri-i-i-ght..."

Colin ignored Melton's sarcastic tone and leaned forward, eager to discuss any evidence that Keegan had gathered regarding Joshua's kidnapping. "Sir, I believe that we should consider Russell Quill as the primary suspect in this case."

"Well, you would, wouldn't you?" the man spoke dryly as he stood up, signaling the end of their meeting.

"We were going to discuss the investigation into Joshua's kidnapping..." Colin protested.

"You will leave the investigation of Joshua's alleged kidnapping and confinement in the hands of Constable Littledeer," Sergeant Melton stated. "He will be given assistance from the Criminal Investigation Branch. As for you—you will remain in Kenora while these charges are being investigated. No more skipping town!" He glanced meaningfully at Sammy. "These are some *very* serious charges and if we have to upgrade them to manslaughter or murder..." He sighed heavily, his meaning clear.

Colin sat frozen to his chair as the sergeant walked from behind his desk and shook Sammy's hand. "It's been nice to see you again. If you'll be here in town a while, maybe we could go out on the lake sometime..."

Colin rose shakily to his feet as the two older men chatted. *Manslaughter... Murder...*

Then the sergeant was opening the office door and striding out ahead of them. Sammy put a hand on Colin's back and spoke gently to him. "We should go now."

"Go?" Colin looked wildly about. What was Sammy implying?

"Go out of the office," Sammy said, a low chuckle rising in his throat.

Colin groaned. Then he caught Sammy's eye and smiled weakly.

Out in the corridor, the sergeant was barking out orders. "Get him a computer and a place to work!"

Colin glanced around at the faces staring back at him—his colleagues—perhaps now his *former* colleagues...

"And everyone back to work!" Sergeant Melton shouted. "This ain't no sideshow!"

An officer came towards them, pushing a computer cart and Sammy reached out to shake Colin's hand in parting. It was a firm handclasp meant to convey support and reassurance. "I'll call Sarah with an update once I've booked us into a hotel," he said.

chapter twenty-two

Sarah had been anxiously awaiting word from Colin. The afternoon had turned out to be hot and sunny, typical for this late in July, and they'd decided to take the girls down to the lake for a swim.

Sarah sat in a lawn chair, her cell phone at the ready, with Jamie in another deck chair beside her.

It had taken a while for Verena and Emmeline to even want to put their feet in the water and Sarah wondered if they'd ever been to the beach before. Rosalee and Michael had finally coaxed them in up to their knees but they stood there like little statues as the two young people laughed and splashed each other.

"Rosie and Michael seem to be spending a lot of time together," Sarah remarked.

"Yes, well, they've always been good friends," Jamie replied.

Sarah laughed. "Well, don't be too surprised if they stop being 'just good friends' and start being a little bit more than that."

Jamie looked startled. "Do you really think so?"

Sarah grinned at her sister-in-law.

"They do seem to be having fun," Jamie observed thoughtfully.

Sarah's attention went back to the two little girls. Her voice was sad as she remarked, "Emmeline and Verena don't seem to know how to have fun."

The two girls were still standing in the water just up to their knees, staring at Rosalee and Michael but not responding at all when they were invited to join with them.

"Well, they've only got about three or four more weeks to get used to the water," Jamie said. "Then it'll be too cold to swim."

Three or four weeks... Sarah was afraid to think that far ahead. She was afraid to think past this moment. Colin was never far from her mind and she prayed silently now for him.

Her cell phone rang, startling Sarah even though she'd been waiting for a call. She snatched it up eagerly, "Yes?"

It was Sammy. "How're you doing?"

"I'm fine," Sarah answered quickly. "Where's Colin? Can I talk to him?"

"He's writing up a report at the police station. He'll probably be able to call you later on tonight."

"Sammy..." Sarah tried to keep her voice steady. "How are things going?"

There was the briefest of hesitations before the older man answered in a carefully modulated voice, "They're going fine." Then Sammy quickly changed the subject. "How're the girls?"

"They're out swimming." Sarah struggled to keep her voice steady. *What wasn't Sammy telling her?*

"That's great," he said. "Will you all be staying at Jamie and Bill's house tonight?"

"Yes," Sarah replied.

"Good. Well, I'll let you go then. If Colin doesn't get a chance to call you tonight..."

"Oh!" Sarah cried. "They'll let him have at least one phone call..."

Jamie grasped Sarah's arm. She'd been hanging on every word that her sister-in-law said.

"He'll be able to call you," Sammy reassured her.

Sarah thanked him for his support. "I really appreciate you going with Colin. I would have but..."

"No," he told her, "you just take care of those little girls of yours."

Sarah thanked him again and they said goodbye to each other.

Those little girls of yours... Please, Lord, let it be true... Give us the opportunity to provide a permanent home to these two little ones...

Sarah continued to pray earnestly as she gazed at Emmeline and Verena who were now being shown how to skip rocks. Michael was searching for the flattest rocks and Rosalee was showing the girls how to hold the stones and snap their wrists back in just the right way. Sarah smiled—Rosalee was famous for her rock skipping.

Jamie wanted to know what Sammy had said and Sarah told her.

They sat quietly, each with their own thoughts for some time after that.

Finally Jamie said, "I should really start thinking about supper soon..."

Sarah tried to think of what she might have at her house. Unfortunately, there wasn't much. They'd been in Winnipeg for the weekend and then there had been the funeral...

Then she remembered. "I've got some frozen pizza we could throw in the oven."

"Yeah, that would work," Jamie said. "It's such a beautiful day. We can just cook them up and bring them out here to eat."

Sarah offered to walk over and get them. Then she hesitated, looking at the girls.

"There are three of us," Jamie reminded her. "We'll take good care of them while you're gone." She smiled. "They've got to get to know their Aunt Jamie soon, anyway."

Sarah appreciated her sister-in-law's encouraging words but as she headed off on the path towards her house, Sarah wondered what the future held for all of them.

A cloud drifted over the sun and with the thick foliage overhead, it seemed to Sarah that it grew suddenly dark. Her thoughts grew darker as well.

Would God really bring these children into their lives just to take them away? She had never understood why He'd never given her and Colin a child. So many people had children who didn't even want them! Or were unable to give them proper care... She and Colin would have been good parents.

And now they had these two precious little ones. Sarah didn't know if she could handle it if they were taken away. Would God really expect this of her—of them? Colin would be devastated.

Sarah didn't even want to think about the possibility of Colin losing his job as a police officer, or worse, much worse... Colin being imprisoned.

She was so preoccupied with her thoughts of Colin and the girls that it took her a few minutes to become aware of the birds that were around her.

Not just one or two birds, as would be usual in the bush, but a whole flock. And they seemed to be keeping pace with her! Sarah watched in amazement as the tiny birds hopped and then flew around her. They scratched and pecked at the bits of gravel that lined the pathway, but as she walked they seemed to follow her, flying for a bit and then stopping to peck again.

Sarah looked at their distinctive black and white plumage. Snow Buntings! But it was the wrong time of the year for them to be this far south!

Then a still, small voice spoke and Sarah stopped to listen to the gentle refrain: "Don't be afraid. You are worth much more than many sparrows. Don't be afraid..."

"Chi, chi, churee!" the little birds chirped, flocking around her.

Sarah laughed out loud. How like the Lord to send a flock of these tiny birds just for her! As the birds continued to chirp, Sarah recalled Jesus' words recorded by Luke, and she recited them softly:

> "Aren't five sparrows sold for two pennies?
> Yet not one sparrow is forgotten by God.
> Even the hairs of your head have all been
> counted. So do not be afraid; you are worth
> much more than many sparrows!"

The flock of birds rose in unison, their wingtips flashing black on white and Sarah's heart soared with them. Songs of praise rose to her lips and Sarah sang the whole rest of the way to her house and back to Jamie's again.

"Somebody's cheerful!" Michael exclaimed.

They had come up from the lake and were sitting together on the deck.

"Anybody hungry?" Sarah asked.

A chorus of voices answered her in the affirmative.

Sarah laughed. "Well, I guess I'd better get cooking!" she declared.

Jamie followed her into the house. "Did you hear from Colin?" she asked.

Sarah smiled. "No, but I think maybe I heard from the Lord." She told Jamie about the birds.

"They're usually not this far south until September or sometimes even October," Jamie agreed.

Sarah turned on the oven as Jamie began to unwrap the pizzas.

"I know the Lord loves those little girls even more than I do," Sarah spoke softly. "And He loves Colin too. We just need to trust Him."

chapter twenty-three

Mommy and Daddy were yelling at each other! And now the baby was crying! That always made Daddy angrier! Oh, no! He was picking up the baby by her arm. He threw her against the wall! Gotta help her... Mommy, Daddy, stop fighting! Mommy, no! Not the knife! No! No! Blood spurting everywhere... No! Oh, no! Mommy... Mommy... Mommy...

"Joshua! Joshua! Wake up! Wake up, now. Everything's fine. You're okay now..."

Panting hard, Joshua sat up straight in bed, and stared wildly around. His mother was not lying in a pool of her own blood. His baby sister was not crying in fear and pain. His father... His father wasn't there either.

"You okay, man?"

Joshua stared up at the male nurse. He tried to speak but couldn't. It had been so real... *so real!*

"He should be in the psych ward, if you ask me..."

"Nobody asked you, Matt."

"You gotta move him outta here! Or move me!" Matt loudly demanded. "It's not enough that he's been keeping me awake all night with his yelling and hollering. But when a grown man starts crying like a baby for his Mommy..."

"Shut up, Matt!" the male nurse ordered.

"Look, I got a whole week left in here till this leg heals—and I ain't spending it with him!"

Joshua turned towards the young man sitting up in bed, his leg in a cast, his arms crossed and a look of utter disgust on his face. Joshua wished there was a hole he could go crawl into. "I'm really sorry," he rasped in a hoarse voice. He swallowed, realizing that Matt hadn't been exaggerating; he must have been yelling or crying or both, for his voice to be like this.

"This doesn't happen very often," Joshua sought to explain. "It probably has to do with the... uh... recent events in my life."

"He was kidnapped and bound hand and foot for fifty-three hours!" The nurse directed his comments towards Matt. "A normal reaction to that kind of trauma would be nightmares, or night terrors, which is likely what Joshua experienced."

Joshua appreciated the man defending him but thought that Matt had a point as well. He could see that it was still dark out. "Look, maybe I should go down to the lounge for a while. Matt could get some sleep."

The nurse hesitated only a moment before agreeing to help Joshua out to the lounge. Joshua wished that he had the strength to move around on his own. It was frustrating for him to still feel so weak!

And as he sat in the lounge, staring out over the city, Joshua wished that he wasn't so emotionally weak, either. It had been such a long time since he'd had that dream... No, not a dream... A true record of events that had haunted his childhood as a recurring dream, the truth lying hidden from him for so many years...

When he'd been four years old, he and his sister, Rebecca, had been sent to stay with their Aunt Yvonne and she had simply told him that his mommy and daddy had gone away. His sister's broken arm had healed and their lives had gone on much as they had before. Yvonne, like her brother Amos, had a filthy temper that was often directed towards the two young children. Joshua and Rebecca soon learned to read the warning signs and would escape from the house, hiding in the bush till it seemed safe to come back. Their aunt also often forgot to feed them. Joshua remembered enduring the hollow ache in his stomach through long days at school, only to many times come home and find the house empty of both his aunt and food. But worst of all were the visits from their older half-brothers, who inflicted deep lasting wounds in their younger siblings through their verbal, physical and sexual abuse of them.

Joshua was nine and his sister five when, without warning, their father had walked through the door of their aunt's house and told the two children he was taking them home.

Joshua remembered his youthful innocence and the excitement he had felt at that moment. *His father was back!* Joshua had eagerly snatched up his sister's and his meager belongings, grabbed her hand and hurried out the door after him. *If their father was back, maybe their mother was too!*

She hadn't been in the kitchen or living room. Joshua had run down the hallway, calling out "Mommy! Mommy!" as he looked into each room, and had arrived back in the kitchen, feeling a huge weight of disappointment and a mounting sense of dread. Joshua's father had stood angrily in the middle of the floor, waiting for him. Normally, Joshua wouldn't dare to speak to him when he looked like that but he'd just *had to know*! "Where is she?" he'd asked.

His father had lunged towards him, cursing loudly, and with an open palm had struck Joshua so hard on the side of his head that he'd flown across the room, and banged his head on the kitchen cabinets. Though blood was dripping from the cut on his forehead and his ear ringing, Joshua had clearly understood his father telling him that if he ever spoke about "that woman" again, he would end up just as dead as she was.

That was the year Joshua's drinking began to get out of control. Liquor had always flowed freely in the Quill house and Joshua's brothers had gotten a kick out of getting him drunk and showing him off to their friends. But it was Amos' return that had finally driven Joshua into seeking the bottle himself in a desperate attempt to numb the fear and torment in his life.

Colin had tried to help and so had Grandpa Pipe. But Tom Peters was the one who'd finally been able to reach him... just after Rebecca's death when he was fourteen.

His sister had killed herself after being raped by their father. Her death had been devastating, especially as Joshua had been the one who found her body. Then when Amos had also committed suicide just days later, using the same weapon as Rebecca, it had been more than Joshua had been able to handle.

But Tom had been there for him, had stood by him through the hard years of healing, and had not only been a father to him but had directed Joshua to the Heavenly Father.

Tom had also helped bring Joshua's nightmares into the light. Together they had gone down to the police station to talk with Sammy Rae. He had been on duty the night that Joshua's mother had died, and so was able to fill in the details of the horrible "nightmare" that had haunted Joshua since he'd been a small child.

Sammy revealed that after Amos threw Rebecca against the wall, Joshua's mother had finally snapped; grabbing up a filleting knife she had gone after Amos. In the ensuing struggle, Amos turned the knife on her. Although initially charged with murder, it had been reduced to manslaughter, and so Amos had only served five years in prison.

Finding out that his nightmare was really a memory had begun the healing process for Joshua. Embraced by Tom and his family, and with his new faith in Jesus, Joshua had grown to believe that he had left the old life behind him for good. Tom, with his great physical, emotional and spiritual strength, had been a bulwark to him and Joshua had felt safe for the first time in his life. And as the years had passed, he had felt safe enough, and self-confident enough, to pursue his dream of marrying Missy, and directing a youth ministry.

Now as he watched the gray dawn slowly breaking over the concrete and grime of the city, Joshua bitterly acknowledged that it had all been just an illusion. Nothing had really changed. He was still weak and powerless, still at the mercy of his older brothers…

A voice startled Joshua out of his reverie. "Heard you had a rough night. Doctor Peters did leave a PRN order for some pain medication if you need it."

It wasn't that kind of pain…

Joshua smiled half-heartedly at the young nurse's aide. "Thanks, but I'm okay."

"I'll leave your breakfast here," she said cheerfully, setting down a tray on the table near where he was sitting.

255

The food looked real enough but smelled artificial, as if the flavors were an afterthought mixed together and sprayed on top of everything just before being delivered to the patient. Joshua turned away. Maybe he just wasn't hungry.

He looked out the window but could see nothing except the other sides of the hospital. He moved his chair a little closer and looked down into the courtyard but that wasn't very cheering either. It seemed to be almost entirely composed of hard, cold brick and stone. Even the few plants that were there were set into concrete pots. A fountain of water shot up from the middle of the courtyard splashing back down into a concrete pool with a stone wall built around it. There were concrete benches where people could sit. Few people were sitting, though. Most were scurrying about as if they had urgent business elsewhere, some carrying briefcases, some wearing white coats, some in suits. Joshua thought they looked like ants—or perhaps squirrels—chattering into their cell phones as they ran from one place to the other.

Why had he ever let Missy and her father talk him into coming here? This wasn't the place for him. He didn't belong here.

"Josh, are you in here?"

Joshua turned to see Missy standing hesitantly in the doorway, her ever-present backpack slung over her shoulder. Her hair hung loosely about her shoulders and she was wearing a San Jose Sharks T-shirt and a pair of blue jeans. She looked young and vulnerable. And there was nothing that Joshua could do to protect her. *Nothing!*

"I was just out jogging with Jasmine. It's a beautiful day outside. Josh...?"

I'm the wrong person for you!

256

"Joshua?"

Just go away! Go away!

Missy's voice began to rise and it shook just a little. "Maybe you went to the bathroom... or maybe you're asleep...?"

Joshua could stand it no longer. "I'm here," he said quietly.

He saw her face crumple, but in sorrow rather than relief, and he was immediately repentant. "I'm sorry."

She began to walk toward him. "You were sleeping?" she asked, a hopeful note in her voice.

He hesitated just a moment before answering her honestly. "No."

Joshua could see that he had hurt her deeply and every part of his being cried out to wrap her in his arms, to ease away the pain etched onto her face.

"Coffee table—left knee!" Joshua exclaimed suddenly.

Missy moved a little to her right, avoiding the coffee table that she had been about to walk into. "At least you'll still tell me that."

"You don't have your cane," Joshua said defensively. *This was the city—how did she expect to get around without her white cane amidst such chaos?*

"I have it folded up in my backpack," Missy said quietly, still moving slowly towards Joshua as she spoke. "And I'm quite familiar with this hospital. Dad's worked here for—"

"That chair's empty," he interrupted her. "I'm just beyond it, in a chair by the window."

Missy moved in front of the big fake leather chair but remained standing. "I heard that you had a rough night..." she began in a gentle voice.

Joshua shook his head angrily. "Word spreads quicker here than in Rabbit Lake."

Missy winced as if he'd struck her. "I asked the nurses," she said.

Joshua looked out over the city of glass and concrete. "I don't belong here," he muttered.

"I know," Missy said softly, reaching out for his hand. "We'll head back soon."

Joshua pulled away. "There's no *we*, Missy!"

He expected her to cry, to maybe run away to her family...

But he should have known better.

Missy raised her chin and declared, "There will always be a *we*, because I'll never stop loving you, Joshua. If this whole thing had happened two weeks from now, we would have already been married. What would have happened then—would you have asked me for a divorce?"

Joshua bowed his head. "I don't know what I would have done," he whispered.

Missy placed a hand on his shoulder and gently rubbed it. "Are you still having muscle spasms?" she asked.

"Just if I move suddenly." Joshua paused and added wryly, "I probably had some last night. It would account for some of the 'yelling and hollering' my roommate accused me of."

"Did you have bad dreams as well?" Missy asked cautiously.

He flinched under her gentle touch. "Cried like a baby, they told me." He grabbed her hand and pulled it away from his shoulder, squeezing it hard as he asked, "Is that what you want, Missy? A man who cries in the night for his mommy. Is that what you want?"

She sat down on the chair beside him and put her other hand over their clasped ones. "I want *you*, Joshua Quill. Everything that you were and are and will be." She smiled ruefully. "You didn't get such a perfect package either, you know."

Pulling her hands away, she reached up and began to remove one of her prosthetic eyes. With a groan, Joshua gently put his hands over hers again. "Don't..." he said in a heart-broken whisper. "I get it."

She adjusted her prosthetic eye back into place and continued in a gentler voice. "I can't even see you, Joshua. I can't share a sunrise with you. I don't know what you look like. *I don't even know what I look like!*"

"*Missy!*" Joshua agonized. "I'd give you my eyes if I could!"

She smiled wanly. "And I'd give you my dreamless nights."

She was wearing down his resolve. "I can't protect you..." he began.

"No, you can't," she said in a gentle voice.

"It's too dangerous for you to live at Rabbit Lake."

"It's dangerous everywhere, Joshua. Are you actually suggesting that downtown Chicago is less dangerous than a small community in Northern Ontario?"

"Sometimes," he replied sadly, "yes, sometimes it is."

Missy shook her head stubbornly. "Taking proper precautions is one thing..." She smiled and took out her white cane, snapping it out to full length. "But living in fear—that I won't do."

Joshua was becoming angry with her nonchalant attitude. "That's because you don't know what real fear is!"

"That's not fair Joshua," she said in a quiet voice that rose gradually as she continued. "Do you know what it's like to be at the mercy of others every day of your life? To not know when some bozo is going to decide it's pick-on-a-blind-person day? To be 'accidentally' bumped into or have someone think it's a big

259

joke to sneak up on you and scare the living daylights out of you. To—to walk into a room and call out and not know if someone is there—because they don't answer..."

As her voice trailed off, the last of Joshua's anger ebbed away, to be replaced by shame. He put out his hands to her and once more asked for her forgiveness.

"There's—there's so few people in this world that I can trust," she said, allowing him to take her hands in his. "Ever since I first met you, I knew that I could trust you. Do you remember when I invited you to sit down and you were already sitting down on the sand beside me? And you simply told me that you were already sitting. You didn't laugh at me or ask stupid questions. You just told me. And when I bumped my glasses and they fell off, you just handed them back."

Joshua smiled at the memory of their first meeting. "Actually," he said, "I do remember teasing you just a wee bit..."

Missy smiled too, her face softening as she reminisced. "But not about my eyesight. I think it had something to do with my haughty, snobbish attitude."

Joshua smiled. Yes, it had been something like that!

Missy leaned forward, her voice earnest. "It was a defense mechanism that I used when I was afraid."

"I was a stranger..." Joshua spoke slowly, understanding for the first time how Missy had felt that day that they'd met on the beach.

"Yes," she answered softly, "and I couldn't even tell if you were sitting or standing." Missy shook her head. "I shouldn't have gone there alone. It was just that I thought no one else ever went there."

M. D. MEYER

"Missy," Joshua began in a tentative voice, "don't you understand? That's what I mean. You could be just walking on the beach or down the road and someone could—could hurt you."

Missy pulled away, tears running down her face, her voice trembling. "And you would take away the one person that I trust—that could be there for me every day—that *promised* to be there for me every day!"

261

chapter twenty-four

Missy swiped at the tears flowing down her cheeks and tried to focus on Joshua's words, even as her heart was breaking. "I was offering you a false protection, Missy," he said. "I thought that it was me but really it was Tom protecting us both. As soon as he was gone, I was a sitting duck. And those that I care about—you, the kids that will come to the camp, the staff—they'll be sitting ducks, too."

"*Joshua!*" Missy felt as if she could shake him! "Can't you understand? We're *all* just sitting ducks. To be human is to be vulnerable. We don't come built with a coat of armor on us. We're weak and powerless against so many things. But as we trust in our Creator and in each other, we become strong."

"But I *was* trusting..." Joshua protested weakly.

Missy leaned towards him and grasped his hands. "Bad things still happen," she said. "We're not invincible. We don't live forever. And sometimes suffering is a part of God's plan. Look at my mom. She didn't grow up with an older brother like Russell. She wasn't blind like me but still she's suffering..."

"And your mom didn't have it all that easy when she was young either," a voice spoke from close to the doorway.

"Dad!" Missy exclaimed, wondering how long he had been standing there listening.

"Missy," he responded with affection, touching her shoulder in passing. When he spoke again, Missy could tell that he was sitting down with them. "You made some very good points, honey," he said.

Missy was surprised that he would agree with her, but should have known that he wasn't finished...

"I also agree with Joshua... by refusing to testify against his kidnappers and bring them to justice, even though he knows who they are, he remains in danger—as do all those he cares about."

"You're letting fear rule your decisions, too!" Missy declared.

"I'm just saying that you would be safer living down here."

"And I agree," Joshua added.

Missy stood to her feet. "Well, I'm glad that you are finally agreeing with each other—about *my* life!"

Her father sighed deeply. "You're very precious to me, sweetheart."

"And to me," Joshua said.

Missy was so angry, she was shaking. "Well, you two just have a nice little cozy chat!" She grabbed for her white cane and began to tap around her, so upset that she couldn't remember where any of the furniture was.

"Missy, wait, honey," her dad entreated gently.

"Your backpack..." Joshua reminded her.

So he didn't mind if she left—*as long as she took her backpack with her!*

So much for the undying love they had for each other! All those fine words he had told her! Their dreams for the future! Their wonderful life together as husband and wife!

263

Missy kept on walking out of the door. He could keep her backpack if he was so concerned about it. Keep it as a souvenir of the breaking of their engagement!

She didn't know where she was going—only that it was away from the two of them!

But suddenly, Missy realized that she had taken the flight of steps down one floor and was heading towards her mother's room.

She stopped outside the door to compose herself, not wanting to upset her mother, who already had far too many burdens. After wiping the tears from her face and clearing her throat, she stepped inside and called out softly, "Mom?"

"Come in, dear!"

Missy was pleased that her mother sounded stronger and happier than she had the day before. Missy sat down on a chair by her bed and tried to put a smile on her face.

She should have known she couldn't fool her mom. "Honey, what's wrong?" she immediately asked.

"Nothing." Missy shook her head and swallowed past the lump in her throat. "Nothing's wrong." But even as she spoke, she could feel the tears begin to trickle down her cheeks.

"Honey, tell me…"

As she felt her mother's hand gentle on her arm, the last of Missy's resolve melted away. "Oh, Mom! I don't know what to do. Joshua—Joshua wants me to stay down here. He doesn't want me to go back to Rabbit Lake with him. He's—he's even talking about breaking off our engagement…"

She felt her mother's soft hand gently wiping the tears off her cheek. "Missy, honey, Joshua *loves* you."

"I—I know," Missy said, her voice breaking again. "And—and he thinks he's showing love to me by making me stay down here. He thinks I'll be safer. But he wouldn't be making me do this if I wasn't blind. He thinks I'm helpless…"

"Missy, honey, listen to me…"

"I—I'm listening," she said after a moment, accepting the Kleenex that was pressed into her hand.

"Dad and I, we've had our doubts about you and Joshua. He's—he's not maybe exactly who we would have chosen as a husband for you."

"Mom!" Missy protested, feeling betrayed. *First Joshua, then her dad, and now her mother—how could she say, or even think, such things?* Missy tried hard to not let her anger show as her mom continued.

"I guess maybe we would have wished for someone with a better family background…"

"You mean, if he came from some rich doctor's family—"

"No, that's not what I'm talking about. I'm talking about someone who can provide a stable home for you and for your children. Someone who can protect you—"

"I don't need protection!" Missy shouted. "I'm not a baby! I'm blind. That's all. I'm just blind…" Missy's voice trailed off. That was what was at the heart of the issue, she knew. Everyone wouldn't be so worried about her safety if she was sighted.

"Honey, it's not just that. I guess we as parents just want things to be easy for our children. And things will not necessarily be easy for you being married to Joshua. He has a lot of baggage from his past. It's possible that he might even turn back to alcohol in times of great stress…"

"If you believe that, then you don't know the first thing about Joshua!"

Her mother sighed. "You're so much like your dad—and your grandpa."

"It would be an honor to be like Grandpa!"

"Yes." Her mother sighed again. "But just this once, honey... It's just that I don't have a lot of strength... and if I spend it all on arguing with you..."

Missy was chagrined. "Mom, I'm sorry. You talk and I'll listen. I promise."

"Okay." This time the sigh sounded like one of relief, not frustration or weariness. "What I'm trying to say is that my attitude toward Joshua has changed over the years. And, believe it or not, your dad has become more accepting of Joshua, too."

"Right!' Missy said sarcastically.

"It's true. Before this recent incident, your father—"

"It wasn't Joshua's fault!"

"Missy..."

She could hear the pain and fatigue in her mother's voice and Missy's heart was smitten again. *She had promised not to argue.*

"Mom..." she said, tears flowing down her cheeks once more. "It's just that our wedding is only nine days away. *Nine days!* And Dad and Joshua seem to be in some kind of league plotting against it—and—and against our marriage."

She could feel her mother's hand again, gently squeezing hers. "Missy, honey, even if the wedding is postponed temporarily, it doesn't mean that you won't ever get married."

"But I wanted *you* there, Mom!"

"I know you wanted me there, honey. But I'm not sure that I could be there, even if it was today. I don't think..." She paused before continuing in a quieter voice. "I don't want you to be alarmed, Missy, but I don't think I'm going to leave the hospital this time."

It took a moment for Missy to absorb what her mother had said. It felt too soon—*too soon*—to be talking about such things!

"You're going to get better, Mom!" Missy declared.

"Honey..."

"I'm just not ready!"

"Honey, remember when I first got diagnosed with cancer. That was a really hard time. Do you remember what we used to say together?"

Missy nodded.

Her mother began in a gentle prompting voice, "Life is hard..."

Missy managed a little smile as she finished the sentence, "...But God is good."

"Hold onto that, sweetheart. There will be rough times up ahead. But God loves you—and He loves Joshua. He's got some great things in store for you both. The youth program that you're going to do—"

"Joshua's given up on that, too!"

Her mother paused a moment before speaking gently. "Joshua is really beat down at the moment—but he will stand again. Till then, you need to stand for him and with him. Remind him of your love and of the Lord's love. He's going to need a lot of encouragement to get back on his feet again."

"You're talking as if—as if you really believe we'll still get married and do the youth program and everything..."

"Of course you will, honey. True love like you and Joshua have—it doesn't die. You're going through a really difficult time right now but I have no doubt that you love Joshua—and that Joshua loves you."

"Do you really, really believe that, Mom?"

"Yes, honey, I do. I see it every time he looks at you. The love he has for you is so clear in his eyes."

"I wish that I could see that!" Missy cried. *"I wish that I could see!"*

There was a longer pause than Missy expected before her mother spoke again. "Your dad didn't tell you yet, did he?"

Missy's heart began to thump wildly. "Tell me what? I—I couldn't possibly handle any more bad news..."

"This is good news."

"Then why are you not sounding happy?"

"I'm just worried that your dad hasn't told you yet. He's— he's kind of been against it from the beginning. We've discussed it at length on a number of occasions."

Missy was getting more worried by the moment. *"What?"* she exclaimed.

"I want to give you my eyes," her mother spoke in a rush of words.

Missy gasped. Her mother couldn't possibly mean what she had just said! "Your—your eyes?"

"Yes, dear, my eyes," her mother answered calmly. "I have talked it over with Doctor Pegrew and he's ready to do the operations whenever you're ready."

"But—you're still—I mean—you're not—"

"I'm not *dead* yet," her mom filled in gently.

Missy swallowed hard. "Yeah. But then... I don't understand..."

"I would like the operation to be now while I still have the strength to go through with it. And there's more of a possibility of it being successful if the organs are… if I'm still alive. And Missy…"

"Yes," she whispered.

"I also want it to be while I'm still alive because I want to experience this with you. I want to hear your voice when you see for the first time. I want to be a part of this gift that I'm giving to you."

"No!" Missy cried out, everything in her protesting against the idea. "No! Mom, I can't let you do this!"

Her mother's voice remained calm and gentle. "Honey, I know that you need time to get used to the idea. I've had a lot of time to think about it."

"But it's *wrong!*" Missy protested.

"If I were donating a kidney or bone marrow to you…"

"Yes, but you could go on the same as normal afterwards."

"You speak as if there's never any risk or hardship in donating an organ."

"But Mom—*your eyes…*"

"My darling, come closer… please."

Missy carefully embraced her mother and felt her thin arms wrap around her.

"I *want* to," her mother said in a voice that was hoarse with emotion.

And suddenly Missy felt huge sobs tearing up from deep within her. Everything that had happened in the past week crashed down upon her—her Grandpa's death, Joshua's disappearance, their broken engagement—and now *this!* She wanted so very desperately to be able to see—but to rob her dying mother of *her*

269

eyesight? *How could that be right?* But would it be worse to refuse this gift—this wonderful gift that her mother was holding out to her?

"I want to do this," her mother said again, as Missy's sobs gradually subsided.

"Thank you," Missy whispered in a trembling voice.

She felt her mother's arms fall away and gently eased her own arms from around her and took her mother's hand instead.

"Doctor Pegrew will talk to you whenever you're ready, hon. But, please make it soon…"

"Oh, Mom, I don't know if I'll ever be ready. I don't know if I can let you do this."

"Please just talk to him. Do it for me."

Her mother's voice was weakening and Missy knew that she needed to rest. She bent over her mother and kissed her. "I will talk to him," she promised.

Colin had slept poorly and woken early. Not wanting to disturb Sammy, he quietly left the room, wandering around the hotel, haunting the front desk for messages from Sergeant Melton. After the third request in thirty minutes, the front desk attendant had taken to shaking his head in response to Colin's questioning glance when he passed through the lobby. Each time Colin felt a plethora of emotions, vacillating from relief to anxiety. He was anxious to get it over with but also filled with terror at the possible outcome. *There was just so much at stake!*

Sammy found him in the hotel restaurant, drinking his third cup of coffee and trying to focus his thoughts enough to read the latest edition of the Kenora Enterprise, a newspaper he usually enjoyed.

"Anything new?" Sammy asked.

Colin shrugged and handed him the paper. "Maybe I'll just go check and see if there are any messages..."

Sammy grabbed him by the arm. "I just checked," he said. "Relax. Have you eaten yet?"

Colin shook his head. The thought of food made him feel ill.

Sammy ordered breakfast for them both and when it arrived, dug in with gusto. Colin managed to swallow a few bites of toast and, despite Sammy's protests, got up twice to check for messages.

"You're going to wear a path in the carpet," Sammy said with a grin. "And that guy at the desk is starting to duck every time he sees you coming."

Colin couldn't find one ounce of humor in the situation. "Why hasn't he called yet?"

Sammy's eyes filled with compassion. "Look, try to get some more food down. I'll phone the station, and find out what the delay is."

Colin focused in on every word that Sammy spoke into his cell phone but it was obvious even before he hung up that Sergeant Melton wasn't ready for them yet.

"Some more reports to look through. He'll call us..."

They paid for their meals and Sammy suggested that they go for a walk down at the harbor front; they could leave their cell phone numbers at the front desk.

Colin's spirits revived a little as they followed the pathway that circled around the lake. Gazing out over the water that sparkled in the morning sunshine, reminded him that God, the Creator of the universe, still had everything under control. He just needed to trust Him...

When the call finally came, requesting their presence down at the station, it was close to ten o'clock. Colin immediately raced for the car, and insisted on driving, and Sammy had to remind him several times to stick to the speed limit. However, as they neared the station and turned into the parking lot, Colin slowed the car to a crawl, suddenly consumed by fear again. *This was it!*

"C'mon," Sammy said in a gentle voice.

They walked straight through past the curious stares of the other officers, and down the corridor to Sergeant Melton's office. He didn't stand up but waved them silently in, passing over a sheet of paper to Colin as soon as they were seated.

Colin's heart started racing when he saw the letterhead at the top of the fax—it was from the hospital where Russell had been admitted. Something of his fear must have shown in his face because Sammy laid a hand on his shoulder. Colin, grateful for his support, found the courage to read on.

Russell was doing better! Colin almost collapsed with relief.

"Looks like Somebody's watching out for him—or for you," the sergeant commented.

"Yes," Colin replied, glancing briefly up at him before returning to read the report in detail. Russell had showed such "remarkable improvement" that the doctors had released him at eight o'clock that morning!

Colin handed the report to Sammy who read it with a growing smile. His eyes twinkled as he declared, "Somebody's watching out for *him* and for *you*."

Sergeant Melton put up his hand. "Not quite time for celebrations yet."

Colin groaned inwardly as the older man continued in a grim voice. "We're still in the middle of an investigation into possible misconduct, excessive use of force, criminal negligence causing bodily harm, aggravated assault, refusing to cooperate with an investigation, resisting arrest and escaping custody. Although..."

Colin hardly dared to glance up.

"Although," the sergeant repeated with a sigh, "I think we can safely dismiss some of these charges."

Colin did look up then. Sergeant Melton was regarding him closely. Their eyes met and the older man shook his head. "What'd you do that upset this Adams fellow so much?"

Colin shook his head. "I don't honestly know, sir."

"Well, you still have friends up there, that's for sure. I have been in communication with Constable Littledeer. He has also been reporting directly to the Commissioner on this. There have been a lot of faxes, phone calls and emails sent on your behalf. Specifically with regards to the 'refusing to cooperate with an investigation' and 'escaping custody' charges, I have been advised that Constable Littledeer, as acting Chief of Police in the community, had ordered you to go home to be with your family. Constable Littledeer also claimed responsibility for... hitting the power button on the computer. Constable Adams was, as I understand it, attempting to interrogate you at that time."

"Uh, yes, sir," Colin replied hesitantly. The last thing he wanted to do was implicate Keegan in any of this!

"And as we established last night, you were not 'resisting arrest' as there had been no formal arrest charges made by Constable Adams."

"That is correct, sir," Colin said.

"And regarding the 'criminal negligence causing bodily harm' you have reported that your sister did call an ambulance and was interrupted before she could apply first aid—by Constable Adams—who then turned over the task to Constable Quequish." The sergeant looked up inquiringly. "Any reason why you didn't do this yourself?"

"It all happened pretty fast," Colin explained. "The subject was subdued but unpredictable. I was guarding him until backup arrived. My sister, a nurse, had already briefly examined the subject before going to get the first aid kit. She had also already called an ambulance; it arrived shortly after Constables Adams and Quequish got there."

The sergeant nodded, seemingly satisfied, and for the first time since he'd walked into the police station the day before, Colin felt a flicker of hope. Maybe he wouldn't end up in prison. Maybe he'd get to keep his position as Chief of Police in Rabbit Lake...

"So there remains the 'excessive use of force' charge..."

"I had already determined—" Colin began.

The sergeant waved away his protests. "Yes, yes, I have it all on record."

The sergeant leaned back in his chair and regarded Colin. "Thing is..." he said, "I know your record. And I know Sammy even better than I know you. And he wouldn't be here if he didn't believe in you."

Colin glanced at Sammy who smiled encouragingly at him. Colin smiled wanly back. The sergeant wasn't finished yet...

He sighed deeply. "Thing is... the final decision is not mine. But the commissioner is making this a top priority. She has all of the reports, including the one from the hospital that you've just read."

The intercom buzzed. "Commissioner Brighton on line one, sir."

Sergeant Melton exclaimed, "Good timing!" before picking up the phone on his desk. His end of the conversation, and his facial expression, provided no clues whatsoever on what the Commissioner had decided. "Yes... uh-huh... okay... yeah, I agree... sure..." His eyes rested on Colin as he spoke and it was almost more than Colin could bear to not know what was being said on the other end of the line!

Finally the sergeant spoke his farewells, hung up the phone and looked across at him.

Colin held his breath.

"All charges are dropped, effective immediately."

Sammy leapt out of his chair and wrapped his arms around Colin in a big bear hug. Colin somehow managed to return the hug, so overwhelmed with relief that his muscles felt as limp as overcooked noodles. Sammy released him and began to pump his hand as Colin thanked him in a trembling voice.

Sergeant Melton rose to shake his hand also.

"Thank you!" Colin exclaimed, wondering if there was any way to adequately express his gratitude.

Sergeant Melton waved it away. "Just keep doing your job. If half my men were as dedicated as you, it'd sure make my job a whole lot easier."

The sergeant turned to Sammy. "Keep looking out for him. It's the good ones that get kicked in the shins."

Colin stood shakily to his feet, still unable to completely grasp that his ordeal was over. He looked at Sergeant Melton and uncertainty swept over him. "May I leave—right now—or—or do you need me for something else—another report?"

The sergeant shook his head and smiled. "No, you're free to go. I'm sure your wife is anxiously waiting for you."

Sarah—and Emmeline and Verena!

Colin looked anxiously at Sammy, who was sitting down again, leaning back in the chair with a huge grin on his face. "We could leave now, couldn't we?" Colin asked.

Sammy took his time about answering. "Nope!" he finally said, shaking his head.

"What...?" Colin asked weakly.

"I was actually sorta thinking about taking Paul up on his offer to go fishing—if I can persuade him to take a break from dealing with dangerous criminals such as yourself." As Colin opened his mouth to protest, Sammy waved a hand to forestall him.

"Rental car's outside. I'll give Jason a call—see if he's got all his shopping done and is ready to fly back." Sammy smiled reassuringly at Colin then dialed a number on his cell phone.

After the flight arrangements were confirmed, Colin was shooed out of the office by the two older men, who were already trying to outdo each other with fishing stories. As Colin headed for the front door, he managed to rein in his urge to run, and nodded politely to passing officers and staff. But as soon as he set foot outside the building, he sprinted towards the rental car, whooping with joy.

He was on his way! On his way to Sarah—and the girls—and home!

chapter twenty-five

When Sarah woke, her first thoughts were of Colin, and she prayed silently for him as she carefully slid down off the top bunk, trying to avoid waking Emmeline, who was sleeping in the bottom bunk.

But her efforts were in vain. Emmeline was wide awake by the time Sarah's feet touched the floor, and her eyes were wide and fearful.

"I'm just going to the bathroom," Sarah explained gently.

The relief on the little girl's face was heartbreaking.

Sarah continued on her way, walking quietly to avoid waking anyone else. Her fifteen-year-old niece, Kaitlyn, was asleep on the couch and Rosalee was in Andrew's bedroom, sleeping on the top bunk with Verena on the bottom. Sarah felt grateful to Jamie and Bill for opening their home to them; they didn't have a big house and if Andrew hadn't been away at school…

"No! No!" Clapping a hand over her mouth, Sarah made a dash for the bathroom and threw up in the toilet.

She was standing, weak and trembling, holding onto the sink when Jamie approached her from behind, her reflected image revealing her concern. "Are you okay?" she asked, gently rubbing Sarah's back.

Sarah started to nod but burst into tears instead.

"Shhh, it's going to be okay. Colin—"

"Verena—Verena—not Colin," Sarah gasped.

"Verena?"

"In—in the kitchen…"

Jamie left. A few seconds later, Sarah heard her groan and then speak in a sad, quiet voice. "Verena, you don't have to eat that. It's all covered with coffee grounds and egg shells…"

Sarah almost threw up again but took a couple of deep breaths instead.

"I'll make you some breakfast, Verena. What would you like? Maybe some cereal, or toast and eggs, or maybe some pancakes and sausages…?"

Sarah quickly pushed the door shut.

A few moments later, she splashed some water over her face, rinsed out her mouth with mouthwash, and made her way out into the kitchen. She pulled her worn terry-cloth housecoat closer to ward off the chill she felt, even though it was a warm summer's morning.

Everyone else was awake now, too. Kaitlyn was sitting up on the couch, sleepily rubbing her eyes. Bill was making some coffee. Jamie was buttering toast. Sarah looked quickly away from the sight of the melting butter towards Rosalee, who was brushing Verena's hair. Emmeline sat close by, her eyes wide with concern as they focused on Sarah. And suddenly, everyone else was staring at her too.

"I'm okay," Sarah said weakly. "Probably just a touch of the flu or something…"

As Bill rushed to pull a chair out for her, Jamie commented on how pale she looked. "Do you need to lie down again? I'll watch the girls," she offered.

Sarah sank down into the chair, feeling incapable of making any decisions at that moment.

"Tea might help to settle your stomach a little," Jamie suggested. "You just stay right there and I'll make you some."

"And I could buy you some ginger ale when the stores open," Rosalee offered.

"Thanks." Sarah smiled at each of them in turn.

"You looked chilled," Jamie said, feeling her forehead. "Would a hot shower help, do you think?"

"Maybe later…" Sarah replied distractedly. Bill was frying bacon now and she was starting to feel ill again. She rose on trembling legs, desperate to escape the overpowering smell of the bacon grease, but a glance at Verena and Emmeline's anxious little faces made her decide against retreating to the bedroom. She smiled reassuringly at the two girls and said in as cheerful a voice as she could muster, "Maybe I'll just lie down for a couple of minutes."

Sarah made her way across the room and sank down onto the couch recently vacated by Kaitlyn, thankful for the pillow and blankets that her niece had left there.

She lay down and smiled again at the girls before closing her eyes. *Just a bit of rest,* she told herself *then I'll feel better. It's just a touch of the flu, or too much worrying and not enough sleep the past few days… just a few minutes of rest is all I need…*

"So how are my girls?"

She was dreaming. She had to be!

Sarah forced her eyes open, clawing her way up out of a deep sleep, as she heard Emmeline and Verena's frightened cries.

No! No! It couldn't be!

Squinting at the silhouette framed in the doorway, Sarah struggled to sit up, entangled in the blanket. Suddenly two small bodies burrowed in close to her. Sarah looked down. Verena was hiding her face in the blanket, but Emmeline was staring warily at her father as he stepped further into the room.

"I've brought some gifts for you—for both of you."

Sarah watched in shocked silence as the man held out two brightly colored bags. It couldn't be Russell. It just couldn't be! Colin had told her just last night that he was in critical condition in a hospital in Winnipeg. Maybe she was having one of those waking dreams that Colin sometimes had...

Russell was dressed impeccably as always: a cream colored shirt tucked into beige pants, and brown suede loafers on his feet. The rings on his fingers gleamed in the sunshine coming through the living room window. A white gauze bandage wrapped around his head stood out in stark relief against the darkness of his hair. The bruise on his jaw was blue and puffy, and there were dark circles under his eyes, evidence of his recent close brush with death.

Yes, he was real enough—but different somehow, too. There was a strange aura of vulnerability in his manner and his words as he set the bags down in front of them and repeated what he'd said earlier, "I brought some gifts—for both of you."

Verena was trembling violently now and seemed to be trying to bury her whole body into the couch. Sarah quickly pulled the covers up around her, effectively blocking the little girl from view.

Russell stared hard at Verena's covered form, then at Emmeline sitting unnaturally still, but obviously poised for flight.

"They're afraid of me," Russell said accusingly.

Sarah looked up at the man towering above them. "Y-yes," she stammered. *And so am I!*

Russell stood a moment longer, his eyes dark and his jaw clenched with some suppressed emotion. Then he spun on his heels and walked out the door.

Sarah was too stunned to move but Jamie had been in the kitchen behind Russell, inching her way towards the phone. Now she pounced on it, dialed a number and ran towards the door, the phone pressed to her ear. She slid the big easy chair in front of the door as her husband came on the line.

"Bill!" Jamie exclaimed. "Bill—come home right away—please!"

Sarah drew the blanket down and bent her head towards Verena. "He's gone," she whispered softly. "You're safe now—he's gone."

The little girl pulled her head out from behind Sarah but still kept her body molded fast to hers. Her eyes were puffy and red, and her breath came in little shuddering gasps as the trembling gradually decreased.

They all stiffened again, though, when a car pulled up outside, followed by the door rattling.

"It's me, Jamie." *It was Bill!* "Are you alright? C'mon, open up!"

Jamie pushed the big chair away, unlocked the door and Bill burst in. Jamie rushed into his arms. "What happened?" Bill asked anxiously as she pulled away.

"Russell!" Jamie spat his name with distaste. "That's *who* happened." Moving away from Bill, she locked the door again and pushed the chair back in front of it.

"But he's in the hospital! How could he...?" Bill didn't bother finishing the question as he put a comforting arm around Jamie and anxiously asked, "Did he hurt you?"

His eyes swept the room, taking in Sarah and the two children as well. "Is everyone okay?"

"Yes, we're okay," Sarah replied, summoning a reassuring smile.

"Well, I'm gonna stay home for the rest of the day," Bill announced, punching in a number on his cell phone. "I was going to fly a group down to International Falls but I'll arrange for someone else to do it."

Jamie gave him a light kiss on the cheek. "Thanks," she said. "I'll make us some coffee—or tea if you'd prefer, Sarah."

"Coffee will be fine," Sarah assured her.

"You feeling a bit better?" Bill asked.

"Yeah, I feel a lot better actually. I guess that sleep helped." Sarah glanced down at her watch and exclaimed. "Eleven o'clock! I didn't mean to sleep that long!"

"You must have needed it," Bill said.

A knock on the door caused everyone to jump, and there was a noticeable pause before Bill finally moved into action, shifting the chair aside and unlocking the door.

A woman that Sarah had never seen before was poised on the doorstep. She was middle-aged, had short auburn hair, and was wearing a crisp blue business suit and clutching a briefcase. The scowl on her face was so fierce that Bill took an inadvertent step backwards.

"Are you in the habit of barricading your door in the middle of the day?" she demanded frostily as she shoved her way past him.

Bill grabbed the easy chair and pushed it back into its usual place and it was then that Sarah noticed that Russell had returned! He had followed the stranger through the doorway, but then hesitated, hanging back instead of asserting his presence as he normally would have done.

The woman strode past Jamie, who was standing in the kitchen holding the empty coffeepot in her hand, and chose a chair that allowed her a full view of everyone in the room. She set her briefcase on the table, snapped it open and took out a sheaf of papers. Sarah watched in amazement as the woman nodded in Russell's direction, indicating that he should take a chair opposite her.

Russell walked in, glanced at the untouched gift bags in front of the couch, and sat down, still without speaking.

The woman looked up at the others. "Which one of you is Sarah Hill?"

"Me," Sarah said hesitantly. "I—I'm Sarah Hill."

The woman stared contemptuously at her, sweeping her eyes down the length of the old housecoat. "You don't feel it necessary to dress during the day?"

"Look, who are you?" Jamie interjected angrily. "And what do you want?"

The woman shifted her attention to Jamie, studied her from head to toe then seemingly dismissed her as not being worth her time. Without bothering to answer Jamie, the stranger directed her next comment to Russell.

"These are the children in question?" she asked, looking towards the couch.

The children in question? Sarah's heart filled with fear as she echoed Jamie's demand. "Who are you? What are you doing here? What do you want?"

"My name is Ms. Richards. Mr. Quill's lawyers have been negotiating with our agency for Mr. Quill to regain custody of his children. Fortunately we had most of the paperwork completed when he arrived at our agency early this morning. A grave injustice was enacted on Mr. Quill when his children were snatched away based on one flimsy report from his estranged and obviously mentally ill spouse. As it is our agency's policy that children remain with their natural parents whenever possible, we cooperated fully with Mr. Quill's lawyers."

Estranged...? Mentally ill spouse...? Sarah tried to piece together this version of the account.

"But there is clear evidence of child abuse!" Jamie protested.

Ms. Richards threw her a look of utter disdain before turning back to Sarah. "There is no question that Mr. Quill is the victim in this situation, as I also have a report from a Constable Adams that Mr. Quill was assaulted by one of the current foster parents." She raised her eyebrows inquiringly towards Sarah. "I'm assuming that is not you."

"My—my husband. But he didn't—"

Ms. Richards put up her hand. "No, I am not here to discuss an ongoing investigation. I'm sure the police are dealing with this in an appropriate manner. The only thing I require is for you to sign these papers, stating how many hours the children were in your care. You will be properly compensated of course."

Sarah rose unsteadily to her feet. Everything was spinning out of control, the faces around her blurring. "Compensated?" she whispered hoarsely. "But—but you're not taking them...?"

Ms. Richards shook her head in disbelief. "Of course we're taking them. Haven't you been listening at all? The children are being returned to their father effective immediately. Please pack all of their..."

The words faded into a white wall of silence and Sarah felt herself falling into a bottomless cavern.

chapter twenty-six

As Sarah fainted, she bumped against the easy chair, which slid into the floor lamp and toppled it over with a crash. Ms. Richards was forced to stop talking as Jamie and Bill rushed to Sarah's aid. Verena and Emmeline leapt off the couch and knelt beside her inert form, tears rolling down their cheeks as they cried, "Mommy! Mommy!"

"How inappropriate." Ms. Richards sniffed disdainfully.

Jamie turned and glared at the woman in disbelief. Never in all of her years of being a foster parent had she met a social worker like this! Stifling her anger, Jamie turned her attention back to Sarah, feeling for her pulse, noting her pale but dry skin, and her still closed eyes. "Sarah?" she called. "Sarah, can you hear me?"

Her eyelids fluttered open. "What happened?" she asked weakly. "Why am I lying on the floor?"

The little girls threw themselves on her, but Jamie and Bill gently pulled them off. "Let Mommy get up, okay. You can hug her after we get her onto the couch."

Ms. Richards babbled on in the background. "Mr. Quill, I do want you to understand that we never *ever* advise our foster parents to assume the title of *Mommy* or *Daddy*. It is very confusing for young children, especially in cases, such as yours, where the children are only in temporary foster care—"

Jamie gritted her teeth, fighting the urge to scream "Shut up" at the obnoxious woman.

"—And we usually have a very thorough screening process beforehand. I can't imagine how these two got accepted. I suppose it has something to do with the agency's policy of wanting First Nations children to be placed in a First Nations foster home. But let me assure you, Mr. Quill, that if we'd had any idea that the Hills were as bad as this... They looked so good on paper: there was no mention of Mr. Hill's tendency towards violence, or Mrs. Hill's laziness—"

Jamie shot to her feet, unable to take it anymore. "Colin is not violent!" she shouted, drowning out whatever Ms. Richards had been trying to say next. "And Sarah is not lazy! She just has the flu. Everyone gets the flu—even foster parents!"

Ms. Richards huffed indignantly, her face turning red. Bill helped Sarah up onto the couch as Emmeline and Verena peppered him with questions. "What's wrong with Mommy? Why did she fall? Is she going to die?"

Jamie removed her glare from Ms. Richards, and quickly turned to the children. "She's not going to die, Verena. She's just a little bit sick right now but she'll get better."

Ms. Richards stood to her feet and advanced towards them. "Now, children," she said in the high pitched tone usually reserved for babies, "you don't need to call this woman *Mommy*. You know she really isn't your mommy. And it's all going to be better now—back to the way it was before all these bad things happened to you. Your daddy is here to take you home with him."

"Nooo!" Verena wailed. "No! I don't want my old daddy! I want my new daddy!"

Emmeline declared angrily, "You can't make us! We won't go!"

Ms. Richards clamped her hands down on the girls' shoulders. Emmeline escaped by viciously kicking the social worker in the shins but Verena stood trembling in place, silent tears rolling down her thin cheeks.

Russell, quietly watching until now, stood suddenly to his feet and strode towards them. "*Let go* of my daughter," he ordered.

Ms. Richards gave a startled gasp and released Verena, who dove into Sarah's arms and buried herself once more beneath the blankets.

Russell frowned at the little girl, looked briefly at Sarah and Emmeline and then ran his eyes over Jamie and Bill, standing guard on either side of Sarah and the girls.

Jamie glared at him, ready to fight if necessary, but Russell had something else on his mind. "I think we should give these people a bit more time."

"*What?*" the social worker exclaimed.

Jamie eyed Russell suspiciously. *Now, what was he playing at?*

"We'll come back later this afternoon," Russell said. "It'll give everyone time to get ready." His eyes flicked to the gift bags on the floor again and then to Sarah. "Maybe you need time to pack their stuff."

"Yes—yes, I would like more time!" Sarah said eagerly.

"I have a very tight schedule," Ms. Richards said, her mouth thinning in frustration. "When this situation arose, it took priority, but I really cannot allow it to jeopardize the services to my other clients."

THE LITTLE ONES

Russell ignored her, focusing his attention on Sarah. "I'd like another chance—to be a good father."

If Jamie hadn't known him all these years, she would have been impressed by the sincerity in his voice. But she knew what he'd done to Colin and Joshua and so many others...

Sarah's eyes filled with tears as she drew the children closer.

"Two o'clock," Ms. Richards snapped. She walked briskly to the table, stuffed the papers in her briefcase and turned towards Sarah. "You *will* have the children ready to turn over to their father by that time. And rest assured, I will personally see to it that you are never again entrusted with the care of any foster children!" She took one last disdainful look around then strode out of the door.

Russell looked at Sarah and the girls again, and opened his mouth as if he was about to say something. Then with a small sigh and a slight shake of his head, he instead turned and walked out of the door, shutting it quietly behind him.

The tension in the air quivered momentarily then fell away.

Jamie looked at her sister-in-law's pale face and said, "Sarah, I'm concerned about this fainting spell. It isn't like you at all. If you feel well enough to get showered and dressed, I'd like to take you to the Health Center. Doctor Tanabe is in today. We could run a few tests..."

"Oh, I'm okay," Sarah protested.

"It might be a good idea," Bill interjected.

Sarah looked up at him, tears hovering in her eyes once more. "She said two o'clock. She's coming back for them at two o'clock..."

"That gives us almost two hours," Jamie said in a brisk, no-nonsense voice, helping Sarah to her feet.

Sarah looked back at the two children. "But I don't want to leave them. We have such a short time!"

"You should go see the doctor," Emmeline said in a decisive voice.

"And we'll go with you, Mommy," Verena added.

Sarah couldn't help laughing. "Okay, okay, I'll go. I know when I'm outvoted."

After the difficult conversation with her mother, Missy retreated to the hospital chapel, a small room that afforded a quiet place away from the noise and bustle of the big city hospital.

She made her way to the second of three pews on her right hand side, softly calling out, "Anyone here?" before sitting down. Usually she could tell by the slight rustlings that people always made but she just wanted to be sure.

It felt good to be alone. Things had been happening much too quickly and Missy was feeling overwhelmed.

Although she had talked to Doctor Pegrew many times through the years about his research, and had been excited about the theoretical possibilities of blind people becoming sighted, she had never allowed herself to imagine that it could really happen to her. Every day of her life had been a struggle and the only way she could go on was to tell herself that life as a blind person was good and full and rich. She didn't *need* to be sighted to go to college or to get married or to help run a youth program at Goldrock Lodge. She was content.

But now, as she allowed the possibility to enter her mind and penetrate deep into her heart, it consumed her with a desire that was almost overwhelming. To be able to see all the beautiful things around her that people tried in vain to describe... To be able to pick out her own clothes and check her appearance in a mirror instead of asking someone else... To be able to see Joshua... To see that love in his eyes that her mom had described to her... Yes, it would be wonderful to see Joshua...

Missy heard the heavy oak door creak as someone entered the chapel but she didn't feel obliged to acknowledge them. The chapel was a place where people came to meditate, to be alone with their thoughts and to pray. She was surprised when the bench she was on squeaked with the weight of another person—people usually sat alone—and she was relieved when she heard her father's voice.

"Missy..."

He sounded so sad. Missy instinctively reached for his hand. They both had such strong personalities that they'd often clashed through the years but always they reconciled, confident in each other's love.

Missy thought that he would bring up their last confrontation, so she was surprised when instead he talked about her mother.

"I'd do anything for her," he said in a broken whisper. "If I could take away the cancer and the pain... I would gladly die in her place."

Missy moved closer to him, entwining her arm with his and resting her head on his shoulder. Her father continued hesitantly, "Your mother really wants to have this surgery. To—to..."

"To give me her eyes," Missy finished in a hushed voice.

He squeezed her hand. "Yes."

"Daddy, I really don't know if I can," Missy said, swallowing back tears. "She's already in so much pain—I don't want to hurt her any more."

Her father sighed deeply. "I don't either, honey. But I think we'd be hurting her more if we didn't let her do it."

Missy nodded thoughtfully.

"Sometimes…" her dad began again. "Sometimes we need to rethink things that we thought we'd already made up our minds about. Things like this surgery… and your relationship with Joshua."

"Daddy!" Missy exclaimed, hope rising in her heart.

"Now, I didn't say that I thought it was a good idea for you to be marrying the guy. I just said that maybe I needed to rethink a few things."

Missy bit her lip, trying hard to keep from smiling. So much, *so very much,* she wanted her father's blessing on their marriage!

"I don't want to be fighting against God," her father continued gruffly. "I just want what's best for you. You know that, don't you?"

"Yes." Missy threw her arms around him. "Yes, I do know that, Dad."

Her father returned her hug and then pulling away, said, "I'd like to go with you when you talk to Doctor Pegrew, if that's alright with you? I've always been a little too resistant on the subject before to really take in what he was telling me. But I'd like to know as much beforehand as I possibly can…"

Missy was already nodding her agreement even before he'd finished speaking. "Thanks, Dad. It will be good to have you with me. It's kinda scary thinking about it all. Do you know how soon Doctor Pegrew would like to—to do this?"

"He's just waiting for your consent, honey. He's quite anxious to talk to you. We can meet with him right now if you like. Everything's ready for the operation to take place tomorrow morning."

Missy gasped. "So soon!"

Her father squeezed her hand. "Yes, he feels we should do it soon—for your mother's sake."

Missy shook her head. "It all feels so *rushed!* What if—what if I say no?" she whispered.

"Then it won't happen," her dad said in a firm voice. "This is your choice." He sighed. "And Mom's. The two of you—no one else."

"Mom wants it to happen."

"Yes," he replied in a heavy voice. "Yes, she does."

"Then I guess I want it, too." And suddenly the reality of it burst upon her and she asked excitedly, "Dad, do you think I'll really be able to see?"

She could hear the smile in his voice. "I hope so, honey."

Missy sighed. "It would be so wonderful."

Her dad stood up. "Are you ready to go talk to Doctor Pegrew now?"

Missy smiled up at him. "Yes," she said, standing to her feet also.

They linked arms as together they walked out of the chapel and into a whole new future.

Colin gazed out of the plane's small window, watching the Kenora airfield shrink into the distance. The pilot had been ready to head out straightaway, so Colin hadn't taken the time to call Sarah from the airport. Maybe he should have, he thought, settling back into his seat; it would have helped put her mind at ease to know he was on his way home.

Home... What a wonderful word. And he and Sarah would make it a good home for Emmeline and Verena. Sarah would be a great mom. He'd always known that. She had so much love to give...

No one was waiting for him as he stepped off the plane and Colin felt a lurch of disappointment. But it was his own fault—he should have called ahead. He pulled out his cell phone and tried Sarah's mobile number, but wasn't all that surprised when she didn't answer—she often forgot to take her phone with her when she went somewhere. He tried their home number and let it ring for quite a while then he tried calling Jamie and Bill. Finally, in desperation, he called the lodge, but Michael said he hadn't seen or heard from Sarah since the evening before.

Colin set off on foot towards Jamie and Bill's house—maybe everyone was down at the lake, like they'd been the day before.

He couldn't spot anyone outside, so he called out as he entered the house—"Hello. Sarah? Jamie? Anyone?" There was no answer and Colin's heart began to beat faster. What if something was wrong? What if something had happened to Sarah or one of the girls?

As Colin looked wildly about, trying to find some clue of what had happened, his eyes fell on a note propped up on the table. It was addressed to Kaitlyn, but as Colin leaned over to look closer, Sarah's name jumped out at him. He quickly scanned it, his heart racing again: *Jamie and Bill had taken Sarah to the Health Center!*

With his heart in his throat, Colin raced out the door and ran up hill the two blocks to the Health Center.

"Where's Sarah?" he demanded of the receptionist. "What's wrong with her? What happened?"

She smiled and calmly said, "Your wife is in Room 2; I'll go with you."

But Colin was already running.

He burst into the room without knocking.

"Daddy!" two little voices cried in unison.

"You're back!" Sarah exclaimed.

"Sarah, you're okay. You're not hurt!" Colin spoke in short gasps, still trying to catch his breath.

The little room seemed crowded. Colin glanced quickly around. The doctor was sitting in his chair, smiling. Jamie was leaning against the wall, smiling. Sarah... Sarah looked radiant!

She was sitting up on the examination table, one little girl on each side of her. "Colin..."

He was drawn to her like a moth to light.

"Sarah..."

She took his hands and drew him closer. And suddenly, no one else in the room existed. She smiled tenderly at him and placed his hands on her belly.

"I have some news for you."

chapter twenty-seven

He didn't dare to hope. Not after all these years...

"I'm pregnant," Sarah said, erasing all doubt.

"We're going to have a baby!" Colin exclaimed, his heart filled with wonder. "I'm going to have a son..."

"Now, hold on there..." The doctor's voice sounded from behind him. "We don't know yet if it's a boy or a girl."

Colin flashed a grin at the doctor before turning back to Sarah. Then, for the first time, he noticed the sad expressions on the two children beside her. He remembered their joyous greeting when he'd walked into the room and suddenly realized that he had not even acknowledged their presence; all his attention had been focused on Sarah and on the news of their child. And he'd talked about a son...

Lifting an eyebrow he grinned at Emmeline, and then Verena. "It's gotta be a boy," he declared, "because I already have two wonderful girls!"

Their faces lit up and they both clamored to speak with him at once.

"I have your card, Daddy."

"I have your badge."

"Did you arrest any criminals?" Colin asked.

As Emmeline giggled in response, Colin noticed the doctor leaving and suddenly the room went quiet... too quiet. Colin glanced quickly around. *Something was wrong.*

He turned back to Sarah, who was biting her lip, trying hard not to cry as she drew the two little girls close to her side in a tight embrace.

"Sarah, what's wrong?"

She looked up at the clock on the wall, and tears started to flow down her cheeks.

Colin's heart was in his throat. *"Sarah!"*

Bill put a hand on his shoulder as Jamie said, "Russell's back."

Colin spun around. "He can't hurt us anymore!" Colin's eyes swept over the children. "He can't hurt them anymore! We'll stand together! I'm going to go see Joshua—persuade him and Missy to come back. We can't let him intimidate us anymore!"

"He's been granted custody of the children."

Colin heard Jamie's words but his heart refused to acknowledge them.

It was impossible!

Colin felt Bill guiding him into a chair and was grateful. His legs felt like rubber. His heart was hammering in his chest. Slowly, he lifted his eyes up to face Verena and Emmeline.

He wouldn't let it happen—*couldn't* let it happen!

"At two o'clock," Sarah whispered.

"It's not going to happen," Colin assured her.

"What—what can we do?" Sarah asked.

Colin looked around, including Jamie and Bill when he spoke. "Tell me what happened—why two o'clock?"

As they took turns explaining what had happened, Colin kept his eyes fixed on Sarah and the two girls. When they'd finished, Colin glanced down at his watch—just a few minutes before one. He looked up at Bill. "I'll need your help."

Bill nodded nervously. "Where will you take them?"

"Winnipeg," Colin answered. Bill visibly relaxed and Colin lifted an eyebrow and grinned. "You thought maybe I'd flee the country?"

"The—uh—thought did cross my mind."

"No," Colin said with a deep sigh. "We'll do this the legal way as far as we can. If we can talk to the same people that we did when we got the girls..." He looked up at Jamie. "If you could give Keegan a call. Explain the situation to him and tell him it's urgent that we get enough evidence to convict Russell on the charge of kidnapping Joshua. And Jamie, ask him if he could please put a call through to Sergeant Melton in Kenora. I may need his support if things get sticky. And if you could get some people together to pray..."

Jamie gave her brother a hug and Colin knew that he could count on her to follow through on what he had asked her to do.

Bill stepped forward. "Jamie, I don't like to leave you to face Ms. Richards—and Russell—alone."

"Ms. Richards, I can handle," Jamie said. "As to Russell..." She hesitated then smiled. "Maybe we'll already be started with our prayer meeting when they get there. And I'll invite Keegan and Constable Quequish and Michael and Pastor Thomas and..."

"We get the idea," Colin said with a grin, feeling better now that a plan was in place. He turned to face Sarah. "Ready?"

She smiled and nodded through her tears.

He reached out to Emmeline and Verena, folding their small hands into his much larger ones. "How about it, you guys? Do you want to go for another plane ride?"

"With you?" Emmeline asked.

Looking into their anxious faces Colin said softly. "Yes, with me—and Mommy." A sudden thought hit him and he turned quickly to ask Jamie, "This won't hurt the baby, will it?"

She laughed. "No, I flew with Bill during every one of my pregnancies."

"Okay," Colin declared, "Let's roll!"

While Bill helped Sarah and Colin pack up the girls' belongings and drove them to the airport, Jamie got busy organizing the impromptu prayer meeting. To each person she called, Jamie gave a quick explanation of the situation. Some hadn't even been aware that Colin and Sarah had taken in foster children, but all of them knew Colin and Sarah and their great capacity for love. Many had been on the receiving end of their generosity and concern at one time or another.

People began gathering right away and by the time that Bill's plane took off a few minutes before two o'clock, the little house was full. Chairs were brought in from the kitchen and some of the younger ones, like Michael and Rosalee, sat on the floor.

Pastor Thomas got everyone's attention. An older man, who had lived all his life in Rabbit Lake, Pastor Thomas was well respected in the community. He didn't bother to retell the story of why they were there and he didn't feel the need to add anything to it. He simply said, "Let's pray," and began:

"Lord, we ask for Your hand of protection upon Colin and Sarah. You know their hearts, Lord, and this love that You've given them for these children in such a short time—it must surely come from You. Bless Colin and Sarah as they come before the authorities. Give them the right words to say and the right attitudes and actions. And we pray for Verena and Emmeline. These two little girls have had a rough time of it so far. Colin and Sarah would be good parents. Help them to have the chance to do it. And... Lord, for Russell too... I pray that you would somehow melt the ice that's in his heart, heal the hurts from his past, and draw him to Yourself. We ask these things in Jesus' name. Amen."

There was a lengthy silence after Pastor Thomas finished praying and Jamie knew she was not the only one who had felt a stab of conviction when he'd prayed for Russell. It had never *ever* occurred to Jamie to pray for him. Though she would not have admitted that any person was beyond God's saving grace, she would nevertheless have considered her prayers to be a waste of time where Russell was concerned. But as she felt the stirring of the Holy Spirit in her and around her, Jamie began to speak in a slow, hesitant voice, "Oh God, I too pray for Russell, that if it's possible for him to turn towards You, that You would work that miracle in his life—and in the lives of his children. Those kids deserve a second chance..."

Jamie suddenly remembered Russell's plea: *I'd like another chance—to be a good father.* Confusion flooded over her. *No, that couldn't possibly be what God had in mind... could it?*

301

Into the silence, someone else began to pray for Russell, and for Colin and Sarah and the two girls. And then another prayed and another...

Even though Jamie was expecting it, the loud knock at the door startled her. Everyone looked up as the door was impatiently thrust open and Ms. Richards strode into the room. Russell was behind her but after a quick glance around, stopped and remained where he was, framed in the doorway.

"What's going on here?" Ms. Richards demanded. "Where are the children? Where is Mrs. Hill?" Her lips were pursed and her eyes narrowed as she surveyed the group. "Who are you—what are you all doing here?"

Pastor Thomas smiled. "We're having a prayer meeting," he said.

"In the middle of the day—in a house?" Ms. Richards' voice was filled with disdain. "What kind of religion are you?"

Pastor Thomas chuckled. "We believe that God can hear and answer our prayers wherever and whenever we pray." He looked past her to the figure standing in the doorway. "Hello, Russell."

His greeting was met with a silent nod.

"We were praying for your children—and for you."

Russell flinched as if he'd been struck. "For me?"

"Where are the children?" Ms Richards' strident voice pierced the air.

Jamie stood to her feet. "They are on their way to Winnipeg," she said, "where I'm sure all of this will be cleared up." She turned to Russell. "Colin and Sarah will be good foster parents to your two girls."

"I want to be—" Russell began hesitantly.

"They had no right to—" Ms Richards interrupted.

Russell spun angrily towards her. "I think it would be good if you left now."

Ms Richards took a step back. "But your children..." she said.

"*My* children."

Ms Richards lifted her chin. "I will speak to my superiors..."

Russell turned away from her dismissively and focused his attention on Pastor Thomas. "I appreciate your prayers."

Ms Richards slammed the door loudly behind her as she left.

Pastor Thomas stood to his feet and said to Russell in a voice filled with compassion, "Jesus loves you."

Jamie watched in disbelief as Russell's face softened. "I know," he said.

His quietly spoken words were met with shocked silence. As Russell glanced around at the disbelieving stares, something like his usual smirk crossed his face. Then he shook his head slightly, turned and walked out the door.

A kind of collective sigh went up from the assembled group, almost as if everyone had been holding their breath.

Jamie thought that if Russell was faking it, then it was his best performance yet!

Pastor Thomas looked around the room, smiled, and said, "Let's continue to pray."

When they landed at the airport, Colin asked Bill if he would stay and wait with them. He willingly agreed and asked how long they thought they might be—and if he should perhaps book a hotel room for them.

But Colin and Sarah had no idea how long they would be at the agency. If they could talk to the right people—someone who would hear their case—and understand...

Bill finally made the decision for them, taking Colin and Sarah's suitcases and optimistically, Verena and Emmeline's also. "I'll bring them back if they're needed," he said. "And I'll be back to pick you guys up whenever you're ready." His smile included them all.

As they walked in through the doors of the agency building, Sarah wished she shared Bill's optimism.

And as the friendly receptionist smiled at them and greeted them, Sarah thought that perhaps everything would be alright, after all. But as soon as Colin introduced himself, the woman's demeanor changed. She spoke urgently into her headset. "Mrs. Kenyon—they're *here!*"

After a short pause while she obviously received instructions, the receptionist eyed them warily and said in a tightly controlled voice, "Have a seat, please. Someone will be with you in a moment."

They sat silently huddled together on two large chairs, Emmeline and Verena both clinging to them fearfully. It had been sweltering outside but the air conditioning was going full blast inside the building. Sarah shivered and wished she'd brought a sweater. Then, as a well dressed woman approached them, she wished for a completely different outfit. In their hurry to leave Rabbit Lake, she had hastily donned a pair of jeans and a bright blue plaid shirt; she'd barely had time to run a brush through her tangled curls, let alone put on makeup.

Sarah glanced down at Emmeline and Verena. At least they were neat and presentable. But Colin looked like Sarah… tired and disheveled.

"The director will see you now," the woman said. Sarah rose unsteadily to her feet and was grateful when Colin clasped her hand and whispered, "It's going to be fine, Sarah. The Lord is with us."

She glanced up at him, took in his encouraging smile, and felt her strength returning. Emmeline was holding tightly to her other hand and Verena was clinging to Colin's hand on the other side. They were a family, and they would face this challenge together.

"The Hills," announced their escort at an open door, and stood aside to let them enter, then closed the door after them.

A middle-aged woman wearing a sage green suit rose from behind her desk to greet them, introducing herself as Mrs. Kenyon.

She sat back down into her plush, navy blue office chair, and waved them towards two matching seats facing her desk. "Excuse me," she said, then spoke into the intercom, "Claire, can you bring in two extra chairs, please?"

Sarah collapsed gratefully into the chair, feeling the faint stirrings of nausea again. She hoped it wasn't all-day morning sickness… it was probably just the tension getting to her. As Colin collected the chairs off Claire, Sarah looked around the office. Along one wall, a large window offered a view over a manicured lawn but on the other side of the office, the curtains on another large window were tightly closed. The office was pleasantly decorated with live plants and beautiful pictures on the walls. Alongside the flat screen monitor on Mrs. Kenyon's polished wooden desk were two framed photos of laughing children, and a big vase of orange Tiger Lilies.

"Shall we continue?" she asked, as Colin positioned the extra chairs. But Verena refused to sit, clinging desperately to Colin until he finally sat down and hoisted her onto his lap. Emmeline also refused, standing silently with her brows knit and her lips drawn into a firm line, holding so tightly to Sarah's hand that it hurt.

For a moment, Sarah was at a loss what to do. Then an idea hit her. She bent her face close to Emmeline's, lowered her voice, raised her eyebrows and grinned as she whispered, "Emmygojumpin' that chair!"

The words worked like magic. Emmeline flashed a grin back at her, put her hands on the arms of the chair and bounced herself up into it.

"What did you promise her?" Mrs. Kenyon chuckled. "A chocolate bar or an ice cream cone?"

Sarah just shook her head and smiled.

Mrs. Kenyon surveyed the four of them thoughtfully. "You seem to have developed a very strong bond in a remarkably short period of time," she commented.

"Yes," Sarah spoke eagerly, "we almost feel as if they belong to us already!"

"Which they don't," Mrs. Kenyon replied dryly.

"But we'd like them to!" Colin said earnestly.

"That's why we're here," Sarah added.

Mrs. Kenyon smiled wryly. "No, the reason that you're here is that you are disputing a custody order that was being acted upon through our office."

Sarah's heart sank. *They weren't going to let them keep Emmeline and Verena...*

"You do realize that we are well within our rights to press kidnapping charges against you both."

Kidnapping! Sarah inhaled sharply and reached out for Colin's hand.

He smiled wearily at Mrs. Kenyon. "I don't think I could handle that just now, if you don't mind."

There was compassion in the older woman's face as she looked back at him. "I just wanted to make certain that you knew how seriously the law regards your actions. Our agency is committed to upholding the laws of this land."

"As am I," Colin replied evenly.

Mrs. Kenyon nodded. "Yes," she said, glancing over one of the papers on her desk, "your reputation precedes you. There is a commendation here from Sergeant Melton and a copy of a citation from the Commissioner of Police dated five months ago."

Sarah glanced down at the girls. Verena had her eyes shut, her face turned into Colin's chest, tuning out the world. But Emmeline was trying valiantly to follow the conversation and was looking anxiously at Mrs. Kenyon.

Sarah leaned over to her. "She just said that Daddy is a good police officer."

Mrs. Kenyon cleared her throat, and Sarah looked up and blushed—she'd obviously heard what Sarah had whispered. The older woman smiled and said, "Emmeline, isn't it? I'm sorry that I haven't been including you in our discussion. I will try to remedy that situation."

"Now," she began again, "it is the policy of our office to keep children with their birth parents whenever possible." She turned to Emmeline and spoke in a slightly higher pitch. "Little kids should be with their own mommies and own daddies."

Emmeline stood to her feet, her arms folded and her eyes narrowed. "My mommy is dead and my daddy hurts us. I want to be with my new mommy and new daddy. You can't take us away. I won't let you!"

"Emmeline!" Colin protested gently.

Sarah put her arm around her. "Sweetheart..."

"Emmeline, honey, we're going to talk to this lady and see if she'll let us keep you," Colin explained.

"Sit back down, sweetheart," Sarah said, gently guiding her back down into the chair.

Mrs. Kenyon turned to Colin, a touch of impatience in her voice. "You seem to have some high expectations of me."

"We *are* hoping that you will be able to help us."

Mrs. Kenyon folded her hands on her desk and said. "The decision has already been made."

"But you can't seriously be planning to return them to their father!" Colin protested.

Mrs. Kenyon glanced down at the file on her desk. "On July 25th, exactly one week ago, the children were removed from their father's custody based on an accusation of child abuse. It is now clear that this was a false accusation filed by a person who was quite obviously suffering from a mental illness and was quite likely herself responsible for the abuse."

"You're—you're blaming *her!*" Sarah sputtered furiously. *Easy enough to blame Russell's wife since she was no longer around to defend herself!*

"Not I," Mrs. Kenyon corrected. "There have been extensive reports. Psychiatrists have been consulted. Mr. Quill's lawyers have—"

"Exactly! *Mr. Quill's lawyers*—can't you see what's happening here?"

"No, Mrs. Hill, I cannot see *what's happening here*—are you actually implying that you know more than all of the experts that have been consulted—more than my staff who are highly trained and more than qualified—"

"What I am saying," Sarah stated, "is that this man is unfit to be a parent. He is a convicted sexual offender, a pedophile and—"

"Mrs. Hill! Are you forgetting that his children are present?"

Sarah glanced at Verena, who still had her eyes shut, and at Emmeline who was anxiously looking back and forward between her and Mrs. Kenyon. "No," she said with a deep sigh, "I'm not forgetting that they are here. I just don't understand how you could return the children to someone who has been in prison—"

Mrs. Kenyon held her hand up to silence her. "We do have men and women who have served time in the past and now make excellent parents. There are no previous reports of any complaints regarding Mr. Quill and the children in question. He is a businessman with a good income and well able to provide for his family—"

Sarah couldn't hold back any longer. "Are you blind—or are you just stupid?"

"Sarah!" Colin gasped.

But she couldn't stop now. "You must be blind if you can't see that these children have been neglected, abused, abandoned, mistreated—"

"Mrs. Hill! Please control yourself!"

But it was becoming all too clear now that the two girls were going to be thrust back into the hell that they had been so recently plucked out of. Sarah felt a crushing pain in her chest. "Please..." she pleaded. "Please don't send them back there..."

"I promised her..." Colin said in a broken voice, as he looked down at Verena.

Mrs. Kenyon stood to her feet. "You both can leave now. We will keep the children here until—"

Sarah didn't hear any more as uncontrollable sobs shook her body. "No, no, no..." she cried.

Colin put his arm around her and Emmeline came to stand close beside her. "Don't cry, Mommy," she said. "I won't let them take us away from you."

Sarah took a shuddering breath and reined in her emotions. *Oh, Emmeline...* She managed a tremulous smile for the brave little girl at her side.

But when Verena slid away from the safety of Colin's lap to comfort her also, Sarah almost broke down again. Verena, it seemed, had no idea of what had just been decided about her future.

"Mommy?" she said, thrusting her little face in close to Sarah's. "What's wrong, Mommy? Are you feeling sick again?"

chapter twenty-eight

"We—we have to say goodbye to you, Verena," Sarah said.

The little girl spun around, seeking confirmation from Colin. "Like—like before?" she asked. "Can I have your card again?"

Sarah looked over at Colin. He had tears in his eyes. Verena had grabbed hold of his arm and was hanging on for dear life.

"We need more time," Colin pleaded.

Sarah looked across the desk at the director. Could they expect mercy where there was no justice?

"You were given time," she said, obviously referring to the two o'clock deadline given by Ms. Richards. Mrs. Kenyon stared at them for a long time as they huddled together. "You've booked a hotel for tonight?" she finally asked.

Sarah nodded faintly. *What did it matter?*

"You can have till ten o'clock tomorrow morning. Ms. Richards and Mr. Quill are both flying in this evening." She paused before continuing. "You *must* have those children ready at that time. Have I made myself very, very clear?"

Sarah bowed her head. She heard Colin giving his assent but everything in her rose up in protest against the injustice of it all.

"Sarah!"

She heard the desperation in Colin's voice and lifted her head to meet his tear-filled eyes. "Yes," she said. "We will do as you say."

"And I'm sure you will understand why we are removing your name from the list of prospective foster parents and prospective adoptive parents. I'm very sorry but I'm sure that you can understand."

Sarah knew that she *didn't* understand, but she was suddenly desperate to leave this office, so that they could spend what short time they had left together as a family.

Colin, at Mrs. Kenyon's request, called Bill's cell phone to ask the room number and name of their hotel. Bill gave him the information, adding that he was out in the lobby waiting for them, whenever they were ready to go.

"Ten o'clock!" the director reminded them as they hurried together out the door.

"So, what's the plan?" Bill quipped, once they were all back in the rental car. "Please tell me it's not 'next stop: Mexico'."

Sarah was in no mood for Bill's humor. She let Colin answer him. "Just back to the hotel will be fine for now."

There was a lengthy silence in the car as Bill wound through the downtown rush-hour traffic.

"They're being returned to Russell," Colin said in a bleak voice, just as they turned off Portage Avenue into the parking lot of the hotel.

"What!" The car swerved dangerously, narrowly missing a row of parked vehicles. Bill pulled the car into a parking spot and turned off the ignition. "You've got to be kidding!" he exclaimed, turning so that he could see both Colin in the front seat and Sarah in the back.

"We need to have them back at the agency in the morning," Sarah said wearily.

Bill took a moment to digest the information. Then in a voice filled with compassion, he asked, "What can I do to help?"

"There's nothing," Sarah said sadly.

Colin laid a hand on Bill's shoulder. "We really appreciate everything that you and Jamie have already done."

"You're—you're not going to fight it?" Bill asked.

Sarah shook her head.

"I think we've kinda tried that already," Colin said in a weary voice.

No one spoke again until they were inside the hotel lobby. Then Bill asked, "So, what are your plans for the rest of the day?"

"Guess we'll take the girls somewhere special. Maybe the Assiniboine Zoo." Colin smiled down at Emmeline and Verena. "What do you say? Would you like to go to the zoo? I think you'll like it. I remember my mom and dad taking me there when I was your age."

For a moment Sarah couldn't swallow past the lump in her throat. If Colin had been about the same age as the girls, that placed the zoo visit not long before his parents died in a plane crash when he was seven. The zoo obviously held bittersweet memories for him. "Are you sure," she asked gently.

He smiled at her. "Yes," he said decisively. And Sarah understood. This was his farewell gift to the girls, sharing with them a favorite place, and happy memories, from his childhood.

"I just booked the one room," Bill said, handing them a keycard. "Unless you need me here..."

"No, we'll be fine," Colin said. "Thanks for everything."

Bill handed him the rental car keys also. "I can just take the airport shuttle," he said.

Colin and Sarah thanked him again and headed out to the car.

The children were quiet on the way there but once they reached the zoo, they quickly lost their solemnity, eagerly pulling Sarah and Colin from one exhibit to the next. They saw various kinds of bears, the "Down Under" exhibit with kangaroos and wallabies, and as they walked further along, owls and pheasants and eagles. But the part that Emmeline and Verena most enjoyed was the monkeys. Sarah watched with delight as the girls pointed and giggled at the monkeys' antics.

By the time their journey had taken them to the Animal Tracks Café, Sarah was more than ready for a break. And it seemed everyone had worked up an appetite, eagerly consuming hamburgers and French fries and juice.

Colin had picked up a zoo map and had been poring over it as they ate. "I knew it!" he exclaimed suddenly, as Sarah dampened a napkin and wiped ketchup from around the girls' mouths.

Sarah grinned at him. "What?"

"I thought I remembered a train ride that I took when I was here as a kid. Look, here it is!"

Caught up in his excitement, they walked back to the parking lot and drove over to the miniature train station, where they bought tickets and climbed aboard for a ride. The brightly painted metal cars were open on the sides, affording a beautiful view of the park as they rode through it. As they rounded a bend, the train whistle sounded and Sarah exchanged happy smiles with Colin and the girls.

After the ride was over, they drove back and continued their tour of the zoo, starting at the Tropical House, where Emmeline in particular was impressed with all the snakes and lizards and other "creepy crawlies" as Sarah called them.

Suddenly, they heard an announcement that the zoo would be closing in fifteen minutes! "But we didn't get to see everything yet!" Colin exclaimed.

"We have to go?" Emmeline asked, her face mirroring her disappointment.

"Can we come back tomorrow?" Verena asked, with a quivering lip.

"No, stupid!" Emmeline snapped. "They have to give us back tomorrow."

"Emmeline…" Sarah gently rebuked. "Don't call your sister bad names. No, I'm sorry, Verena; we can't come back tomorrow."

They started walking towards the exit, the girls' excitement forgotten, their faces downcast. Then Colin saw the Zootique Gift Shop, and pointed it out to Sarah. "Maybe we could buy something to remember our day together," he suggested.

Emmeline and Verena perked up a little as they began to shop. Sarah chose T-shirts for all of them, Emmeline picked out a stuffed toy tiger for herself, and Verena chose a monkey. As they headed to the checkout to pay, Colin stopped in front of a display of cute animal-themed flotation devices. He nudged Sarah and said in a low voice, "You brought their swimsuits, right?"

Sarah nodded. "Yes, but—oh, what a good idea! I was thinking we might try out the hotel pool when we get back and these flotation devices are perfect… maybe it will help Emmeline and Verena to not be so afraid of the water."

The girls helped pick out a couple of friendly looking inflatable crocodiles and happily carried them back to the rental car.

Arriving back at their hotel, Sarah felt a sudden wave of fatigue and eyed the beds with longing... they looked so comfortable. "Can we maybe just rest a wee bit before we go swimming?" she asked. "Maybe watch a little TV?"

"Sure," Colin agreed. "I do want to talk to the girls anyway. Maybe now would be a good time."

Sarah needed no further encouragement. She eased down onto one of the beds and propped herself up in a sitting position with a couple of pillows. Emmeline grabbed a pillow from the other bed and climbed up beside her. "Where's the remote?" she asked.

Colin pulled up a chair close beside the bed. "Wait, honey, I want to talk a bit with you and Verana first, okay?"

Verena, somehow sensing that the "talk" would once more be focused on their leaving, came up beside Colin and said in a quavering voice, "I want to go see the pool."

"We will soon, honey," Colin said, pulling her up onto his lap. "Come and sit here for just a minute."

Sarah reached over and squeezed his hand as Colin began in a hesitant voice. "Sometimes, we can't always be with the people that we love..."

Verena turned her face into his shoulder. Colin gently pulled her away and looked lovingly into her eyes as he continued, "But even if we can't be with you anymore, we can pray for you and ask God to take care of you." He glanced over at Emmeline, including her as he continued, "While we're apart, we're going to pray for you every single day."

"And God will do what you tell Him to do?" Emmeline asked.

"Not exactly," Colin said with a faint smile. "He's still the boss. And sometimes we think we know what's best and we don't really. But it says in the Bible that God does want to give us the things that we ask for, just like a father..." his voice broke, and the last words emerged as a hoarse whisper "...wants to give good gifts to his children."

"Why don't you ask Him then?" Emmeline demanded.

Sarah looked over at Colin, but he was still struggling to get his emotions under control, so she said, "Ask Him what, honey?"

"You know!" Emmeline retorted angrily. "Why don't you ask Him to make us stay with you?"

Sarah searched her heart for an answer to the little girl's question. *We did ask. We did pray...but they're still going to take you away from us...*

"Oh, Emmy..." she said, feeling at a loss for words.

Verena asked again in a sad, quiet, voice, "Can we go see the pool now?"

Sarah glanced over at Colin, who shook his head. "Just a little bit longer..." He looked down at Verena and then at Emmeline. "What I want you both to know," he said gently, "is that God loves you. He loves you even more than Sarah and I do. But the bad things that we have done make a break in our friendship with God... but He loved us so much that He made a way for us to be friends with Him again. God became a man—His name was Jesus—and He took *all* of the blame for *all* of the bad things that *all* of the people in the world have done. And because He took the blame for all the bad things we have done, He also had to take the punishment for all of those things, which was death."

"So the bad things that I've done made Jesus die?" Emmeline exclaimed.

Colin nodded. "And the bad things that I've done and the bad things that Sarah has done—and the bad things that Verena has done. But, honey, the reason Jesus took the punishment was so that we could be friends with God again. That's what He wanted—that's why He did it—so that we could be forgiven."

Emmeline scrunched up her nose. "Forgiven?"

"Yes, when God forgives us, the bad things that we have done don't get in the way of us being friends with God. The Bible says that God doesn't remember them anymore. He buries them in the deepest sea. He makes them as far away as the east is from the west."

Emmeline scrunched up her nose again as she looked in one direction and then another. Sarah smiled. She could just about see the little wheels turning in Emmeline's head! Suddenly, a huge grin burst over the little girl's face. "I get it!" she exclaimed.

Colin laughed. "It's pretty far away, isn't it?"

Emmeline nodded, happy to share the moment with him. But then her face fell. "I don't think I'm forgiven. I've done lots of bad stuff."

Colin smiled gently at her. "The Bible says that if we tell God about all that bad stuff, He will make things right between us again. It's like if you broke something special that belonged to Sarah, and she knew you did it, but you never ever said sorry—you would both stay sad about it. But if you talked to Sarah about it, then she could tell you that she forgives you—and that she will always, always love you." Colin leaned towards the little girl. "Emmeline, do you want to be friends with God?"

The little girl considered. "Is He like you?"

Colin smiled and shook his head. "No, honey, but I hope that I'm just a little bit like Him. I do want to be as much like Jesus as I can."

"Then He took the children in His arms, placed His hands on each of them, and blessed them," Emmeline quoted from memory.

"Yes," Colin said softly. He gently placed one hand on Verena's shoulder and one on Emmeline's, and with a shaky voice, began to pray. "O God, You know how much I love these kids. I pray Your blessing on them. I pray that good will come to them. That they will have happiness and—and that no one will hurt them…"

"Ask Him," Emmeline urged.

"You can pray too, Emmy," Sarah said gently.

"Okay." The little girl began, speaking each word slowly and thoughtfully. "Dear Jesus, I want to live forever and ever with my new Mommy and my new Daddy—or maybe just till I grow up. That bad lady wants to take us away. Can you make her dead or something?"

"Emmy—no!" Sarah gasped.

"Well—maybe just sick then."

"No, Emmy," Sarah said, but had to bite her lip to keep back a smile. "Just ask God for what you want and let Him figure out how to do it, okay?"

"Okay," Emmeline said in a resigned tone. "Dear God, I guess I already told You what I want but maybe You won't listen 'cause I've been bad."

Sarah was about to interrupt again but felt a slight pressure on her hand from Colin. He was right; this was Emmeline's conversation with the Lord and she *was* interrupting.

"I hurt Rosalee," the little girl confessed, "but I won't do that again because Rosalee is really nice. And I broke Mommy's dishes and messed up the kitchen but Michael and me cleaned it all up. And I hurt my other baby-sitters before and those kids that came over one time. And I hurt my sister, Verena. I don't want to hurt her anymore. I want to take care of her and not let her eat garbage anymore 'cause she's not garbage. And I hurt Mommy, too—my other Mommy—the one that's dead. Maybe I made her get dead..."

"No!" This time both Sarah and Colin cried out.

Emmeline folded her arms in front of her and stared at her feet. "I can't pray," she said angrily. "I don't know how to pray."

"Oh, Emmy, I'm so sorry for interrupting you again," Sarah said. "But honey, you have to know that it wasn't your fault that your mother died. And it wasn't your fault either, Verena. And you were praying just fine, Emmeline. Praying is just talking to God. I guess it's not so bad that I interrupted you, either, because we can talk to God, and then to each other, and then to God again."

"I wasn't done," Emmeline said in a tiny, sad voice.

Colin and Sarah locked eyes, and Sarah wondered if he was thinking the same thing that she was. *What more was this little girl carrying around on her conscience?*

"I did bad things with Daddy," Emmeline whispered, with downcast eyes.

Sarah felt her heart breaking as Colin gently said, "That wasn't your fault either."

"And now I hate him. I hate him! *I hate him!*" Emmeline shouted.

Verena began to weep, as she turned her face into Colin's shoulder, away from the storm of her sister's emotions.

"It's bad to hate. But I don't care," Emmeline said fiercely. "I still hate him."

"Oh, Emmy," Sarah gently stroked the little girl's hair away from her face, "what you're feeling is *anger* towards your father. And you *should* be angry, because he hurt you when he should have been protecting you and taking good care of you." She tipped Emmeline's chin up, and gazed into her pain-filled eyes. "It makes *me* angry, too."

"And me, too," Colin said in a hoarse whisper.

Verena raised her head and declared fiercely, "Me too!"

Sarah smiled through her tears. "Emmy, did you know that God gets angry, too? And He hates, too. He doesn't hate people but He hates the bad things that they do to each other, and He especially hates it when people hurt little kids. Do you know what Jesus said about that?"

"No," Emmeline answered in a wondering voice.

"He said that somebody who hurts little kids would be better off having a great big stone tied around their neck and being drowned in the bottom of the ocean."

Emmeline was silent for a moment. Then a big smile came on her face. "God must be really big and strong."

"Yes, He is," Sarah said, smiling back at her.

"Can we go see the pool now?" Emmeline asked.

Colin laughed, and wiped tears from the corners of his eyes. "Yes, we can go see the pool now." He stood to his feet, lowering Verena to the floor as he did so. "How about you, kiddo?" he asked her, remaining crouched down at her eye level. "Do you know that you can talk to Jesus anytime and anywhere? You don't

321

have to be with us and you don't even have to talk out loud when you pray."

Verena nodded her head, a little smile beginning to chase away the sadness on her face and in her eyes. "I'm going to pray that I can stay with you, Daddy," she declared solemnly.

Colin wrapped her tightly in his arms. "So am I, honey. So am I."

"Colin..." Sarah cautioned gently.

He drew in a deep breath, his eyes clouded with pain. Then he pulled away from Verena a little so he could see her face as he said, "Even if you don't get to stay with us, you remember that you're never alone. You can always, always pray and ask God to help you. And remember that I'll always, always love you, no matter what."

Verena flew back into his arms. "And I love you too, Daddy."

Sarah gave Emmeline a hug. "And I love you, too."

"And I love you, too." Colin let go of Verena to embrace Emmeline.

"And I love you, too," Emmeline said. Then she began to giggle as Sarah said the same words to Verena and she said them back.

Colin's eyes were shining with love as he and Sarah exchanged the words as solemnly as if they were wedding vows.

And finally, in quiet, shy voices, Emmeline and Verena said to each other, "I love you, too."

Joy flooded Sarah's heart as she laughingly declared. "*Now* let's go check out that pool!"

chapter twenty-nine

As Sarah opened their suitcases to get out the girls' swimsuits, she saw the gift bags from Russell that she'd hastily packed in on top of their clothes. Emmeline and Verena had so far shown no interest in opening them. *Maybe they can open them when they're back with Russell...* Her mind recoiled at the thought and she quickly snatched out their swimsuits and closed the lids of the suitcases. If this was their last evening together, Sarah was determined to make it a good one.

They took the elevator from the third floor down to the first, squeezing into the small space with the two freshly inflated grinning crocodiles.

As they walked through the glass door to the heated indoor pool area, Sarah looked around appreciatively. The atmosphere was that of a tropical oasis. Large potted ferns and umbrella trees surrounded the deck chairs and tall fig trees reached towards the skylights set into the high ceiling. They were the only ones there on this Thursday evening; likely the pool would become a lot busier on the weekend.

Colin set the two crocodiles down and with a loud whoop, took a run for it and cannon-balled into the middle of the pool.

Sarah laughed at his antics but the girls, huddled close around her, stared wide-eyed at him and at the large pool of water before them. Colin grinned at the trio. "C'mon in!" he called.

Sarah knelt and put an arm around each girl. "Ready to go in?" she asked cheerily.

But they both shook their heads. Sarah sat down on the edge of the pool and gently pulled them down with her. "Let's just sit here for a while and dangle our feet in the water," she suggested.

After some persuasion, the girls first gingerly touched the surface of the water before letting their feet and ankles get wet.

Colin swam over to them. "You guys have never been to a pool before, have you?"

Emmeline and Verena shook their heads.

"But you've been to a lake...?"

"With Rosalee and Michael," Emmeline answered. "But it was kind of scary—for Verena."

Colin smiled at her. "Maybe it won't be so scary for Verena—and for you—if I'm in here with you." He reached out and pulled the two floatation devices into the water. "Of course, you know..." he drawled in a deep, theatrical voice. "These here waters are infested with crocodiles."

That produced a giggle from Emmeline and a shy smile from Verena. Colin, thus encouraged, assumed now the voice of a circus ring leader, challenging his audience—"So which of you fine young ladies will dare to venture into this crocodile infested swamp and..." With a raised eyebrow and a wicked grin, he swept a pointing finger at them. "Who will dare to ride inside this man-eating crocodile?"

Emmeline giggled. "I'll go. If he's just a *man*-eating crocodile."

Colin threw back his head and laughed. Then he reached up and put his arms around her waist. He held her high in the air so her feet still just touched the water before gently lowering her down into the pocket seat of the floatation device.

He didn't release her right away but held her until she smiled and said, "It's okay, Daddy." She began to move her dangling legs and paddle with her arms on either side of the floating toy as Colin watched approvingly.

Sarah clapped from the sidelines and congratulated Emmeline on her fine crocodile-riding skills. Colin swam back over to Verena. "You next?" he asked, putting his arms around her waist. Verena smiled as he lifted her high into the air and then slowly lowered her into the other floatation device. Sarah exchanged happy grins with Colin and slid down into the pool to join them.

It didn't take long before Verena was confident enough to paddle along on her own, too. Then Colin and Verena teamed up against Sarah and Emmeline for the "Ultimate Crocodile War" which involved a lot of splashing, laughter and fun.

"Okay, okay, I surrender!" Sarah finally called.

"Hey, you can't quit yet," Colin protested.

She leaned across and kissed him. "I'm declaring a truce. That chair over there is calling my name," she said, pointing to a lounge chair by the edge of the pool.

"Okay," Colin conceded. "But you girls aren't going to abandon ship, are you?"

"No, Daddy!" they both chorused.

The laughter and splashing had already resumed even before Sarah pulled herself up out of the pool and sank down into a lounge chair. She glanced around the room, thankful that they still had the whole place to themselves—the girls might not be able to relax and enjoy themselves the same way if there were strangers around.

But there was someone—staring at them through the glass door... *No, it couldn't be! Not him. Not here. Not now!*

Her first impulse was to turn and warn Colin, but then her eyes met Russell's, and something in his demeanor held her back. Then he suddenly turned and walked away. Sarah glanced towards the pool where Colin and the two children were still playing— they obviously hadn't seen Russell. *How long had he been standing there watching them?* Had he purposely chosen to stay at the same hotel as them? But how could he have known?

She bit her lip in indecision. Should she tell Colin? What if Russell tried to forcefully take the children? No—he didn't need to—the law had given him custody.

She tried to relax while keeping an eye on the spot where he'd stood, silently praying that he wouldn't return.

Finally she could stand it no longer. "Hey, guys!" she called. "Can we go back to our room soon? Maybe we can rent a movie and order a pizza?"

Colin swam over to her, trailing the two child-filled crocodiles with him. "You sure are hungry these days, Mrs. Hill," he said with a wide grin. "Eating for two, are you?"

"And I'm making up for all the food I don't get to eat in the mornings," Sarah said.

"Well, let's go feed Mom and the baby!" Colin lifted each of the girls out and set them on the pool deck.

As they headed off to their room, Sarah decided not to say anything about Russell. They would be safe enough locked securely in their hotel room. And she didn't want anything to ruin their last evening together.

Russell barely made it back to his room before uncontrollable sobs burst out of him. *What was happening to him? He never cried! Never!* Not since he was a little kid—not since he was six, when he'd found his mother's lifeless body hanging out in the woodshed.

He'd run to fetch his father, who had cut the rope and callously let her body drop to the sawdust covered floor. He had been unable to stop crying even though his father ordered him to. Amos had found a way to make him stop, though—he'd beaten him until he'd fallen unconscious to the floor beside his mother's body. When he came to, in a bed at his aunt's house, alone and afraid, he vowed that as long as he lived, he would never again shed a single tear.

And he had kept that vow... until the night before, lying in the hospital near to death. And now. Now he was sobbing like— *like a six-year-old!* It angered Russell to feel so out of control, *so helpless!*

And all these tears simply because he'd witnessed joy on his children's faces! It didn't make sense. Why was it tearing him apart—breaking his heart!

They were having such a good time with Colin and Sarah...

Russell groaned. *That was it!* That was what pierced through his soul like a knife—they were laughing and having a good time with Colin and Sarah—*but they had cowered and run away from him!*

With a sudden, sharp clarity, Russell knew that he was not fit to be a father.

And as the memory of that awful day so long ago flashed through his mind once more, Russell wondered if his delight in hurting other people had begun then. He recalled that as he'd lain bruised and bleeding in his aunt's house, his younger brothers, Garby and Bryan, had come trailing into the room, crying and babbling that Mommy was dead. A dark anger had enveloped him and he'd dragged himself off the bed and beaten the five and three year old into terrified silence. He remembered smiling afterwards, not knowing why—but feeling strangely content. Now Russell realized that something human had died in him that day—some necessary ingredient that he needed to be a good father.

Since then he had hurt so many others, always those who were weaker than him. It had made him feel strong—strong enough to face the next day and the next. He had lived for the intoxicating rush that came from beating someone into submission, whether verbally, physically or both. And he'd delighted in the easy destruction of sexual abuse: so little effort was required to wreak such great devastation.

His cruelty robbed all those around him of their strength and confidence, yet even as he achieved his goal, and his victims cowered before him in fear, he'd despised and mocked their weakness, insisting that they should be strong—like him!

He'd done that with Verena—he could see that now. He'd not given her a chance to be anything but fearful and then he'd despised her because of that fear. And Emmeline... Emmeline was going to be just like him. Strong, addicted to power... Cruel and cold-hearted...

He'd done this to them—he had destroyed his children's lives...

Once more, the unbearable weight of his sins crushed him into a sobbing, crumpled heap on the hotel room floor.

chapter thirty

Even though the children's movie that they'd rented was only half over, Sarah and the children were already asleep. Colin eased off the bed, careful not to wake anyone. He turned off the television before scooping up Verena and Emmeline and tucking them into the other big double bed, glad that they were already wearing their pajamas.

Sarah in her nightshirt was also ready for bed. He shook her gently, softly calling her name. She awoke enough to climb under the covers then her eyes promptly closed again. Colin tenderly pulled the covers up around her, smoothed her hair back and kissed her on the cheek.

He'd been tired during the day, but now felt too restless and anxious for sleep. Quietly he moved the desk chair over by the wall opposite the bathroom, where they'd left a light on for the girls, and in the muted glow began to read his Bible.

Still thinking about his earlier conversation with Emmeline about prayer, he opened up the eleventh chapter of Luke and read the first verse, where the disciples asked Jesus to teach them to pray. Then he read through the next four verses—the familiar "Lord's Prayer." But his eyes kept being drawn back to the one phrase, "Forgive us our sins, for we forgive everyone who does us wrong." Then his focus was narrowed down to just the words: "for we forgive everyone who does us wrong."

He recognized the voice of the Holy Spirit asking, "Are you ready to forgive, Colin?"

And his heart cried out, *"No! No! I can't!"*

Then the story of the Apostle Paul's conversion came to Colin's mind, and he flipped through the pages until he reached the ninth chapter of Acts. Paul had thrown many followers of Christ into prison, and had even persecuted some Christians to death. But after Paul was himself converted, through a miraculous vision of Jesus on the road to Emmaus, the Christians did not immediately accept him. They were afraid of him; they didn't believe that he had really become a follower of Christ, and feared that he meant to betray them all. But finally, one man believed him, forgave him, and spoke up on his behalf to the leaders of the church...

Colin abruptly stood up, a great battle raging within him. What was the Lord trying to get through to him—was He really asking him to forgive Russell, as Barnabas had forgiven Paul?

But he's shown no signs of repentance, he thought frantically.

A small still voice whispered, *What if he did?*

"I wouldn't believe him!" Quickly he looked around the room, checking that his outburst hadn't disturbed anybody.

Then the phone rang and Colin leapt forward to silence it.

"Hello," he whispered, glancing over towards the beds, where Emmeline now lay awake, watching his every move. He smiled reassuringly at her but as the voice on the other end spoke his name, Colin turned quickly away so she wouldn't see the fear that was knotting his stomach and tightening his chest. *No, he wouldn't give in to it!*

Angrily, he hissed into the phone. "What do you want?"

"Just to talk with you," Russell answered quietly. "I'm in room 304."

Colin's heart beat wildly. *Russell was here, right now, in this very hotel and on the same floor as them!* Talking with him was the very last thing he wanted to do, but what if he refused? Would Russell come to their room, bang on the door, demand to be admitted? Thinking quickly, Colin realized he'd have to ensure the confrontation happened away from Sarah and the children.

"I'll meet you at the front desk," he finally whispered into the phone, and hung up. At least there'd be someone to call the police if he needed assistance...

He said a quick prayer then walked quietly over to Emmeline with what he hoped was a reassuring smile on his face. "You should be sleeping, sweetie," he said.

"Are you okay, Daddy?" she asked, a pensive look on her little face.

Colin perched on the edge of her bed, and smoothed back her hair. "Yes, everything's fine. You go back to sleep now and don't worry."

Emmeline yawned. "I'm not worried, Daddy. I prayed to God and He's going to make us live with you. Nobody's going to take us away from you."

Her eyes drooped shut and even after he knew that she was asleep, Colin stayed by her side for a few more minutes, thinking that though he'd been a follower of Jesus for many years now, his faith was nowhere near what this little child's was!

Eventually he took a deep breath and stood up—Russell was waiting. Pocketing the keycard, he slipped quietly out of the room, carefully closing the door behind him, and walked quickly down the hallway towards the elevator.

At the last moment he decided to take the stairs instead, worried that the elevator might take too long and that the few minutes he'd spent with Emmeline might have already taxed Russell's patience. Colin ran down the two flights of stairs, envisioning Russell storming up to their room and pounding on the door.

But when Colin arrived breathless in the hotel lobby, he found Russell sitting quietly, reading a paper. He stood to his feet with a sardonic smile when he saw Colin. "Thought maybe you weren't coming."

"I'm here," Colin said, struggling to bring his breathing under control. "What do you want?"

Russell took a step towards him. "Just to talk with you."

He seemed so sincere! But Russell had always been a world-class actor.

"So talk," Colin said impatiently.

Russell sighed and glanced over at the desk attendant. "It's kinda private. Can we go to my room?"

Colin stared at him. "You've *got* to be kidding!"

"I know you have no reason to trust me…"

Colin couldn't quell the anger that was rising up within him. After all the terrible things that Russell had done to him, and to so many of the people that Colin cared for, now he wanted Colin to *trust* him?

"Please… I won't hurt you. I really do just want to talk."

Colin, remembering his vow that he would no longer live in fear of this man, struggled to know how to respond. If he refused to go to his room, would that make him *afraid*... or just smart? Finally he nodded his assent. But frustration boiled up inside him and he spat out the words, "You always get what you want, don't you?"

Russell lowered his eyes, staring at the floor that stretched between them. "No, not always." He glanced up. "I wanted a second chance..." His eyes fell to the floor again. "But it's not for me."

You got that right! You don't deserve a second chance!

Colin turned angrily away, determined again to leave, when Russell suddenly cried out, "Please, Colin! I don't know anyone else that I can talk to. I tried to call Pastor Thomas but there was no answer."

Colin turned back. "Why would you want to talk to him?"

Russell's eyes burned with intensity. "I want to confess my sins. I want to—*have to*—tell someone that I'm sorry for what I did."

Colin's heart raced and he could feel his throat closing up.

Now, Colin. Now's the time.

But still Colin struggled. *No, I can't. I can't!* But he willed his voice to speak a single word—"Okay."

The relief was so obvious on Russell's face that Colin wondered, for an instant, if he might really be sincere.

Neither of them spoke as they rode up to the third floor on the elevator and then walked down the hall. Before following Russell in, Colin quickly scanned the room... but there was no accomplice lying in wait. Stepping in, he shook his head when Russell offered him the one chair in the room; he'd stand.

Russell smiled wanly and took the chair himself. But now that he had Colin in the room with him, he seemed at a loss for words.

Colin, anxious to get the visit over with, broke the silence. "So why the sudden urge to confess your sins?" he asked, unable to keep the sarcasm out of his voice.

Russell stared at the floor again and was silent for a long time. When he finally looked up, there were tears in his eyes. "I saw Jesus," he said.

Colin shook his head angrily. "There's no one here but us, Russell. There's no one to impress. You've already got custody of your kids again."

"I don't want them!" Russell cried, jumping to his feet.

Colin, with a great effort, remained where he was. "I *know* you don't want them. But you don't want me to have them, either."

"No! It's not like that!" Russell almost shouted the words in a voice choked with tears. "I'm going to sign a paper tomorrow. I want you to adopt them."

Colin felt his heart begin to beat faster. Could it really be true?

He'd never seen Russell this emotional even when he was... "Are you drunk?"

Russell groaned and walked unsteadily past him to the door. "Maybe—maybe I'll wait for Pastor Thomas..."

Colin's conscience smote him. What if Russell really was sincere?

"Russell..."

He was leaning against the wall by the door, and didn't turn around as Colin spoke in a halting voice. "I'm listening—if you want to talk."

335

When Russell swung around, the ravaged look on his face startled Colin... he looked much older than his 41 years. With a stab of guilt, Colin remembered that Russell had been in critical care just the night before...

"Why don't you sit back down again," he said. "Would you like a glass of water or something?"

Russell shook his head. "There's some Pepsi in the little bar fridge over there though, if you want some."

As Colin bent down to retrieve a couple of bottles, Russell collapsed back into the chair. Colin opened one and handed it to Russell, who absently took a sip and then set it down again.

"Colin, I really did see Jesus," he began again in an earnest voice.

Colin's heart was beating like a jackhammer but he merely nodded and said, "Can you tell me about it?"

Russell smiled nervously. "This is kind of hard for me, you know..."

He sounded so sincere. *Maybe he was sincere.* Colin nodded again.

"It's when I was in the hospital—yesterday." Russell shook his head. "It seems like a lifetime ago."

Colin's throat felt dry. He unscrewed the lid from the Pepsi and took a swallow.

"I think that I really did come close to dying," Russell continued. "At least I thought that I was going to die and maybe that's all that matters. The doctors and nurses had been coming in non-stop it seemed but suddenly, it was all quiet and I felt as if I was completely alone. Then like some movie trailer, I saw my whole life in a series of flashes from when I was a little kid up till now. I saw the things that I'd done." Russell bowed his head.

"And I saw all the kids that I'd hurt." Russell raised his eyes for an instant and then winced and lowered them again. "You were there, too," he said.

Everything in Colin was shouting, telling him *Run! Run! He's just stringing you a line—the best one yet!* But another quieter voice rose slowly above it. *The Lord is with you. Don't be afraid. The Lord is with you.*

Russell was speaking again, his eyes still cast down. "I heard them crying. All the children crying. And my own kids too. Crying and crying... 'No, Daddy! Stop! Stop!' Crying... and pleading with me..."

A very vivid picture of tormented children, pleading for Russell to stop, flashed through Colin's mind, dissolving any ounce of sympathy he might have felt for the man. He watched dispassionately as Russell swiped at the tears that were cascading down his cheeks.

"Then..." Russell swallowed hard and made a visible effort to control his emotions enough to speak. "Then everything got really quiet—and—and I saw *Him.*"

Russell was looking at Colin now, waiting... Colin forced himself to look steadily back and nod, indicating that Russell should continue.

"I—I couldn't see His face or anything but I knew—*I just knew somehow*—that it was Jesus. And—and He loved me. *He loved me!*"

Colin blinked and swallowed hard, trying to keep sudden tears from welling up in his own eyes. He could feel the fear in his heart melting into hope—and something more.

"I couldn't believe it," Russell continued in a hoarse whisper. "I knew that He forgave me. *I hadn't even asked Him!* He knew that I wouldn't dare to ask." Russell searched Colin's eyes. "It's so hard to explain. It all happened in a moment of time and He didn't even have to say anything. It was just like I suddenly knew and could feel that He loved me—and that He'd forgiven me."

"I do know what you mean," Colin acknowledged softly, no longer fighting the tears for there was no mistaking the character and presence of Jesus in Russell's vision. Colin himself had encountered that same unconditional love.

The gratitude in Russell's eyes was undeniably genuine.

"There's more," he said.

"More?" Colin asked incredulously. What more could there possibly be?

Russell's face lit up with a beautiful smile. "He spoke to me."

"But I thought you said..."

"That was about me," Russell said in a soft voice. "And it all happened in an instant. But when He spoke—it was about my kids."

Colin's heart started to beat faster again. *Emmeline... Verena...*

"The words that Jesus said were, 'Give your kids a second chance.'"

Colin couldn't speak—could barely even breathe.

"I thought he was talking about me," Russell said sadly. "Then I saw the kids at Jamie's house and I wasn't so sure anymore. Then, earlier this evening, I watched you guys in the pool—and that's when I knew. He meant that I should give them a second chance—with you and Sarah."

"But—I—do you mean...?"

"I mean that I will do everything in my power to ensure that you and Sarah are the ones who raise my daughters," Russell confirmed.

"But—you've been given custody..."

338

Russell smiled sadly. "I think they'll be changing their minds in just a short while."

Colin felt as if he was swimming through molasses. His brain simply refused to accept what Russell was saying. "They've already made the decision..."

The corners of Russell's mouth twitched into a semblance of a smile. "I'm planning on doing some confessing, as I told you before. Somebody might like to arrest me afterwards." He lifted an eyebrow. "Maybe it'll be you."

"I don't know if I could do that now."

"Oh, you probably could," Russell replied sardonically. Then he shook his head as if to clear his thoughts and began again in a gentler tone of voice. "I told you that you were one of the kids in my vision. When I saw my whole life... I saw you crying. You'd just lost your parents..."

Colin's mind flashed back to the day when his whole world had fallen apart.

Russell turned away as he continued. "I remember you cried every single night. I'd yell at you and hit you, and you'd be quiet—but the next night it would be the same thing all over again."

The pain of those nights rose up fresh in Colin's heart. "I—I felt so alone. So abandoned..."

"I'm sorry."

Colin stared at him in disbelief.

A wry smile just touched Russell's lips and was gone. "I don't expect you to believe me," he said in a sad, quiet voice, "but I really am sorry. I wish I could go back and undo all the terrible things I did to the people around me—so many people that I've hurt..." His voice trailed off as Russell bowed his head.

But Colin suddenly remembered another time—a time when Russell had been the one who was hurt. "I remember..." he said hesitantly, "just after I'd come to live at your house. You'd been out canoeing, hadn't pulled the canoe up far enough on the shore, and it had drifted away. Your father was so angry with you that he grabbed you by the neck and started banging your head against the wall. I hid behind the couch but I could hear your head hitting the wall over and over again. When I heard him slam the door as he left, I came out, and you were lying on the floor and I couldn't wake you up. That's when I ran and got your aunt..."

Great gasping sobs were shaking Russell's body and Colin longed to put a hand on his shoulder, to comfort him. But years of intimidation and fear were not so easily cast aside.

Finally Russell looked up and stared at Colin through pain-filled eyes. "I tried *so* hard to please him!" His voice was thick with anguish. "All I wanted was for him—just once—to be proud of me."

For a moment, Colin was too overcome to speak. But he knew he had to try. "Your daughters..." Colin swallowed back the tears. Soon they would be *his* daughters. "Emmeline and Verena—I will always tell them how precious they are—and that—I am very proud of them."

Russell leaned forward and stretched out his hand towards Colin. Colin clasped it, and Russell shook his hand firmly. "Thank you," he said.

They both rose to their feet and Russell shook his hand again.

If it had been anyone else, Colin knew, he would have given him a hug. But he couldn't do that to Russell—not yet—maybe not ever.

Russell seemed reluctant to let go of Colin's hand, to let him leave. Colin realized that it was probably the first time that he'd ever shared his heart with anyone.

"So I guess I'll see you in the morning..."

Russell nodded. "We're supposed to be there at nine-thirty."

Colin's heart skipped a beat. "We were told to be there at ten o'clock."

They would be waiting for them... waiting to take the children back.

"Colin..."

He looked into Russell's eyes and was amazed to find compassion there!

"If it's the last thing I do, I'll make sure that you get custody. I saw you with them in the pool. *They were laughing...*"

Russell's voice broke. Then he shook his head and attempted a smile. "And I'm going to end up crying again if I keep this up!"

Colin opened the door. "I'd better say goodnight then— brother."

Russell nodded solemnly and shook Colin's hand one last time. "Goodnight, brother."

As Colin returned to his own room, he felt like whooping and hollering and dancing and singing! He looked over at the two sleeping children and felt as if his heart would burst with joy. *Emmeline! Verena! I'm going to be your Daddy!* He wanted to wake them all up and tell them—but there would be time enough for that in the morning.

chapter thirty-one

Once again, Sarah woke up feeling ill. But unlike the morning before, she didn't find Verena eating from the garbage. Sarah prayed silently that she would never wake to that sight again.

Then, with a groan of dismay, she realized that she would never again wake to *any* view of the two girls. Today was the day...

They were still sleeping soundly, worn out from the day before Sarah guessed with a little smile. Then her smile faded. *Today was the day.*

Colin was still sleeping too. Sleeping like a baby...

Sarah placed a gentle hand on her still flat tummy... soon they would have their own child. For so many years she had longed to hold a baby in her arms—hers and Colin's. But now she wanted to hold Verena and Emmeline in her arms, too. She wanted to teach them how to swim and ride a bike and bake cookies. And she wanted to help them shop for school clothes and read them stories and help them with their homework and pack their lunches... Despair filled her heart and tears fell as she looked over at the sleeping girls. Today was the day when they were going to be returned to their father. Today was the day that they were going to be thrust back into a life of fear and pain and torment. Sarah shut her eyes again, feeling the crushing weariness of despair.

She must have drifted off to sleep again because when she next opened her eyes, Colin and the girls were already dressed and half-way through their breakfast, talking in hushed voices as they ate.

Colin noticed she was awake and leapt to his feet. "Good morning, sweetheart. Hope we didn't wake you. We were trying our best to be quiet as little mice."

Sarah stared at her husband. He was grinning from ear to ear! *What was the matter with him? Didn't he remember?*

"No, you didn't wake me," Sarah said moodily. It didn't help that she still felt nauseated, even after the extra sleep. She grabbed up some clothes and went to the bathroom, emerging a few minutes later, dressed and ready for the day.

Emmeline and Verena were finished eating and Colin was moving about the room, getting things packed up again.

"C'mon, girls," Sarah said. "You can brush your teeth while Da—while Colin—is finishing up here."

They obediently followed her into the bathroom, Sarah squeezed toothpaste onto their brushes, and they began to clean their teeth, looking into the wide mirror above the sink as they worked. Suddenly, another face appeared above theirs.

"You girls are doing a great job!" he told their reflections. Then he grinned at Sarah. "And the name's 'Daddy.'"

"Oh, Colin," she pleaded, "don't make this harder than it is."

"Sarah..." He drew her closer. "I'm sorry. I didn't mean to hurt you. But something happened last night. Something wonderful..."

"God answered my prayer!" Emmeline declared, her eyes shining with joy.

"Our old daddy's going to give us back to you," Verena said.

"What! How?" Sarah stammered, looking from one of them to the other. "But that's impossible!"

When Colin got done describing his visit with Russell, including Russell's vision of Jesus and the message to give his kids a second chance, Sarah was even more skeptical than before. This sure didn't sound like the Russell she knew!

Sarah glanced at the children's beaming faces and then back up at Colin again. "You believe him?" she asked doubtfully.

"Yeah," Colin said, "I really do."

Sarah shook her head. It still seemed so impossible! Maybe if she'd been there and heard for herself... But Colin knew Russell way better than she did—and Colin was no fool—he wouldn't be taken in by some fancy story that Russell had concocted.

"It's just really hard for me to believe," she said. "And what about the agency? Everything's already been decided. I don't think they're going to change their minds..."

Colin lovingly brushed back some curls from off her forehead. "I know, I know," he said softly. "But Sarah, we have to hang onto hope. Right now, it's all we have. But maybe it's enough. The Bible says that there is nothing that God cannot do."

"Show me, Daddy," Emmeline said.

Colin smiled happily and went to get the Gideon Bible from the drawer of the night table. Sarah and the girls followed after him as he flipped it open onto the desk top. "It's in the first chapter of the book of Luke and the thirty-seventh verse." Emmeline watched intently as Colin pointed to each word. "For there is nothing that God cannot do."

Emmeline's face broke into a huge smile. "I like that one," she said.

Colin grinned at her. "Me too. Now, who's going to help me pack up the last of our stuff?" Both girls clamored to help, and Sarah was relegated to resting on the bed until it was time to check out.

Upon their arrival at the agency, they were ushered into a room that they had never seen before. It was brightly decorated and contained comfortable chairs and lots of toys.

"But we were supposed to report to the director..." Sarah said.

Their escort nodded. "Yes, but the director has been unavoidably delayed. She requested that you wait for her in here."

Colin smiled reassuringly at Sarah and gave her a quick hug. Then he took Emmeline and Verena's hands and pulled them further into the room. "Wow!" he exclaimed, "a whole room full of toys! We don't mind waiting here for a while, do we girls?"

They seemed a little nervous at first but Colin's enthusiasm was contagious and soon they were all laughing and playing as if they didn't have a care in the world.

On the other side of the two-way mirror, a heated discussion was taking place.

"You see what I mean," Russell said wearily to Mrs. Kenyon, frustrated with her attitude and tired of arguing with her. Who did she think she was anyway? These were *his* kids. And he wanted them to be raised by Colin and Sarah. What was the problem?

For what seemed like the hundredth time, Mrs. Kenyon said, "But you are their father and you have been granted full custody."

Russell turned to face her. He had kept himself well under control so far, but felt as if the dam was about to burst. He tried to keep his voice down as he told her, "Later on today, or perhaps tomorrow, I am going to be walking into a police station and confessing to enough crimes to qualify me as an unfit parent for the entire remainder of my natural life. Before I do that, I want to ensure that my children will be safe and well cared for. What part of this are you having a problem with?"

Mrs. Kenyon retreated quickly behind her desk, putting a barrier between them. "You will need a lawyer," she said primly.

"I can get a dozen of them down here in five minutes. Where do you want them?"

She seemed even more taken aback. "They—they can meet here, I guess. But I think that perhaps just one will do."

"Fine," he replied impatiently, sitting down in one of the plush blue chairs and putting his feet up on the other, as he pulled out his cell phone.

"Yes," he said, "Tim Miller... no, I don't care that he's in a meeting. Tell him Russell Quill's on the line." Tim Miller was a brilliant lawyer, but one that he usually avoided like the plague; he was one of those "bleeding heart" types that Russell usually despised. But he figured that in this situation, that particular characteristic would work in his favor.

"Mr. Quill," a voice said coldly on the other end of the line. "What can I do for you?"

Russell wasted no time getting to the point, but it took a fair amount of convincing before Tim could wrap his head around the idea that Russell could—and did—genuinely care about someone besides himself.

Russell knew he'd succeeded when Tim started listing all the forms he would need to fill out. "You do realize that this could take some time," he said cautiously.

"I don't have time," Russell snapped.

Tim sounded more relieved than anything to hear the familiar tone from Russell. "I'll see what I can do," he said.

Russell was suddenly desperate. "I need everything settled *today*, Tim."

There was silence on the line then the young lawyer said slowly, "You do realize there will be some extra fees to fast-track the process."

Russell knew all about *extra fees* and he knew all about *fast-tracking,* too.

"Today, Tim," he repeated.

"Give me an hour to get things together."

Russell rang off and turned towards Mrs. Kenyon who was waiting expectantly. "Is there a computer I can use?" he asked.

The extreme look of alarm on her face answered his question. Russell rolled his eyes. "I wasn't planning on hacking into your system," he said sarcastically. "Just doing a few money transfers." He sighed dramatically. "Perhaps there's a fax machine that I can use?"

Mrs. Kenyon lifted her chin indignantly. "You may use this phone and this fax machine," she said, pointing to the equipment. "Anything else?"

Russell regarded her with amusement and shook his head slightly.

She sidled past him and opened the office door.

"Wait!" he called.

She startled and turned slowly around, her eyes fixed warily on him.

Russell smiled sardonically. "Just wanted to know if they could eat in there." He gestured towards the room on the other side of the mirror.

"Yes, I suppose so," Mrs. Kenyon said hesitantly. "What did you have in mind?"

Russell drew out a thick wallet and watched the woman's eyes grow wide at the sight of it. "I was thinking of coffee, juice and donuts for now, and some pizza at noon."

Mrs. Kenyon gladly relieved him of the hundred dollar bill he held out to her. "My secretary will certainly be able to see to this," she said, hurrying from the room.

Money talks, Russell thought grimly. And he'd better get a bit more of it flowing before his assets were frozen...

He had money salted away in a dozen accounts in different banks. Russell used his cell phone to call the banks and they agreed to fax over money transfer forms for him to sign and return to them.

As Russell made the phone calls, he walked over to the two-way mirror again to watch his children, knowing it might be a very long time before he saw them again—perhaps even forever. No, not forever. If nothing else, they would someday be reunited in heaven. There would be nothing between them then—no past sins. Russell knew enough now about Jesus to know that all would be forgiven—the slate wiped clean. He could freely love and be loved...

Russell watched in satisfaction as the donuts and juice arrived in the next room. But he suddenly noticed that there was something strange about the way that Verena was covertly trying to eat. It reminded him of...

He groaned in dismay as he remembered.

He would have been only about five when he'd befriended that stray dog. His mother used to sneak him scraps now and then to feed her—a *pregnant* her as he soon discovered. He'd eagerly waited for the puppies to be born and when they were, had been amazed at how skinny his dog became—he'd been able to count all her ribs! The puppies clambered for milk but it had been obvious that the mother didn't have enough to give. It had reminded him so much of his own life... his mother tried to look after them, tried to provide for them, but his father spent all the money on booze, leaving them all dirt poor and hungry.

As the puppies tumbled over each other and fought for the little bit of milk that their mother could give them, she would abruptly stand up, shake them off and walk away. The stronger puppies would tumble along after her until she laid down somewhere again but the weaker ones were unable to follow and, to Russell's dismay, one by one, they died. One day, when only two puppies were left, Russell watched as the mother dog walked slowly off into the bush, her head bent low. He waited for her to come back but she never did.

Determined to save the remaining puppies, Russell had soaked scraps of bread in water for them. Having learned the hard way that only the strongest survive, the puppies continued to fight each other as they ate. They would grab up a piece of soaked bread and instead of chewing it, would swallow it whole, all the time casting furtive glances at the other dog. And before those two puppies were even six weeks old, his father had caught Russell feeding them and had killed them both.

349

Russell felt tears rolling down his cheeks as he looked through the glass at Verena. She was like one of those puppies, stuffing her food into her mouth when no one was looking, furtively glancing around as if it would be snatched away at any moment. Russell shuddered—*had he done this to her?*

He knew he had.

Just then a courier arrived from Tim Miller's office and Russell quickly wiped away the tears, angry with himself for showing any sign of weakness. He had to be strong and fight for his kids!

Soon there was a steady stream of couriers coming and going, bearing multiple copies of documents from banks and lawyers. Then Tim Miller arrived with papers for Colin and Sarah to fill out. He also needed the agency to provide him with all the information and background checks that they held on Colin and Sarah, as he had already secured a judge who was willing to look over everything and make a decision before the end of the day.

The promised pizza was delivered at noon. Mrs. Kenyon had surrendered her office to Russell and Tim, so while they worked, Russell was able to continue observing the family in the next room. Colin remained fairly relaxed throughout, and it amused Russell to see the confidence that Colin was placing in him—so different from the hostility and suspicion that had been present such a short while ago. Sarah, though, looked like she still didn't dare to believe what was happening. Only after Tim had stopped in with the first set of papers they needed to fill out, had her tension seemed to ease, and a hopeful smile appear on her worried face.

Tim had brought his own laptop computer and his notarizing stamp, and Mrs. Kenyon, becoming more gracious and helpful as the day progressed, had provided a printer and scanner for him to use. The whole agency staff, in fact, seemed to be caught up in the excitement of the moment. Their tasks were wearisome enough most days, often filled with disappointment and heartbreak. Here was a "happy ending" story unfolding before them! The couriers were ushered in, hot coffee and doughnuts were kept in constant supply, and everyone was anxious to help in any way they could.

Russell, though he didn't show it, felt a strange mix of emotions. Things were working out even better than expected—everyone bustling around him, seeking to accomplish what had before seemed impossible. But the next step in Russell's plans loomed over him like a dark specter. Russell mentally checked off what he still needed to do before taking that final step...

Get someone to clean out and empty his house—that needed to be done without delay. Russell dialed the number of a person that he knew he could trust to do the job right. Besides getting rid of anything of interest to the police, "Bones" would also find ready customers for Russell's vehicle, expensive clothes and jewelry. Not that Russell needed the cash anymore either—at least he wouldn't after tomorrow.

He made a few more phone calls, using his cell phone to ensure privacy, and paid off his outstanding debts, canceled orders and effectively closed his "business."

With most of the loose ends tied up, Russell ordered a chartered flight into Rabbit Lake for that evening, knowing that if he waited until the next day, he might lose his courage to go through with what next needed to be done.

chapter thirty-two

Joshua was also planning to return to Rabbit Lake that evening.

But although typically a detail-oriented person who planned things ahead of time, Joshua had yet to make any travel arrangements. He had enough money to charter a plane if he decided to do that. Or he could just go to the airport and take his chances on whatever flights were available. Even stop overnight somewhere if he had to... The problem was that he seemed incapable of making any decisions at all.

He'd told Missy he was going to leave as soon as he was discharged—and that had already happened. One of Doctor Peters' colleagues had stopped by shortly before 8:00 am and informed Joshua that he was well enough to go home.

He'd gotten dressed in his street clothes and his bag was packed and ready.

He'd told Missy he was going to leave...

Joshua picked up his bag, set it down again, paced the length of the room and then sat down on a chair and stared out the window.

Today... Today, Missy would see the world for the very first time... see the brilliant blue sky, the emerald green grass... see cars and people and buildings...

"But what I most want to see is *you*," she'd told him.

She hadn't listened to Joshua's repeated entreaties that she should forget all about him. The engagement was off. The relationship was over.

Missy's words echoed in his mind: "It will never be over, Joshua. I will always love you. Always..."

She'd popped back into his room a dozen times, bubbling over with excitement about something she'd thought of that she would be able to do once she could see. She had so many wonderful plans—and they all included him!

Joshua had grown tired of protesting that he was no longer a part of her future. And he'd been unable to bring himself to completely dampen her enthusiasm. It was indeed a very wonderful thing and he couldn't help but be happy for her.

When her father had stopped by, they'd talked about the operation. Doctor Peters was intrigued by the concept of using an electronic interface between the optic nerve and the brain. To Joshua, it just sounded dangerous. What if the doctors messed up somehow?

Jeff Peters enthusiastically explained the process to him. "Visual input goes from the eye to the lateral geniculate nucleus, which is the primary processing center for visual information and from there it goes to the primary visual cortex. The electrical nerve impulses between the LGN and the primary visual cortex..."

Joshua had tuned him out. What did it matter how they were going to do it? "What are the chances that she'll be able to see?" he'd asked when Doctor Peters paused in his long dissertation.

"Doctor Pegrew and his team are quite confident that she'll be able to see something right away but it may take days or even weeks while the computer technicians synchronize the eye to the brain so the brain understands what the eye is seeing."

As Doctor Peters had rambled on about calibration and interfaces and programming, Joshua had pulled out what he needed to know—Missy would not immediately be able to make sense of the world around her, and the whole thing would be a long, slow and quite likely, frustrating process for her.

As the morning wore on, Joshua wondering how she was faring. He was thankful that Jasmine was with her for the operation. Missy's father would be preoccupied with his wife...

His thoughts were interrupted as a young man dashed into his room.

"Are you Joshua Quill?" he demanded abruptly.

Joshua glanced at the man's name tag: *Rick Thompson, RN.* "Yes, I am. Why?"

"You're needed down in Emerg—come with me."

"What?" His first thought was of Missy. As Joshua hurried out of the room after the nurse, he peppered him with questions. "Did something go wrong with the operation? Why'd they bring her down to the emergency room? *What's going on?"*

They'd reached the elevator and Rick waited until they were alone inside before turning towards Joshua and answering his questions. "I don't know what operation you're talking about. She was brought into the emergency room at 7:30 am. And

354

apparently, you're the closest family member that she has available right now."

Joshua's head was reeling. "Who...?" he asked weakly.

The elevator doors opened and the nurse walked quickly out, Joshua hurrying after him. "*Who* are you talking about?" Joshua asked again.

Rick stopped abruptly and turned around, almost colliding with Joshua. "Didn't I tell you?—Jasmine Peters."

"No," Joshua said pointedly, "you *didn't* tell me. What happened to her?"

Rick shook his head. "Think I'd better let her tell you that," he said, turning and walking away again.

With a frustrated sigh, Joshua followed him into the emergency department.

He was shocked at the sight of her. Jasmine had always seemed so delicate and beautiful, seemingly untouched by the harsher realities of life. She was barely recognizable now, her face swollen and bruised, as she lay flat on the gurney with her eyes closed and a thin white sheet covering her almost to the neck, a hospital gown barely visible above it.

Joshua spoke her name in a trembling voice and Jasmine slowly opened her eyes.

The bleak despair that he saw there broke his heart.

He leaned over her. "What happened, Jas?"

A voice spoke from behind him. "She needs a woman at a time like this."

Joshua spun around to see a tall, dark-haired woman, wearing a white lab coat. "At a time like *what*?" Joshua demanded.

The woman looked at Jasmine. "It's up to you, my dear," she said.

Jasmine nodded her consent and the woman turned to Joshua. "She was raped."

The words slashed through Joshua like a grizzly bear's paw, cutting deep into his soul. His groan of anguish was followed by a deluge of tears.

She'd been lying frozen in position on the gurney but as Joshua dropped into the chair beside her, Jasmine turned towards him, curled into a fetal position and burst into sobs. Joshua put his arm around her, and cried with her.

For the past two hours, Jeff had been trying to be in two places at once. He'd stayed with Jenny until the general anesthetic had taken effect and then he'd rushed over to be with Missy as her operation began.

He simply couldn't understand what had happened to Jasmine. When he'd talked to her early that morning, she'd been planning to go for a quick jog but had promised to be at the hospital by eight o'clock at the latest. As that hour came and went, Jeff's mild annoyance had turned to worry. He had trying calling her but got no answer at their house or on Jasmine's mobile phone.

By ten o'clock, Jenny's surgery was finished and she was in the Recovery Room. As Jeff stood helplessly by her side, he felt as if his own eyes had been plucked out and as the anesthetic wore off, he felt her pain as if it was his own. Jeff was thankful at least that she hadn't needed to be awake for the surgery so he hadn't had to be there—and watch as they used a scalpel on her. He wasn't about to leave her now, though. He couldn't let her wake up alone... Missy would just have to do without him.

It was tearing him apart though, knowing that Missy was alone. And his anxiety over Jasmine was about to turn into full-fledged panic. He'd even tried to contact Joshua, thinking he might be able to convince him to sit with Missy for a whie but he had apparently already left.

"She'll need some clothes."

Joshua glanced up at the nurse who was standing nearby.

Jasmine's tears had subsided but she was shivering uncontrollably now. Joshua rubbed her arm. "Maybe a blanket for now," Joshua suggested.

As the nurse left to get one, Joshua said, "Sounds like they're ready to discharge you. Have the police already been here?"

"Yes," Jasmine said in a voice that was hoarse from crying, "and the doctors have been here—and the nurses—and the lab technicians—and I don't know who else. It seemed as if people would never stop coming and asking stupid questions and doing stupid things."

Joshua recognized anger as a healthy part of the grieving process. He was starting to feel a little angry himself. He remembered Rick had said that she'd arrived at 7:30. Joshua glanced down at his watch; she'd been in the emergency department for *two and a half hours!*

"Why didn't they call me sooner?" he asked.

Fresh tears fell from Jasmine's eyes. "I don't know," she said weakly. "There were things they had to do and..." Her voice trailed off.

"Jasmine, they said you need clothes..."

She nodded. "They took mine. Said they needed them for evidence."

Joshua thought quickly. "You and Missy are about the same size. They admitted her last night so she'd be ready for pre-op this morning. There's probably an overnight bag in her room. I'm sure Missy wouldn't mind..."

Jasmine nodded again. "I helped her pack a couple of extra outfits. It's in the closet in her room. Could—could you go get it, please?"

The nurse arrived back as Joshua was leaving. She'd brought a heated blanket for Jasmine, and Joshua thanked her before hurrying up to Missy's room.

He found the overnight bag where Jasmine had said it would be and as he slung it over his shoulder, he felt a brief instant of profound gratitude—Missy was safe. Just yesterday, she'd gone jogging with her sister. If she hadn't had the operation today, maybe they would both have been attacked. Jasmine hadn't said if there was more than one assailant. Maybe there had been a group...

The bag dropped off his shoulder and Joshua sank weak-kneed down onto the bed as the sudden realization hit him. Missy wasn't any safer in Chicago than she was in Rabbit Lake!

Her words echoed through his mind. *We're all just sitting ducks.*

Yes, Joshua thought bitterly, that was certainly true.

But Missy had also talked about trusting in God...

But even for those who were trusting in God, bad things still happened. "We're not invincible," she'd said. "We don't live forever. And sometimes suffering is a part of God's plan..."

Joshua didn't know what possible plan God could be shaping up out of this mess. He still didn't understand why he'd had to go through the terrible things that he had in his life—and for sure he didn't understand why Jasmine would have to go through what she was going through.

And even Jenny, dying of cancer...

Joshua shook his head, trying to clear his thoughts. He'd known all his life that there was pain and suffering in this world. And as a Christian, he'd learned to trust God in spite of, or perhaps even because of, the pain. Where he'd gotten derailed was in thinking that somehow he could manipulate events to prevent anything bad happening to those he loved.

But forcing Missy to stay in Chicago—or to stay away from him—wouldn't guarantee her safety any more than it had guaranteed Jasmine's safety.

The only thing it would guarantee would be that he wouldn't be by her side when something bad did happen...

Joshua groaned as the full realization of what he'd done sunk in. Trying to protect Missy, he'd instead hurt her, leaving her to face the operation alone... Leaving her to face life alone...

Joshua stood quickly to his feet and picked up the bag again. First, he had to do what he could to help Jasmine...

She was curled up under the blanket with her eyes closed again.

"Jas..." he said gently, "I have some clothes for you."

The nurse reappeared at that moment. "I'll help her," she said, taking the bag from him and pulling the curtain closed.

When Jasmine appeared a few moments later, she looked more fragile than ever. Joshua slung the bag over his shoulder and took her arm.

"I'm so worried about Missy," she whispered in a voice still hoarse from crying.

"It's okay," Joshua said gently. "I'm going to be with her as soon as I get you settled in somewhere. Do you want to go home or...?"

"My mother's room," Jasmine said. "Her nurses know me and they won't mind if I wait there. She probably won't be up for a while yet."

There was a cot in Jenny's room; Jeff had spent the past two nights there. Jasmine looked so done in that Joshua suggested that she lie down again. Jasmine wearily agreed.

"May I tell the nurse in charge what happened?" he asked. "And I can dim the lights and shut the door for you."

The gratitude in her voice was obvious. "Thank you, Joshua," she said, fresh tears rolling down her cheeks.

He bent over and hugged her. "Just get some rest, okay."

"Wait!" Jasmine called as he turned to go. "Make sure they let me know when my mom is on her way up. I need time..."

"I'll tell them," Joshua said softly.

Missy felt as if her whole world was crashing down around her. She had hoped against hope that Joshua would show up at the last moment. And she'd been absolutely counting on having Jasmine to support her if Joshua didn't. Now even her father was gone.

She didn't begrudge his absence—her mother needed him more than she did at the moment—but she felt so terribly alone and abandoned!

And even though they had given her a local anesthetic, Missy could still feel them working inside her head and it scared her. How she longed for someone to be there... to hold her hand and speak comforting words....

Now they were asking her questions, asking her if she could see anything yet. But it was just as before—a world of nothingness. Missy was beginning to fear that her mother had given her eyes for nothing.

Then it happened!

"I see..." Missy exclaimed but her voice trailed off immediately.

"What do you see?" they asked excitedly.

She couldn't tell them!

"What colors do you see?"

"What shapes?"

"Can you see my fingers? How many am I holding up?"

"I don't know!" she cried. "I don't know!"

"Of course she doesn't know. She's never seen anything before in her life. What kind of doctors are you?"

Joshua...

"Joshua!" she cried out. "Help me!"

She felt his hand and heard his voice again. This time it was gentle. "Close your eyes, honey. That's it. Just close them for now."

Missy felt instant relief. The confusing mass of moving things disappeared.

"What do you think you're doing?"

"Who are you?"

"How did you get in here?"

"I'm her fiancé," Joshua stated calmly. "Can we maybe just take this a little bit slower? And don't all talk at once. It's very confusing—especially for a blind person."

Missy felt her heart swell with pride. *Way to go, Joshua!* And he said he was her fiancé! *Joshua, oh Joshua, my love...*

A deep-throated chuckle sounded off to Missy's right and she recognized it as belonging to Doctor Pegrew. "He's right, you know. Well done, young man. And you're going to marry her, are you? Congratulations!"

Missy could hear the smile in Joshua's voice. "Yes sir, I am."

Joy bubbled up inside her as she felt him squeeze her hand. "Josh!" she whispered happily.

He bent closer to her and said in a low voice. "I was a fool to believe that I could prevent anything bad from happening to you. I just want to be there for you, whatever happens to you, good or bad. I love you, Missy. I want to spend the rest of my life with you." He kissed her softly on the lips.

"Be careful!" One of the other doctors growled.

Doctor Pegrew's voice remained calm. "Don't worry. He knows what he's doing. Let's all just take a five minute break, shall we."

"But what if he...?"

"He won't."

Missy felt surge of pure, sweet joy. Doctor Pegrew was a wonderful doctor. *And Joshua was here!*

Missy could hear the scrape of stools and the doctors' voices off to her right.

"Joshua..." Missy whispered.

"Just rest for a moment," he said gently. "I need to think about this."

She smiled and kept her eyes shut.

"Okay," he said. "Now, I'm going to take your hand and put it in front of your eyes. I want you to move your fingers slowly one by one."

Joshua positioned her right hand and then told her to open her eyes.

"Just close them again if it gets too overwhelming. There's no rush."

Missy watched as her fingers moved one by one. Then she used her left hand to touch each finger on her right. She had known how they felt. Now she knew how they looked.

"Okay, close your eyes again," Joshua instructed. But now his voice was trembling. "I'm going to lean forward and I want you to touch my face."

She did. There were tears on his cheeks.

"Missy, when you're ready, open your eyes." He chuckled softly. "But be ready to close them again. I'm kind of an ugly mug."

Missy opened her eyes and gently traced Joshua's hair, his forehead, his eyebrows and then down around his cheeks, across his nose and over his mouth to his chin. "You're beautiful," she said.

She felt and saw Joshua's lips curve into a smile. "Sorry, Doc," he said. "The operation was a failure. She thinks I'm beautiful."

The doctors rushed back, all talking at once.

"It's wonderful!"

"She's progressing so much faster than we'd thought..."

"Close your eyes, Missy!" Joshua commanded.

The frightening cacophony of movement disappeared.

"One at a time," Joshua said, and the voices ceased as well.

"May I be the next one?" a familiar voice asked.

"Daddy!" Missy exclaimed.

Of all the faces in the world, she knew his the best. Even as a baby, she had reached her hands up to "feel" his smile. And he was the one who had made sure that there was nothing between them and then had told her to run into his arms. He had been the one to give her a normal happy childhood in spite of her blindness. Missy opened her eyes and traced his features as she had Joshua's. "You're beautiful, too," she whispered.

He threw back his head and laughed. Then he was moving away from her. "I've got to go tell your mom. She's going to be so happy."

"Wait!" Missy called. There was something she had been wondering about all her life. "Please let me see your hand. And yours too, Joshua." Missy looked carefully at their hands comparing them to hers and to each other.

Skin color—she'd heard about it all her life. "So this is what all the fuss is about," she said and looked again at Joshua's face and then at her Dad's. "Silly world we live in!" Joshua and her Dad each clasped one of her hands and heartily agreed with her.

Doctor Pegrew asked her if she was ready to see her reflection in a mirror.

"Yes!" Missy exclaimed eagerly.

With the mirror in front of her, Missy traced out her features, "recognizing" each part, her brain connecting and "calibrating" as Doctor Pegrew had hoped it would.

"The most beautiful woman in the world!" Joshua declared.

"The *second* most beautiful woman in the world," her father said.

Missy laughed. She knew that her Mom would always be first in her Dad's eyes.

"I have to go tell her," he said. "She'll be back in her room by now."

Joshua's face moved suddenly and his smile disappeared. "I have to go with you," he said. "Missy, I'm sorry. Will you be okay? I just need to talk to your Dad about something..."

"Yes," she assured him. "I'll be fine now. Take as long as you want." Joshua leaned forward to kiss her and Missy whispered, "Tell him that he'd better get used to the idea of you being his son-in-law."

Joshua smiled. Then his head moved and Missy watched as his lips formed words. "You'll go slow with her—not try to rush things?" he asked in a stern voice.

"Don't worry, young man," Doctor Pegrew said with a chuckle. "We'll take good care of her."

Joshua kissed her again and smiled in farewell.

He had to hurry to catch up with Doctor Peters.

The older man didn't stop till he got to the elevator. "If you want to tell me that your engagement is on again, don't bother." He turned towards Joshua and softened his words with a smile. "I can't believe I was such a fool as to believe that it could ever be off." He paused as they stepped into the elevator. "You did good in there," he said gently. "I was proud of you."

Joshua let the unexpected words sink in for a moment. "Then you approve of our marriage?" he asked hopefully.

Doctor Peters laughed. "Let's just say that I bow to the inevitable."

They were the only ones in the elevator. Joshua knew that he needed to tell him—and quickly. "We need to talk—not about Missy."

"I need to go see my wife," Doctor Peters countered.

"It's about Jasmine."

The older man turned pale. "What about her?" he demanded.

But Joshua didn't want him to find out as abruptly as he had. "Do you have somewhere private where we could talk?"

"Just tell me!" Doctor Peters shouted, grabbing Joshua's shirt.

The elevator opened and a crowd of people stared at the two of them.

Doctor Peters let go of Joshua and pressed the button for the first floor, where he led the way into an empty doctor's lounge. "Now what's this all about?" he demanded as he turned the occupied sign over.

"Jasmine has been hurt," Joshua began.

Doctor Peters flew to the door. "Where is she?"

Joshua grabbed his arm. "There's more. Now, sit down—please."

Doctor Peters moved shakily towards a chair and looked fearfully up at him. "She's not—she's not—dead, is she?"

Joshua pulled up a chair beside him. "No, but it's bad."

Doctor Peters started to rise to his feet again. "I can help her. I'm a doctor."

Joshua pushed him back down. "She doesn't need medical help." Joshua struggled to find the right words to say and realized there were no "right" words. "She was attacked while out jogging," he said, "and she was sexually assaulted."

"No! No! Not Jasmine." Jeff Peters' voice shook as he began to tremble uncontrollably. "It's impossible! Not her. No! No!"

Joshua watched the older man carefully, wondering if he needed to call for help. This day had already been taxing enough for Doctor Peters with both his wife and daughter in surgery. And his father had just recently died. How much more could the man take?

"Where—where—is she?"

"She was going to wait in your wife's room."

"She can't tell Jenny! It'll kill her!"

He started to stand up again and Joshua placed his hands on the older man's shoulders. "She won't," he reassured him calmly.

Joshua knew that Doctor Peters was only in his late 40's but at that moment, he could easily have passed for a 60 year old. "I'll go up and check on them both if you like," Joshua volunteered. "It will give you time to…"

But Doctor Peters was nodding for him to go, tears already flooding his eyes. Joshua granted him his privacy and went to see Mrs. Peters—and Jasmine.

She was sitting by her mother's side. "Joshua's here," she said.

There was a wide bandage around Mrs. Peters' eyes. She looked frail and her voice was weak. But she smiled as she asked eagerly, "How's Missy? Can she see yet?"

"Yes," Joshua replied carefully, "but how are you both doing?"

Mrs. Peters said, "I'm doing fine. But Jasmine here seems to be more upset about all this than I am. She feels bad that I've lost my eyes. But I'm just so happy that Missy will be able to see everything now. Her wedding dress and her flowers and of course, you Joshua... I was thinking that maybe you could get married right here in the chapel and then I could for sure be there. But tell us about Missy. I wish that I could have been there..."

Joshua exchanged glances with Jasmine. Tears were streaming down her cheeks and Joshua was thankful that Jenny couldn't see her. There would be no mistaking the abject grief in her eyes. But she smiled and spoke in a clear voice, "Yes, tell us about Missy, Joshua. Can she really see?"

Joshua gave Jasmine a quick hug and pulled up a chair beside her. "It was a little frightening for her at first..." he began.

chapter thirty-three

Russell watched through the two-way mirror as Tim entered the next room and excitedly announced to Colin and Sarah that he was there to drive them to court, to have the judge officially declare that the adoptions were complete.

Russell had been observing them throughout the day, watching Colin and Sarah's joy and wonder grow as each stage of the adoption process was completed. Sarah had become more relaxed, settling into the situation, reading stories to the children and playing simple table games with them.

Meanwhile, Colin's demeanor had changed from quiet confidence into joyful exuberance. They'd even turned some music on at one point and Colin had danced with the two girls and finally pulled Sarah in to join them as well.

Russell had kept the intercom turned off most of the day in the busy office but when he'd caught sight of Verena bursting into laughter at Colin's one-man puppet show, Russell had quickly stepped over and turned up the volume. The sound of her laughter had given him hope and the confidence he needed to follow through on what had to be done next.

Mrs. Kenyon came up behind him. "They've gone," she said quietly. "And when they come back, your two girls will be officially adopted."

There was frank admiration in her voice—and Russell was tempted once again to remind her that he was a criminal, not a hero. But it felt good to have someone to share the joy of this moment with.

"I just don't know how you did it!" Mrs. Kenyon continued. "*Five hours!* It usually takes five months or five years!"

Russell remained silent. She didn't really need an explanation. She'd been watching every step of the way. Had seen the money changing hands. Had watched as Russell had wheedled his way or commanded with authority, as the need arose for one or the other. And Tim had done his job well, working harder perhaps than he had any other day of his life. And Russell couldn't forget the office staff and Mrs. Kenyon herself. It seemed as if all of them had cast non-urgent duties aside, combining their efforts together towards this one common goal.

A goal that had been accomplished! Tim had assured Russell that the actual court proceedings were a formality—the judge never brought the children and the adoptive parents into the courtroom until he was very certain that everything was finalized.

Colin, Sarah, and the girls were gone for less than an hour and Russell knew the instant that they arrived back. Even without the office door open, he would have been able to hear them—Colin was whooping and hollering like a crazy man! And as Russell leaned out of the doorway a little, he could see that Colin's enthusiasm was contagious—the new family was being mobbed by agency staff, all wanting to congratulate them, shaking their hands, hugging them, patting them on the back.

Russell had hoped to stay out of view but suddenly Colin was looking directly at him. Russell ducked back into the room. He'd already said his goodbyes.

But an instant later, Colin burst into the office and threw his arms around him. Russell had no idea what to do with a hug and stood like a frozen statue. Then he slowly pushed Colin away and they grinned at each other like two Cheshire cats.

Colin began pumping his hand. "You did it!" he exclaimed joyously. "You did it!"

Russell grinned sardonically. "You doubted me?"

With tears in his eyes, Colin hugged him again, and this time Russell hesitantly returned the embrace for a brief second before dropping his arms and stepping backward.

"I've chartered a flight into Rabbit Lake this evening," Russell said. "Pastor Thomas has agreed to meet with me. After that, I'll be turning myself in to the police. You'll have a lot of reports to write."

Colin shook his head. "Not me," he said. "Someone else."

They both stood there awkwardly for a moment before Russell smiled faintly and said, "Goodbye, Colin."

Voices out in the hallway could be heard. "Daddy! Daddy!" and "Colin, where are you?"

"Go!" Russell said gently.

"But... what about the girls? Aren't you going to say goodbye to them?"

"No," Russell said, steering him towards the door. "They're afraid of me—and rightly so."

"But this is a new beginning," Colin protested.

Russell pushed him out the door and with a final pat on the shoulder said, "Then let it begin."

371

It had taken all of Colin's willpower to hold off from contacting anyone in Rabbit Lake throughout the day but the instant the judge had finalized the adoptions, he'd whipped out his cell phone and called Jamie. And he gave her free rein to pass the word, knowing he could rely on the "moccasin telegraph" to get their good news spread around Rabbit Lake.

Jamie called while they were en route back to the agency, to say that Bill was already on his way to get them and that she was throwing together a potluck supper at the church in their honor. Many of the people who had been at the prayer meeting the day before would be present, with their families, to congratulate Colin, Sarah, Emmeline and Verena.

Colin had been afraid that the two girls would be overwhelmed by such a large crowd but it seemed to be for them, as it was for Colin and Sarah, the perfect ending to a perfect day. Emmeline was happy to be the focus of so much attention and Verena was content as long as she was holding on tight to either Colin or Sarah's hand.

Besides quickly preparing sandwiches and desserts, people had also hurried out and purchased gifts for the girls and some of the young people had even blown up balloons and put up streamers!

Towards the end of the evening, just as Colin was thinking that it was time to get the girls home and tucked into bed, Pastor Thomas approached him with a grave look on his face. As the older man drew him aside, Colin braced himself for bad news.

"Russell made an appointment with me..." Pastor Thomas began.

Colin steered the pastor further away from the group clustered around his family.

"...To confess his sins," Pastor Thomas continued.

"Yes...?" Colin prompted, feeling more anxious by the moment.

Pastor Thomas waved his hand towards Sarah and the girls. "I hate to take you away..."

Colin's heart was beating faster. "It's okay," he said. "Just tell me what happened!"

Pastor Thomas looked confused. "He said that he'd already told you."

Colin shook his head in frustration. "Is Russell okay or not?" he demanded.

"Well... he's pretty upset."

Colin let out the breath he'd been holding, in a deep sigh.

Pastor Thomas looked at him carefully. "You were afraid that he'd... injured himself?"

Colin nodded, still too relieved to speak. It wasn't something he could have put into words anyways. It had been just a feeling he'd had. Something about the way that Russell was tidying up his life, rushing the adoption through, confessing his sins... as if he was preparing for death.

Colin was surprised at how much it mattered to him that Russell had not taken his own life. But he was a little annoyed at himself also for jumping to conclusions. "So, what do you need me for?" he asked bluntly.

"It will be quiet at my house. We'll be undisturbed..."

Colin nodded impatiently. Yes it likely would be quiet there. Pastor Thomas, a widower for many years, lived alone. Perhaps, that was it—was he afraid to be alone with Russell? Colin could hardly blame him for that. But if it was police protection that he wanted...

"I think it would be good if you were there also—when he confesses."

Colin shook his head. "Why?"

"For support—and to help counsel and pray with him. You have personal experience with... with the sins that he's confessing."

Colin shook his head again. "A good reason for me to stay away!"

The older man's eyes were filled with compassion. "A good reason for you to be there," he said gently.

Colin turned and looked back at his family, laughing and celebrating. It would be so easy to say no. Perhaps it was even the right thing to do...

With a heavy heart, he walked over to Sarah and the girls. "Pastor Thomas needs me to go over to his house for a little while," he said.

"Now?" Sarah asked incredulously.

Colin nodded and bent down to hug each of the girls.

"I won't be back until late," he told them. "So I'll say goodnight now and I'll see you guys in the morning, okay?"

"You gonna arrest some bad guys, Daddy?" Emmeline asked.

No, not me. When it came time for Russell to make an official statement, Colin would let someone else do it—likely Keegan.

"Not tonight, sweetheart," he said.

Tonight, he would not represent the law, but the church. It was an odd role for him, one that he was unaccustomed to.

And later, as he listened to Russell recounting his many sins, Colin thought it was a role that he was particularly ill suited for.

Unlike Pastor Thomas, who remained calm throughout, Colin often felt his emotions spiraling out of control. At times, he felt close to vomiting. At other times he wanted to throttle Russell and scream, *How could you do that? How could you do that to an innocent child?*

And often, Colin simply had to leave the room—take a break for a while—and wrestle it out with God. Over and over the words, "he doesn't *deserve* to be forgiven!" had raged in his heart, and over and over again the Holy Spirit had whispered softly into his soul, "*No one* deserves to be forgiven, Colin. It's mercy— God's unmerited favor."

Russell, too, seemed to being having doubts about God's ability to forgive him.

Colin thought that perhaps Pastor Thomas would reassure Russell by reminding him of the vision of Jesus that he'd had. But instead, the older man had opened up his well-worn Bible and pointed out to Russell that it was a stated fact that God would forgive if we confessed our sins.

Pastor Thomas asked Russell to read the words aloud and later he got him to write them down. Then each time that Russell would have doubts, Pastor Thomas would point to the words from the first book of John, the first chapter and the ninth verse: "But if we confess our sins to God, he will keep his promise and do what is right: he will forgive us our sins and purify us from all our wrongdoing."

As Pastor Thomas emphasized the concept of forgiveness, everything in Colin longed to cry out, "But what about justice?" And he wondered if Russell would make good on his promise to turn himself in to the police. He found himself not wanting Russell to feel forgiven and "purified from all wrongdoing." He didn't want him to feel released from the guilt and weight of his sin. The victims had not got off so easy—why should Russell?

But it became obvious as the night wore on that Russell was not being let off easily. It seemed the more he confessed, the more tender his heart became. And as God's love saturated his soul, Russell in turn felt true love and compassion for his victims and deep remorse for the pain he had caused them.

With each successive confession followed by an assurance of forgiveness, Russell became more and more of a broken man. Huge gut-wrenching sobs and steadily flowing tears many times made words impossible.

And as his heart became further softened, Russell began to ask about the victims. How were they coping? Was there anything he could do to help?

Colin felt compelled to mention that if Russell turned himself in and served a lengthy prison term, it would go a long ways to bringing closure for people.

Russell wanted to go and turn himself in right then and there but Pastor Thomas said that there would be time enough for that in the morning. He would go with Russell down to the police station then.

"But there is another way that you could help," Pastor Thomas said thoughtfully.

Colin watched as Russell turned puffy, red eyes towards the pastor and asked in a voice that was hoarse from crying, "What? I'll do anything! Just tell me."

"I think that you need to confess to the people whom you have hurt…"

"Yes," Russell agreed eagerly. "I know that would help! It would help… me… to know that they forgave… me." His voice trailed off, Russell obviously aware of how selfish his thoughts still were.

"It would help them, too," Pastor Thomas reassured him.

"You can't offer any excuses," Colin interjected.

"I won't," Russell promised.

"Or blame them in any way."

Russell nodded. "I know. I've gotten very good at making people do what I want them to do. It wasn't their fault that they did it." He paused, considering, then looked intently at Colin. "Do you feel to blame for the things I made you do?"

Colin stiffened. Then, as he answered honestly, his eyes fell to the floor. "Sometimes."

"It wasn't your fault. It was mine," Russell said.

Colin felt as if a giant fist had struck him in the stomach. The sob that tore its way up into his throat and drove him to his knees, released a deluge of tears, and Colin found himself struggling for each breath, feeling as if he were drowning in a sea of pain.

It was a few moments before he realized that he had two comforters, both men kneeling beside him with a hand on each of his shoulders. Pastor Thomas was praying for him, asking for God's healing touch.

When Colin finally looked up, there were fresh tears in Russell's eyes.

"I'm sorry," Russell said.

Colin opened his mouth and the words flowed from his heart. "I forgive you."

Russell didn't speak but silently nodded, obviously overcome with emotion.

They rose to their feet and Pastor Thomas advised that they take a break and get a few hours sleep. It was almost three in the morning.

But Russell was still anxious to talk, wanting to know more about how he should confess to the people whom he had hurt.

As he and Pastor Thomas talked about calling the individual victims and setting up times when they and their family could meet, Colin suddenly realized that, although this was a good plan, there was a need for something more.

"This thing—this sexual abuse," he began haltingly. Both men turned their attention to Colin as he continued. "The reason it has such a hold on people—it's because it's done in secret and people suffer the shame of it in secret. They don't tell anyone and so there is no support, no help given. They carry the blame alone. And often they can't even admit to themselves that it happened and so they think it's their own fault that they're all messed up with alcohol and drugs and stuff. They can't see that it's the abuse that is crippling them, devastating them, keeping them prisoners in the darkness. What we need to do is bring this evil out into the light of day and face it together as a community."

"You're right!" Pastor Thomas said.

"I agree." Russell nodded solemnly. "And I will do this. Not for me... But for all of the people whom I have hurt."

"It won't be easy," Pastor Thomas cautioned.

A shadow of Russell's former smirk crossed his face. "I know how hard it will be," he said.

"And on that note," Pastor Thomas said wearily, "we all need to get some rest. Tomorrow is going to be a very long and difficult day. Russell, I have a guest room that you can use…"

Russell gave his statement in the morning to Keegan Littledeer, and although officially in police custody from that point on, he was able to travel around with Pastor Thomas to talk to the victims and their families. Colin accompanied them, dressed in his uniform and Russell, though he was not required to wear handcuffs at all times, chose to do so, as a further reassurance to the victims.

The visits went on longer than expected as old wounds were reopened and Pastor Thomas and Colin prayed and counseled with the victims and their families. The public meeting which had originally been set for that afternoon was moved to the following day, Sunday at 3:00 p.m.

Even before the appointed hour, the little church was packed. Extra chairs had been borrowed from the Community Center and added to the ones that were usually set out on a Sunday morning. There was one long aisle leading from the back to the front, and ushers were on hand to ensure that there were no empty seats among the 150 that were set out, but still there were people standing at the back, and along the sides.

At the front of the church, on a low platform that ran the width of the building, there was a hand-hewn pulpit and a simple wooden cross suspended on the wall behind it. A small band was softly playing some old hymns that were easily recognizable to the assembled crowd and there was a hushed atmosphere in the building, as people conversed with each other in quiet whispers.

Russell, wearing handcuffs, sat on a chair in the front row, flanked by Keegan Littledeer and Jonathan Quequish, who were both in uniform. Pastor Thomas was seated by Jonathan, and Colin sat on the other side of Keegan beside Sarah

Colin had chosen not to wear his uniform that day. He'd also decided to leave Emmeline and Verena with Jamie. They'd had a brief explanation of what was happening in the meeting but Colin didn't feel that they needed to be exposed to a rendition of all the horrible things that their father had done to other people.

At three o'clock, the band stopped playing and walked off the stage. Pastor Thomas took his place behind the pulpit and picked up the hand-held microphone that was lying there. He looked exhausted but his voice was strong and full of compassion as he invited everyone to join with him in prayer.

"Precious Lord, we come before You today, asking for Your healing mercy to be upon each one of us. There are so many of Your children here today that are in terrible pain. Oh God, we ask that You would comfort them and heal them. Lord, we know this healing process is a journey, one that can take many years. For some that journey has already begun. For others, it is just beginning today.

"And we pray, too, for those of us who have not been sexually abused as children, that we would be a comfort and a support to those in our community who have endured such suffering—often alone. We are breaking the silence today, piercing the darkness with light—with the light of Your love.

"Bless us now as we begin. Strengthen our brother, Russell, as he comes forward now to speak. We ask these things in Jesus name, Amen."

He then addressed the audience, telling them that it was an open meeting and that the ushers had microphones that they could pass around if anyone wished to speak. He also made it clear that people were free to not participate as they wished. And he reminded them that there were trained counselors in the community and in the church that were available and that his door was always open, also.

Then he nodded towards Keegan who accompanied Russell onto the stage. Pastor Thomas handed Russell the microphone and he held it in his cuffed hands.

Keegan and Pastor Thomas walked off the stage, leaving Russell alone at the pulpit. Seeing him standing there, Colin marveled at the change that had taken place in Russell in just four short days. His eyes were red-rimmed and his shoulders sagged, the old arrogance gone. Russell looked completely beaten down, as if he were at the end of all his emotional and physical strength.

He leaned heavily on the pulpit, as if for support, as he looked out over the crowd. Colin shifted a little in his seat so that he could follow Russell's gaze and it was obvious that he was not just seeing a crowd but individual people whom he had hurt.

As Russell's eyes lingered for a moment on each person before going on to the next, it seemed as if he absorbed their sorrow, the weight of it crushing him further and further down. Tears streamed from his eyes and his chest began to heave.

When he finally spoke, it was a hoarse, rasping sound that echoed through the room. "I'm sorry," he said. "I'm sorry." He fell to his knees and began sobbing, a broken man.

Colin glanced over at Pastor Thomas but his head was bowed and his eyes closed.

Colin willed Russell to rise to his feet again, to speak to the crowd, to do what he had promised he would do! But as Russell continued to weep, Colin realized that his former foster brother needed his help.

He walked onto the stage, picked up the fallen microphone and knelt beside him. "Russell..." he prompted. Colin's voice echoed around the room and for an instant, he was tempted to turn off the microphone but knew that for there to be a community healing, there needed to be community participation, at every stage of the process. It was important that everyone could hear all that was being said in the meeting that day.

Colin put his arm around Russell, and it seemed to give him the strength to finally speak a few words. "I—I've hurt so many people," he whispered hoarsely, lifting tear-filled eyes towards the crowd again. "So—so much pain."

"Russell," Colin said, "if you want to help..."

Russell turned imploring eyes towards him. "Yes," he gasped.

"It will help people on their healing journey if you will confess your sins."

Slowly, Russell nodded. Colin helped him to his feet, rested a comforting hand on his shoulder and held the microphone for him.

Russell took a deep breath as if to gather strength. Then he looked steadily at Colin and began in a slow, halting voice. "When you were a foster child in our home, I abused you verbally—and physically—and sexually. Since that time, I have continued to be verbally and physically abusive to you. I am only now beginning to comprehend a little of the—the devastating effects of that abuse.

Colin... I am so sorry. I wish that I could undo what I have done. I wish that I could be the big brother to you that I should have been—the hero that you needed me to be. Instead, I hurt you in such horrible ways. Colin, I take full responsibility for every sexual act that I committed against you. None of it was your fault. You were just a little kid. I should never have demanded that you do or see or experience the things that you did. It was a sin that was against our Creator and His teachings..." He glanced down towards his cuffed hands. "And it was also a crime that was committed against you."

Even though he had heard much of Russell's confession before, the words, publicly spoken, released another torrent of emotions in Colin. He felt an incredible surge of joy and a feeling of release, as if a great weight had been lifted off his shoulders.

He couldn't get the words out fast enough. "I forgive you, Russell. I *forgive* you."

"Thank you," Russell murmured hoarsely.

He turned to face the people of his community once more. His eyes scanned the crowd, stopping at a man leaning up against the back wall, close to the door.

"Garby," Russell said in a sad, quiet voice, "as your older brother, I should have set an example for you to follow. Instead, I dragged you into a lot of things that I shouldn't have. And I hurt you when you were little. When our—our mother—died—and you were crying and I hit you to make you stop... I'm—I'm sorry for that—and for all the other things I did to you when you were just a kid. I take responsibility for the things that I made you do. It wasn't your fault."

Garby pulled himself away from the wall, spat on the floor and swore loudly. He took a step towards the stage and shouted up at Russell. "I told you I wouldn't have any part of this—and I won't! You're crazy." His eyes swept across the room. "You're all crazy!" He walked angrily out of the church, slamming the door hard behind him.

Russell looked as if he'd been struck. He swayed a little as if he might fall and Colin reached out a hand to steady him.

"You're doing fine," he said in a comforting voice.

The dazed look in Russell's eyes cleared to be replaced with gratitude. He looked out over the crowd once more, focusing this time on Bobby Peters, who was accompanied by his mother, Martha.

A very vivid image of Bobby being held captive in an old abandoned cabin rose in Colin's mind. He'd been the one to find the frightened boy, blindfolded and tied up to an old bunk bed. Fresh anger rose up in Colin's heart as he remembered the pain and confusion in the young boy's eyes. "Dey hurt me Colwin. I call, 'Daddy, come help me.' I call him and call him. Why dey hurt me, Colwin?"

His hand dropped away from Russell's shoulder but he held the microphone steady as Russell confessed to kidnapping Bobby.

Colin wondered if perhaps Martha had made a mistake bringing Bobby to the meeting. With his father's death so recent, it seemed unfair that he should also have to revisit the memories of the kidnapping that had happened so many years before. Colin also wondered if the whole thing might be too difficult for him to understand.

But he'd underestimated Bobby. The young man rose confidently to his feet and took the microphone. "Russthel, Jesthus wuves you and stho do I. And..." Bobby carefully enunciated the word he had likely practiced until he got it right. "I

for-give you. I for-give you for awl bad fings you done to me."
Then he handed the microphone back to the usher and walked
boldly up to the stage and threw his arms around Russell.

Unable to hug Bobby back with his hands in cuffs, Russell, in a
voice choked with tears, thanked the young man instead.

Bobby's words and actions caused a chain reaction throughout
the crowd. Other people stood to their feet and began to speak
what was in their hearts. Many shared how Russell's private and
public confession had helped in their healing process. Some,
desiring to speak their forgiveness in a public setting, did so.
Others around the room broke down in sobs and people gathered
around them to offer comfort and prayer.

Suddenly Colin saw Jamie walking down the aisle towards
him *with Emmeline and Verena!* Colin stepped down off the stage. "I
told you not to bring them!"

Jamie stood her ground. "It would have helped you—when
you were a kid. It would have helped you to have someone say
that it was wrong and..." She glanced past him up to the stage and
her voice softened. "...And it would have helped to have had
someone ask you to forgive them. Maybe you wouldn't have
started drinking. Maybe you would have healed sooner."

Colin looked back at Russell, who was watching them, tears
streaming down his cheeks. Pastor Thomas had come up on the
stage to stand beside him. Colin looked beyond them both to the
wooden cross, and thought again about God's love and mercy. It
was a message that Verena and Emmeline needed to hear and
understand.

"But I want them to stay back here!" Colin said, ushering them
away from the front of the church. "And the moment that they
want to leave, you take them out of here. No questions asked."

"Daddy…" Emmeline tugged at his sleeve.

Colin bent down to her level.

"We're not afraid, Daddy," she said. "We think that our old Daddy should say sorry to us. He hurt me a lot but he hurt Verena more."

Colin heard the echo of her voice and suddenly realized that he hadn't turned off the microphone and when he'd bent down, he'd placed it at her level.

Colin looked up to the stage. Russell had fallen to his knees, his face in his hands, and was sobbing loudly.

A hush had fallen over the crowd, everyone's attention once more drawn to the front of the room. Russell looked down at his daughters and in a trembling, tear-filled voice, began to speak. "Emmeline, it was wrong what I did to you and the things that I asked you to do. None of it was your fault. I am to blame for everything. As your father, I should have been the one to show you the right things to do. I'm sorry. I'm so sorry…"

Emmeline said in a clear, confident voice, "I forgive you."

Broken sobs of anguish filled the room. Colin glanced back and saw Pastor Thomas with his arm around Russell, comforting him and for an instant Colin thought that maybe Russell would once again ignore his eldest daughter…

But then Russell took a deep shuddering breath and began to speak again. "Verena, what I did to you was wrong. I should have protected you. I should have loved you. You were a precious gift given to me by the Creator. Instead of taking care of you the way that a daddy should, I hurt you so many times in so many ways. Verena, you didn't deserve any of the bad things I did to you. It was all my fault. Every single thing! You are not to blame. It was all my fault. And I'm so sorry. I'm so sorry…"

Colin watched the little girl closely, wondering how much she was taking in. He didn't want to pressure her to speak or do anything at all. But as soon as Russell finished, Verena smiled up at Colin and pulled the microphone closer. Her sweet clear voice filled the room as she said the healing words, "I forgive you."

And suddenly it seemed as if the Holy Spirit filled the entire room with His presence. The microphones were passed quickly from person to person, and the words rose and fell like ripples on the water, each voice blending with the next. "I forgive you... I forgive you... I forgive you..."

Slowly Russell stood to his feet. Joy and peace shone out from his eyes. He looked as if he'd seen the face of God. And perhaps he had...

And suddenly a lone voice began to sing: "Amazing Grace, how sweet the sound that saved a wretch like me." The voice was joined by another and then another. "I once was lost but now am found. Was blind but now I see."

As the last notes of the song quivered in the air, Pastor Thomas made an announcement. "We will be concluding our meeting at Sandy Point. You are all welcome to attend the baptism that will take place as soon as we can all get over there."

Colin was surprised by the announcement and further taken aback when Pastor Thomas approached him with a request. "Will you assist me?" he asked.

Colin shook his head in wonder. A week ago—even a few days ago!—he would never have dreamed of doing such a thing. The *possibility* of it would never have even crossed his mind! But God—the God of the universe—had come crashing down into their lives, shaking up their very foundations and replacing all that

Colin thought he knew with something he could never ever have imagined.

"Yes," he declared, as a swell of joy rose up within him.

The water was warm and as Colin waded in with Russell and Pastor Thomas, he felt the sun shining down warm upon them too, as if heaven itself was adding its blessing. Colin stood on one side of Russell, and the pastor on the other, supporting him as they lowered him into the water. "In the name of the Father and of the Son and of the Holy Spirit..."

As they raised him up again, Russell lifted his face to the sky and his smile was one of pure joy.

Colin knew, of course, that there would still be many difficult days ahead for Russell, days when he'd be tempted to fall back into his old lifestyle, especially in the brutal dog-eat-dog environment of prison. He was going to need a lot of teaching, love and support.

But today... today was a celebration of new life... a new beginning!

They waded out of the water and were promptly surrounded by well-wishers who wanted to shake Russell's hand or give him a hug. Colin glanced over at Keegan, who was standing ready to replace the cuffs as soon as the ceremony was over.

It was Russell who made the first move. He separated himself from the group and walked with his palms together and his arms stretched out towards Keegan. Colin hurried towards them. Just a few short days ago, he'd been all for locking him up and throwing away the key! Now, for an instant, Colin wondered if it was right for Russell to spend the rest of his life in prison... since God had wiped the slate clean, shouldn't man?

"I'll visit you," he said helplessly, as Russell was led away. "We'll all visit you... we won't forget you." Russell glanced back and smiled reassuringly.

Colin stared after them until he felt a little tug on his arm. He looked down to see Emmeline, with Verena standing close behind her.

"Is our old daddy going to jail?" Emmeline asked.

"Yes," Colin said quietly.

"Cause of the bad things he did to us?" Verena asked timidly.

Colin swallowed past the lump in his throat. "Yes."

"That's good," Emmeline said, as the police car carrying Russell pulled away.

"He won't be able to hurt us anymore," Verena added.

Colin put his arms around both of them. "That's right," he said in a hoarse voice.

There had been mercy and now there was justice.

Sarah joined them. Her smile was filled with compassion as she looked at Colin, and he felt a sudden burst of love for her. Sarah—his dear, precious wife—and now the *mother of his children!*

He grinned at each of them and said, "Let's go home!"

For suddenly, it was the only place that Colin wanted to be— home with his family. Home to a new beginning.

"Stop your noisy songs;
I do not want to listen to your harps.
Instead, let justice flow like a stream,
and righteousness like a river that
never goes dry."

— the Lord, whose name is Almighty God.
(Amos 5:23, 24, 27b)

Author's Note

If you have been sexually abused, it is very important that you talk to someone you trust: a teacher or your pastor or youth counselor.

If you know of someone under the age of 14 who is being sexually abused, it is against the law to not report it to the authorities: the police or a social agency.

If you have been sexually abused in the past, the first step on your journey of healing will be to acknowledge that it happened and that it is affecting you today. You need to look honestly at the problems in your life and be willing to accept the help and counsel of others.

To know Jesus is to know the Great Healer. The Bible says that God loves you. He loves you so much that He sent Jesus to pay the price for your sin (it's like somebody taking your jail sentence for you so you can go free). Speaking of Himself in John 10:10 and 11, Jesus said: "I came that they might have life, a great full life. I am the Good Shepherd. The Good Shepherd gives His life for the sheep."

Jesus gave His life for you. But the Good News is that He didn't stay dead. He came alive again after 3 days. The Bible says that He "swallowed up death in victory"! (Isaiah 25:8 and I Corinthians 15:54, KJV).

He only asks us to trust Him. A simple but often difficult decision for someone who has been betrayed by those whom they should have been able to trust. Though your earthly father may have hurt you, your Heavenly Father loves you and because He is perfect, His love for you is perfect.

Life here on earth may be difficult but it is a journey we all must take. There is Someone who wants to walk beside us. When we talk to God and tell Him of our troubles, He hears us and the Bible says that the Holy Spirit is there to comfort us. As you read more of the Bible, you will learn more about God and He will speak truth to your mind and to your heart.

The Lord bless you!

M. Dorene Meyer

Recommended Resources

1. The Bible—available in many versions. Find one that's easy for you to read.
2. Visit www.risingabove.ca—excellent site that will direct you towards resources, conferences in your area, and hope and healing.
3. *Hope for the Hurting* by Howard Jolly published by Rising Above Counseling Agency in 1996
4. *How to Counsel a Sexually Abused Person* by Selma Poulin, also published by Rising Above Counseling Agency.
5. *Helping Victims of Sexual Abuse* by Lynn Heitritter and Jeanette Vought, published by Bethany House Publishers in 1989.
6. *A Door of Hope* by Jan Frank, published by Thomas Nelson Publishers in 1993.
7. *Breaking the Silence* by Rose-Aimee Bordeleau, published by Raphah Worldwide Ministries in 2002 and available from www.raphah.org.

Dorene would like to thank Lisa Holliday
for editing this manuscript.

About the Author

M. D. Meyer grew up in Lac Seul and in Sioux Lookout, Ontario. Over the years, she has lived in Winnipeg, Red Lake, Thunder Bay and in Nova Scotia, New Brunswick and Indiana.

Dorene has five previously published books:

Deep Waters (a contemporary novel)
Colin's Choice (a young adult novel),
Get Lost! (a children's chapter book),
Pilot Error (a children's chapter book) and
Meet Manitoba Children's Authors (a reference book).

She has also edited five anthologies of Manitoba authors:

Prairie Writers, Volumes 1, 2 and *3*
The Voice Behind the Mask and
Northern Writers, Volume 1.

Dorene mentors and teaches novice and emerging writers. She is currently residing in Norway House, Manitoba.

You can visit Dorene's website at:
www.dorenemeyer.com
or email her at:
dorene@dorenemeyer.com